STEFANIE BARNFATHER

BENEATH
THE BIRCH TREES

a romantic tragedy

*Paulette,
Thank you for
helping this
book grow.*

BARNFATHER BOOKS
Calgary, Canada

BENEATH THE BIRCH TREES

a romantic tragedy

STEFANIE BARNFATHER

Print edition ISBN: 978-1-7381481-3-4
eBook edition ISBN: 978-1-7381481-4-1

This book is a work of fiction. Names, characters, events, and incidents are products of the author's imagination. Any resemblance to actual persons (except for satirical purposes) is coincidental. The author in no way represents the companies, corporations, brands, or historical figures mentioned in this story.

In the spirit of respect, reciprocity, and truth, Barnfather Books honours and acknowledges Moh'-kinsstis, and the traditional Treaty 7 territory and oral practices of the Blackfoot confederacy: Siksika, Kainai, Piikani, as well as the Îyâxe Nakoda and Tsuut'ina nations. Barnfather Books acknowledges that it operates in the territory that is home to the Métis Nation of Fairfield, Region 3, within the historical Northwest Métis homeland. Finally, Barnfather Books acknowledges all Nations—Indigenous and non—who live, work, and play on this land, and honour and celebrate this territory.

Copyright © 2024 Stefanie Barnfather
Barnfather Books supports copyright.
Thank you for buying an authorized edition of this book and complying with copyright laws by not reproducing, scanning, or distributing any part of it in any form without permission. Your decision allows Barnfather Books and Stefanie Barnfather to continue to share stories.

Designed by Barnfather Books
www.barnfatherbooks.com

*For Jason,
who–despite everything–is a realist.
Wink.*

MAPS of the WORLD

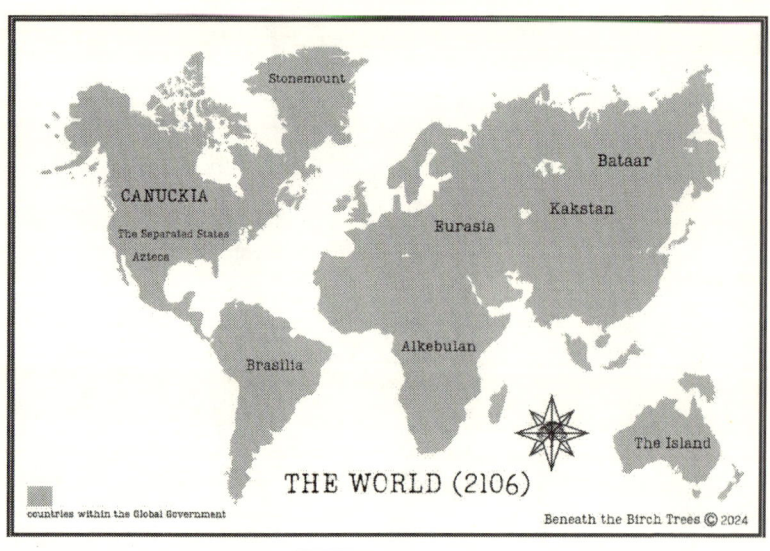

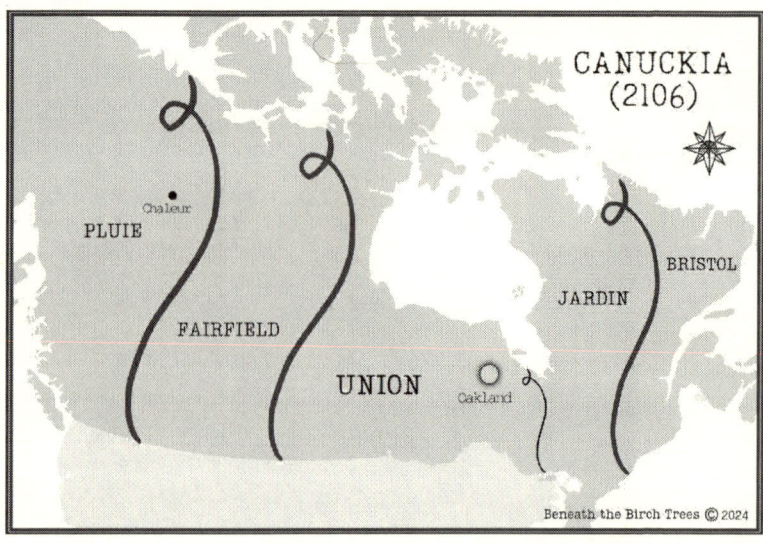

TIMELINE of the WORLD

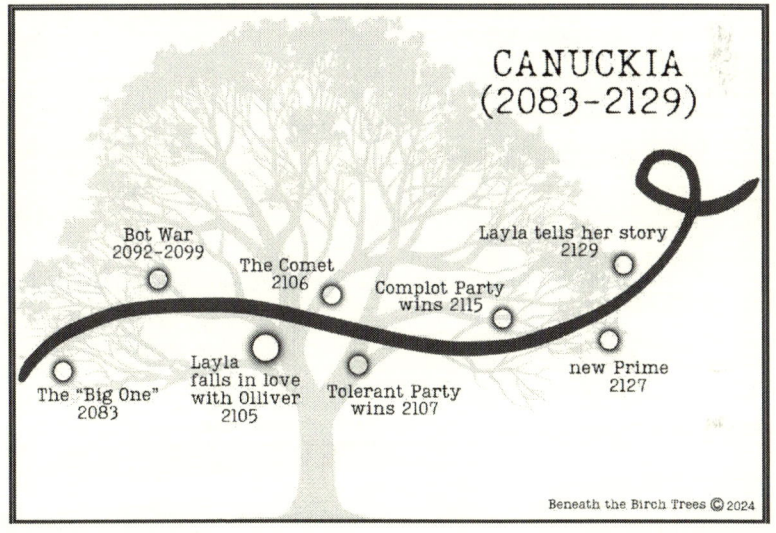

PART ONE

"I never wondered if Olliver loved me."

Layla Caitir Douglas

CHAPTER ONE

I never wondered if Oliver loved me.

Not once. I never doubted his devotion. And I never wondered if I should love him back. The second we met I knew we belonged together. I knew Oliver knew it, too. I saw it in his eyes. The eyes I instantly adored.

The eyes everyone else in our town feared.

Oliver and I dated for a year before I understood why people were afraid of him. I saw the first glimpse of his potential the day his mom walked into my grove and interrupted us—

Well, you know. Doing the thing two lovers did when we could catch a moment alone.

I almost missed the flash of fury that lit Oliver's face. I was too busy straightening my shirt. But I happened to look up at the exact moment his mom—the mayor—told us about the Champions, and the fire they started on Simone Rogers' property. Oliver's expression twisted into something feral, something primal, before slipping back into its typical calm.

When I saw my partner change—when I saw him reveal his true nature—I should have been worried. I should have been afraid, too. But I wasn't. I trusted Oliver.

We were in love.

I was innocent when Oliver and I met. I wasn't young—nobody was young in 2105—but I believed the world was a beautiful place. It was easy to believe in its beauty. I was surrounded by it.

I was born in Pluie, the westernmost province in the cold northern country of Canuckia. I grew up in a tiny town called Chaleur. The mountainous land was covered in forest: densely packed trees that shrouded a landscape flourishing with life. The rocky, green-covered world defined my days, so I was happy. Or, I thought I was happy. After all, I—Layla Caitir Douglas—was a citizen who'd survived the Bot War: the mechanical uprising that overtook the planet from 2092 to 2099.

In 2105, Pluie was peaceful. Well, sort-of peaceful. Canuckia was still recovering after the Bot battles killed thousands of citizens. Even though Pluie's forests protected Chaleur—because the giant Artificially Intelligent Bots couldn't navigate the province's greenery—my community had spent a decade surviving on rations, living under curfew, and working in careers that supported the war effort. But despite our regrowth fatigue, Pluie thrived. And I had my trees.

I loved trees.

Cedar, fir, hemlock.

Pine, spruce, alder.

I had a special connection with a birch tree that grew in the grove behind my home: *my* grove. I adored that tree. When I wasn't managing the administrative tasks for the Compassion Coplot—Canuckia's newest up-and-coming political party that hoped to bring the peaceful lifestyle of Pluie to every province in the country—I managed my birch's health. Nothing made me feel more grounded than when its marbled trunk shone in the winter darkness, or its roots crackled during the spring thaw, or its mint green, heart-shaped leaves shook within the summer rain.

But I tried not to discriminate. I loved every tree. My happiest moments were spent smelling the conifers' overwhelming scent of pine, and feeling the poke of their needles. I squirmed with joy whenever deciduous branches rustled in the breeze, or when helpful insects made bark their home.

I—also—loved the mountains. I scaled stony cliffs and skipped over moss. I threw pebbles into ponds, and flitted in and out of sunbeams when light streamed through the forest canopy. I wrapped my callused, tree-climbing fingers around pine trees' trunks, then pulled my strong body up into their branches. Within the boughs, I watched citizens travelling below, shuffling along the cultivated pathways that connected the homes, markets, cabins, and farms populating the mountainside.

I loved, and *was* loved. I was a cherished member of Chaleur's community. I organized emergency response drills, and delivered plant-based recovery rations to citizens who lived in the lowlands. People slipped bran muffins and sweet potato chips into my treetop playgrounds when Madame Perrault, the local grocer, wasn't looking. They asked me which seeds they should plant during what season, and how to tell if weeds were overtaking their gardens.

That answer was easy. Weeds persistently choked everything in nature that was beautiful, so citizens had to get rid of them.

I hated weeds.

But I had a good life. I *thought* I was happy.

Except I wasn't. I didn't know happiness until I met Oliver. I knew peace, nothing more. I wasn't alive. I wasn't awake in my world. But I woke up when Oliver's stooped shape stalked beneath my birch tree on a rare warm day at the end of spring.

Hidden by the branches, I shifted my position on my perch to see him better, and a shower of leaves fell on Oliver's head. He looked up—and I knew real love. Romantic love. Soul-squeezing, spark-igniting love. My future took root when I gazed at Oliver's sand-coloured hair (that needed a trim), his hunched shoulders (bent as though his responsibilities were too heavy to carry), and his thick brows that scowled above his shining eyes.

His angry eyes.

But I didn't see his anger—not on the day we met—so I was happy. Truly happy. I realized I'd lived a half-life, even though it had been beautiful. I knew Oliver and I were supposed to be together.

I knew.

But knowing is different than *knowing,* you know? You can feel something real, in your gut and in your soul, and not realize its importance right away. Which is why Oliver simply blinked at my shadowed body—high in my birch tree—before he brushed leaves off his fruit-fiber sweater and walked away. I was left alone, awake and alive, but not sure if what I thought had happened had *actually* happened.

It wouldn't be long before I was certain, though.

Swinging out of my tree, I balanced on a thick, sturdy root that poked out of the mossy undergrowth. Then I shook out my sheet of walnut-coloured hair and headed for the town. The Compassion Coplot had a gathering scheduled that evening, and I never missed a meeting. My duties were too important.

The Coplot was run by the mayor, Amelie Billadeau, and her son, Oliver Billadeau, created the policies the collective planned to implement once we were granted official Party status by the current government: the Reclamation Party. I hadn't spoken to Oliver before—our separate roles kept us apart—but I knew I had to introduce myself that night. He'd fall in love with me, we'd bond, then we'd spend the rest of our lives working together. We'd make the country a better place as a team. I knew we would.

But I wouldn't realize how wrong I'd been on that warm spring day until Mayor Billadeau appeared in my grove a year later. And I wouldn't *regret* that day until ash fell from the sky and indigo fire destroyed the world.

I strode through the forest, sure-footed in my heavy hiking boots. The trees thinned as I neared the main street that ran through the centre of Chaleur. Citizens smiled at me as they made their way towards the wooden cabin that hosted the Compassion Coplot's meetings. Tugging on the end of my hair, I joined the stragglers, and we slipped through the cabin door just before the gathering began. I took my seat at the back of the room—and tried not to stare at Oliver.

An hour passed. Assignments were, well, assigned. I rose from my chair as the meeting ended and the cabin emptied, with only a few zealous Coplot members staying behind. Three young citizens—the town's twins and an older, blonde girl—dallied in the space, tossing chairs into the storage room. I ignored the children's chaotic clatter and kept my focus on Oliver. Mayor Billadeau waved out the girls, then followed them onto the main road. She didn't see me stay behind, and she didn't say good-bye to Oliver who remained in the cabin, sitting at a long retractable table reserved exclusively for the Coplot's leadership team. Oliver always lingered after meetings, scrawling on a chalkboard as he noted his newest idea.

I waited until Oliver finished scribbling: until he pulled back from the table and stretched his hands over his head, cracking his hunched back. Then, as Oliver headed for the exit, I inserted myself in his path.

Oliver raised his eyes off the floor and onto my smiling face. He frowned, then stepped to the side. I stepped with him.

I quietly—and confidently—cleared my throat. "Can we talk?"

Oliver's eyes narrowed, then he side-stepped again. "You can send today's meeting minutes to my mother." He jerked his chin out the opened door and towards Mayor Billadeau, who was entering her office across the street. "She'll contact you if she needs anything else."

"I don't want to talk about the Coplot," I said, pulling on my hair. "I want to talk about this afternoon."

Oliver shifted from one foot to the other, clearly itching to be on his way. "I don't know what you mean."

"I think you do." Taking a risk, I stretched my fingers towards Oliver's arm, but didn't make contact. "You saw me in my tree. You know why I'm here."

Two bright spots appeared on Oliver's angular cheeks. "I need to—need to go." He stuttered when he got nervous.

I stretched my fingers farther. "Please. I've—" I dropped my hand, suddenly short of breath. Then I remembered the joy I'd felt when I saw Oliver under my birch; and I found my voice. "I've been waiting for you. I know that doesn't make sense, because we've lived in Chaleur our whole lives and we haven't spoken before today. But I waited for you. And you were waiting for me. We're supposed to be together, for the rest of our lives. And you know it." I nodded, made braver by the fact that Oliver was listening to my rambling. "I came here to, well, *start* the rest of our lives. Right now. Because once you know who you're destined to love, you can't be apart from them a second longer."

Oliver disagreed. With a pink-cheeked frown, he backed out of the cabin and onto a pathway that wound into the surrounding forest.

My feelings weren't hurt. Oliver was notoriously shy. I would wait and—when he was ready—Oliver would find me.

I didn't have to wait long.

The next morning I was back in my birch, whistling a melody that had played inside my head since the night before. I'd dreamed of Oliver. Nothing sexual, though a tingling in my belly leapt wickedly when I thought about him. In my dream I stroked Oliver's cheeks. His face softened under my touch and tears welled in his eyes. Instead of feeling sad for his sorrow, I felt empowered by Oliver's emotion. The depth of his feelings strengthened the depth of our bond and made my head sing. So, the next morning, when Oliver strode along the footpath directly underneath my tree, I wasn't surprised to see him there.

And I wasn't surprised when he stopped beneath my bough.

Oliver looked up. "What's your name?"

"Layla." I wrapped my fingers around a branch and swung to the forest floor. My boots landed on a mound of leaves with a soft *thud!* "Layla Douglas."

Oliver's eyes snapped to my face. His gaze sharpened. "You're Cole Douglas' daughter?"

I ignored the thump in my chest—which happened every time I spoke to a townsperson about my dad—and said, "I live with my cousin." I pointed towards Hope Ridge, the second largest mountain in Chaleur. "In the big house by the river."

"I knew your father," Oliver said. "He worked with my mother before the war." He looked me up and down, frowning at my torn trousers, mud-splattered shirt, and the leaves sticking out of my hair. His eyes settled on my face, then Oliver said, "Has your father messaged you? Since he—since he went away?"

"No," I said curtly. "He hasn't talked to anyone in Chaleur for fifteen years."

Oliver's stare softened. Then he stepped towards my tree and placed his hand on the trunk. "Why haven't we met before if—if you live in the big house by the river? We're neighbours."

I blinked. Most citizens peppered me with questions when they found out my dad was Cole Douglas: the scientist the Canuckian Prime had dubbed, 'the male who will change history.' Before the Bot War, my dad worked for a subdivision of Military Intelligence: Space Intelligence. Their department tried to contact extraterrestrials in order to grow Earth's orbital footprint. But it wasn't successful, and when the war started my dad left.

It didn't matter. I'd made my peace with it, even though the community still fixated on the story like it was juicy gossip instead of my life. But not Oliver.

"Layla?" His voice quieted as he repeated his question. "Why haven't we met before?"

I leaned against my birch for balance. Oliver's gaze made me dizzy. "I keep mostly to myself."

"Right." Oliver's eyes narrowed as he stepped closer. "Me too. Why didn't you talk to me before—before yesterday."

"I didn't know you." A breeze rustled the branches over my head and lifted the ends of my hair. "Before yesterday."

Oliver nodded. "Right."

We stood in the grove a moment longer, then Oliver jerked his head towards a space in the ring of pines that surrounded the grove. "You coming?"

Without waiting to see if I would follow, Oliver stalked into the forest.

I hurried after him. Thrilled. "Where are we going?"

"I have things to do," Oliver said. "For the Coplot."

I stayed by his side, allowing my fingers to graze Oliver's arm. He leaned into my touch.

As my heart leapt and my stomach swooped I said, "Can't wait." It didn't matter what Oliver had to do. From that moment on, we were inseparable.

If only I'd known better.

CHAPTER TWO

That first year was one I'll never forget.

I followed Oliver everywhere, and he would have found me if I'd climbed to the top of Mount Ryndle, the largest mountain in Pluie. We explored caves. Grottos. Stony summits. We roasted spun sugar on sticks over campfires. Waded through thigh-high rivers. Bathed nude in the sulphur ponds that dotted mountain pastures.

Our favourite place was the library built into the back of the Coplot cabin: a room filled with stories protected by laminate plastic so they'd survive the passage of time. I wasn't a reader—I preferred being out in the natural world instead of inside a fictional one—but when it rained too hard, or the winter winds trapped the town indoors for days at a time, Oliver and I hid in the room of books to flip the slippery, plastic pages.

Oliver read political espionage novels. I preferred fantasies: spirits, and creatures, and magic wielded by witches. But, every now and then, when Chaleur was draped in mist and the mood was right, I'd pull out a romance.

Romance stories always included a passage where the lovers, well, fell in love. Time blurred, and moments strung together, and before the couple knew it they were bonded more tightly than sap on a maple trunk.

Oliver and I lived that passage. We spent that year not falling in love, but *being* in love. And time didn't blur. Every moment was clear and distinct.

"Why do you like trees so much?" Oliver asked me one day, months into our relationship. "Especially this one." He nodded at the tree in the centre of my grove. "The birch."

It was a humid summer afternoon, and the grove smelled like soured apples: sweet with a hint of a bite. I leaned against my birch's trunk with Oliver's head in my lap. He stared at me—unblinking—as I gazed into the branches above our heads, watching a leaf spiral to the flowered floor.

I stroked Oliver's hair, letting my fingers linger behind his unshaven neck. "I like that they're connected to each other. And to us." I glanced at the white and black marbling behind my back. "Do you know anything about lateral root systems?"

Oliver slowly shook his sand-coloured head.

"Lateral roots grow outward, from the trunk," I said. "Right under the soil's surface. Not only do they anchor the trees into the ground, but they absorb moisture and nutrients to keep the trees alive. And!—" I sat straighter, "—lateral roots overlap other roots. They connect with other trees. They pass along nutrients to plants that are sick so the whole forest thrives. That's how our woods have survived fire, and drought, and insect attacks for thousands of years. And survived the Bot War, I guess. Trees are safe."

Oliver patted my leg. Patiently. "Right."

"And," I said, pinching the tip of Oliver's nose, "my birch tree speaks to me."

"It talks?"

"Sure," I said. "Listen."

We sat in silence. Then the wind picked up, rustling the pale green leaves above our heads. The grove came alive.

Branches sighed. Roots crackled. I touched my tree trunk and a spark ignited under my fingers.

"Ouch!" I laughed, stroking my birch fondly. "What are you trying to tell me, friend? Is a storm on the way?"

Oliver grinned. "Trees can't predict the weather."

"No, but they can warn other trees if predators are nearby. When insects eat them, birch trees turn their bark pure white to alert the rest of the family. Immediately, the trees start storing nutrients so they can survive a long insect attack."

"That can't be true."

"It is. And some trees let off a smell—a stink—if bigger bugs go after their leaves. The toxin makes the insects ill." I waved my hand, smiling. "Bye bugs."

Oliver shook his head, then wound his fingers through mine.

We sat quietly, letting the warmth of our hands combine as I watched the sunlight speckle my birch's bark. "That's why tree communities are safe. My birch protects me." I lifted my face towards the overhanging branches. "I've always loved it."

Oliver unwound his fingers, then rolled on his side. "More than me?"

"Weeell," I drawled, knowing my false insincerity would prick Oliver's pride. In a cute way. "I've liked trees my whole life. You've only been around for an instant. No time at all, really."

Oliver's mouth turned down into the pout that drove me wild. I wanted to nip his lower lip, but anyone could wander through the grove, and I didn't want to get caught with my trousers pushed below my hips and Oliver's hand up my shirt. Again. So, instead, I watched my lover's mouth form the words, "That's not fair. I've been here your whole life. You never noticed me."

"You didn't notice me, either." This was a regular argument: whose fault it was we hadn't paired up sooner. "I've been here, watching everything. You never looked up from your chalkboard."

"Right." Grinning, Oliver flopped onto my lap.

Almost as though they had a mind of their own, our fingers drifted together.

"You should like me more than trees now, though," Oliver said. "I can give you things your birch never could."

"Like what?"

"You know." Oliver blushed. "Things."

"Jewelry? Carob? Lectures about economic inequity?"

"No!" Oliver slid his hand up my shirt and cupped my breast. He squeezed, then withdrew his hand. His red blushes fanned down his neck. "Private things."

I grinned. Oliver was a male of contradictions. He was shy and sensitive most of the time, but when we were alone he—

Well. You know.

My longing surged as I thought about our first time together.

Together, together. I'd been with boys before—males in age, but youths in maturity—but I hadn't physically connected with anyone like I had with Oliver.

He'd arrived at my house for our typical talk and fondle session but, soon, our passionate kisses and fumbling fingers became urgent. It was lucky I always kept protection in my bedside drawer—and my cousin was at the Billadeau's mountain mansion—because the moody evening light and promise of hours alone created the perfect setting for me and Oliver to explore the next phase of our growing affection.

My fingers found Oliver's hand as I luxuriated in the memory of that night: stripping off our clothes, sweat soaking the blankets, and Oliver's mouth touching places I'd only allowed myself to stroke when I was alone.

Our first time had been clumsy, and involved more pokes and jabs than I'd expected, but it was with Oliver, so it was magic.

My thoughts spiraled back to the present moment—and my tree—as my hands moved on top of Oliver's chest, tingling with desire as I thought about our second time *together* together. Oliver melted in my hands, then lifted his chin.

I lowered my lips to his, and our discussion was done for the day.

Well. Almost.

"I don't like trees more than you. I adore trees. I always will," I said, my mouth hovering above Oliver's to allow time for his arousal to grow. "But what we have is special."

Oliver smiled as our lips touched. I knew his eyes were smiling, too. Like me, he was remembering our second time together. I knew.

Our second time had been more than magic. It was perfection.

It happened a few weeks into the relationship, and a few days after our first fumbling attempt at intimacy. I'd taken Oliver to my cave: a secret hideaway at the top of Mount Ryndle. Dried moss and brush had blown through the cavern's mouth, leaving the dirt floor under the rounded overhang cozy and comfortable.

After I pulled down a drape of weeds (I hated weeds) and ducked through the cave's opening, Oliver followed. He straightened as I walked deeper into the cavern.

I blinked my eyes rapidly to adjust to the darkness, then smiled at my lover. "Well? Do you like it?"

Oliver squinted as he turned in a slow circle, examining the space.

Unsure if he liked my cave or not, I blinked again; and adjusted a set of clear communication lenses covering my corneas.

The eyelinks.

Eyelinks were the only Com Tech that worked without assisted Artificial Intelligence, so they were the only technology Canuckian's used after the war. The eyelinks allowed wearers to read the thoughts and feelings—or 'glints'—of other wearers, and made it possible for people to sense the auras of nearby citizens. Auras were wavelengths of sound—undetectable to human ears—that shared energy resonance between wearers. When I spent time in the town, instead of in my trees, the community's combined auras hummed in my head like an active hive: a calm hive.

I happened to be very good at reading glints and sensing auras, which made me the ideal administrative assistant to the Coplot's leadership team. Mayor Billadeau's oldest son, Khleo, was as dense as a dung beetle, and the other leaders—the mayor, my cousin, and Oliver—weren't much better.

I fluttered my eyelashes as Oliver stopped his circle spin, hoping my eyelinks would give me some insight into his observations. Oliver wasn't wearing his eyelinks—he never wore the eyelinks because (he claimed) they distracted him from his duties —but I could sense something—something!—flowing out of Oliver anyway. His aura sounded like a zooming nest of hornets and he sort-of vibrated.

Which shouldn't have been possible. No one could sense another person's aura without assisted technology. Our bond must have been stronger than I realized.

I turned to Oliver to tell him that but, instead, let out a gasp as he swept me off my feet (like a couple in one of the sillier romance stories). With my laughter echoing in the domed enclosure, I clung to Oliver's shoulders as he knelt on the ground. Then, with a sensual voracity I'd suspected he had—though hadn't yet experienced—Oliver slipped his hands under and up my shirt to slide it over my shoulders.

I giggled as my shirt rose over my head, and Oliver's hands moved to cover my exposed nipples. Gently, he rubbed my skin. Then Oliver's mouth replaced his fingers, tongue flickering as his hands palmed the sides of my breasts. My nipples hardened. I arched my back and moaned.

"Oliver," I said. "Lower."

Oliver raised his face—eyes locking on my face—and a slow smile split his angular cheeks. He wound his arm behind my head to prop me up, then his free hand snaked across my breasts before settling on my stomach. "Here?"

I moaned again, then slid my trousers down to my calves. I pushed myself higher, into the crook of Oliver's arm, and spread my knees so they flanked his thigh. Biting my lip, I said, "Lower."

Oliver's smile grew as his hand moved. Teasingly slow, his fingers traveled over the downy hair growing between my legs.

I lifted my hips, pursing my mouth to keep from mewling. Even though the cave's location was far away from Chaleur, anyone could walk by and investigate. Especially if they heard me whimpering in ecstasy.

But my climax was reaching its peak, so I stopped caring.

As I shuddered and gasped, Oliver withdrew his fingers. He mumbled, "Good?"

I couldn't speak. I couldn't open my eyes. All I could do was enjoy the ripple of pleasure coursing through my body.

Oliver straightened. He pulled his shirt over his head, wiggled out of his trousers, then slipped off my pants, which had gathered around my ankles.

I pushed my sweat-soaked hair away from my face as my heart pounded. "Your turn."

"Or—" Oliver said, placing his hands on my knees, "—it could be your turn again."

"Um, you just made me, well—" I tried to ignore the heat infusing my face, but my rising exhilaration was difficult to control. I swallowed as Oliver massaged the back of my thighs. "That was the best I've ever had. You have to let me, um—"

Oliver kissed me.

He more than kissed me. He consumed me.

He moved inside me.

Soon, we were caught in each other's rhythm. Oliver shivered, and a low moan escaped his mouth. He fell on top of me. Spent. The electricity from my release rippled through my body, then rippled again. We stayed pressed together, breathing hard, until I opened my eyes.

I found Oliver's hand and squeezed it. "I had no idea I could feel like—"

Oliver looked up, smiling. "That?"

I nodded. "That *much*. I—" I stopped, then coyly dropped my gaze. "I'm pretty sure you could do that again. Right now. And I would feel that again. Like, right *now*, right now."

Oliver kissed me, long and slow. Then he lowered his head to my belly. While his lips hovered above my stomach, tantalizingly hot, he said, "You are beautiful."

My head spun. Nothing made me dizzier than a compliment from Oliver. With a burst of confidence, I grabbed his waist and rolled him over so I could straddle his hips. I nuzzled Oliver's neck with my nose as I ran my fingers along his shaft, sliding him inside my core. Leaning back for balance, I tightened my knees. "I love you, you know."

Oliver nodded—speechless—as I began to rock.

He knew.

I shuddered as another wave of pleasure crested, then receded. Then I stared out the cave's opening, up at the midnight sky and the stars winking overhead. A neon light crawled over the canopy, casting a purple glow on the trees that climbed the mountainside:

the Northern Lights were stunning in the summer. With beauty in my mind and peace in my heart, I closed my eyes and succumbed to my desire.

During that first year, Oliver and I did more than make love. In fact, we rarely made love. We made out—a lot—but finding the time and space to fully physically connect was difficult in a tiny town. So Oliver and I spent most of our time being, well, stupid. Immature. Ridiculously foolish, like only new lovers could be. I dragged Oliver to my favourite places: into unexplored crevices and up hills he was reluctant to climb. He never joined me in my trees, but he'd run along the footpaths as I swung from branch to branch. Sometimes, Oliver jumped up and reached for my legs as I flew overhead, but I never let him catch me. As much as I loved him, I couldn't give Oliver the satisfaction of besting me in my world.

He won enough in his.

Oliver's world was the Compassion Coplot. At the meetings, and with his mom, he was a prince. Citizens respected him because of his principled ideas for change, and he was admired for his passionate equity advocacy. The Bot War had split the country into multiple factions (rural vs. municipal vs. provincial vs. federal) but Oliver wanted everyone to unite.

I wanted a united Canuckia, too. Regardless the obvious differences between my life and Oliver's, I happily followed his lead when it came to the Coplot. I didn't mind Oliver's obsessive nature, and he tolerated my obsession *with* nature. Actually, he did more than tolerate. He embraced my world, however reluctantly. Because Oliver's preference was always—always!—to work.

But outside of the Compassion Coplot, Oliver's reputation in the town was less-than-desirable. Whenever I picked up my weekly food order from the market, Madame Perrault—the grocer—would say to me, "You're only twenty-four. That's so young. Why would you let that toxic tick stick to your side?"

Oliver *was* sort-of like a tick: buried deeply in his duties. But the town didn't see him when we were alone. How could they? We were, well, alone. Oliver melted when he was with me. He softened, becoming pliable in my tree-climbing hands. His voice changed. It grew lighter, and more tilted toward laughter. He was a good listener. He, well, *listened*.

Oliver didn't listen to anyone, but he listened to me. Oliver let me talk for hours, and he could repeat back every word I said.

I wasn't shy. I had no problem chatting with anyone who was around. It was part of my job. But I wasn't used to being listened to. Oliver treated me like I was important. And I listened to him, too.

Sometimes, during the Coplot meetings, I'd forget to do my administrative tasks because I was too busy staring at him: watching his mouth stretch wide when he shared a new idea, then purse tightly when his brother told him to ease up. I watched Oliver's thin shoulders hunch when other citizens spoke, then straighten when someone asked for his advice. I watched his rigid hands gesticulate, knowing they would turn into silk when we were alone.

Oliver's hands—loving when they touched me—revealed his frustration when he was around other people. They clenched in his lap when someone said something sarcastic, and balled into fists when his mom publicly praised his brother.

But he was always gentle with me. Always.

Then, after a year of blurred time and achingly acute moments, Mayor Billadeau changed everything.

Oliver and I were in my grove—talking, like always—when reality (aka the mayor) stepped in.

"Do you like me more than your tree now?" Oliver pressed his back against the birch's trunk as I lay in his lap.

"I love you, but my birch has grown a lot," I said. "I might love you and trees the same, now. And that means something. The trees are my family, after all."

Oliver grinned. He smiled easily after a year spent in my arms. "What if the birches weren't yours? What if the trees belonged to us?"

"Oh, I like that," I said. "This land is ours. This forest is ours.

This birch is—"

"Ours." Oliver stood, then pulled a lighter out of his pocket. He flicked open the heat source and a thin flame spouted out the top. "Let's make it permanent. We'll brand it with our initials. Then, no matter how much time passes, when the tree grows our love will grow with it."

The tree flexed its roots.

It hadn't done that before.

"Don't." I pushed myself to my feet. "Branding trees hurts them."

Wind rushed through the grove, wavering the light in Oliver's hand. "Trees are wood," he said. "They can't feel."

"Please don't. Can't we just say the birch belongs to us? We don't have to mark it."

"What's wrong with marks?" Oliver lifted his face, and the lighter went out. He pointed to a scar that ran under his chin.

"What is that?" I cupped Oliver's jaw with my hand.

He jerked away: he didn't like my calluses. Then he melted, and wrapped his arm around my waist.

Comforted by our closeness, I said, "I know every inch of you and I've never seen that scar." Gently, I touched the thin, brown line. "How did you get it?"

"During the war," Oliver said. "After the Total Tech Takedown. When the Bots were disabled my mother was in the valley, on the front line. Her eyelinks weren't working, so she asked a scout to message my father so he could bring her a new pair. We were at home, hiding. My father didn't want to leave me with Khleo—I was too young—so he brought us along. When the explosions started—"

I winced. I remembered that day. I hadn't left Hope Ridge until the Bots lost power. One of my most vivid memories was walking to the border between Pluie and the neighbouring province of Fairfield—in the valley—and seeing the giant Bots broken on the ground, smoking from the impact of their crashing.

"—Khleo started crying," Oliver continued. "My mother left

her post to soothe him, and my parents forgot about me. So, I ran towards the Bots. I'd never seen anything like it: the giant machines falling over, destroying the earth, smashing into each other. It was amazing. But I got too—" His hand tightened around my waist. I knew he was trying not to stutter. "I got too close. A Bot fell and a piece of metal sheared off its chassis when it hit the ground. The metal spun towards me, so my father pushed me out of the way. He'd run into the valley when he saw me down below, on the battlefield. The metal killed him."

"What?" I gasped. "I didn't know that! Why didn't you tell me?"

"Lots of people died in the war." Oliver shrugged. "My father was one of them."

"Is that why you understood about my dad? How I felt when he left?" I reached for Oliver's cheek. "Oli—"

"When my father pushed me, I scraped my chin on a rock. There was blood everywhere." Oliver's arm shook. "From my face and from my—my father. I hated it. To this day I don't do blood. I can't." His eyes darkened. "I—I can't."

"I get it," I said. "Holy holly berries, do I get it."

I didn't get it.

"But there's nothing wrong with your mark." I stroked Oliver's scarred chin. "Your mark of bravery."

Oliver pulled away. "I wasn't brave."

"You were," I said, surprised by his sudden movement. "It must have been awful watching your dad die. Mine left willingly, so I never had to—"

"If we're not going to mark your birch tree, then every tree should belong to us." Oliver turned away and slipped the lighter in his pocket.

I moved forward to comfort him—

—and stopped.

Oliver's aura zoomed, even though he wasn't wearing his eyelinks. I blinked, then stepped back. If Oliver's frantic aura was an indication of his inner distress, he must have been really upset. He needed me to be patient.

So I smiled; and gestured around the grove. "The whole world can be ours, Oli. Every tree, in every forest."

Oliver glanced at me, then grinned. "I knew you were ambitious."

"What?" I laughed. "I'm kidding. I'm happy with you—and my birch—and nothing else."

"No," Oliver said playfully. He grabbed my hand and pulled me into his arms. "You're just like me. And my mother." Oliver lowered his lips to my neck and mumbled, "You want to rule the country."

"Oli!" I squirmed as he kissed behind my ear.

"You want power," Oliver murmured. "You want—"

"Oli!"

We were standing in that pose—me giggling while Oliver kissed my neck—when the mayor walked into the grove.

And the end began.

CHAPTER THREE

Birch trees were the most beautiful plants within the Betula genus and there wasn't a lovelier species than the Silver.

Their white bark contained crystalline cellular deposits that made them shine, even when it was dark outside. The pale colour reflected the winter sun, so birch trees were able to grow year round, despite the high northern altitude. Their refreshing scent—wintergreen mint with a splash of vanilla—added to their splendour. My grove held an air of opulence unmatched in any other Canuckian forest.

But when Mayor Billadeau walked into it, the birches sagged.

"I knew I'd find you here." Usually, Mayor Billadeau bounced around Chaleur with an aura that thrummed like a bee, but that afternoon she was quiet. Too quiet.

It worried me.

I stepped closer to Oliver as Mayor Billadeau said, "Sorry to interrupt, but I need you. Both of you. I've called an emergency meeting of the Compassion Coplot."

Without hesitating, Oliver strode towards his mom. "What's wrong?"

I didn't move. I couldn't look away from Mayor Billadeau, who ran her hand through her short hair before replying, "It's the Champions. That upstart leader of theirs—Zekiul Cox, I think his name is—brought his rebels to Pluie. He set up camp in our mountains. And, last night, he set fire to Simone Rogers' farm."

Holy holly berries. The Champions had been on the Reclamation Party's radar for years. They were infamous on the News Alert network: the virtual social centre citizens accessed with the eyelinks. The Champions' rebellion started when the war ended. They protested every move the federal government made. But the rebels were based in Jardin, the province sandwiched between Union—

the capital—and the sea-bordering territory of Bristol.

Straightening my shirt, I absorbed this new development. And I looked at Oliver's face.

That was the moment. That was when I should have walked away. Run, actually. When I saw Oliver's expression crumble and contort—when his eyes burned as though they were lit by a hidden inner fire—I should have clipped a bud from my birch, tucked it in my pocket, and disappeared. Like my dad.

But I stayed. I watched Oliver's face smooth, and his hand drop on his mom's arm protectively. "What's the plan?"

Mayor Billadeau smiled. "That's why I need you, Monsieur Brilliant. Our Reclamation Party representative messaged me." She tapped her temple, indicating her eyelinks. "They asked me to tackle this little problem. So, of course, I want the Coplot's help. Get that noggin in gear, my dear boy, and start thinking of solutions." Mayor Billadeau glanced at me, then held out her hand. "You too, Layla. We need to you pay special attention in tonight's meeting. If you can record everyone's glints, we might find a non-confrontational way to put out the Champion's fire before they start another one." Holding onto Oliver's elbow, the mayor guided her son towards the break in the pine trees, chuckling. "Metaphorical fires, that is."

Swallowing my worry—and the image of Oliver's eyes that continued to spin in my head—I followed them. I had no idea what was coming or if I could handle it, but I followed.

I was sort-of excited. After years of sitting on the sidelines, the Compassion Coplot could finally do something about the conflict affecting Canuckians, instead of preparing for the 2107 election year when we planned to submit for official Party status. And *I* could help. My ability to read multiple citizens' glints meant I could provide the leaders with the collective's subconscious ideas: ideas their minds forgot the second they had them. And!—it might be fun to be active. Anything was better than waiting patiently before we could kick out the current government.

The Reclamation Party took over in 2099 when the previous

leadership failed to navigate citizens through the war. The party was competent, but there were problems spanning the land that needed to be addressed, like the hulking metal Bot bodies that rusted on the landscape like bronzed blights, and the lack of skilled labour—nationwide—that was needed to replace the Artificially Intelligent workforce. The quality of education and health care across the country was inconsistent, and a citizen could consider themself lucky if they lived in a town, or city, that had people who knew how to teach and heal.

Which was why the Compassion Coplot was so important. Mayor Billadeau and her family created policies designed to help Canuckia return to its previous state of wellbeing: the time before the Bots revolted and humans had to destroy them to survive. And!—the Coplot's plans worked. Chaleur thrived under the mayor's guidance, and her methodologies were being adopted across Pluie. With the Coplot proving the effectiveness of its strategies locally, it wouldn't be long before we grew, ousted the Reclamation Party, and Mayor Amelie Billadeau became the next leader of Canuckia: the Prime.

With her children by her side.

I smiled as I followed Oliver—and his mom—to the Coplot's cabin. Mayor Billadeau had prepared for a post-war reality before the Bot battles ended, and she started the Compassion Coplot in 2100. She asked both of her children to join her so she could teach them how to lead. Which they did, with enthusiasm. Oliver inherited his mom's passion for politics. His older brother, Khleo, had Mayor Billadeau's bee-like energy: he couldn't stay still—or serious—if his life depended on it.

Which Khleo proved the second the three of us entered the cabin.

"For the love of leaves, what took you so long?" Khleo wiggled on his chair as he hollered across the room. "Were you two screwing again?" He leaned over the leadership table, pointing his finger at my face. "Dimitri's told you a thousand times: the world could end at any minute, so you can't let Oli's dick distract—"

Oliver's muddy boot hit his brother squarely in the middle of his forehead.

"Nice," Khleo said as Oliver hopped across the room on one foot to retrieve his shoe. Khleo smirked at me. "Really, that was his best act of aggression yet." He wiped mud off his stubby nose. "Why Mom didn't enlist him in the military still baffles me—"

His words were cut off again as Oliver shoved the back of Khleo's chair, tipping his older brother onto the floor. With a growl, Khleo rolled onto his feet and wrapped his arm around Oliver's head, subjecting him to a noogie.

"Are you finished?" Mayor Billadeau waited patiently behind the table. "Or should I sell tickets so I can profit off your wrestling match? Winner has to stay late, since you're making us wait."

"Sorry, Mumsy," Khleo said as Oliver's head twisted in his arm. "Sorry Oli's such a shit."

"Watch your language," Mayor Billadeau said. "The rest of the Coplot will be here any minute."

Oliver pulled away from his brother, then sank onto his chair. Khleo blew him a kiss.

I bit back a grin as members of the collective filed into the cabin. Taking my place at the back of the room (next to the library) I focused my attention on the people filing into the space. Then my cousin—Dimitri—walked through the front door, and I tried not to flinch. My cousin had a perpetually pessimistic attitude, and his aura's fly-like buzzing infected the gentle hum of the community. But he was the last to arrive, so I was able to ignore him and widen my eyes so my eyelinks could record a vid of the discussion.

Vid recordings were an efficient way to take meeting minutes. After every gathering, I sent the vids to the mayor so she could review the collective's talking points at her convenience.

Mayor Billadeau waved everyone to their seats. The Compassion Coplot settled onto chairs placed in rows facing the table while the leaders arranged themselves *around* the table: the mayor facing the audience, Oliver to her right, Khleo lounging *on* the table, and Dimitri leaning against the wall that held the cabin's one window.

Keeping my gaze on Mayor Billadeau's face, my eyelinks recorded every word she said: from her introduction, and a quick reminder to share Coplot announcements on the News Alert network, to the urgent topic of the hour: the Champions.

"—but it wasn't until this morning—when Councillor Whitley reached out to me—that we realized the magnitude of the problem we're facing." Mayor Billadeau sat on the edge of the table. "The Champions have been on the federal government's watch list for years, but this escalation of violent, rebellious behaviour caught everyone off guard. We have to discuss—seriously—what to do. I suggest—"

Mayor Billadeau's voice settled into a pleasant thrum. My vision sharpened as I stared at the short female with her sandy shock of hair that curled over her ears, and the love handles that peeked over the waistband of her trousers. The mayor's voice seemed to emerge from her body as though her stomach was a bellow blowing air into the room: air that soothed. Then Mayor Billadeau turned her back to the audience and pressed her temple. She squinted, and her eyelinks projected an action list onto the wall behind the table titled, 'Putting Out (Metaphorical) Fires. Ha Ha Ha.'

A male sniffed above my head. I looked up, into Dimitri's disdainful gaze. He stood beside my chair, staring down at me. "Your relationship is unhealthy," he whispered as he nudged my ankle with his toe. "You two never take your eyes off each other."

"What are you talking about?" I whispered back, keeping my eyes on the mayor. "I'm working, not looking at Oli. And he's definitely not looking at me."

I stole a glance at my partner. He *wasn't* looking at me. Oliver wrote on his chalkboard as he chomped on the side of his tongue.

"When we aren't in meetings he watches you," Dimitri said, crossing his arms. "It's concerning."

I glared at my cousin. His high-pitched aura filled my head. Dimitri didn't understand my attachment to Oliver, but I didn't care.

"If you ever loved something the way Oliver and I love each other, you'd know we aren't concerning," I said. "We're admirable. You're just jealous."

"Jealous? You two are obsessed," Dimitri said. "I've known true love. You and Oliver act like you own each other. Love isn't possession."

"Loving your designs doesn't count," I said. "Loving a person is much more meaningful than loving a thing. Or an idea. Or, whatever it is you like."

Dimitri sniffed. "Trust me, the way you two behave is . . ." He nudged my leg. "It can't last, Layla. It won't last."

I ignored my cousin, which was the best thing to do when he got doom and gloomy.

But he wouldn't let me.

Leaning over to murmur in my ear, Dimitri said, "Who are the Champions? What did they do?"

"The Champions cause chaos." I adjusted my mind's focus so I could keep recording the Coplot's glints—and the mayor's speech—as I said to Dimitri, "Haven't you heard about their rebellion?"

Dimitri squinted his sharp green eyes: eyes that burned against his brown skin. "Just tell me—"

He shut his mouth as Mayor Billadeau looked over at us. Quizzically. "Is there a problem, Dimitri? Layla?"

"I was just asking our assistant for a recap, Madame Mayor," Dimitri said as he straightened. "My apologies for interrupting."

"No trouble," Mayor Billadeau said. "No trouble at all. Last night, the Champions set Madame Rogers' mushroom farm on fire. They destroyed her entire crop."

Dimitri pasted on a look of fake concern. I knew it was fake, because his glints were panicking and a stream of words had taken over his mind: *Stop embarrassing yourself in front of everyone, Mitty. Stop being stupid, or they'll hate you like—*

I muted Dimitri's glints. I'd lived with my cousin for years and, by that point, his constant self-recrimination was more annoying than it was pitiable.

Out loud, Dimitri said, "Did the fire spread? No. Never mind." He pinched the bridge of his brown nose. "The town would have been evacuated."

"The fire department put out the blaze right away," Mayor Billadeau said. "The Champions messaged them to claim ownership of the act as soon as their instigators left Madame Rogers' property."

"And, uh, who are the Champions?"

"They're the renegade group who've been actively undermining the Reclamation Party. You must have seen their vids on the News Alert network. The ones they posted from Jardin?"

"Definitely," Dimitri lied as he crossed his arms. "But I've never taken the vids seriously. I thought they were parody posts."

"Their posts are foolish, but their behaviour is downright disturbing," Mayor Billadeau said. "In real life, the Champions protest the Prime's politics. They recently moved to Pluie, but we didn't realize how close their new headquarters was to Chaleur until—"

"Last night." I clapped my hand over my mouth. My job was to listen and record, not comment. But Dimitri's delays made my skin crawl. Most things Dimitri did bothered me.

"Exactly." Mayor Billadeau smiled. "Thank you, Layla. Now! Questions, anyone? No? Well, then." She nodded at the wall, where her action list still hovered. "What option should we go with?"

A blonde girl sitting in the middle of audience raised her hand. "Do we have permission from the provincial government to engage with the rebels?"

Mayor Billadeau beamed at the girl. "Great question. We're allowed to respond to the Champions' stunt ourselves. Since the Compassion Coplot's applying for Party status in the new year, Councillor Whitley is more than willing to let us address this teeny, tiny, town problem. Like a kind of test. You get me?" She winked. "We need to win in the small arena before we enter the big one."

28   STEFANIE BARNFATHER | Beneath the Birch Trees

"If it's a test," the blonde girl said, "we should go with the last suggestion on your list and take out the Champions' leader. Now."

"That's somewhat extreme." Dimitri walked towards the front of the room to resume his typical stiff stance by the window. "We should follow protocol: go through Amelie's action options in order, starting with diplomacy. Banishment should be our last resort."

The girl raised her plucked eyebrows, muttering, "I didn't say we should banish the Champions' leader."

"What was that?" Dimitri rubbed his temple. "Did you glint something?"

"Me?" The girl smiled at my cousin. "I don't think so."

Sometimes, citizens' words didn't align with their glints, which caused fuzzy disturbances over the eyelinks. But I was paying close attention to the auras humming in the room, and nothing unusual resonated inside the girl. Nothing noticeable, anyway. Like always, Dimitri had made a mistake.

And he refused to own up to it. "I could have sworn I sensed an odd—"

"So, if I'm hearing this right, we have one member who wants the immediate ejection of the Champions' leader from Canuckia," Mayor Billadeau said, "and one member who'd like us to follow standard de-escalation practices and ask the rebels to meet with our envoy."

"Nope," Khleo said. "That idea is shit."

"Language," Mayor Billadeau muttered.

"That idea is crap," Khleo amended. "Our envoy leader is Oli. Can you imagine the rebel retaliation if we sent Monsieur Grump to negotiate peace terms?"

"Peace terms?" Oliver's hunch deepened. "We aren't at war. The Champions set some mushrooms on fire."

"All my mushrooms," Rogers said from her place at the front of the audience. "And I have the biggest farm in Pluie. We have to go without meat flavouring for the rest of the year."

That set off a chorus of grumbles in the room.

Mayor Billadeau took command. "We've survived worse. And Simone is receiving full financial compensation for her loss. But we can't let the Champions do something like this again."

"Then don't send Oliver to talk to them." Khleo crossed his powerful legs with dramatic abandon, kicking Oliver's chalkboard off the table. "Send me. I'm so irresistible the rebels will bow down before us." He winked, looking exactly like his mom. "Nobody can resist my tooth-ache charm."

"Tooth-ache charm?" Oliver turned on his chair: not to grab his chalkboard but to glare at Khleo. "People can't resist you because you hurt their mouths?"

"Nope." Khleo wiggled his shoes. "People can't resist me because I'm sweet. Tasty. Everyone wants a piece."

Khleo's canvas sneakers were covered in sparkling sequins that day, specially imported from the capital. His shoe addiction was out of control, but Mayor Billadeau loved indulging her eldest's whims. She used her connections within the government to supply Khleo with frequent sneaker deliveries, and he had so many pairs he was able to wear new designs every day. As Khleo shook his feet the sequins caught the overhead light and sent bright dots onto Oliver's forehead. Khleo grinned as Oliver wrenched his face to the side, shutting his eyes to protect them from the glare.

"Oliver is our envoy leader." Mayor Billadeau bent over and grabbed the chalkboard, handing it to her second son. "And he'll be fine. *If* that's the course of action we choose to take, of course."

"Speaking with the Champions is smart," Dimitri said. "I vote we follow that route."

"Are we voting? Already?" The blonde girl pitched her voice so it soared over the audience. "I thought we were going through the options."

"I'm ready to vote," Khleo said. "But only if Oliver isn't the envoy leader."

"Oliver *is* the envoy leader." Mayor Billadeau rifled Khleo's hair affectionately. "You get me?"

"Then Layla has to go with him." Khleo pointed his sparkly

sneaker in my direction before aiming his toe at Dimitri. "I'll second Dimitri's vote if Oliver takes his better half."

I sat up. I'd watched the leadership team plan adventures for years, but I never imagined I'd get to join them. If they thought I could help, I'd gladly trade my eyelinks for a seat at the table and—

"Layla can't come." Oliver leaned back on his chair. It creaked under his weight. "It's too dangerous."

I slumped. So much for that.

"Oh, blah," Khleo said. "She's braver than you. And smarter. And she smells better—"

"Layla accompanying Oliver to the envoy meeting is a wonderful idea. Her observational skills are just what we need." Mayor Billadeau stood on her toes and peered over the audience, smiling at me. "Layla? What do you think?"

I half-stood, pushing back my chair. The legs scraped the floor, but I ignored the squeal of metal on wood. "I'd love to go—if everyone else is okay with it?"

"Everyone else?" Mayor Billadeau grinned around the room. "We're okay with it, right? Am I reading our glints correctly?"

She *was* reading the collective correctly. The Compassion Coplot's acceptance swelled over the eyelinks.

I sat on my seat, strangely touched. I had no idea the community had so much faith in me. I figured they saw me as nothing more than a tree girl, the person who preferred plants to public speaking. The meeting continued, but I forgot to restart the vid recording. I was too busy basking in the warmth of my own glints: my pride and internal affirmations. The Coplot thinks I have potential. Maybe I could do more than speak with rebels. Maybe I could—

If I hadn't been distracted, I might have noticed the dangerous glint threading through the Coplot's support. But I didn't notice.

And I didn't see Oliver watching me, his eyes glittering with barely-controlled malice.

CHAPTER FOUR

After the meeting ended, Oliver and I stayed behind to shoo out the girls who lingered in the cabin.

Then we shut down the space: me carefully stacking the chairs in the storage room, and Oliver slamming the leadership table's legs flat while he scanned the notes he'd written on his chalkboard. Then, together, we flicked off the lamps that dotted the wood-paneled ceiling and stepped into the night. It wasn't late, just dark. It always got dark early—dark and cold—and the rain made us hurry home as though it were well past midnight.

Seeing my shivers, Oliver threw his sweater over my shoulders as we hurried up the path that led to Dimitri's mountain estate: my home.

Dimitri designed the place. Before the war, he and my dad worked together, but when the Reclamation Party deemed Space Intelligence a useless department—because the interstellar skies continued to be populated by non-sentient gas instead of alien species—Dimitri turned stargazing into a hobby and started his architectural career. After the war he became a nationwide success: *Dimitri Simard,* the designer who sky-rocketed to popularity because there weren't any Bots left to create buildings. He'd built our artistically flawless house into the side of Hope Ridge.

I disliked Dimitri (*really* disliked him) but I loved the home's oak floorboards, cedar-stripped walls, and wooden staircase that ascended two stories.

As Oliver and I sloshed across the field growing in front of the Ridge—which was wet from the evening rainfall—Oliver hugged me close and pressed his lips to my forehead. "What would you do without me?"

Even though I couldn't see Oliver's face, I knew he was happy.

I shrugged into Oliver's sweater, then wound my arm through his. "I would be colder."

Oliver stayed quiet. He never responded when I replied to his rhetorical questions as though they were literal.

"Anything I need to know," I asked as we neared my front door, "about envoy meetings?"

"No," Oliver said. "They're easy. We meet, we negotiate, and we try not to kill the other side. We'll be in and out in twenty minutes."

"You've negotiated with renegade groups before?"

"None—yet—but my mother trained me in the fine art of peacekeeping."

"The fine art of peacekeeping? How exciting." We paused on my front step. "I didn't know politics was so refined."

The light above the door sent shadows across Oliver's furrowed forehead. "You need to take this seriously, Layla. My mother is worried."

I pressed my temple: eyelink wearers used the physical action to focus their minds. "She didn't seem worried to me."

"The Champions are acting out of character," Oliver said, as though I hadn't spoken. "Rebels who target big issues, like the Reclamation Party's policies, don't set farmers' fields on fire. They know it won't help their cause."

"What is their cause?"

"Overthrowing the government," Oliver said. "Which is ridiculous. Change doesn't happen by storming the Capitol and screaming. You have to be patient, and *earn* the power to make a difference. But over the past few years, the Champions have done nothing except protest the Prime."

"I know," I said, widening my eyes and tapping my temple pointedly. "I go on the network."

"And they haven't declared an official agenda," Oliver said, *again* as though I hadn't spoken. *He* was acting out of character. "They don't have a specific platform. Without an agenda, it's hard to support them."

"Not everyone has an official agenda. Most people aren't as organized as the great Oliver Billadeau."

"Right." Oliver stepped off my front stoop. He was genuinely concerned, but I had no idea why. His mom had been confident about the envoy decision when she dismissed the Coplot for the evening.

"Why do they call themselves the Champions?" I reached for Oliver's sleeve, trying to reconnect. "Who are they championing?"

"They claim they champion Canuckians, but—like I already said—they haven't declared an official agenda, so I'm not sure. I guess we'll find out tomorrow." Oliver tucked his hands into his trouser pockets and peered into the forest. "I need to get back. My mother is expecting me."

"You have to stay the night." I grasped Oliver's shirt. "You have to fill me in."

Oliver arched his eyebrow. "Is that what we're calling it now?"

"Calling it?" I laughed, realizing what he meant. "No! Not that."

Oliver blushed so deeply I could see his cheeks redden in the stoop's shadows. "You meant the envoy meeting."

"You could fill *both* of those ins." I pulled Oliver close and snuggled into his chest. "You could tell me what I need to know about tomorrow, then fill in my—"

"You don't have to be on the envoy team, you know. Dimitri said he'd be my second." Oliver's body felt like a plank: he was that tense. "If you'd rather remain in your assistant role, you can stay home. Or go gardening."

"I don't want to garden. I *don't* garden. I want to go with you."

Oliver melted. "Right." Playing with the end of my long hair, he said, "There's no shame in being an administrative assistant, Layla. You're good at it."

"I know," I said, pretending his sort-of dismissal didn't sting. "But Dimitri? Your second?" I pulled my hair out of Oliver's hand. "Don't be stupid. You want a resolution. Dimitri will make things worse. And I'm an excellent assistant. I could also be an excellent negotiator."

"I could ask Khleo to come, but he's more of a cheerleader than a leader." Oliver stared over my shoulder, at the forest. "Yes. It's better if Khleo stays away from active—active—" He frowned. "Active activities. He's unpredictable."

"Khleo?" I giggled. "He's harmless. Loud, but harmless."

"Trust me," Oliver said. "I know him."

My chest gave a thud—*I* knew people better than anyone—but I kept quiet. Then I wrapped my hands around Oliver's lower back so he couldn't escape my grasp, no matter how much he squirmed. "Forget about Khleo. Forget about Dimitri. You have me. And I'm coming to the envoy meeting."

"Layla—"

The front door swung open. Dimitri stood on the threshold, backlit by the light in the foyer. "It's freezing out. Get inside."

"See you tomorrow." Oliver shrugged out of my arms, then backed across the field.

"Hold on. I'll come with you." Dimitri disappeared into the house, sending his voice out the opened door. "I have some questions for Amelie." He jogged down the steps as he put on his jacket. "There's leftover cauli-steaks in the cold cupboard, Layla. Heat them up until they steam."

"I'm coming, too," I said, pulling the door shut. "I'm part of the envoy team."

"Stay," Oliver called over his shoulder as he and Dimitri moved towards the forest. "We'll talk tomorrow when I pick you up. Early."

"It'd better be really early," I yelled, pausing on my front stoop. "I want everything filled in before we meet the Champions."

"She's still coming with us?" Dimitri asked as the two males jogged away.

"Layla will be useful," Oliver said. "Admit it."

Hugging Oliver's sweater around my body, I laughed quietly at his final statement. I'd definitely be at the envoy meeting. They needed me.

I entered my house. Pulling off Oliver's sweater, I pressed the orange fruit-fibre to my face and breathed in Oliver's scent (made sharper by the citrusy shirt). Then I tossed the sweater on Dimitri's drafting desk—which he'd placed by the door so guests would have to ask about his current projects—and made my way to the kitchen. Dimitri had a stash of broccoli florets hidden at the back of the cold cupboard, and the fresh, green vegetables would make a much better dinner than reheated leftovers.

As I waited for water to boil so I could steam the broccoli, I stared at a painting hanging above our sink. I didn't know how Dimitri had managed to snag an oil-on-canvas piece by the famous Artist, MIRÆ, but—at that moment—I was grateful. MIRÆ's bold brushstrokes depicted the stormy indifference of the sea, and her artwork provided a calming backdrop for my mind to replay moments from the Coplot meeting. Then Oliver's loving face floated to the surface of my mind, and I forgot about the painting. And the Champions, and the Coplot. And my broccoli, which turned to mush as my thoughts swirled. But didn't matter. I'd happily eat limp veggies in exchange for pleasant rumination about Oliver.

Then Oliver's angry expression from the grove smashed apart my memories. When Dimitri arrived home, hours later, I was still in the kitchen, sitting behind the counter pushing florets around my plate. I couldn't understand Oliver's sudden temperament change. I'd known him for a year—a year!—and even though he could be moody at times, he never lost his cool.

What was it about the Champions that upset him so much?

Dimitri sniffed.

I looked up at my cousin; and erased Oliver's anger from my mind. I'd find out why he hated the Champions at the envoy meeting. If negotiations were as easy as Oliver claimed, I'd have plenty of time to analyze him.

"Layla," Dimitri barked. "Are you awake?"

With a defiant smile, I lifted my fork and placed an ice-cold floret on my tongue.

Dimitri wrinkled his nose and grabbed my plate off the kitchen counter. He stormed towards the sink. "Disgusting."

I smirked. I was being childish, but I didn't care. Dimitri yanked my filaments. It was about time I started yanking his.

My cousin never really liked me. We lived in the same house, but we didn't spend any time together. Dimitri had a telescope attached to the roof, so when our paths crossed—usually after the sun set—he'd hide outside, pretending he could learn things from the cosmos instead of suffering from my company. Dimitri's architectural designs—and his astrological projects—were the only things that made him happy.

I frowned. Astronomical projects? I could never remember how astronomy and astrology were different. I was an Earth expert, not a space cadet.

It didn't matter. I didn't care. I didn't need Dimitri to like me. The town took care of me, and the trees. And Oliver.

Grabbing my water glass, I pushed away from the counter and dropped my cup in the sink.

I was halfway out of the kitchen when Dimitri stepped in front of me, green eyes flashing. "For the last time, Layla, I'm not doing your chores. I don't mind washing a few dishes, every now and then, but you need to be more responsible. You have to take care of yourself."

"I've been taking care of myself since my dad left," I said, snapping. "The least you can do is clean up, since you've ignored me for over a decade."

Dimitri's jaw dropped. "Layla!"

I never spoke to him that way—I didn't snap at anybody!—but between Oliver's anger and the Champions' drama it was becoming difficult to stay composed. "You know you're going to keep washing my dishes, and you're going to do the rest of the chores, too. If we run out of plates, I'll eat at Oliver's. And if I run out of clean clothes, I'll walk around naked."

Dimitri followed me into the living room, practically spitting. "You will not. You'll freeze."

"Good point. Oliver will make sure I have plenty of outfits." I glided towards the staircase that led to my upper-floor bedroom, grabbing Oliver's sweater off the drafting desk as I sauntered by. I waved it in Dimitri's face. "See?"

"Layla Caitir Douglas!" She can't speak to me like that! How dare she? Doesn't she understand how hard it's been—

Dimitri's use of my full name—and his glints—stopped my snapping. I turned around, shooting Dimitri an *I'm-sorry* smile.

His anxious mind-chatter disappeared and his high-pitched aura quieted. "I need to talk to you." Dimitri pinched the bridge of his nose. "But if you don't want to talk, I can send you my glints. You need to see what happened at the Billadeaus. And it's a clear night, so I want to get upstairs. Jupiter might show his face before the clouds come back."

Willing to do anything to keep Dimitri calm, I nodded. I could receive his memories much faster than he could explain them, so I sat on the living room couch and readied my mind. Dimitri sank onto the couch's armrest. Wearily. Then he removed a small tube from his pocket and took out his eyelinks, which he placed over his corneas.

I pulled away. "Wait. Did you—were you *not* wearing your eyelinks? Just now?" I looked around the room, like answers might be hiding behind the canary-wood columns flanking the front door. There was no way—no way!—I could have read Dimitri's glints without technology. But I had. His emotions and thoughts had been as clear as the surface of a spring pond. And somehow, I'd heard his aura.

Dimitri stared at me like I'd grown an extra ear, and—honestly —it felt as though I had. "What wrong?"

"Nothing," I said. "It's nothing. I'll figure it out, um. Later. Never mind. Show me what happened at the Billadeaus."

"I can send you my glints tomorrow." Dimitri squinted. "Before the envoy meeting."

"No, that's too early," I said. "And, um. I'm tired. Sleep will be good. Please, send me your glints."

Dimitri shrugged, then pressed his temple. His aura peaked

before condensing into a rod. The rod snaked towards me and knocked on my mind. It didn't hurt. The knocking was an internal concept, not an actual sensation: it was a request to let Dimitri share a memory. I opened my mind, and received Dimitri's recollection of his time at the Billadeau's.

Well, Dimitri's interpretation of his recollection.

CHAPTER FIVE

DIMITRI ORION SIMARD
SEPTEMBER 22, 2106

Layla is pushing me off a cliff.

Not literally. She's pushing me off an emotional cliff. Living with her is terrible.

Layla is irresponsible and selfish, which are problematic personality traits I *know* will lead to painful disappointment. But does she listen to me? Of course not. Even though I stuck around after—

It's not important. I can't worry about Layla right now.

Oliver walks into the forest, but I catch up to him. Lowering my head so it doesn't brush the trees' branches—a common problem when you're tall—I ask, "She's still coming with us?"

Oliver knows who 'she' is. There is no other 'she' with him.

"Layla will be useful," Oliver says. "Admit it."

I sniff. The only thing Layla can do well is sit with her mouth closed while she records the rest of us. I can't tell her true love that, though. Oliver is a good guy, but he'd strike me senseless if I insulted *his* true love.

Hmph. True love. They don't know true love.

Oliver picks up his pace, navigating the densely packed trees with ease. He's surprisingly agile for someone so stooped. I hurry to catch up.

We arrive at Amelie's house a few minutes later. As always, my breath catches when her lovely home appears in the mountainside: Niccola Peak. Amelie's property is one of my finest creations. It has front facing windows ensconced by rock, speckled panels of wood shaped like trees, and an entryway arched by a tunnel, built to blend in with the natural stone overhang. The house looks like a fantastical fortress.

I didn't intend to design Amelie's home in the trending style of the day: 'Safehouse Chic.' We live in peaceful times, after all, but some inner desire for privacy must have affected my imagination when she hired me to take on the project. In a worst-case scenario, the Billadeau property could operate as a sanctuary. In a best-case scenario? It will solidify my status as an architectural genius.

I smile up at my handiwork as Oliver leads us towards the entryway.

"Did your mother send a message to the Champions' leader?" I ask as we pass under the tunnel and into the Billadeau's home. The overhead lights make me blink. They're searchlight bright.

"His name is Zekiul Cox," Oliver says.

We cross the entryway's onyx floor, following the midnight-blue walls that lead to Amelie's den: a Hunter-green room filled with a squishy sofa and heavy, maple furniture. Wincing, I duck through the den's door. Amelie and Khleo are short—and Oliver's stooped shoulders lower him to their height—so the mayor asked for a dropped ceiling to be put in the den to create a comfortable atmosphere. Oliver, who is used to the room's splendour, strides into the space without stopping, but I pause to admire my design. The den is definitely comfortable.

Then I remember why we're there. "Whose name is Zekiul Cox?"

"The Champions' leader," Oliver says as he takes his usual position on his usual chair: a high-backed seat that sits straight and spindly. "You need to remember that."

"Yes, the Champions are prickly about their titles." Amelie walks into the den and claps me on the back. "Tagged along, huh? After this one—" she smiles at her emotionless son, "—escorted the oh-so delightful Layla home?"

I shake Amelie's hand. "You look better. I was worried about you after tonight's meeting."

Amelie's laugh lines deepen as she clasps her hands around mine, then she moves to *her* usual place: the sofa with its plump cushions. With a sigh—followed by a tired groan—Amelie lowers onto the couch. "Every time disaster strikes I get a little older." Her russet-brown eyes settle on my face as I sit beside her. "You get me?"

"Did you find out which Champions are attending the envoy meeting?" As always, Oliver skips conversational pleasantries. "We need to know their names. We can't make etiquette mistakes like other diplomacy organizations. It's the details that matter in negotiations."

"I'll send you the details—both of you the details—later." Amelie settles deeper into the sofa. "But I'm not all that worried about tomorrow. Despite the complaints made in the meeting—by Khleo—you can handle the Champions. And Layla has real potential."

Oliver grins. "Don't tell her I said this, but I wouldn't be surprised if she convinced the Champions to become mercenaries for peace. Ten minutes with Layla, and the fire-starting rebels will be planting crops with Madame Rogers instead of destroying them."

I disagree with Oliver's assessment of Layla. She's annoying, not convincing: but I don't share that glint out loud. It's good if Oliver is confident about tomorrow. Despite Amelie's belief in her youngest son, Oliver's cynicism often adds unnecessary complications to simple schemes.

I keep that glint quiet, too. Amelie is besotted with her boys—like any good mother—and I never want to disrespect the mayor. She's been my closest friend since—

It's not important.

"I agree, Oli," Amelie says. "Your gal is one of a kind."

"If we aren't going to discuss tomorrow, I have a few questions about recruitment." I squint so I can see Amelie better. Part of the room's comfortable atmosphere is achieved by dim lighting.

"The Compassion Coplot's growth has been stagnant for weeks," I said, "and we need more members if we're going to run in the next election."

"Yes, yes. Yes." Amelie waves her hand. "We can chat about recruitment. But first, I'd like to hear your opinion about another Coplot complication. I'm concerned."

Amelie wants *my* opinion? How kind of her. "What's wrong?"

Amelie glances at her son. "Did you sense that strange glint over the eyelinks?"

"When?" Oliver shifts on his chair. "In the meeting?"

Oliver doesn't wear the eyelinks: Amelie should know that. But I do—most of the time—and I happened to note a disconcerting glint. "I picked up on it," I say. "What did you sense, Amelie?"

"Something worrisome. Anger tinged with—" She looks down at her hands, then rubs her thighs. "I'm a little embarrassed to say this, because it's such a strange combination of glints, but I swear I felt excitement. Excitement mixed up in the anger."

"Excitement?" I squint. "You must have felt nervousness. Someone was probably upset and they didn't want everyone to know about it."

"No, no. No," Amelie says. "I recognize nerves. You're glinting them right now."

"Dimitri's not nervous," Oliver says. "He's impatient. So am I. Why are you worried?"

"The last time I noticed that particular combination of anger and excitement was, well—" Amelie laughs, quick and low. "I don't want to create a fuss over nothing, and this is probably nothing."

"Just tell us," Oliver says. "We can't fix your problem if we don't know what the problem is."

"That's part of the problem," Amelie says. "There might not be a problem. I've been tired lately—damned tired—so there's a chance I used the eyelinks incorrectly—"

"Tell us, Mother! When was the last time you sensed those glints?"

I pinch my nose. Oliver can be terribly impolite.

But Amelie ignores her son's abrupt interruption. "The last time I felt anger mixed with excitement was at the end of the Bot War, when the Global President signed off on the Total Tech Takedown."

Oliver and I squirm. The Global President in 2099 was Min RoboReiwa. After the Bots were destroyed, RoboReiwa was proven to be a psychopath. She took pleasure in destruction, felt no remorse for causing pain—to human or Bot—and she was the strongest natural glint reader in a century. She possessed unheard-of power: she could read the glints and sense the auras of every sentient being on the planet at the same time. *Without* wearing her eyelinks. And she could project her glints into others' minds. The whole planet sensed her warped intentions the day the war ended: when she agreed to Reset the Bots, despite knowing how much they would suffer. Fortunately, RoboReiwa was replaced weeks later. Thank goodness.

"Former President RoboReiwa is in prison," Oliver says. "She wasn't in tonight's meeting."

"I know she wasn't in our meeting." Amelie pushes out of the sofa to pace in front of her magnificent maple bookshelf. "But if someone in the Coplot has a similar personality type—"

"Then a rebel group burning down a field of mushrooms isn't our only problem," I say as the full weight of Amelie's concern lands. "We might have an ambitious troublemaker in Chaleur."

"Not possible," Oliver says. "We know everyone in Chaleur. We'd know if there was a potential Min RoboReiwa in our midst."

"That was poetic, my dear boy," Amelie says, mid-stride. "I haven't heard 'midst' used in a sentence since—well. Never." She stops pacing and smiles. "Your time spent in the library with Layla is paying off."

Amelie likes relieving tension, especially the tension created by her offspring. But her light-hearted jibe doesn't work this time. In fact, it sends a streak of crimson under Oliver's eyes.

Oliver is still blushing when Amelie's other offspring appears.

"Did Oli say something smart?" Khleo places his hands on the back of the sofa, then flips over to sprawl on the cushions.

I move to the armrest to avoid being kicked by Khleo's large, sneaker-clad feet. He's terribly inconsiderate.

"Why wasn't I invited to your conference?" Khleo smirks. "Is it a secret conference? Are you inventing a secret handshake?"

"Go away, Khleo," Oliver says. "This doesn't concern you."

"I agree." Amelie pats her eldest's head. "I love you, Le-Le. But go away. Have a snack and a soak. We'll talk later."

Unlike Layla, Khleo knows when he's not wanted. Grinning at Oliver over his broad shoulder, he heads out of the den. "You know I'll read your glints while I eat my sandwich and enjoy my bubbles."

"Uh, I don't think so," Amelie says. "Reading glints without permission is dangerously close to glint-snatching."

"Nuh uh," Khleo calls from the hallway. "Reading your family's glints is allowed. And Dimitri's practically family."

"Illegal is illegal, Le-Le. And glint-snatching is illegal."

I pinch my nose. Glint-snatching makes me feel nauseated. The idea that someone could access my glints—and my entire lifetime of memories—to peruse without permission is heinous. It's breach of privacy, which is why it's illegal. Fortunately, you have to be a very strong glint reader—Min RoboReiwa strong—to snatch someone's glints without them knowing. Which is why people like Khleo make jokes about the practise. It rarely happens.

Insensitive whippersnapper.

I keep that glint to myself.

However, I don't know Khleo very well. He might be secretly strong. So I whisper to Amelie, "Is he really going to read our glints? Should I take out my eyelinks?"

"I wouldn't worry," Amelie says. "Khleo's never shown an

aptitude for glint-reading. No matter what he says, most of his blustering is fluff and nonsense."

I want to trust Amelie, but she's proven she lacks awareness of her sons' peculiarities. Khleo could be reading my glints as we speak, so I remove my eyelinks and slide them into their carrying case: a tube filled with salient solution to keep the lenses moist.

Amelie's glints disappear.

"Who do you think the ill-intended citizen is?" I settle on the sofa's armrest. "Has anyone in the town displayed psychopathic tendencies?"

"Yes," Oliver mutters, his voice laden with sarcasm. "Just the other day I caught Madame Forsyth butchering radishes for fun. You should have heard the screams from her vegetable patch. I almost called the Provincial Police—"

"If there were any obvious signs of psychosis in a townsperson, I'd know about it," Amelie says. "But I've heard nothing. I've seen nothing. Not until tonight."

"Let's go through the possible suspects, then," I say. "Who attended tonight's meeting?"

"Layla isn't a suspect," Oliver says. "Or Khleo."

"Khleo. Yes. We should discuss Khleo." I lean towards Amelie, lowering my voice, "I hate to implicate family, but Khleo is irresponsible. What if he—"

"My son isn't the problem," Amelie says firmly. "The troublemaker isn't one of us. But they *are* in the Coplot. One of the regulars."

Amelie presses her temple. Names and pictures project onto the wall beside the bookshelf. As she speaks, the names leap around: some disappearing, some becoming obscured by a thick line through their centre, and some pictures shifting to the side under a column labelled, 'Actual Suspects (Not My Babies).' I stare at the remaining names and faces: the three people Amelie thinks could be the problem.

"Wait." Oliver pushes off his chair to jab the list. "Who did you eliminate? We have to consider every member. You can't arbitrarily cut people."

"I removed the people who didn't attend tonight's gathering," Amelie says, "and the members it couldn't possibly be. Like Madame Flanagan, who's ninety-six—and the sweetest old bitty on the planet. And the kids: the Boucher twins, and the Kovalchuk siblings, and Madame Graham's daughter, and the gaggle of wee ones the Landry's foster. Oh!—and Mixeur Templeton. They were chatting with the Forest's Department over the eyelinks during the meeting."

"What about everyone else?" Oliver points at the wall. "There are over fifty people in the Coplot. Three is not fifty."

"Most of the people in the Compassion Coplot glint goodness on a regular basis," Amelie says. "Relax, Oli. We can't assume everyone is disturbed."

Oliver humphs, then flops onto his chair. "But one of those three could be our villain?"

"Villain?" Amelie raises her thick, burnt-umber brows. "Well, now."

"Definitely." I walk to the wall, then trace the list with my finger. "You are correct about these members." Staring at the pic of a male more stooped than Oliver, I aim my voice at Amelie. "Justin Kendle: Local hermit who hates trespassers on his property. He even turns away the Xander kids when they go door-to-door sharing baked goods."

Amelie nods. A pic of a redhead jumps to the projection's foreground. "Don't forget Ashleigh Smyth, the gal who pilfered that scarf from Madame Perrault's market."

"And Madame Perrault." Oliver spits his words at the pic of the grocer, an older female with a flint-grey coiffure who could take out a rebel group—like the Champions—using only her pinched expression. "Peevish Pear looks for trouble."

"Peevish Pear?" Amelie smiles. "That's funny. When did you come up with that flattering nickname?"

Oliver shrugs, noncommittally. He stares at the grocer's face. "Layla calls her that. It fits though, right? She has that strand of hair that sticks out the top of her head like a stem, and nobody is as nosy as Madame Perrault. Layla wanted to call her 'Pervy Perrault,' but I talked her out of it."

I almost laugh at that comment, but—fortunately—I'm able to maintain my usual frown. When Oliver and Layla started dating, Madame Perrault was the first person to spot them kissing in the woods. Amelie spent hours explaining to the grocer that her adult son's business wasn't *her* business, even *if* Madame Perrault decided that Amelie's child entering into a relationship with the local orphan was a scandalous affair.

My frown deepens. I'd also spent hours explaining to Madame Perrault that Layla's business was her own, and asking the grocer to please stop referring to Layla as an orphan since she was raised by a competent caregiver: me. Since everyone knew orphans couldn't fit in society due to their traumatic upbringing away from functional adults, it was inappropriate to assume—

I blinked, then shook my head to erase Dimitri's point-of-view. "Is that it?"

Dimitri shifted on the couch, frowning. "Is what it?"

"Is that all you talked about?" I grinned. "Don't worry, Dimitri. I know you're a good caregiver. And a discriminatory weevil." I swatted his shoulder. "Orphans can fit into society. And I don't need to see the replay of you rubbing Peevish Pear's ignorance in her face, especially since you should visit the learning shop yourself." I hopped to my feet. Pleased.

I liked the spice that had gotten into me that evening.

Heading for the stairs, I kept up my confident swagger. "I already flagged Kendle, Ashleigh, and the Pear as problem people. Honestly, I am so far ahead of the 'smart' citizens in this town it's embarrassing."

"Layla Caitir—" Dimitri half-rose to his feet, then sat back down. "You knew about the strange glint?"

"No," I said, shrugging, "but people have strange glints all the time. It doesn't mean they're going to murder someone." I paused on the landing at the top of the stairs, one foot in my room and the other lightly kicking my doorframe. "Can I go to bed now? In case you've forgotten, we have to meet with the Champions in the morning and negotiate world peace. Or, whatever."

"Layla!"

"Don't forget to send me their names, *if* you remembered to get the list of attendees. The Champions are prickly about their titles, right?"

Ignoring the sound of Dimitri sputtering with annoyance, I shut my bedroom door. Within seconds, my cousin's buzzing rod snaked under my door and knocked on my mind. Grinning, I sent back through the rod, May I help you?

I did get the list, he shot up at me. Here.

A digifile stamped with the mayor's seal of office flowed through the rod: the details about the Champions' envoy.

Dimitri's voice slammed after it. Your majesty.

I like that, I sent. You can call me that tomorrow. The Champions need to know who runs things around here. Then I pushed away Dimitri's rod and shut my mind.

Lying on my mattress, I placed my hands behind my head and closed my eyes. I waited until Dimitri finished banging around down below—he had such an awful temper—then I opened the digifile.

The Champions' leader was a male named Zekiul Cox, like Mayor Billadeau—and Oliver—had said. Major Zekiul Cox.

Pushing up on my elbows, I took a closer look at the file. The major was young: twenty, practically a youth. The pic underneath his title showed a dark-skinned male with a muscular build and a thin, intelligent face. And—this surprised me—his face seemed kind. Too kind to match the vision I'd already formed of the rebel who, in my imagination, was a viscous predator-type.

The other Champion attending the envoy meeting seemed

much more rebel-y. She was a female with shoulders thick enough to belong to a big-headed ground beetle: a female named Jolene. Just Jolene.

A single name? I bit back a smile. That had to be fake. Though, maybe two names were too difficult for someone like Jolene to remember.

Just Jolene.

I giggled, then removed my eyelinks; and my laughter faded away. As I placed the Com Tech in their case, I remembered how I'd read Dimitri's glints when he wasn't wearing the devices.

Dimitri had been right in his memory. Nobody—except abnormally strong natural glint-readers—could sense other people's thoughts and feeling without the eyelinks. The ability only showed up once or twice in a century, and Min RoboReiwa had enough strength for three powerful readers. But was there a chance—a small chance—that I could be a strong natural glint-reader, too?

I shivered, then burrowed under my river reed blanket. The power was dangerous. If I could read glints without technology, I didn't need citizens' permission to peruse their minds. And!—I might be able to *snatch* glints. Snatching glints gave the snatcher ownership of their victim's source thoughts, feelings, and memories; and the snatcher could manipulate the glints any way they wanted. Min RoboReiwa snatched her cabinet's glints so they'd approve every policy she wanted to pass. She made her opponents believe her ideas were the best course of action. At one point, she convinced the Global Government to hire the Bots as space mercenaries so she could conquer interplanetary society—before she realized there was nothing up there but stars and moon rocks.

But I wasn't like RoboReiwa. I didn't want to hurt anyone. So—maybe—if I *was* a strong natural glint-reader, I could use the power to help people. But—

—no. I couldn't do that. Not without invading their privacy.

Then I laughed. Me? A glint-reader with the strength of Min RoboReiwa? I really did need some sleep.

Shaking my head, I crawled out from under my coves and

slipped into my night shirt. I scrubbed my teeth and skin, then combed my long hair with a bristlegrass brush. As I untangled my walnut-brown tresses, I thought about Oliver. The second I placed my head on my pillow I drifted into dreamland, lulled by the memory of my partner.

Turns out, I *was* an abnormally strong natural glint-reader. But I was also human. So, after I fell asleep, I forgot about the town's troublemaker.

And Oliver's unusual expression in my grove.

CHAPTER SIX

The next morning dawned cold and crisp.
    And early. I shivered in Oliver's sweater. And his coat. And his toque and mittens.
    We'd risen before the sun, and were now waiting in the agreed-upon meeting spot: an outdoor amphitheatre with a sliced tree trunk in its centre that operated as a speaking platform. Small stone slabs rose in a ring around the space. Rain dripped from the branches of the trees that surrounded the amphitheatre, but it didn't fall on me or Oliver. Or Dimitri, who was with us. The canopy covered the area, protecting us from milder weather. But the crown of the forest didn't shield us from the wind, which pushed through the trees' trunks to lick the bodies of people stupid enough to spend time in the early-morning elements.
    "Stop that." Dimitri glared at me as my teeth chattered. "You're going to annoy the Champions' leader."
    "Annoy their leader—" I said, "—or annoy you?"
    I'd woken up that morning in the same headspace as the night before. Spicy. Treating Dimitri the way he'd treated me for the past fifteen years was satisfying. I liked fighting back when he insulted me, instead feeling sour. I liked digging in.
    "Do you care who you annoy?" Dimitri breathed on his hands, coaxing warmth into his fingers. "You frequently annoy everyone. Why should the rep for the rebel rebellion be any different?"
    "Reb-beb-beble rebellion." I giggled at my shaky pronunciation. "Reb-beb-beble. Reb-beb—"
    "Can't you shut her up, Oliver?"
    Oliver ignored most things, but not someone being rude to me. He shifted his stance on the stage as he scowled at Dimitri. "I could shut you up."
    "Nobody needs to shut-tu-tup. Shut-tu-tup. Shut-tu—Oh, this

is sil-lil-lilly." I grabbed my face, stilling my jaw. "Everyone shut up."

"This is a disaster." Dimitri peered through the trees. "The Champions' leader isn't going to negotiate with us. He won't take us seriously."

"Cox," I said. "His name is Zekiul Cox. Major Zekiul Cox. Ze-ze-Zekiul—"

"Layla!" Dimitri stomped his feet, then slipped on the wet stage. He refused to put on hiking boots, and his cactus-leather loafers had no grip. "Where is he anyway? Major Cox?"

I snorted, then clapped my hand over my face. I wasn't a snorter, but Dimitri's tongue-slip innuendo was funny. "For the love of leaves, don't call him Major Cox. All I'll think about—the whole meeting—is Major Cox's major—"

"Layla!"

But I couldn't seem to stop. "Come on." I nudged Dimitri with my elbow. "Major. Large. Cox. Peni—"

"Shut *up*, Layla."

"You're thinking about Major Cox's major cock right now. Admit it." He was! Dimitri's glints radiated with desire and a dark, oblong image that was sharpening into a—

Dimitri spun around on his heels. His shoes squeaked. "Glint-snatching is illegal, Layla."

"I would never snatch someone's glints. Your glints aren't hard to read—unlike the stiffness in the image solidifying in your mind."

"Holy holly berries!" Dimitri pinched the bridge of his nose. "Stop!"

I smirked at my irate cousin. "It's such a shame you aren't a morning person."

"I'm not a morning-with-Layla person," Dimitri said. "You're usually in the forest by the time I wake up. Usually, I start my day happily. Without you in it."

"Aw, Dimitri, you're too good to me. I'm so glad my dad went gallivanting around the globe so you could have the pleasure of patronizing his only child—"

Oliver pulled me to the side. "Leave him alone, please. I know Dimitri bothers you—and, apparently, you've started bothering him—but can you pause your poking so we can focus on what's important?"

Whoops. I'd gone too far. I sighed, and my long hair flipped around my face. "Sorry. I can focus." I kissed Oliver's cheek, then shook out my shoulders.

I was prepared. I could handle this. How difficult could one conversation with two rebels be?

As tall, menacing bodies stepped out of the tree line opposite where we stood, I gulped. Looking at the hardened renegades the Champions sent to negotiate, I realized the meeting might be trickier than I'd thought.

Then I realized I could get rid of my worries by testing out my new (theoretical) glint-reading power. So as the Champions walked across the amphitheatre to join us on the thousand-year-old trunk ground flat by inclement weather, I reached out—tentatively—to read the glints of Just Jolene and Zekiul (I couldn't think of him as Major Cox without giggling).

My test worked.

Zekiul was smart—I could see the advanced connections his mind made as he assessed us—but he was exhausted, which made him pliable. But not too pliable. Despite his inner fatigue, Zekiul's body was fit and strong. And attractive. Really attractive.

He was attractive.

Zekiul's pale brown eyes shone in his dark face like polished sandstone, and the half-unzipped jacket he wore over his toned body showed off his muscled chest. His black, spiraled curls were cut close to his scalp, and he stood taller than Dimitri. Zekiul's defined chin tilted towards the canopy, but it wasn't an arrogant tilt. It conveyed confidence, without bravado. As he analyzed the amphitheatre, Zekiul's aura floated to my ears. It zoomed like Oliver's, but the quality of the sound fluttered like a moth. It was sort-of beautiful.

My stomach swooped. In a good way.

Well, *not* in a good way. In a very, very wrong way. I was in love with Oliver. He was the only male on the planet who made my stomach swoop. The familiar feeling inspired by Zekiul had to be surprise: surprise that the Champions' leader wasn't dangerous. Or, *bad* dangerous. Major Zekiul Cox was good dangerous.

Very good.

Swallowing, I glanced at the other Champion; and my stomach stabilized. Just Jolene *did* look like a ground beetle. Her flat face showed no emotion, except for the rapid movement of her darting eyes. Jolene's wide body was corded with muscle—like Zekiul—but her glints were barely readable. She had a weak mind. Oliver would have no problem getting her to negotiate.

"Thank you for speaking with us today," he said, stepping forward. "We understand you feel your actions were justified two nights ago when you set Simone Rogers' field on fire. We're here to understand why, and to craft a resolution—together—so this doesn't happen again."

"You assume we *don't* want this to happen again." Zekiul widened his stance, holding his hands behind his back.

I caught myself leaning towards the major. Unintentionally. When Zekiul spoke, his fluttering aura quieted to a thin, sharp tone. Oliver didn't notice—without the eyelinks, he couldn't read the major—but he seemed to have some awareness of Zekiul's internal focus. Oliver cricked his neck, then shifted his weight from side to side. He really *did* have a problem with the Champions.

That wasn't good. A shifty Oliver was an uneasy Oliver, and an uneasy Oliver meant—

"You're going to burn down more mushroom crops?" Oliver took a step towards Zekiul. "What? Is your big, rebellious plan to make food less appetizing? I know citizens would be upset if they didn't have umami flavour to balance their dinner recipes, but—"

"What Oliver is trying to say—" Dimitri placed his hand on Oliver's bristled shoulder, "—is that we'd like to understand what happened so the Compassion Coplot can support you."

Zekiul's lip stretched into a sideways sneer. "Compassion Coplot? That's what you call yourselves?" He leaned back on his heels, sending a glance towards Just Jolene as she barked out a loud, "HEH." Then Zekiul mimicked, "What? Was the Hugs and Kisses Society already registered with the business bureau?"

"We wanted to call ourselves something pretentious, like the Champions—" Oliver shot back, "—but we had to settle for a name that represented our goals instead of one that made us seem like heroes: if heroes did nothing but share lies on the News network."

Zekiul stepped away, his dark face flushing. "We don't share lies."

"You don't post facts," Oliver said. "And your shares that include a little truth are so twisted they might as well be lies."

"We share source stories," Zekiul said. "From real people, with real lives. People who get their hands dirty." He nodded at Oliver's clean, quivering fingers. "People you know nothing about."

"You think you're so noble, but you're nothing but an idealistic idiot. You have no clue how the world works." Oliver sneered. "The real world."

Zekiul breathed in through his nose. "You don't know anything about the Champions. You're the idiot if you've drawn conclusions because of a few posts and your obvious biases."

Holy holly berries. This interchange was hot. Too hot. If my lover, Oliver, and the majorly cocked Zekiul kept up this intelligent—and feverish—back and forth I was going to combust in a puff of erotic steam.

I rubbed my sweating palms on the back of my trousers.

"Right," Oliver said, flexing his fingers. "Help us out, then. Tell us your agenda."

"Why should I tell you our agenda?"

"So we can fix your mess."

"Fix it? Fix it how? And what mess? As far as the Champions are concerned, setting the field on fire was necessary."

"Don't you understand?" Oliver's hands shook. He was trying so hard to stay in control. "You attacked a farmer. A *farmer*: someone who was supposed to be on your side. Before the fire, you targeted Cabinet Members in the Capitol. The Champions' picketing and protesting could have been construed as heroic, but now you look like petty renegades who go after harmless, hardworking citizens." Oliver's voice wavered. "Is that who you are, Cox? A petty renegade? Because after the fire, that's how Canuckia sees you. You aren't a hero. You're an ass."

The forest quieted.

Oliver stared at the stage. "If you told us what you really wanted—what you're trying to accomplish—the Coplot could make this fire incident go away. If you tell us agenda, and your agenda is honourable, the mayor will talk to our provincial rep and they'll downplay your transgression. Then you can leave Pluie and go back to canvassing the Capitol. The Compassion Coplot doesn't want another *real* person's livelihood destroyed because you don't know how to lead an advocacy organization."

Zekiul watched Oliver without moving. Then he nodded. "Fine. I'll tell you our agenda."

The wind died. The canopy settled, and everyone held their breath. Even the rain lessened. I leaned towards the major again, captivated by the stillness that had settled over the amphitheatre, seemingly because of Zekiul's energy shift.

Zekiul spoke from a place deep within his chest. "Canuckians are suffering, even though the Bot War ended years ago. The Reclamation Party has tried to address the problems in our country —the poverty, and institutional failings—but the government is struggling, too. The Champions want the federal government to work with the municipalities. We want them to rebuild trust with civilians by talking with us about what we want, and what they can provide. The Reclamation Party should help us build a Canuckian future that considers the diverse desires of complex communities. But the government won't. Our Prime—and the cabinet members—hide in the Capitols like they're above the rest of us. Like they're better than the people they promised to serve." He shook his head, then looked around as though he'd forgotten where he was. Flushing, Zekiul shrugged. "The Champions remind the Reclamation Party that they're failing. And they need to do better."

My heart pounded. Forget the Compassion Coplot! I wanted to become a Champion.

Oliver didn't share my enthusiasm. "Do you always use fancy words to avoid answering direct questions?" He smirked. "Why did you set fire to Madame Rogers' field, Cox?"

Jolene lurched forward—

—then she stopped as Zekiul raised his finger.

Tightening his grip on Oliver's shoulder, Dimitri said, "It might be a good idea if our leader and local mayor, Amelie Billadeau, heard more about your organization. We should arrange another meeting."

Zekiul's lip lifted. "Why would we do that?"

"Mayor Billadeau supports Canuckians' wellbeing, and you threaten that wellbeing."

"We don't harm Canuckians," Zekiul said. "The Champions help Canuckians. Didn't you listen to what I just said?"

"So, you were helping Madame Rogers when you burned down her field?" Oliver shook out of Dimitri's grip. "Right. Farmers are so frightening. I'm glad the Champions saved the country from evil Rogers and her forest of fungus."

I snorted, then covered my mouth with my hand. I had to stop laughing out loud or Oliver wouldn't let me leave my seat at the back of the Coplot cabin ever again.

Zekiul dropped his finger and Jolene lumbered forwards, snarling.

For the love of leaves. So much for trying not to kill each other.

I inserted myself neatly between the two groups as they closed the gap in the amphitheatre. Raising my hands, I said, "Alright. Let's relax, and—"

I didn't get to finish my sentence. Dimitri pulled back his fist, hollering, and threw himself at Jolene. Oliver reached over my outstretched arms to grasp at Zekiul's face. With a snarl, the major ducked, then darted around me to—

STOP!

The Champions—and Dimitri—froze. With a gasp, they bent over, clutching their heads. Startled, Oliver paused. He looked me. I blinked.

I'd stopped the fight. With my power.

In my fear—and frustration—I'd reacted to the violence, and the surge of accompanying strength forced my glints into the minds of the Champions. And Dimitri. I'd stopped them!—and they knew it. Sure enough, one by one, everyone plucked the eyelinks off their corneas to prevent another intrusion. As they placed the Com Tech in their salient tubes, I swallowed, then sent a small smile towards Oliver.

Who stared at me. Confused.

I understood. The power *was* confusing, but I couldn't explain anything to Oliver until I figured out what was going on myself. So I pretended everything was normal by gesturing towards the slabbed seats that ringed the amphitheatre's stage. "We're civilized citizens. Let's sit and continue the conversation." I swallowed. "Civilly?"

Shooting side glances at me—like I was a scorpion, or something—Zekiul, Just Jolene, Dimitri, and Oliver settled on the stone slabs.

"Alright." I took a breath, then stood in front of the group, trying to tap into the cool confidence I'd woken up with. Swinging my hair over my shoulder, I turned to Zekiul and said, "Why did you burn down Madame Rogers' mushroom field?"

Zekiul placed his hands on the grass behind the rocky riser. Smiling, he unzipped his jacket and revealed his chiseled chest.

I pretended I didn't notice.

"Rogers went after our News Alert network posts," Zekiul said. "Intentionally. Every time a Champion shared something important—like a failure the Reclamation Party tried to cover up—Rogers called our posts 'propaganda,' and the Provincial Police pulled them down." His lip curled. "Then she went after us. She spread lies about our friends and family, and shared private information about our kids: photos and addresses. She encouraged Jardinians to harass the kids in real life in order to 'get us where it hurts.'" He looked at his feet. "I don't care if Rogers is a farmer. She's a terrible person."

Oliver and Dimitri sat up, clearly surprised by the major's story. Then Dimitri slipped on his eyelinks, pressed his temple, and scanned Rogers' account on the News Alert network to verify Zekiul's accusation.

"Well?" I asked, after Dimitri spent what felt like a year searching the News.

Dimitri dropped his hand. "He's correct. Zekiul Cox—"

"*Major* Cox," the leader said.

I giggled. Damn it.

Dimitri glared at me, then continued. "The Major is correct. Madame Rogers reposted pics of the Champions' children with their full names and whereabouts."

Jolene let out a loud, "HEH."

Oliver muttered to Dimitri, "My mother is going to tear Simone to pieces."

"Now that we've cleared up this misunderstanding, may we go?" Zekiul rose, flicking his finger at Jolene, who stood at the major's command. "Rogers is who you want, so we have nothing more to say."

"One moment." Dimitri scrambled to his feet. His loafers slipped on the stone slabs. "We haven't resolved anything. You can't respond to harassment however you want. You should have spoken with Madame Rogers before you retaliated, or talked to Mayor Billadeau. Everyone knows Chaleur is her jurisdiction. Or you could have reported Madame Rogers to the Provincial Police—"

Zekiul turned his back on Dimitri and made his way towards the surrounding forest. As Jolene lumbered after him, Zekiul called, "And after we sat down with the corrupt cops we could have had tea and scones, then talked about what an unusually dry spring 'twas."

The Champions laughed, then disappeared into the trees, leaving Dimitri to sputter over their abrupt departure.

Now that the meeting was over, *I* could laugh. Loudly. "He's funny. Really funny." I grinned at my cousin, who glared at the canopy overhead. "Why can't you be funny like Major Cox?"

"Shut up."

"Chore negotiations would be simple if you had a sense of humour."

"Our arguments about chores aren't negotiations. Unless you think domestic dictating is a bartering tactic."

"That is going on my gravestone." Oddly cheerful, I raised my voice so my words echoed across the amphitheatre. "Layla Caitir Douglas! Domestic Dictator!"

"Don't forget 'dominatrix,'" Oliver called to me, smiling.

"Ooo! Yes!" I giggled, then twirled my hips. "Douglas the Domestic Dictating Dominatrix: The female who avoided chores with subversive sadomasochism."

"For goodness sake." Dimitri pinched the bridge of his nose. "Are we done here?"

"We know why the Champions targeted Madame Rogers." Oliver slid down the hill and grabbed my hand, pulling me towards the forest as Dimitri followed behind. "My mother will handle it."

"Will your mother also handle Layla? She used the eyelinks to stop the fight." Dimitri tapped his temple as he scowled at me. "You can't do that."

"You should be thanking me," I deflected, as though breaking into someone's mind was a typical, everyday occurrence. If Dimitri wasn't going to question how I'd prevented the fight, I wasn't going to tell him the truth: that I'd somehow tapped into a strange new power. "If I hadn't intervened, Jolene would have you in a headlock right now."

"That's not the point. You physically stopped us. I didn't even know that was possible."

"If you can't handle the Com Tech, don't use it. Like Oli."

"I can handle the technology," Oliver said. "I just don't like the technology."

Dimitri groaned, then stopped under a rocky overhang. "We took our eyelinks out. We don't have an official record of the meeting."

"Dimitri." I patted my cousin's arm. "Poor, poor Dimitri."

"Don't 'poor Dimitri' me. Say what you have to say."

I tapped my temple. "When you took out your eyelinks, mine stayed in. Which means—"

"You have memories of the meeting: a recording of Major Cox—I mean, the major—making his claim against Simone." Dimitri sighed with relief. "Nicely done, Layla."

I flipped my hair over my shoulder, then sauntered along the forest path. "Oli told you I'd be useful."

Oliver hurried after me. He grabbed my hand and raised my knuckles to his lips. "We were wrong to mischaracterize you."

As Oliver's mouth brushed my hand my body tingled. "That's going on my gravestone, too. Layla Douglas: The Domineering Dictator Who Was Constantly Mischaracterized."

Oliver smiled. We kept walking and—soon—the Billadeau's mountain home appeared between the trees. Oliver squeezed my hand and said, "I love you, you know."

I wound my fingers through his. "I know."

CHAPTER SEVEN

I lay on my back on Oliver's bed in his attic bedroom.

Later that day. Well, no, it was later that evening. Or—I glanced at the time blinking on Oliver's clock—it was *late* in the evening. The wind, for once, wasn't howling outside Oliver's window (the window built into Niccola Peak), but rain dripped from the fir trees brushing up against the glass.

I barely noticed the dripping rain. It was such a constant in my life—like the trees themselves—that the sound of *plunk! plunk!* plunking water mixed with the steady plodding of my thoughts. And my thoughts were plodding steadily that night. No—that *evening*.

Late that evening.

Early that *morning*, after the envoy meeting, Oliver and I—and Dimitri—dried off in the Billadeau's kitchen, then scarfed down some bean bread before joining the mayor and Khleo in the den to debrief.

I sat on Mayor Billadeau's giant couch, which was so large an armrest touched the bookshelf on the far side of the room. His mom presided over the gathering behind her large, maplewood desk. Khleo sprawled beside me with one rainbow-striped sneaker thrown over the back of the couch and his arm around my shoulders. It was comfortable, even though Oliver kept looking at me like I needed protection. Khleo took up space, and he never had a problem draping himself over people who happened to be *in* his space. Dimitri, on the other hand, looked tenser than ever as he perched on a straight-backed chair. His aura buzzed like a yellowjacket.

Oliver recounted, verbally, what happened when we met with the Champions, then—with a quick nod at the wall—he sat on Mayor Billadeau's desk and asked me to share my vid recording of the envoy meeting.

Leaping into action—or, sitting up, because straightening my back was the only action I could manage with Khleo's heavy limbs on my lap—I scanned my memories and pressed my temple. With a flicker, the wall lit up, playing my perceptions.

ME
SEPTEMBER 23, 2106

Dimitri, as usual, doesn't know what's going on. "Cox," I say, respectfully keeping him on track, even though I should be finding ways to warm up. "His name is Major Cox—"

"Layla!" Dimitri slips on the wet stage. He's wearing his loafers again, even though he lectures me all the time about responsibility—

~~~

"Layla? Pause the playback, please," Mayor Billadeau said. "Just for a minute."

The vid froze as I touched my temple. "What's wrong?"

"Nothing's wrong," Mayor Billadeau said kindly. "But can you edit out a few of your interpretations?"

"Especially the ones of you insulting me," Dimitri said. "I have feelings, you know."

"We don't need the commentary, Layla," Mayor Billadeau said. "Just the sequence of events."

"Whoops." I shifted on the couch. "I'll play the dialogue."

"Nope!" Khleo shoved his hand in the air. "We need to see the Champions' body language, too. That's my specialty. I can tell what our enemies are glinting when they move."

"You can't interpret glints based on body language," Oliver said. "That's ridiculous."

"Oli's right, Le-Le," Mayor Billadeau said. "Movement rarely reveals true nature. For example—" She raised her sandy eyebrow. "What am I glinting right now?"

Khleo grinned. "You want Oliver to shut the fuck up."

"No, you want Khleo to go away," Oliver said. "That's what everyone wants."

Mayor Billadeau chuckled. "Wrong. Both of you."

I eyed Khleo closely. Oliver's brother had always been a bit of a mystery. I didn't get his sort-of crude sense of humour, and his glints weren't easy to read. But with my power, maybe I could understand him better. So, as Oliver and Khleo continued bickering, I subtly reached out to read Khleo's glints.

Wrong? Khleo thought. Moi? Never! "Wrong?" Khleo fake-gasped, half-a-second later. "Moi? Never!"

"I know, Le-le," Mayor Billadeau said. "Your judgement is usually impeccable. But, yes. You are wrong about this."

Oh, please. It's obvious Mom thinks Oli's yap is better trapped. "Oh, please." Khleo snorted. "It's obvious you think Oli's yap is better trapped."

"For the love of leaves, Khleo," Oliver said. "Stop talking."

I'll stop talking when the planet stops turning. "I'll stop talking when the planet stops—"

Biting back a smile, I realized why Khleo's glints seemed so elusive: his thoughts and feelings exactly matched his words and behaviour. Khleo wasn't a mystery. He was assertive.

"—so just admit it, Oli. I'm an analytical expert and you're plain old obtuse." I *am* an analytic expert and Oliver *is* obtuse.

"May we continue, please?" Dimitri pinched his nose. "I'm getting a headache."

"Include your whole memory in the playback, Layla," Mayor Billadeau said. "But cut the commentary. You get me?"

"I got you." I reviewed my memory, then replaced the vid with a slightly-altered one: a trick I often used to cut filler glints from the meeting minutes. "Okay," I said once I was finished. "I did the best I could, but some of my interpretations were hard to erase."

"That's fine. A few comments are fine."

The vid resumed, playing the edited version on the wall.

ME
SEPTEMBER 23, 2106

We're waiting for the Champions. It's too early to function.

Dimitri is grumpy, but Oli looks cute in his canvas trousers that pull tightly across his crotch—

"Layla!"

I paused the vid. "Sorry, sorry, sorry. That glint snuck in."

"Let it play, Mumsy," Khleo said. "We know how Layla feels about Oliver. You can handle a look-see at her obsession."

Oliver rolled his eyes. "I don't know if *I* can handle a look-see at Layla's obsession."

Khleo and the mayor rolled their eyes. The glare was a family trait, like the Billadeaus' blonde hair and sarcasm. I smiled, then played the edited memory vid again.

ME
SEPTEMBER 23, 2106

—and Oli looks cute in his canvas trousers that—

GREY FUZZZZZZZ]

Dimitri, as usual, doesn't know what's going on. "Cox," I say with supreme patience. "His name is Zekiul Cox."

"Layla!" Dimitri slips.

[*editing fuzz*

smushy grayscale images]

Two people step out of the trees [*fuzzy fuzz*] and I have a bad feeling about them. I'd better read their glints to make sure—

"Layla?"

I blinked.

"Did you snatch the Champions' glints?" Mayor Billadeau leaned over her desk, frowning. "That's illegal."

"No, I—" Whoops. I scrunched up my nose, searching for a way to *not* lie to the mayor. "I didn't snatch anything. Um. You see—"

"With all due respect, Amelie, I'd appreciate it if we could continue without interruption. Unless you're okay with me vomiting on your carpet." Dimitri lifted his hand to his forehead, which had turned a delicate shade of tan.

Oliver glanced at his brother. "What could Dimitri possibly mean by that body language, Khleo?"

"It means he's sick of you and your—"

"No more interruptions." Mayor Billadeau settled on her chair. "Layla and I will chat about the glint . . . whatever-she-was-doing later. Please, Layla. Continue."

ME
SEPTEMBER 23, 2106

—and I have a bad feeling about them.

GREY FUZZZZZZZ]

Zekiul could be a problem—he's smart—but the other one, Jolene, isn't a threat. We can handle her. Her mind is mush. And her single name is strange.

[*fuzzy fuzz Grayscale Grayscale Grayscale*]

"Thank you for speaking with us today," Oli says. "We understand you feel your actions were justified two nights ago when you set Simone Rogers' field on fire. We're here to craft a resolution—together—so this doesn't happen again."

Oli is such an eloquent speaker. I love when he uses proper grammar.

"You assume we *don't* want this to happen again," Zekiul says.

Uh oh. Zekiul is upsetting Oli, I can tell. And that's not good. An upset Oli is an uneasy Oli, and an uneasy Oli is a—

"I know citizens would be angry without umami to balance their dinner recipes," Oli says, "but—"

"What Oliver is trying to say—" Dimitri interrupts, "—is that we'd like to understand what happened so the Compassion Coplot can support you."

Zekiul glances at Just Jolene, then turns to stare at Oli. "Compassion Coplot? That's what you call yourselves?"

[*rapid fuzz that blurs the grayscale*]

Dimitri grimaces at Zekiul, then says (like he's the boss of everyone), "It might be a good idea if our leader and local mayor, Amelie Billadeau, heard more about your organization. We should arrange another meeting."

"Why would we do that?"

"You threaten Canuckians' wellbeing."

"We don't hurt Canuckians," Zekiul says. "Didn't you listen to what I just said?"

I like him a lot. Zekiul is different. I don't know *how* he's different, but I should find out and—oh! Oli's speaking. "So, you were helping Madame Rogers when you burned down her field?"

Zekiul lunges at Oli. Oli gracefully leaps towards the Champions while Dimitri scuttles behind him like a cockroach, trying to close the gap.

This is stupid.

I move between the advancing antagonists. Lifting my hands, I say in a calm and reasonable manner, "Let's relax, and—"

Zekiul moves, or something, because Oli reaches out to save me. Zekiul growls. Dimitri is a millisecond away from getting trampled by Jolene, so I—

[FUZZZZZZZZ

SMASH]

—stand in front of the group and say to Zekiul, "Why did you burn down Madame Rogers' mushroom field?"

Zekiul leans backwards. "Rogers went on the News Alert network and told Jardinians to harass our kids in real life in order to 'get us where it hurts.' She posted their names and addresses."

Oli and Dimitri sit up. Then Dimitri slips on his eyelinks, presses his temple, and scans Rogers' account on the network.

"Well?" I say to Dimitri. He's been looking at the News for an eternity.

Dimitri sighs dramatically. "The major is correct."

[*fuzz fuzz fuzz fuzz fuzz*

GREYSCALE SMASH]

"Ooo! Yes!" I giggle as I twirl my hips. My footing is sure on the flattened tree trunk. I don't slide around at all, even though the surface is slippery. "Douglas the Domestic Dictating Dominatrix: The female who avoided chores with subversive sadomasochism."

Dimitri glares at me. "For goodness sake."

—⚘—

"For goodness sake," Dimitri said, standing. "Amelie?" He gave a short, rigid nod to the mayor. "I'll speak with you tomorrow. Have a good evening."

"Did I show too much?" I asked as Dimitri stalked out of the den. I pressed my temple and the vid disappeared, plunging the room into darkness. Or, its typical low lighting.

"Never mind Dimitri," Khleo said as he swung his sneakers onto the floor. "Rogers harassed the Champions? Rogers?"

"Well, I'll be damned." Mayor Billadeau rubbed her fringe of hair. "I thought I knew everyone in our community. I never would've guessed Simone started the conflict with the Champions. I'll have to speak with her. Her offence is so severe we might have to report her to the Provincial Police."

"Are we sure Cox is telling the truth?" Oliver said. "If Madame Rogers could hide her true nature from us, Cox could have lied."

"Um, no," I said as I sidled up to the mayor's desk. "Zekiul told the truth. I'm the best eyelink user in Chaleur. Records don't lie." I sat next to Oliver and squeezed his knee. I couldn't tell him —yet—about the glints I'd read without the Champions knowing: Zekiul was sincere.

Oliver placed his hand over mine. "Let's say you did make a mistake, though."

"I didn't."

"But let's say you did," Oliver said. "If your interpretation of Cox—and the meeting—is wrong, and Cox lied, we can't accuse Madame Rogers of a crime she didn't commit. That would create more problems, which would distract us from what's important."

I nodded solemnly. "Taking care of my birch trees."

Mayor Billadeau cleared her throat. "We can trust Layla, Oli."

"Yes! You can." I wrapped my arm around Oliver's neck and beamed at the mayor, thrilled she approved. Maybe she'd ask me to take on more Coplot tasks. And bigger responsibilities. And—

"Layla is excellent at recording accurate vids. The Coplot would be a disaster without her as our assistant," Mayor Billadeau said, deflating my dreams a little bit. "We don't know the Champions—though I think I should set up a private meeting with Cox, like Dimitri suggested—but we know Layla. And if Layla believes Cox is—"

Oliver tensed. "Scum?"

"If Layla believes Cox is telling the truth, I believe her." Knees creaking, Mayor Billadeau rose off her chair. "I'll talk to Simone."

Khleo—who'd been remarkably quiet since Dimitri stormed off—raised his hand and caught his mom's attention. "Do you have to talk to Rogers?"

"I can't let something like this go," Mayor Billadeau said. "The conflict could escalate more than it already has."

"Maybe." Khleo flapped his multicoloured foot up and down. "Or, it could drive the Champions away."

"Drive them away?" Oliver leaned towards Khleo. "How?"

Khleo sat up, then crossed his legs at the ankles, tucking his rainbow shoes together. "If Rogers keeps attacking the Champions on the network, they might leave Canuckia. For good. I hate to disagree with the Coplot leadership team, but I think Rogers *should* go after the Champions. They post crap content all the time. They lie about everything."

"Zekiul said they aren't lies," I said. "I didn't show that part, though, so you'll have to believe *I'm* not lying."

Oliver grunted. "Eyelinks are so impractical. Once the Coplot's official Party status is approved, we need a better system of sharing information. Instead of relying on a single person who happens to be good at interpreting glints, small groups of people who are loyal to the Coplot should secretly spy on their citizens, then report their evil intentions to the premier. We could have good groups investigating the bad groups all the time. As a preventative measure. And—"

"You work on that, my dear boy, while the rest of us work on this," Mayor Billadeau said indulgently. "Add it to your To Do list."

"Yeah, Oli, add it to your list," Khleo said, "while the rest of us work on the important stuff."

Mayor Billadeau glanced at her eldest son. "What do *you* think is important?"

"The Champions," Khleo said without hesitation. "They're jerks. And, if I'm being completely honest, Cox is shifty."

Oliver blinked—drawn back into the conversation—then nodded. "Right. He *is* shifty."

"Zekiul isn't shifty," I said. "Dimitri is shifty. So's Oli. What?" I looked at Oliver's blank face. "You are shifty. It's cute."

"Do you think Cox is cute?" Oliver asked quietly.

"I'm not going to dignify that question with a response." I hugged Oliver's neck. "It's beneath you. And me."

"Anyway," Khleo said as he, Oliver, and the mayor rolled their eyes in unison. "We should leave Rogers alone. She didn't do anything *really* wrong. If I wasn't busy with my Coplot duties I'd harass the Champions on the network, too."

"Oh, Le-Le." Mayor Billadeau made her way towards the den's doorway, sighing. "It's so nice seeing you embrace the virtues of the *Compassion* Coplot: integrity, and morality, and the ability to welcome differences instead of discriminating against people you know nothing about."

"Which is Mother's way of saying, 'Rogers is screwed.'" Oliver grinned. "The mushroom farmer made a mistake. She has to be held accountable."

"You get me." Mayor Billadeau stopped by the doorway. "When children are used as a bartering tool in conflict—even rebel children—it crosses a line. A big, big line. You know that, Khleo." With a swoop, she opened the door. "You did well today, Oli. You too, Layla. I appreciate you more than you know, but I can take it from here. Shoo."

"What about me?" Khleo hopped to his feet and bounded towards his mom. "Do you appreciate me?"

"Always, Le-Le," Mayor Billadeau said. "Now, go away."

After planting a kiss on his mom's cheek, Khleo flounced out of the den. Oliver slid off the desk, then pulled me towards the mayor. He gave his mom a short nod as he headed for the attached hallway.

I slowed as I neared Mayor Billadeau so I could whisper in her ear, "I know how much you appreciate us." I tapped my temple. "I *know*."

"So you *can* snatch glints." Mayor Billadeau grabbed my elbow, forcing me to stop (and Oliver to drop my arm). She leaned towards me, whispering, "We need to chat. Sooner rather than later." Mayor Billadeau looked at her son, then raised her bushy brows. "Don't you have items to cross off your list?"

Oliver glanced at me, then continued into the hallway without a word.

Mayor Billadeau waited until he was out of earshot, then she said, "How strong are you? How many glints can you snatch at once? This is interesting, Layla. Interesting."

"I can't snatch glints," I said. "At least, I don't think I can. I've never tried. But I am getting better at reading glints. And I can read strong glints without using my eyelinks."

"You can what?!" Mayor Billadeau stumbled backwards, into the doorframe.

"Is there a problem?" Oliver called from the hallway. "Because my work can wait if Layla's in trouble—"

"Do your work, my dear boy." Mayor Billadeau waved at her

son without looking at him. "Layla and I are having girl time: chit-chat that doesn't concern you."

Oliver wrinkled his nose, then walked away.

"I knew that would get rid of him," Mayor Billadeau said softly. "How long has this been going on?"

"Just the last few days," I said. "I don't know much about it. I haven't tested how strong I am or anything."

"Hmm." Mayor Billadeau tapped her chin. "Hmm, hmm." Her eyes glittered as she stared at me. "This could be helpful, Layla. Oliver told you about that disturbed glint, right? The angry-excited one? If you could snatch the community's glints to find the glinter—"

"You want me snatch everyone's glints?" My stomach flipped. "Like, run through the town on a snatching spree?"

"Not a spree, but yes. It would help—a lot—if you could find our secret sicko."

"But I can't snatch glints," I said, recoiling. "And I don't want to. You're right: snatching glints is wrong. I don't want to own someone's memories—and thoughts and feelings—without their permission. All I can do is read glints. Naturally."

"This *is* interesting." Mayor Billadeau smiled. Slowly. "Very interesting. Okay." She clapped her hands together, making me jump. "You don't have to go on a glint-snatching spree. The disturbed glinter can wait. But you're coming with me when I speak with Madame Rogers. You'll read her glints while I talk to her so we can find out if Cox is telling the truth; and find out how powerful you are."

"But, that's kind of like glint-snatching." I edged towards the hallway (and away from Mayor Billadeau). "I'm not as strong as you think I am. Honestly, all I can do is naturally read glints—and auras—when I'm close to someone. That's it."

"So, you didn't use your strength to stop the fight in the envoy meeting?"

I froze. "How do you know about that?"

"Dimitri told me." Mayor Billadeau wound her arm through

mine and led me into the hall. "It's okay, Layla. I'm not mad. I told Dimitri you'd probably lost control after the fight started. You know, like teenagers do when they're going through puberty." She chuckled. "Good gracious, that's a topsy-turvy time. Large glints, wild glints, auras peaking all over the place—"

"But I'm twenty-five!" As Mayor Billadeau guided me away from the den I pursed my lips, then lowered my voice. "I've been in control of my thoughts and feelings for years. Did Dimitri believe you?"

"Dimitri believes anything that comes from the government. One of the perks of being the mayor is having constituents who are loyal to your position, not your person. Oopsy daisies, I've gone off topic." Mayor Billadeau looked over her shoulder, then pulled me into an alcove underneath the main floor staircase.

Boxes of shoes filled the space, stacked against the tiny walls. The mayor threw a pair of bright yellow sneakers into the corner before dragging me behind a tower of crates stamped with the Reclamation Party's official seal.

"If you say you can't snatch glints, then you can't snatch glints, but *reading* Madame Rogers' glints would be a big help. And—" Mayor Billadeau winked, "—if you strengthen your ability to physically stop people when they lose control, I might be able to promote you. How would you like to be on the Coplot's leadership team as our unofficial behavioural bouncer?"

My stomach swooped with excitement. And nerves. "Maybe I can help," I said, after staring at a pile of shoes dumped unceremoniously on the floor while my mind tried to reconcile my desire to be a leader with my need to be a good person. "If we can confirm that Madame Rogers asked the Jardinians to harass the Champions' kids, it would prove that Zekiul told the truth."

Mayor Billadeau clapped her hands. "Yes! You get me!"

"And—" I swallowed, unsure why it felt wrong to admit this, "stopping violence is a good thing. I guess I can practice my power. The, um, physical part of my power."

"Sure, sure. Sure." Mayor Billadeau nodded. "But we can

wade through that river when we get to it. Right now, you reading Madame Rogers' glints is enough. More than enough. And it isn't illegal at all." She paused, then grinned. Widening her eyes pointedly, Mayor Billadeau's glints rose to the surface of her mind, clear as a dew drop. Okay, it's a little illegal. But if you're discreet, and we keep this to ourselves, I don't see why we can't bend the rules. "So?" She blinked, then bounced on the balls of her toes. "What do you say?"

I watched Mayor Billadeau bounce: watched the top of her head come close to hitting the slanted alcove ceiling. Then I nodded. "I can help."

"Wonderful! We'll speak to Madame Rogers first thing tomorrow." Mayor Billadeau ducked out of the alcove, and pointed up the stairs. "Now, git. And tell that son of mine to put away his To Do list and slow down. You, too."

But I couldn't rest—I was too nervous—and Oliver never slowed down. So I spent the day lying on Oliver's bed, staring out his attic window.

CHAPTER EIGHT

Scritch. Scratch. Scritchity-scratch.

Oliver sat behind his desk, scribbling on his chalkboard. His attic bedroom was small, but organized. Oliver valued efficiency, which meant his belongings stayed tucked away unless he needed them. A peaked roof covered the room, which was just large enough to fit Oliver's single bed and his desk. His clothes were in a drawer under the mattress, his spare chalkboards were stacked inside a hollowed-out bench under his window, and his notes—and ideas—were scribbled on an oversized blackboard that doubled as a backsplash.

I'd spent a lot of time staring at Oliver's upside-down agenda when we made love in his attic: me on my back with Oliver on top. Sometimes, after we fell asleep, I'd dream about Oliver, and my sexual fantasies would get mixed up with his politics. I'd woken in terror—more than once—after a nightmare about a Cabinet Member spanking me while they intoned, "A better way, a brighter day, a better way, a brighter day, a better—"

After the dream happened several times, I told Oliver about the unsettling mantra. He wrote down the slogan (he liked the political patter) before wiping the headboard clean. But his stack of chalkboard notes, piled high on his desk, grew taller and taller.

Scrrrrrratch! Oliver flourished his chalk, then placed his most-recently filled board on top of the nearest pile. Without pausing, he grabbed an empty board and kept writing. He never ran out of ideas.

Usually, I supported Oliver when he was in his focused state. I stayed with him when he locked himself in his bedroom, drafting petitions to submit to Pluie's Reclamation Party representative. I researched Canuckian law in the Billadeau's den—the bookshelf was stuffed with government texts—then I'd cart my notes to

Oliver's attic and lay my findings on his desk.

Even when Oliver ignored my efforts, I helped him. I stayed up late: making him snacks, keeping him hydrated, and tucking him under his river reed covers when he passed out from exhaustion. But, sometimes, it was tiring taking care of an adult male who really needed to take care of himself.

"Why do you like work so much?" I asked that rainy evening, turning away from the window. My mind spun from Mayor Billadeau's chit-chat, but I couldn't work through my worries that night. I needed time in my grove to process my whirling glints. But maybe talking would help me fall asleep.

"I don't like work," Oliver mumbled out the side of his mouth. "I love my mother. The Coplot is her whole life, so I work for the Coplot. If we succeed in accomplishing my mother's mission—and if I can help it succeed—that will make her happy." He looked at me and smiled. "I like when the people I love are happy."

"Me, too." I rolled onto my stomach, then propped my elbows on Oliver's bed with my chin resting on my hands. "So, um, what are you doing?"

"Layla—"

"Come on. Talk to me! Your mother will love you—and be happy—even if you don't finish tonight's tasks. In fact—" I pulled my hair over my shoulder, letting it dangle between my breasts. "She said you should take a break. With me."

"Layla—"

"She said that, I swear. She wants you to put down your chalkboard and do me, all night long."

Oliver kept writing. "She didn't say that. And I don't have time to 'do' you. My Coplot tasks are important, and I haven't checked an item off my list in days. The Champions are distracting."

"What about me? Aren't I important?" I flipped on my back and spread my legs, winking at Oliver through my bent knees. "Isn't this important?"

Oliver closed his eyes. "The Coplot is important, too. I want— I want—" He looked at me, and his troubled eyes shone. "I want to create a legacy. A legendary legacy. Something permanent people will talk about for centuries. The Compassion Coplot has the opportunity to change the world, and the Billadeau name needs to be linked to that change. Forever."

"Forever?" I shut my knees and giggled. "Forever's a long time. Your name—and the Compassion Coplot—could be wiped out during forever. Or, well—" I pulled myself backwards until I leaned against Oliver's headboard, "—for as long as forever is recorded."

"That's it! Exactly!" Oliver spun around on his stool. "We have to keep a record of the Billadeau's influence so our name endures. The Bot War taught us that." He crawled across his bed and grabbed my shoulders, turning me to face the window. Oliver pulled my body into his chest, then said, "Like the library, in the Coplot cabin. You know how the books are protected by plastic sheets? Well, I want to create an imprint on our global society that can't be destroyed either." His breath warmed my cheek. "No matter what."

I glanced at his face. "You want to write a book?"

"Nothing that infantile. I want to do something bigger." Oliver breathed in, rough and shaky. "The Compassion Coplot has to be remembered."

I turned in Oliver's arms, forcing him to look at me. "I'll remember you. Isn't that enough?"

"Are you going to live forever?"

"Maybe. You don't know."

Oliver folded into his hunch. "Layla—"

"And anyway, you can't control if you're remembered forever," I said. "Nobody can."

That got Oliver's attention. His eyes narrowed, surprisingly thin. "What do you mean?"

"Well—" I gestured towards Oliver's desk. "This is great—and important, it really is—but nobody gets to determine their legacy. You could be the perfect person, and the Coplot could change the world, and you still might not be remembered. History determines legacies, not the legacy themself. Or itself. Or—" I tilted my head, searching for the best explanation. After finding it, I grinned. "Generations from now, people who feel the impact from a legacy's contribution decide if that person—or Party, or whatever—is worthy of legend. *And* how that legend is remembered. The history files could say the Coplot was a mess, or something, instead of the well-managed organism you and your mom grew."

Oliver stared out the window. Then he let out a huge, soul-purging sigh and moved back to his desk. "Then all we can do is keep working towards our goal, and hope everything goes the way we want." Oliver grabbed his chalkboard. He resumed his focused scratching as though the interruption hadn't happened.

Damn it. I was still wide awake. "Oliver? Can I ask you a question?"

Oliver sighed again. "You just asked me a question. *That* was a question."

"A real question. Not a question about a question."

"Now you know why I'm stressed all the time." This was another regular argument: why Oliver had a near-permanent frown and what I thought he should do to cheer up. "It's impossible for the people I love to be happy if they prioritize different things," he said. "I can't talk to you and help my mother—and the Coplot—at the same time."

"We'll see about that." I knew what I needed to do to feel better, and Oliver's sighs and scribbles weren't going to stop me.

Rain pounded on the roof as I took off my shirt. The cold air seeping through the shoddy window casings brushed my breasts. I slinked across the bed, closer to Oliver. With my nipples hardened from the cold—and from my arousal—I leaned over Oliver's desk.

He didn't look up from his notes. "I know you're good at multi-tasking, but I can't 'do' you and finish this. You could put your considerable talents to work, though." He gestured towards a graph drawn on his board. "I need to find a pattern. Can you spot any similarities between the regions that have seen an increase of citizens living in poverty this season?"

Grinning, I wiggled out of my trousers, then sat—nude—on Oliver's lap. Inspired by my dream, I put on a loud, performative voice (like I was the host of an erotic festival for politicians) and declared, "On this chart, one can see that inflation caused more complaints to be registered in Fairfield than is typically typical."

"This isn't helping."

I tickled Oliver's leg with my foot. "And on this chart—"

"Layla!" Oliver tapped his temple. "Do you want to see my To Do list? The whole thing? It should tire you out. That *is* what you're trying to do, right? Seduce me so you can fall asleep?"

Oliver knew me so well.

"Fine," I said, smiling. "Send me your list. But if I want to talk about your list, you can't stop me."

Oliver stood, dumping me unceremoniously on his bed. Then he stalked to his bedside table, grabbed his eyelinks, and placed the devices over his corneas. Oliver pressed his temple and a digifile knocked on my head. I accepted the digifile; and Oliver slid the eyelinks back into their tube.

A long list of items scrolled through my mind. Frowning, I scanned the file. "You were supposed to do this? Today?"

Oliver eyed my naked body, then sat on his stool. "Mmm."

"Do you have lists like this every day?"

"Mmm," Oliver mumbled, reaching for his chalkboard.

"Oli. I know why you're stressed all the time."

With a raspy laugh—that sparked a fire between my thighs—Oliver threw his chalkboard on his desk and launched across the bed. He hugged me as he kissed my face and neck.

He pressed his thumb between my legs.

I arched my back, then gasped, "I'm not kidding, Oli. You do too much. I'm going to talk to your mom about it."

"Don't," Oliver said as his lips moved to my collarbone. "Don't talk about my mother right now. Don't talk at all."

"Can I talk a little? About—" I closed my eyes and read the first item on Oliver's digifile. "Re-evaluating Justice in a Compassionate Canuckia?"

Oliver laughed. He slid down my body and kissed my stomach. "No."

"What about—?" I read the second item, which slipped from my lips on a moan. "Uuh-pdating the Inclusivity Act: A means to revolutionize systematic acc-eeh-eeh-eptance."

"Layla!" Oliver's mouth lingered around my navel. "Stop."

I clutched Oliver's sandy hair. "Are my political buzzwords too much?"

"Much too much," Oliver mumbled. "I can't handle it."

"What about the third item on your list?" I placed my hand on Oliver's fingers, which were rubbing the wetness between my thighs. "This one is going to drive you wild." I wrapped my ankles around his lower back, raising my hips as I moaned, "Ooo, Transcontinental Transportation: Repurposing the Bot Highways and Subterranean Railways. Ohhh, Oli. Subways are so sexy. And—Oli!" I gasped as Oliver slid his fingers inside me. "Oh, that feels good." I grinned at my lover. "But if I can still read your list, you aren't deep enough. For example, the fourth item analyzes the economic benefits of combining a democracy with an autocrac—ahhh!"

I stopped reading. I stopped thinking. All I could do was feel as Oliver took over.

After we'd both been satisfied, I lay in Oliver's arms, twirling the hair on his chest. "Can we stay here forever?"

Oliver patted my head. "Mmm."

"This could be a great life, Oli," I said. "You, me, here: for always."

"For always," Oliver mumbled. "I like that."

"*We* could be your legacy," I said. "This. Our partnership. I can't think of anything else worth growing."

"Mmm." Oliver sighed as he sunk into his pillow. "Legacy."

I rolled onto my side. "Are you asleep?"

Oliver's soft snore answered.

I brushed hair away from his closed eyes, then crawled under the covers—and closer to him. I thought I'd fall asleep right away

—'midnight exercise' normally tired me out—but, instead, I stared at the ceiling. Then at the rain outside Oliver's window. And at the chalkboard on Oliver's desk.

I cradled my head on the crook of Oliver's warm arm. Lulled by the patter of raindrops, I finally fell asleep.

I slept so soundly I didn't notice when Oliver woke up, slid out from under me, and sat on his stool. The next morning Oliver was still hunched over his desk, dark circles blooming under his eyes as he made notes on his chalkboard.

CHAPTER NINE

The agricultural sector in Pluie was one of the most lucrative postwar industries in Canuckia.

Growing regions were interspersed among the living spaces in every community, and the farms flourished under the canopies. No matter where I walked in Chaleur I could see a farmer's field snuggled along the forest pathways. Even though the properties were occasionally obscured by rain, or autumn fog, I knew if I took a few steps forward an acreage would emerge, teeming with growth. It found comfort in that.

Rogers' property was no different. She'd built her home on a hill (or, her Bot-builder had built her home on a hill). The house was a simple single room with lights dancing in the windows through the rain, fog, and sometimes sun. Beneath Rogers' hill stretched her mushroom field. Usually, the moist earth was dotted with tiny, cream-coloured domes rising out of long wet grass. Pools of water surrounded the mushrooms: repositories filled with oxygenated liquid so the farm held the moisture necessary to grow the crop. Rogers had placed wooden planks cut from the trunks of cherry trees over the pools so she could harvest her mushrooms without stepping on their delicate flesh. Or into the PH-balanced water.

After the fire, the planks were the only part of the farm that remained intact: cherry trees were heat-resistant. Soggy and (somehow) charred grass stuck out of the field, and clumps of dirt floated in the ruined pools. And—strangely—an iridescent liquid clung to the edges of the dirt clods.

As I followed Mayor Billadeau across the planks—and over the fire-destroyed farm—I pinched my nose. The pools smelled acidic. I stopped in the middle of a plank, distracted. The shimmering liquid looked like fuel which, technically, no longer existed in

Canuckia. Where had Rogers gotten gasoline?

"Amelie!" Rogers' wavering voice carried over the field.

Mayor Billadeau leapt off her plank—landing on an untouched section of grass—then she beelined towards Rogers: a rake-thin female with translucent skin who was tearing up the ground underneath a knobbly aspen. I hurried after the mayor, then stopped as we drew close to the farmer. Rogers was covered in dirt, head to toe, and her aura chirped with ant-like frustration: though not at me. Or Mayor Billadeau. Rogers was upset with her equipment. Her nuclear-powered trowel and pickaxe were zooming—haywire—around the base of her tree.

Nuclear tools had been created by the Reclamation Party to replace the Bots, but the technology was underdeveloped, so only government officials and citizens in essential industries were granted access: citizens like Rogers, who was still learning how to operate the equipment. Or, kick the equipment.

"Darn trowel!" Rogers exclaimed as she aimed her boot at the nuclear-powered rotating spade. "Waste of time, waste of money. Ugh!"

"When does the Capitol cleanup crew arrive, Simone?" Mayor Billadeau stepped over a shovel as it frenetically dug into the earth. "You've made a lot of progress, but I imagine you'll welcome the help."

Mayor Billadeau looked around Rogers' property, smiling serenely at the repair efforts that had already been made. Stakes marked the worst damage, and wooden barrels heaping with ravaged soil waited be sent to Chaleur's composting cabin for re-nutrification.

Mayor Billadeau clapped her hands. "Well done, Simone! You did all this by yourself?"

"Kind of." Rogers itched her pale nose, then tilted her canvas hat back on her forehead. "A few of the kids have been coming by to lend a hand, but it's not enough. I can manage the field by myself when its healthy and grown, but fixing it is a whole other story." She slid her hat off her head. "Darn Champions. Can't figure out what they've got against my shrooms. Did they tell you anything? At your envoy meeting?"

"That's why I'm here." Mayor Billadeau clasped Rogers' shoulder. "We need to talk."

"About the Champions?" Rogers glanced at me. "Why is she here?"

"Layla and I have some Coplot chores to take care of after our chat. So, she tagged along." Mayor Billadeau squeezed Rogers' collarbone. "But say the word and Layla will skedaddle. Won't you, Layla?"

I nodded solemnly.

"Well, uh—" Rogers rubbed her dirty cheek. "I guess she can stay. If our 'chat,' as you call it, isn't that big a deal."

"You know what?" I moved closer to the aspen. "While you talk, let me take a look at your tools." I nudged the shovel with my boot. "I might be able to fix them."

Mayor Billadeau smiled, shaking Rogers' shoulder. "Layla has a way with technology, Simone. Nuclear-powered devices should love her."

Rogers shrugged, then turned to Mayor Billadeau—after dismissing me from her mind. Her glints were clear: she didn't care about me. She was worried about her crop and the mayor's hand on her shoulder. Rogers' fear chirped with nattering insistence.

Which was exactly what Mayor Billadeau wanted. With Rogers distracted, I would be free to read her glints.

Grasping the shovel in my hand, I yanked it from the soil, then walked around the aspen to toss the nuclear device into the forest. I didn't have a way with tools—I hated machinery—but the excuse was necessary. If Rogers got upset, or tried something tricky, I was supposed to disappear, and chasing wayward equipment was the perfect excuse to create distance.

"Why did you throw that shovel into the woods?" A girl stepped out of a thick cluster of bushes that ran behind Rogers' hill. She tugged on her shirt—which was torn around the hem—then stood completely still, staring at my face.

I groaned. The girl was one of the twins. Chaleur youths often played on Rogers' property. The mushroom field was a popular hangout for children who liked games: like hopping from plank to plank without falling in the pools, or swallowing handfuls of runty, low-grade mushrooms and immediately puking them back up. Rogers encouraged the play—she said that "laughing kids chased away loneliness"—but I'd assumed that the children had stopped coming after the fire. But no!—here one was. And, unfortunately, it was a twin.

The twins were notorious. Their parents suffered terribly during the war, with their mother giving birth in the middle of the conflict. Due to the strict rations and regulated necessities, the twins didn't receive enough nutrients during their formative years, making them wiry and feral-looking. And detached from reality. Because of their hardships—and the continued struggles of their family—the town took care of the twins, and let them roam where they were happiest. So, wherever one twin went, the other went, too. And where the twins went, their friend followed: the blonde girl.

Sure enough—

"Who are you?" The blonde emerged from the bush.

Oh, good, I thought with a sigh. *Trouble with a capital Teen.* I could hear Mayor Billadeau starting the conversation with Rogers—the conversation I was supposed to be listening to—but with the appearance of the girls, our plan might go up in smoke. *Like Rogers' mushrooms,* I thought, giggling inappropriately.

I had to stop doing that.

"I asked you a question." The blonde stuck out her chest. "Who are you?"

My laughter died. I didn't like the blonde. I knew that wasn't kind, but I couldn't help it. Something about the teen made my stomach clench. Maybe it was how pretty she was (I didn't mind admitting I was jealous of other people—I had assets, but jaw-dropping beauty wasn't one of them). Or maybe I disliked the blonde because she was bossy. She ordered the twins around, and they did whatever she demanded.

It made my skin crawl.

So I had to get rid of her.

"I heard you," I said, using my patient tone of voice: the one that worked when I had to placate members of the Coplot's collective. "But I'm busy right now, so please play somewhere else."

My patient voice worked on most people, but not on the blonde.

She dug her feet deeper into the ground. "Why did you throw that tool at my friend?"

"I didn't," I said. "I'm helping Madame Rogers. I didn't know you were playing back here." I smiled at the staring twin. "I wasn't aiming for you, little bug."

"That tool was sharp." The blonde pulled the twin to her side, glaring. "You could have killed her. Why did you throw it at us?"

For the love of leaves. The blonde's attitude was haughtier than Mount Ryndle. I snapped, "That is none of your business. Go play somewhere else."

The blonde shot me a piercing look, then steered the twin towards Rogers' hill.

I nodded—

—then grabbed my head. A searing bolt of—something!—hit my mind out of nowhere. Then, as suddenly as the pain landed, it disappeared, leaving my head throbbing and my glints in a whirl.

What had happened? What *was* that? The pain didn't feel like a typical headache. It arrived—then left—too quickly. I looked around (did something fall out of the trees and hit me?) but the forest floor was empty, and the farm was silent.

Except for the sound of Mayor Billadeau's chuckle.

Whoops. I was supposed to be reading Rogers' glints. Forgetting about the headache, I inched towards the aspen and peered around its trunk. Rogers was chatting animatedly with the mayor; and her glints were easy to read.

Rogers was *not* a harasser.

She'd fallen into the same communication trap that caught

many citizens: getting pulled into News Alert network anger and its indiscriminate vilification of strangers. Rogers wasn't evil. She was easily impacted by implied rage. She went after the Champions—and shared private information about their children—never dreaming anyone would see it, or that the Champions would retaliate. Rogers was impulsive.

But she wasn't dangerous.

Now that I knew the truth, I could start the second part of Mayor Billadeau's scheme: ending the conversation. I crept through the forest underbrush, found the shovel hacking at a root—bad shovel!—then I walked into Rogers' field.

As I passed the aspen, nuclear shovel in hand, Mayor Billadeau caught my eye. I tossed my hair (our agreed-upon signal to indicate Rogers' innocence) and dropped the shovel on the ground. "Sorry, Madame Rogers, but your tools are impossible. You should ask the cleanup crew to bring you a new set from the Capitol."

"Oh, uh—" Rogers stammered. Her aura chirped. "I, uh—"

"And!—just so you know," I continued, "the twins are playing in the forest."

"The twins?" Rogers looked over her shoulder, towards her hill. "Haven't seen the twins in ages. One of them's been following Erika around but, uh—" She shook her head. "What were you saying, Amelie?"

"I believe you." Mayor Billadeau cuffed Rogers' collarbone. "I know you're a good citizen—" She leaned towards Rogers as though they were conspiring, "—and I know you won't bother the Champions on the network again."

Rogers worried her canvas hat in her hands. "Thanks, Amelie. I appreciate that. You're a great mayor. A *great* mayor."

"Well, now . . ." Mayor Billadeau blushed. "It's easy to be a great mayor in a great town."

"You *are* a great mayor," Rogers said. "Only a great mayor would understand how a citizen can get carried away—"

"Layla and I need to be going." Mayor Billadeau lifted her feet out of the mud and headed for the planked paths. "Good luck,

Simone!"

I shrugged at Rogers, hoping she thought the gesture was sympathetic, then I placed my foot on the nearest plank, the one Mayor Billadeau was already halfway across.

As I stepped onto the wood the sharp pain—the same pain from the forest—hit me between the eyes. Wincing and gasping, I bent over, clutching my face. Then the pain receded like before (unexpectedly) and I could breathe.

"Layla?" Mayor Billadeau called as she waited on the plank. "Is there a problem?"

"I'm fine!" I waved at the mayor as I straightened. "I left my, um. My bag. I left my bag in the woods."

"Your bag?" Mayor Billadeau plodded across the plank, back to the confused Rogers and her aspen tree. As the mayor stepped on the muddy ground, she asked, "Did you bring a bag?"

Rogers swung her crumpled hat onto her head as she frowned at the mayor. "What's wrong now?"

I jogged backwards, towards the forest. I had to find the source of the headache before it happened again, but I didn't want Mayor Billadeau to worry. I headed into the trees, calling, "I won't be a second. I dropped my bag when I was fixing the shovel. Or, trying to fix the shovel."

"Actually, Amelie, if you're going to hang around I have a couple questions for you," Rogers said. "The Reclamation Party rep for our area—uh, Whitley? I think their name is Whitley? Something-or-other Whitley?"

"Yes, yes. Yes. Councillor Whitley."

"Right, well, Whitley said my funds won't kick in until the new year. That's months away. How am I supposed to—"

Their voices died away as I entered the woods. The forest was quiet—no dripping rain, no whirl of wind—and the silence made me shiver. Then I heard a laugh, high and shrill, from behind Rogers' cabin. And I knew who'd caused my headache.

One of the girls must have sent the jolt my way. Youths often caused glint stress inside adult minds. Their inability to understand their inner worlds meant their bursts of extreme feelings—and incoherent thoughts—often went widespread. Sighing with relief, then annoyance, I climbed the hill and headed for the playing children.

Who didn't care about the grief they'd caused. The girls sat in a mound of mud, placing rocks in a circle and using sticks to build triangular tents inside the stony circumference.

I took a breath, then read the girls' glints. Sure enough, the blonde was chaotic: her emotions leapt from wild exultations of joy when the stick tent stabilized to maudlin despair when rocks tumbled out of place. Strangely, the twin's glints were stable. She didn't react to the polarizing reactions of her blonde friend.

But maybe that wasn't so strange. The twins were odd little things. They were consumed by their troubles, oblivious to the goings-on around them.

I smiled at the children. "What are you making?"

The girls looked up, as one. The twin stared, unblinking, but the blonde sneered. "*That* is none of your business."

"For the love of leaves!" I threw my hands in the air, then reigned in my frustration. If I was going to help these girls (because they couldn't keep hurting people) I had to stay in control. I put on my patient smile and knelt in the dirt, meeting the blonde on her level. "I'm sorry I was rude before—"

The blonde huffed, raising her nose to the sky.

"—but I need to tell you something," I finished. "Something you might not know."

That got their attention. The twin dropped her stick and the blonde narrowed her eyes, leaning forward. "What?"

"I can read glints, really well," I said as I tapped my temple. "And when you—" I nodded at the blonde, "—got upset, it caused me pain. In here." I touched my forehead. "It hurt."

The blonde sneered. "Stay away, then. You can't blame me for your weak mind."

"I don't have a weak mind," I said. "You aren't aware of yours. I know how it feels to lose control of my glints. I was a kid once, too. But you can't go around harming people because you haven't matured." I stood, brushing dirt off my trousers. "Alright?"

The blonde's smile twisted. "It wasn't me."

"It had to have been you," I said. "Your glints are violent."

The blonde gasped. "Are you saying I'm a monster?"

"What? No!" I stepped back. A monster? I didn't say she was a monster. She was just a kid. "Everyone's glints are wild when they're young. It's normal."

"I can't believe you're yelling at me." The blonde's lip trembled. "I didn't hurt you. I'd never hurt anyone."

"There's nobody else here." I said with more bite in my voice than I intended. I wasn't yelling at her. I never yelled! I took a breath, then nodded at the twin. "Unless you think she did it?"

"So, *both* of us are monsters?" The blonde buried her face in her hands.

My jaw dropped. What was happening? I was trying to help this girl and she was acting like I'd accused her of committing a crime. Kids were weird.

I preferred plants.

"Ignore her," the twin said, patting the blonde's shoulder. "Everyone knows Layla has a temper."

"Excuse me?" A temper? Me? I was the calmest person in Chaleur! I stamped my foot. "I do not have a temper. Who says I have a temper?"

The blonde howled.

"It's okay," the twin cooed as she rubbed the blonde's back. "I'll get Madame Rogers. She'll make Layla go away."

"No—no, don't do that." I knelt down, waving my hands. I had to fix this mess: I never should have talked to these irritating urchins. "I didn't mean to hurt your feelings. If you say you didn't cause the pain in my head, I believe you. I do, I swear."

As though the blonde had flipped a switch, her cries—and tears—stopped, and her chaotic glints disappeared. Sniffling, she said, "You mean it?"

"Yes," I said. "The pain must have come from somewhere else.

Don't tell Rogers, or anyone, that I lost my temper. Please."

The blonde wiped her cheeks, nodding. "Okay. I won't." She lifted her chin. "What's your name?"

"I'm Layla Douglas." I climbed to my feet, hoping my height would assert authority that stuck. "You can call me Layla, though."

The blonde smiled. "I'll do that." She stood, hoisted the twin to her feet, then nodded down at the solemn youth. "This is Havu Boucher. And *my* name is Erika Graham." Erika fluttered her lashes as she said, sugary sweet, "Now that we know who's who, are you done? Because your drama wrecked our day, and I might have to tell Simone Rogers you attacked us just so I don't have to keep looking at your nature-wrecked face."

Red hot anger exploded behind my ears: anger I didn't know I was capable of feeling. "Hold on one second," I snarled. "You can't talk to me like—"

"Are you yelling at us again? Madame Rogers won't be happy about that." Erika grabbed the twin's tiny hand. "Will she, Havu?"

"No." The twin shook her head grimly. "Madame Rogers takes care of us. She doesn't like when people are mean."

"Yeah," Erika said. "She doesn't like when people are mean." Her mouth widened until the tips of her teeth gleamed under her full upper lip. "You'd better be careful."

Drawing on my new power, I gathered my energy and formed a rod with my mind-strength. Catching—and holding—Erika's gaze, I sent the rod towards the blonde's face and—

Hit an impenetrable barrier.

Erika had shut me out of her mind.

My energy drained from my body: tapping into that amount of power was exhausting. I dropped the rod and bent over, dizzy. "How did you do that?"

Erika lowered her chin. "I'm sorry."

"What?" I gaped, startled by the rapidity of Erika's temperament changes.

"You're right," Erika said. "I'm not in control of my feelings. Or my thoughts. I didn't expect to see you here today, so I got nervous. I've never told you this before, but I look up to you. You're one of the nicest people in Chaleur. You aren't stuffy, like your cousin. Or rude like the grocer, Madame Perrault." She smiled at me with tentative hesitation. "You're special."

My shortened breath caught in my throat. This kid was bizarre. "That's sweet of you to say, I guess." I backed away. I had to get out of there. "I've got to go. I'd hate to ruin more of your day. Or, whatever."

"Layla?" Mayor Billadeau's voice carried through the trees. "Did you find your bag?"

"Coming!" I called before turning back to the girls, who beamed at me innocently. Well, Erika beamed. The twin stared, like the twins always did. Waving at them awkwardly (what else was I supposed to do?) I hustled down the hill.

"—so if you can look into her disappearance, Amelie, I'd really appreciate it," Rogers was saying, wringing her hat in her hands.

"Certainly. I'll speak with the girl's parents."

"Already did. They were out of it. Half-gone." Rogers twirled her finger over her temple. "The war fried them, Amelie. That's why I look after the girls. The Bouchers don't know which way is up, let alone how to take care of their kids."

"I'll look into it." Mayor Billadeau turned to me, eyes twinkling. "Ready?"

"Ready." I smiled, displaying my empty hands. "I couldn't find my bag."

Mayor Billadeau waved at Rogers. "Thanks for clearing the air, Simone. Let me know once the cleanup crew arrives, and I'll send some locals to help restore your field." She grabbed my elbow and steered me towards the plank pathway.

As we made our way through the trees that surrounded the mushroom field, I sent my energy rod towards Mayor Billadeau's head with the last of my strength.

The mayor smiled as I knocked on her mind. "Yes?"

I wasn't looking for my bag, I sent. I didn't bring a bag. Something hit my head. In the forest.

"Are you okay?" Mayor Billadeau looked me up and down, searching for injuries. "Was it a branch? Some of the spruce trees didn't fare well in last night's wind."

It hit my mind, I sent. Inside my head.

Mayor Billadeau stopped. "In the forest?" She whispered, "While you were reading Simone's glints?"

Yes.

Mayor Billadeau pulled me behind a large pine. She widened her eyes, and her glints filled my head. What kind of something? Something like the anger-excitement I sensed the other day?

No, nothing like that, I sent. It wasn't a glint. It was sort-of like when I used my mind to stop the fight at the envoy meeting, but much—much!—more powerful. It hurt, but I'm alright.

"Huh," Mayor Billadeau said out loud. "What could it be?"

"I thought it might be those girls who play on Madame Rogers' property, but I talked to them. They weren't the problem." I stared at my shoes. "They were *a* problem, but for other reasons. Not mind-pain reasons."

"Huh." Mayor Billadeau rubbed her chin. "Well, now." She blinked, and her brown eyes flashed. "You talked to the girls? All of them?"

"I talked to that blonde girl—Erika—and one of the twins. Havu." Distracted, I pulled a weed off the pine tree's trunk. I hated weeds. "I'm sure the other twin was around somewhere. Where one of them goes, the other follows."

"But didn't you hear Simone? The other one—Havu's sister—hasn't been around in a while."

"Madame Rogers must be confused," I said as I ripped the weed in half and threw it on a rock. "I didn't see the other twin, but that doesn't mean she wasn't there."

"Good point," Mayor Billadeau said. "Or she could be at home—sick—and the Bouchers didn't want Simone to know their business when she asked about her. Or the gal could be playing by herself. The Bouchers would've told me if their daughter went missing. I don't care what Simone says, those two love their girls. Even if they're still hurting from the war."

I stared at the torn weed, then tugged on the end of my hair. "Maybe—" I wound my hair around my finger. "Um, I know it isn't my place to give you advice, but maybe you should tell someone. Like the Provincial Police. In case the twin—the other twin—*has* gone missing."

"That's great advice." Mayor Billadeau smiled. "But I don't want to involve the Police before we have to." Her grin twisted into a grimace. "Their presence in Chaleur could make our lives . . . complicated." Mayor Billadeau nodded towards the path, which was lit by a rare beam of sunlight. "Shall we?"

My feet followed the mayor, but my thoughts were elsewhere. "Mayor Billadeau?"

The mayor chuckled as she led us out of the forest. "You can call me Amelie, Layla. Or Mom. You're practically family."

I almost swallowed my tongue. "I can't call you Mom. I appreciate the offer, I do—honestly—but it would be strange. I might call you Amelie." I scrunched up my nose, shaking my head. "Ew. No. You'll always be Mayor Billadeau to me."

The mayor laughed as we walked out of the woods and onto Chaleur's main street. "There are worse things than my son's partner being a tad too polite." She stopped in front of the mayoral offices. A hanging sign swung above the cabin's wraparound porch. "I've got some business to take care of. See you later? At the Coplot meeting?"

"Yes, madame. I mean, Mayor Billadeau." I grinned. "You can count on me."

"Don't forget to tell Oli to take a break," the mayor said as she stepped into her office. "A real break, not a chasing-Layla-through-the-trees break."

"Yes, madame." I saluted her. "Whatever you say, madame. Your whim is my will, mad—"

Mayor Billadeau shut her door. I giggled, but nobody was around, so it was alright.

Then I stopped.

Out of the corner of my eye and in the background of my mind, an intense aura stalked down the mountain. Its sound shadow skulked within the trees, sending ripples of tension into my head. Vibrating oscillations with a moth-like quality fluttered out from the stalker's core as it circled Rogers' mushroom field.

I frowned. The stalker might be the source of my head pain.

I had to find out.

Turning in a slow circle, I breathed into my power. Keeping my face and body relaxed, I hummed the tune I'd dreamed the night I met Oliver, swinging my arms in time with the song's tempo. But under my outward calm, my mind searched the forest.

I gasped. I knew the stalker! And the potential cause of my headaches.

The figure moving around Rogers' property was tall, fit, and young. And they possessed a focused intensity I would recognize anywhere.

The stalker was Major Zekiul Cox.

That should have been the most important news circulating Chaleur that day: Zekiul hanging out in the woods instead of with the Champions at their base? Intriguing! But, fortunately for Zekiul—and unfortunately for everyone else—the Bouchers filed a missing person's report that afternoon. Their daughter, Herra, *was* in trouble.

She'd been gone for days.

Zekiul Cox's stalking had to wait. Finding a child days after she disappeared within the mountainous province of Pluie needed to be the priority.

PART TWO

"Everyone is fucked up."

Khleo Billadeau

CHAPTER TEN

The child hunt began.
Well, no. It didn't actually begin. When a child went missing, people didn't leap into action. They had to plan. And organize. Imagine if a town full of people ran indiscriminately into the forest in a panic, screaming and yelling for a missing child. Adults, in their fear-filled hurry, would get hurt. The mountains were treacherous. It wouldn't take much to sprain an ankle on a loose rock, or pull a hamstring hopping—or sliding—down a slippery cliffside. Running off without guidance was never a good idea. The last thing anyone needed was to lose a team of searchers due to injury. Or, whatever.

So, even though the community was in an uproar, Mayor Billadeau kept the town calm with her firm hand—and her firm glints over the eyelinks—and forced everyone to pause. Then she asked the community to join her in the Coplot cabin.

I was surprised at how quickly the town complied. I was one of the citizens who itched to start the search right away, even though I knew it was a bad idea. I hated that one of the twins was lost in the mountains. The girl could be injured, or—

I swallowed.

Herra could be dead.

I didn't like the twins—nobody liked the staring children with their identical frowns—but I felt bad for them. And my pity, mixed with worry, made me wiggle on my chair as the mayor addressed the community.

Mayor Billadeau laid out a plan: we'd split into teams under the leadership of Oliver, Khleo, and Dimitri, then search quadrants of the town, starting in the centre of Chaleur and moving outwards in concentric circles.

Citizens divided themselves sort-of equitably between the

team leads. I wanted to join Oliver's group, but Mayor Billadeau insisted I partner with Khleo. *You'll keep him in line*, the mayor sent as she stared at me through her widened eyes.

She was still the only person who knew about my burgeoning power; and we agreed that was best. Since I hadn't properly tested my strength, the correct thing to do was to keep quiet about it. Mayor Billadeau and I didn't want to cause additional trouble by misusing my ability: even if glint-reading could have helped find Herra.

So I started the search with Khleo, and the other citizens who liked the eldest Billadeau's carefree leadership approach. Straggling in a clump behind Khleo's shining shoes—metallic overlay that day—our team headed up Mount Ryndle. I wanted to scout ahead, because high in my trees I could see more than a group of people could on the ground, but Khleo told me to stay put. He wanted everyone to stick together, which I sort-of understood.

Our group searched the mountains for an hour. Every team searched for an hour. Then an hour turned into hours, and hours stretched into a full day. Then two. Then, on the morning of the third day, the child search came to a screeching halt.

Not because we found Herra, but because the Champions did something stupid. Again.

"They're harvesting Bot bodies in the valley?" Mayor Billadeau pressed her temple, reading the News Alert network. "What are they doing with the pieces? The Reclamation Party wants the dead Bots to stay untouched until the Reuse, Recycle, Repurpose factories are up and running. *How* are the Champions harvesting Bot bodies? Those bloody Bots are heavy! And why would Cox—that moth-faced miscreant—broadcast his illegal activities? Is he dim? Or is this a scam? Are the Champions trying to get the government's attention to distract them from—from—" She sighed, and leaned against the Coplot cabin's wall. "I have no idea what's happening anymore."

Khleo, who sat behind the leadership table, reached up and patted Mayor Billadeau's forearm. "Mumsy. Everyone is fucked up.

That's why we started the Compassion Coplot."

"Watch your language," Mayor Billadeau snapped. "Don't forget where you are."

Khleo looked around the empty cabin: empty except for his mom, Dimitri, and Oliver.

And me. I waited on my chair, eyes wide as I recorded the unofficial meeting.

I'd woken that morning after a rough shaking from Oliver who'd hissed in my ear that his mother needed us. Now! We grabbed Khleo from his room—bleary-eyed and disheveled—then met Dimitri on the path that led to the town. When we entered the cabin the sun had just risen. It shone through the cabin's window, illuminating the miserable mayor. When Mayor Billadeau told us why we'd gathered before the town arrived to receive their child-hunt assignments for the day, Khleo rolled his eyes, Dimitri leaned his forehead against the window's glass, and Oliver punched the library door.

I tended to Oliver's hand—which was only a little bruised—as Mayor Billadeau projected a vid from her eyelinks onto the wall. Then I fell onto my chair as the problem played out.

In the vid circulating the network, the Champions took credit for carting off six—six!—disabled Bots from the valley. They didn't say where they took the rusting machinery, but they boasted about their triumph. And!—they'd robbed a rations warehouse in Fairfield, close to the foothills. The vid flipped between Zekiul explaining the heroics of the Champions and images of Jolene distributing food to hungry citizens: citizens who looked suspiciously like Champions.

"So, because the Champions stole food from a storage facility, Fairfieldians are going to starve?" Dimitri peered at the wall, staring at an image frozen on its surface (Mayor Billadeau had paused the vid so the leaders could comment). Dimitri sniffed. "Should *we* be saving our supplies? In case the Champions raid Pluie's rations warehouse next?"

"I can steal food from Peevish Pear's market," I said, sort-of joking. "Our house has plenty of places to hoard them."

I wasn't joking.

"We won't starve. And neither will Fairfieldians," Mayor Billadeau said. "The other premiers will skim the top of their provincial warehouses to share with Fairfield. It will be fine."

"It won't be fine," Khleo said. "The whole country will go hungry because the Champions are brainless and don't know they can apply for a rations upgrade. If they want more food, they can have it. They don't need to steal anything." He glanced at Oliver. "What are you going to do about this?"

"Me?" Oliver massaged his hand. "Why me? You're a leader, too. You come up with a plan for once."

"We don't need a plan, my dear boy," Mayor Billadeau said, "because Khleo's right about the Champions, but wrong about going hungry. Nobody will notice if a little food is missing from the weekly rations. There are a lot of people in Canuckia. It won't take much to make up the deficit."

"So what's the problem?" I asked. "If the premiers will fix this—and nobody will really be affected—why are we upset?"

"Citizens will be angry when they see these vids. They don't realize how much the government supports us," Mayor Billadeau said. "Rebel groups, like the Champions, take advantage of Canuckians ignorance by preying on their deepest fear: that they'll suffer because the *government* is taking advantage of them. The Reclamation Party has problems, but they aren't as terrible as the Champions claim."

"Why don't we post that?" I tapped my temple. "On the network? To reassure everyone?"

"Nobody will listen to us," Mayor Billadeau said. "They're too scared. And scared people are illogical people. When fear takes over, gut-sense and fact mean very little. The Champions know that, which is why this News Alert vid is a problem. They're lying to everyone, but the lie is so worrisome people want to believe it."

"Why?" I asked. "Why would citizens believe something scary instead of the truth? Especially when the truth is sort-of nice?"

"Because." Mayor Billadeau shrugged. "They can't help it."

"Think about Dimitri's first reaction when he saw the vid." Oliver nodded at my frowning cousin. "He assumed Fairfieldians would starve, and Khleo assumed the whole country was in trouble. Why? Because starvation is horrible, so they jumped to the worst possible conclusion so they could justify taking action to protect themselves. They didn't care if the information was correct, or consider if hoarding food was the right thing to do, or—"

"I get it." Grinning at Oliver, I said, "Dimitri and Khleo stink."

"And you love it." Khleo lifted his arms. "Take a whiff, Layla. Enjoy the odour of awesomeness."

"No, no. No." Mayor Billadeau smiled. "But you and Dimitri do react like many of our constituents. Some of them, anyway."

"Are you calling us common, Mumsy?" Khleo tapped his metallic heels together as he leaned towards my cousin. "Dimitri? How should we respond this insult?"

Mayor Billadeau ignored her son; and replayed the Champions' vid. "Why are they doing this? It's damned foolish. And Cox isn't a fool. No, he is not."

"Did you meet with him, Amelie?" Dimitri peered out the window. "Before Herra went missing?"

"I sent him a message." Mayor Billadeau tapped her temple. "He didn't answer."

The image of Zekiul skulking through the woods rose to the surface of my thoughts. Because of the child hunt, I hadn't told the mayor—or anyone—what I'd seen. But I hadn't forgotten.

"You need to meet with Cox," Khleo said. "If you think he's a good guy, and Dimitri vouches for him—"

"I don't vouch for that rapscallion." Dimitri whirled around. "Why do you think I vouch for him?"

"I saw your face when Layla showed us her memory of the envoy meeting," Khleo said. "You like him. Or you want to fuck him, which is basically the same thing—"

"Khleo!" Dimitri's voice wavered with mortification. "When Layla showed us her memory all I felt was nausea from my migraine. Major Cox is a scoundrel!"

I giggled, then covered my mouth. "Major Cox," I whispered behind my fingers.

Dimitri continued: "A swindler! A scallywag! A—" As he shouted, Dimitri's glints tried to deny the truth: but he was unsuccessful. He did like Major Cox, both the person and his appendage. *Liked* liked.

I smirked. My power was proving to be more than helpful. It was sort-of fun.

"You need to meet with Cox, Mumsy," Khleo said as Dimitri's rant ended with an abrupt, 'schmuk!' "If you and Layla vouch for him, that's good enough for me."

"I don't count?"

I looked towards the library, where Oliver stood by the door. I hadn't spent a lot of time with him over the past three days, and I hadn't taken a hard look at him in a while.

I looked then.

The bags under Oliver's eyes were deeper. Darker. His lips were cracked and his hair was unwashed. I cursed, inwardly, at his messy state. I'm supposed to look after him. It's my job to make sure he's alright. How could I—

Khleo's response to his brother's question stopped my guilt-laden glints. "Your opinion about hot rebellion leaders never counts. You're about as mature as the twins and—"

"The twins!" Mayor Billadeau groaned. "What time is it?"

I blinked. Whoops. *That* was my job: assisting the Coplot, not Oliver. "The community will be arriving in thirty minutes," I said. "I recommend concluding this conversation after you schedule a time to address your concerns about the Champions at a later date."

"Thank you, Layla." Mayor Billadeau straightened her rumpled shirt: a shirt she'd clearly slept in. Like Oliver, she'd dropped her hygiene regimen when Herra went missing. "Let's finish this chat tomorrow morning. Until then, I don't want anyone in this room gossiping to anyone outside of this room." Mayor Billadeau stared at Khleo. "You get me?"

Unlike the rest of his family, Khleo looked fresh and squeaky clean. He beamed at his mom. "My lips are sealed."

The leaders parted to set up the cabin for the rest of the community. Dimitri—cheeks still burning—yanked the chairs out of the storage room. Mayor Billadeau and Khleo kept talking behind the leadership table. I hopped off my chair to grab Oliver's fingers.

I pulled him into the library, away from the others. "You look awful. When was the last time you showered?"

"Thank you for the compliment." Oliver sunk deeper into his hunch. "Your criticism is just what I need when I'm burnt out."

"I'm sorry. I should have been here for you. What can I do?"

Oliver pulled his fingers out of my grip, mumbling something under his breath.

"What was that?"

"Nothing. I have to get ready for the search."

Stung by his tone, I stepped back. "I'm trying to help you."

"Right. Well, you can't." Oliver brushed past me, out of the library. "Let's talk later."

"Oli," I pleaded, following my partner. "There isn't time to talk later. Tell me what's wrong."

"What's wrong?" Oliver turned around. "Haven't you been paying attention? We're trying to find a missing child and stop a rebellion led by a psychopath you have a crush on—"

"I do not have a crush on Zekiul."

"—and my To-Do list is growing. We have to apply for Party status in the new year. That's only a few months away. What I need is for you to actually help, instead of distracting me with your talking and—and—and whatnot."

Oliver didn't notice as the Coplot's leaders looked his way. His zooming aura was loud enough to wake a hibernating marmorated stink bug. The leaders didn't need to have natural power to know something was wrong.

I reached for Oliver's arm. "Maybe we should discuss this outside."

"No!" Oliver clenched his hands. "I'm tired, Layla. I'm tired of talking, and I'm tired of—"

"Are we late?"

We turned towards the front door. The blonde girl hovered in the entryway with Herra's twin sister standing sullenly behind her.

The blonde smiled, then said, "We heard voices. Have you started the meeting?"

"Not for another half hour, pet." Mayor Billadeau strode towards the girls. "We're still setting up. And you should be at home. Youths aren't assigned to search teams."

"But it's my friend who's missing." The blonde pulled the twin—Havu—further into the cabin. "We can't stay home doing nothing. It's not fair."

"Don't fuss." Mayor Billadeau intercepted the girls and steered them towards the door. "We'll find Herra faster if we're not worried about you two."

"Okay." The blonde's smile broadened as she stared at me—and Oliver—over the mayor's shoulder. "Looks like you have enough to worry about."

Mayor Billadeau shooed the girls outside. Closing the door firmly, then dropping the latch, she looked at her son. "Oli? Take a walk. You don't need to be here for the community preamble. I know how prepared you are for today's search. See you in an hour."

Oliver turned his head. He'd been gazing out the window. His eyes darted to me, and he paled. "Yeah. Yes. That's a—a good idea. Layla?" Oliver opened his mouth, then shut it. Without any emotion he shoved his hands in his pockets, lifted the latch on the door, and walked into the falling rain.

I watched him as he stalked towards the forest: watched Oliver scrub his eyes with his trembling fists.

His sad eyes.

CHAPTER ELEVEN

As though the argument never happened, the rest of the leadership team resumed their tasks.

I breathed in and out to slow my thudding heart, then joined Dimitri as he pushed the chairs into straight lines.

He glared at me.

Abruptly, I changed direction, and marched over to the mayor. "Mayor Billadeau? Can we talk?"

The mayor nodded, confused, as I stepped outside. Holding her hands over her head to protect her face from the downpour, she followed me around the cabin and into a copse of mountain hemlocks.

"These are funny-looking firs," Mayor Billadeau said as I stopped within the cluster of pines. She fingered a branch growing close to her face. "Didn't know we had trees like these in Chaleur. Look at the needles!" The mayor aimed the branch at me, grinning. "They're sticking out all which-way and whatever."

"And they have white on both sides," I said absentmindedly, staring at the hemlocks' reddish-brown bark. "Like racing stripes. The needles are flat and porous."

"You sure know a lot about this stuff." Mayor Billadeau let go of the branch. It swung backwards, then forwards to whack the side of her head. "Ouch! I suppose I deserved that." She raked her fingers through her hair, dislodging a handful of needles. "Here I am, gabbing about nature when you clearly want to chat about something important. Oliver, right?"

"Is he okay? I've never seen him like this." My ears rang and my head felt stuffed. I couldn't get enough air. Watching Oliver wipe his watering eyes hurt. My throat had closed up: like it did when my dad left.

"Never you mind Oli." Mayor Billadeau's aura thrummed with

sympathy. "He gets moody when he's overwhelmed. Has his whole life. It isn't personal, Layla. It's just part of who he is."

"But he was so mad at me." My head started to ache. "He's never been upset with me before. I—"

To my complete horror, tears welled in my eyes. I covered my face with my hands: I couldn't let the mayor see me like this. I'd never be promoted if I couldn't control my glints. Nobody would take me seriously, and Mayor Billadeau certainly wouldn't want my help.

But before I could gulp down my rapidly-rising sobs, Mayor Billadeau wrapped her arms around my shoulders—

—and held me.

I froze, then sagged like a child. All my worry—and built-up loneliness—swelled like a wave to spill out of my soul. I cried in the mayor's embrace.

"Shhh, shhh. It's okay," Mayor Billadeau murmured, rubbing my back. "Let it out. Let it all out."

"I don't know what to do," I said into the mayor's shoulder. "I don't know how to help him."

"Oh, my dear, this isn't about Oliver. Well, not completely. Your dad's absence affected you more than you know." Mayor Billadeau stroked my back: up and down, up and down. As her soothing aura thrummed, my headache eased. "Losing a loved one is a terrible thing. Trust me, when my Harold died—when my boys lost their father—I thought I'd never bond with someone again. But I got better. I fell in love with my babies." The mayor lifted my chin with her finger. "I know you want Oliver to be happy—" she grinned, "—like his mama, but everyone has low moments you can't fix. So, you just have to stick with your partner when they're down in the dirt, and be grateful when life returns to normal. Okay?"

I sniffed, then wiped my face with the back of my hand. "Okay."

"Okay." Mayor Billadeau smoothed my hair, smiling. "I'm proud you're partnered with my boy. You take good care of him, but don't forget to give yourself some loving attention, too. You get me?"

I nodded, my head suddenly lighter. I could breathe again. "I get you."

"Good." Mayor Billadeau wound her arm through mine. "Now, before we head inside to start the search, tell me more about these trees."

I laughed—a shaky laugh—then wiped my nose on my sleeve. "Well," I said, gesturing to the firs, "hemlocks like to grow around other trees. That's why there's a Douglas-fir over there—" I pointed towards the forest, "—and Western Reds over there." I nodded at the town, at the cedars lining the main street. "Hemlocks grow everywhere. But they have shallow root systems, so they fall over a lot."

"Fall *over* fall over? Like, bam! On the ground? Just like that?"

"More like, whoosh!" I mimed a torrent of wind blowing into the copse. "They aren't sturdy like my birch trees."

"Ah, yes. Your birch trees. Oliver's told me about them. They protect you from nasty insects, and spirits who roam the forest." Mayor Billadeau grinned as she tugged me towards the cabin. "Shall we?"

But I stayed put. "Mayor Billadeau, I think you should set up that meeting with Zekiul Cox," I said in a rush. "I saw something the day Herra was reported missing. I think *he* was roaming the forest, around Madame Rogers' farm. I heard his aura."

"Did you now?" Mayor Billadeau paused. "What was Cox doing in our neck of the woods? Especially when he posted vids from the valley a few days later?"

"If you meet with him, I want to help," I said. "Like with Madame Rogers. I can read Zekiul's glints while you two talk."

"I'm sorry, Layla, but no. No, no. Meeting with Cox isn't the same as clearing up a misunderstanding with Simone. Now, come on. The community's going to show soon."

"How is it different?"

Mayor Billadeau sighed. "Persistent, aren't you? Fine. I'll give you the facts. It won't be long before the Provincial Police take over the Champions case. Cox could be arrested for his most recent bought of shenanigans—and tried. You met him at the envoy meeting. You might be called in as a character witness, so you can't snatch his glints. Aside from it being illegal, snatched glints aren't admissible as evidence in a criminal trial at the provincial judicial level."

"But I watched a vid on the network where a criminal's lawyer snatched her glints to prove she bribed a police officer."

"Lawyers are allowed to snatch glints. Not private citizens."

"But I won't snatch Zekiul's glints. I can't. And I won't learn how. I just want to *read* his glints to find out if he was in the woods. That has to be alright."

"As far as I know, there isn't any legal precedence for reading glints without someone knowing. The court might consider reading the same as snatching, if it came down to it."

"But I want to help—"

"Layla?" Mayor Billadeau stepped out of the copse. Within seconds, rain had drenched her sandy hair. "Please. Let's go."

"But the Champions might be connected with Herra's disappearance!"

Mayor Billadeau stopped in the middle of the street, holding her arm in the air to shield her eyes. "In what way?"

I strode to her side. I didn't mind the rain. "If Zekiul was around the mushroom field around the time Herra went missing—and the twins played in the field—and the Champions set fire to the field—the two incidents might be related."

Mayor Billadeau looked over her shoulder. Then she widened her eyes and sent, If that's possible, we have to tell the Provincial Police.

No.

The mayor recoiled. "That's not your call to make, Layla."

Listen to me, please. I gritted my teeth. I couldn't sleep last night, so I did a little reading in your den.

"I thought that was you. I heard someone moving around the

big books, but I knew it couldn't have been my boys because they were put away properly this morning." Mayor Billadeau raised her eyebrow. "A little reading?"

Fine, I read the Canuckian Constitutional Law books: 2023-2083. You were right when you said the Provincial Police make things complicated. The security sector's list of misdemeanours is longer than an ancient oak, and those trees are tall. The Police can't come to Chaleur. Not yet, anyway. I kept my eyes on the mayor's. Do you trust me?

Mayor Billadeau nodded slowly. I've got no reason not to.

Good, I sent. Because I have an idea. An Oliver-style idea.

That grand, huh? Mayor Billadeau led me to the sidewalk and stopped under a Western Red cedar. Tell me quickly. The community is waiting.

I took a breath, then took a chance. Here's what I'd like to do.

CHAPTER TWELVE

The next morning I stood in my grove, waiting for Oliver.

The day *before*—after I explained my idea to Mayor Billadeau—she accepted my idea and we entered the Coplot cabin. I tried to focus on finding Herra during the day's search, but my mind reeled from my rapid pitch by the cedar.

The pitch that changed my life.

I was going to leave Chaleur. *That* was my idea. I was going to travel into the highlands in the Bot-gondola—a metal carriage that used to carry passengers up and down the mountain on wires that ran over the trees—and scan the rocky cliffside for the Champions. With my aura-sensing power, I'd be able to find their new base: the hideaway they'd moved into after they left Jardin.

After that, things would become tricky.

I was going to approach the Champions—and Zekiul Cox—and pretend I'd had enough of the Compassion Coplot. I was going to lie and say I wanted to join the Champions. Then—to gain Zekiul's trust—I'd edit a few of my memories to make it seem like I had intel about potential allies in Eurasia. After Zekiul let me join his ranks, I'd snatch his glints and find out the truth: Was he in Chaleur the day Herra went missing? And was her disappearance connected to the mushroom fire?

To my surprise, Mayor Billadeau loved the idea. She told me to meet her at the Bot-gondola the next morning. She even offered to tell the community I would be going north to meet with the highland farmers, to see if they knew something about Herra's whereabouts. She seemed excited about our little deception.

But I had to deceive Oliver for my idea to work, and I didn't know if I could.

"Can I please tell Oli the truth?" I whispered to Mayor Billadeau as we hovered on the Coplot cabin's threshold, finishing our conversation while Dimitri and Khleo argued about the reasons the Champions were harvesting Bot bodies. "I don't know anything about spying, but Oli might have suggestions. He just read the 'The Five Eyes Alliance' trilogy by Emi Manfling."

"The less people who know what we're up to the better," Mayor Billadeau said. "And Oli would want to go with you—you know how he is—but I need him here, leading his search party. That boy is brilliant at keeping stragglers on task."

"But—"

"Layla. Think about it. If Oli knew you were going to find the Champions' base to spy on Zekiul Cox, do you really think he'd support it? Of course not. He'd tell you stay put."

"What if I told him *part* of the truth. Not the glint-snatching or spying part. Just the part about me looking for the Champions' hideout. Then, when I get home, I can say I accidentally learned the truth about Zekiul after I found his base."

Mayor Billadeau rubbed her wet fringe of hair. "Layla."

She was right. I hated that she was right.

"Don't fret," Mayor Billadeau said, patting my arm. "If you pull this off, I'll put you on the Coplot's leadership team for sure. And who knows? When we win the 2107 election and I become Prime, maybe I'll tell Councillor Whitley to make you the next mayor of Chaleur."

But promises about potential career moves didn't make lying to Oliver any easier.

After the day's search ended I hung around the Coplot cabin, waiting for Oliver and his team to return. But according to Peevish Pear, who'd volunteered to be Oliver's 'search second' (her title, not Mayor Billadeau's), Oliver had dismissed his team in the forest. He went straight home. So I hurried to the Billadeau mansion; and Oliver's attic.

He wasn't there.

"Looking for Oli?" Khleo called up the stairs as he tapped his shiny blue sneakers on the second floor landing. "He isn't here. Do you want to leave a message?"

"How?" I said as I jogged down the staircase. "He isn't wearing his eyelinks."

"You can leave a message with me, Nutty Nitwit." Khleo mimed pulling a piece of chalk out of his pocket. He pretended to scribble in the air. "Dearest Oli Asshole: I miss you terribly, and am seriously considering sleeping with your brother if you continue to ignore me. He's much hotter than you, and I've been dying to know if his huge feet prove he has a huge—"

"Tell Oliver I'm going home." I pushed past Khleo and headed for the foyer. "If he's too busy to see me tonight, he can meet me in my grove tomorrow morning. Early." I paused by the arched exit. "Early, Khleo. Can you remember that?"

Khleo did a shiny two-step down the stairs to land on the foyer floor with a loud *slap!* "You'll be in your grove around noon."

"Early, Khleo."

"Early evening."

"Khleo!"

"You'll be in your grove before the sun crests the top of the majestic Mount Champ. And I'm ginormous, Layla," Khleo called as I hurried away. "You'd be lucky to spend a night with me instead of a lifetime with my bitchy bro."

I waited on my front stoop all afternoon—but Oliver didn't show up.

His mom did, though.

Mayor Billadeau barged into my living room, beaming, and threw camping supplies on my couch. "Ask and ye shall receive," she intoned as cold weather clothes and climbing gear tumbled to the floor. "The community stepped up. I thought I was going to have to raid shops and homes—like the Champions—but when I told the town about your trip, they happily provided the survival equipment you'll need in the tip-tops of Pluie. Now! You pack while I coach."

Out loud, Mayor Billadeau gave me names of the highland farmers who could help me find Herra, but in my mind—over the eyelinks—Mayor Billadeau shared different information:

negotiation tactics, peace-making strategies, and ways of assessing suspicious behaviour so I could escape if it seemed as though the Champions suspected I was there to spy.

But I half-listened to Mayor Billadeau's advice. I could read glints and sense auras. If anyone found out what I was up to, I'd run away. Nobody could catch me when I was in my trees.

After she finished, Mayor Billadeau left the way she'd arrived—abruptly—and I was left alone in my room, wondering if her son would make a similar appearance.

He didn't. And I had no idea if he would show up in my grove the next morning.

Sure enough, as the sun filled the circle of pines with light—and I waited underneath my birch tree—Oliver didn't arrive.

My stomach dropped. My head filled with haze. My throat closed up and tears pricked at my eyelashes.

What was happening? Why was I so upset? I wasn't going to be gone for long—I could live without Oliver for a week or so—and I hadn't done anything to make him mad, so I had nothing to feel bad about. But Oliver's stubborn moodiness made making-up impossible. I was leaving, and I wasn't going to get to say goodbye.

Power pulsed in my belly. As my strength grew, my hazy glints cleared away. I breathed into the power as it filled my chest, then I straightened my shoulders. Encouraged by the confidence, I lifted my chin and—

—my power disappeared, leaving behind a wave of weakness. Ignoring the thud that landed in my gut, I looked up, into the sky.

Clouds gathered, thick and white. The breeze picked up and the air smelled like citrus. My birch creaked and its branches waved. The wind died.

With a thundering *crack!* rain poured from the clouds, hitting my face and wetting my hair.

And washing away my worries.

I was Layla Caitir Douglas, Queen of the Trees and Mistress of the Mountains, and I was going to infiltrate the Champions and find out the truth about Zekiul Cox; and Oliver would apologize after he realized how much he needed me. I wasn't *just* an admin assistant. I was a freaking fantastic admin assistant. And I was going to find Herra.

Or, I'd find out if Zekiul was connected to her disappearance.

So, as the sun sent shadows between the thin trunks of the pines, I said goodbye to my birch. Then I walked to the outskirts of Chaleur where Mayor Billadeau waited by the Bot-gondola.

"Was watching you leave too much for Oli?" Mayor Billadeau asked as I joined her at the bottom of Peter's Peak. The scraggly-faced mountain loomed over our heads.

"Apparently." I swung my survival gear to the ground and squinted at the Bot-gondola's metal carriage. "Saying goodbye was too much, too."

"He didn't meet you at your grove? When I see that boy I'm going to—"

"With all due respect, Amelie, a little quiet if you don't mind." Dimitri's head popped around the side of the gondola, his face smeared with dirt. "I finished installing the navigation controls, but these nuclear batteries are finicky."

"Yes, yes. Yes. We'll cut the chit-chat." Mayor Billadeau lowered her voice. "Whatever you need."

"What's he doing here?" I whispered to the mayor as I nodded at my cousin.

"Without AI, the Bot-gondola is nothing but a useless metal skeleton. It needed power. Dimitri has been tinkering around with nuclear technology, so I asked him to get this baby—" Mayor Billadeau slapped the side of the carriage, "—up and running."

"Amelie!" Dimitri's voice rose as the gondola swung to the side, moved by the force from the mayor's hit.

"Sorry!" Mayor Billadeau nudged my sack with her boot. "You got everything you need?"

"Yup."

Mayor Billadeau widened her eyes. Do you remember the plan?

I hope so. I came up with it.

Yes, yes. Yes. Mayor Billadeau winked. "You'll be splendid."

"That should do it." Dimitri straightened. Walking around the carriage, he eyed the Bot-gondola up and down. "The batteries are installed, and the navigation instructions are inside. You shouldn't have any trouble running the machine." He turned to me and his green eyes narrowed. "Are you sure you don't want someone to go with you? The highland farmers aren't the politest citizens. Maybe Madame Perrault could leave Oliver's search team to accompany you up North."

"Well, now. Let's give Layla a chance." Mayor Billadeau grabbed Dimitri's tool kit off the ground and handed it to my cousin. "She did well at the envoy meeting, and we need every other citizen here."

"But I dealt with the highlanders when I remodeled their central farming shed. They're tough to talk to." Dimitri glanced over his shoulder. "Who is she staying with?"

"Farmer Blair is going to be her highland guide," Mayor Billadeau lied as she steered Dimitri towards the forest. "I messaged the whole clan last night, and they're happy to take on the northern search."

"But—"

"Be there in a minute! Tell Khleo it's okay to start without me," Mayor Billadeau called to Dimitri, who'd given up protesting and was stumbling towards the town. The mayor grinned at me. "Your cousin is too smart for his own good."

"Dimitri's too smart for everyone's good." I grabbed my gear and hoisted the heavy load into the Bot-gondola.

"Good luck, Layla." Mayor Billadeau helped me climb into the carriage. "Stay safe—and get your butt out of there if anything goes awry."

"Mayor Billadeau?" I paused with my hand on the carriage door's handle. "Can you do me a favour?"

"Anything. What do you need?"

"Can you tell Oli that I—um. That I said I'll see him soon?"

"Of course." Mayor Billadeau smiled up at me. "The second

he realizes you're out of his reach he's going to feel like a two-day-old pile of parasite poop. You know that, right?"

"Yeah, but I don't want him to be upset."

"It won't kill Oliver if he misses you a little. Now!" Mayor Billadeau rapped the gondola's metal body with her knuckles. "Find Herra! Or find out what Cox is up to."

I pulled the door closed.

Travelling inside the Bot-gondola was simple. When it was a living machine run by Artificial Intelligence, the gondola carried passengers without them having to do a thing. But with the intelligence core shut down, the Bot-gondola was useless. Fortunately, Dimitri's navigation controls and nuclear batteries made it easy to run by myself. So, after settling on the hard bench that stretched the length of the carriage, I yanked on a lever, powered up the gondola's nuclear core, and let the propulsion system take over.

The wheels running on the wires screeched, and the gondola lurched upwards. With the nuclear batteries doing the work, all I could do was relax; and push the brake when I reached a stopping station (the exit platforms built into Peter's Peak plateaus).

The Bot-gondola moved quickly. It only took a few minutes for it to travel up to—and through—the first stopping station. I watched Chaleur shrink as I climbed higher. It grew colder as the gondola ascended the mountain's rocky face, but I was prepared: I hugged Oliver's fruit-fibre sweater around my body and ate an apricot.

While I snacked, I searched for the Champions' hideaway. I scanned the mountainside for the humming auras of people below, but the only citizens I heard were the highland farmers who were, well, farming.

The highland farmers were a fascinating group. They were Anti-Techs: citizens who rejected technology and wanted Canuckia to revert to an agrarian lifestyle. They used human-made tools to do their work, so the farmers were sweaty, dirty, and nothing-but-muscle. In fact, one was so muscled I mistook him for Zekiul. I almost fell out of the gondola when I leaned out the window to get a better look at the toiling farmer down below, but the highlander was just a highlander, not the Champions' fit leader.

Hours flew by. The Bot-gondola passed through stopping station after stopping station, taking me higher and higher, but I couldn't sense the auras of the renegade rebels: until the gondola paused at a stopping station built into the side of Mount Champ, the mountain nestled between Ryndle and Peter's Peak.

The mountain that housed the Champions' hideout.

I stopped the gondola with a jolt, then hopped onto the stopping station's stone platform. The aural residue from the rebels throbbed along every square metre of the mountainside. I heard the faint pulsing of thumps and wallops left by the hard-edged renegades, and there!—in the middle of the clunking sound—Zekiul Cox's moth-like aura fluttered with insistent rapidity.

The Champions had been there recently: their residue would lead me to their hideout.

I grinned, then slipped my eyelinks off my corneas and into their case. I didn't need them, and I certainly didn't need the Champions accessing my glints. With my defenses up, I hoisted my survival sack onto my shoulders and headed into the forest. Even without my Com Tech, the renegades' aural imprints were loud and clear. The residue led me up, down, and around Mount Champ, then the sound disappeared as I stopped in front of a cave's mouth: an entryway hidden by a curtain of weeds.

I hated weeds.

But not as much as I hated surprises.

"Heh," a voice said right behind my ear.

I spun around and looked up into the blunt face of Just Jolene.

CHAPTER THIRTEEN

Before I could say a word, including, 'Hey! You're just the renegade I wanted to see!' Jolene clutched my bicep and shoved me through the weed curtain.

The trashy plants scraped my face as Jolene pushed me into the cave. Blinking my eyes to adjust to the darkness, I let Jolene shove me into the rocky cavern. We stopped a few strides in.

"Who is this?" Major Zekiul Cox reclined on a large stone seat with his legs spread wide to brace his body against the chair's back. "Who have you captured, Jolene?"

I laughed. Loudly. Amelie and I had agreed that supreme self-confidence was the best way to tackle my introduction.

"Are you trying to be intimidating? Please." I grinned as Jolene released her grip and stepped away. Massaging my arm, I smirked at the Champions' leader. "I thought you knew me better than that, Cox. Theatrics don't impress me."

Zekiul's glints shook—he was confused, which was great—but his expression stayed the same. "Who are you?"

"I'm Layla Douglas," I said, as though I was important or something. "We met at the envoy meeting." I tapped my temple. "I broke your brain, remember?"

Zekiul's lip curled. "I do remember. You're with Oliver Billadeau. Jolene?" He nodded at his second-in-command. "You can go."

Smiling, I watched Jolene lumber out of the cave. Then, as Zekiul watched me, I took a good look around the cave I'd been dragged into. The Champions' hideout within Mount Champ was as large as a canyon.

A monstrous canyon.

Lights hung from wires attached to the walls. The ceiling above my head was so high I couldn't see the stalactites hanging in the air, but I could hear the steady *drip, drip, drip* of water as it rolled down the rods and onto the rocky floor. The canyon looked like a gathering place. On either side of the stone throne, rows of tables ran from one end of the cavern to the other, with spinning stools tucked underneath. The hanging lights swung over the tables, pushed by wind that whistled through the weed curtain. Behind the throne—behind the rows of tables and stools—a large door squatted in the wall, locked with a giant bolt.

Intrigued, I read Zekiul's glints, and found out what the locked door protected.

More canyons.

The Champions' hideout wasn't a poorly-constructed squatters cave like Mayor Billadeau said it might be. It was a technological marvel.

Descending from the base of Mount Champ in recesses set inside the hulking rock, two additional tiers travelled to the root of the mountain, deep within the earth. Each tier was oblong, with tunnels connecting them to each other, and each tier had a different purpose.

The second chamber, just below the first, was an Intelligence Centre. Giant screens showing News from across the globe played on a constant stream, relaying information from every government on the planet. Mounted on the walls between the screens were charging stations for the eyelinks: salient tubes filled with dozens of the devices as they powered up. Alongside the technology I saw plastic maps, and food-preparation spaces, and long corridors that ran out from the Centre like insect legs.

The third and final chamber looked like private quarters: Zekiul's room. A bed sat in the centre, along with a cleansing closet and rest area that ran along the chamber's perimeter. The rest area included a board game table built into the wall adjacent the entryway. Board games! Zekiul collected the old-world entertainment systems.

As I read Zekiul's glints, a memory leapt into his mind: the Champions had harvested Bot-bodies in the valley so they could use the metal to build their paradise. Zekiul Cox was brilliant.

But he couldn't naturally read glints, so I had the advantage; and, at that moment, Zekiul's brilliant mind revealed an image of his chess set. He was visualizing his next move.

I giggled. Zekiul couldn't strategize against me. I could anticipate everything he decided to do, and he was going to find that out. Immediately.

I struck: "Why do you have a trapdoor under your bed? I don't know where the attached tunnel leads, but I bet none of the other Champions know it's there."

Zekiul narrowed his eyes. "Who told you about the tunnel?"

"And I think it's interesting," I said, sauntering along the nearest row of tables, "that the Champions operate as a collective—and you believe in equality—but you have the nicest room in the place while your minions sleep under the stars."

"The Champions don't sleep outside. They have rooms on the second floor. Why would you assume they—you know what? Never mind. I don't care." Zekiul leaned forward, resting his elbows on his knees (and revealing his chiseled chest). "What are you doing here?"

I let my fingers skim the closest tabletop as I swayed towards Zekiul. "I want to talk to you."

"The partner of my enemy's son wants to talk to me?" Zekiul sneered. "What could you possibly have to say that I would want to hear?"

"Amelie Billadeau is your enemy?" I laughed. "Billadeau is a fool. So are her sons. You have a bigger cob of corn to husk than the Billadeau family, Cox."

Zekiul tilted his handsome head. "I do?"

"You do."

"Like who?"

"There's a queue."

"A whole queue?"

"Almost a crew."

"That's untrue."

"I can't tell *you* who your worst enemies are," I concluded, even though I was enjoying the rhyming repartee. "Yet. I just arrived. Give me a good night's rest, and maybe I'll share the list of people who want you dead."

"There isn't a list."

"Uh huh! I know of several Global organizations that would give a lot to see you gone." I held up my hand and ticked off countries on my fingers. "On The Island, in the Separated States, in Bataar, Brasilia, Alkebulan, Stonemount, Azteca—"

"I don't believe you. Why are you actually here?"

"I told you." I hopped onto the nearest table and swung my legs back and forth. "I'm done with the Billadeaus. Amelie is ridiculous, and her boys are annoying. They think they're better than everyone, but—actually—they suck. At the envoy meeting, you proved there's only one group in Canuckia that can actually make a difference." I grinned at Zekiul, then raised my chin. "The Champions."

His lip lifted. Then Zekiul reclined on his throne; and smiled. "*That* I believe." In one elegant move, he leapt off the stone chair and strode towards me, extending his hand. "Welcome to the team, Layla Douglas."

Even though Zekiul's capitulation seemed a bit too easy, I shook his hand; and that was the beginning of my new life. Or, the next few weeks of my life.

CHAPTER FOURTEEN

It didn't take a few weeks to win the loyalties of the Champions, though: or the Champions' leader.

After I settled in, I dropped my false swagger and relaxed, trying to be genuinely friendly. So only a few days passed before I was welcomed into the Champions' inner circle: the small subgroup of renegades responsible for the raids and Bot harvesting. And only a week passed before I snatched Zekiul's glints.

I'd been giving pretend advice about pretend allies in Eurasia to the Champions in the Intelligence Centre when Zekiul suddenly left, claiming he had to meet with Jolene about a potential uprising in Jardin's Capitol. I excused myself as well—claiming I had to pee—when, actually, I had to follow Zekiul.

I knew Jolene was on a scouting mission. I could hear her slithery, slug-like aura as she scaled a cliff. Zekiul had asked her to recruit the highland farmers, even though I told him they wouldn't join the Champions because the highlanders wanted nothing to do with the rest of the world. So, after Zekiul left the second-floor chamber and trotted down the tunnel that connected to the lowest floor, I waited outside his door until I heard soft snoring inside his room.

He was taking a nap!

The poor guy must have been tuckered out from all his evil scheming.

Breathing deeply, I prepared to snatch my first thoughts. The power in my belly burned the instant I opened my mind. It rose into my head and spun into a glowing orb. I sent my energy into the middle of the orb, then used my power to send it towards Zekiul's aura. The orb passed through his chamber door; and I dove into his head. Zekiul's consciousness flooded my mind.

I could see every glint he was having—every glint he'd ever

had!—and the aura imprints he'd left over his lifetime. I knew where Zekiul had been, what he'd thought and felt, and his memories throughout every moment. But it was too much. I couldn't see Zekiul's important glints—or hear his aura—in all the chaos. So I let go of my hold on his mind and pulled back, just a bit. Suddenly, it became easier to select the glints and auras I needed: the strongest memories Zekiul possessed.

His memories appeared and I felt—understood—*knew!*—Zekiul's truth. I recoiled.

Major Zekiul Cox was a good person.

A great person. Not a sort-of nice person like the citizens in Chaleur: friendly people who were kind but complex. Zekiul's heart was pure, his intentions were well-meaning, and he had clever insights about the corruption in Canuckia. He wasn't just a charismatic speaker and chaos instigator. He cared.

And his ideas weren't that different from Oliver's.

After we're finished in Pluie I need to make sure we use the metal we harvested from the Bots to build our next hideout, Zekiul glinted in his sleep. His mind never turned off. *We can't waste resources. The places we live have to be better after we leave them.*

He rolled on his side.

Oh, fuckity-fuck, Zekiul glinted with a delightful display of profanity. *I forgot to tell Jolene to switch to low-power mode during the day. If we use up our energy sources, we're no better than the Reclamation Party.*

He spun onto his back. I could sense drool dribbling out the side of his mouth.

The Inclusivity Act revisions proposed by the government are fine, Zekiul glinted as he remembered a News Alert, *but they can make improvements. I want bylaws put in place that protect the victims of systemic indifference longer than the current Party's power cycle. We need guarantees that promise money, and staff, and supports when the government turns over so new agendas aren't prioritized.*

This changed things.

I couldn't be a spy anymore. I had to become Zekiul's ally.

I spent more time in his company. I asked real questions, and stopped telling lies about intercontinental issues. And, as I let down my guard, Zekiul and I grew closer.

I started to like him.

Zekiul told me about his plans for a better country. We spent hours sitting on the plateau outside Mount Champ's cave mouth, basking in the sun and gabbing about what was possible. Zekiul came alive when he spoke about his vision, and I was enthralled by his optimistic enthusiasm. Being Zekiul's friend was like eating a giant seed enriched with the B12 vitamin. He energized my soul.

Then—during one unusually hot afternoon—when the sky was blue and the sun beamed, Zekiul told me the truth about Rogers' mushroom fire.

He'd received a tip from an anonymous source on the News Alert network about a toxic substance in Rogers' pools. The substance could have poisoned Chaleur's main water supply, so the Champions set the fire. Burning the substance was the best way to get rid of the poison. Hundreds of citizens had been saved. Rogers' *did* share private information about the Champions' children on the network, but that wasn't enough to cause the rebels to burn her livelihood to the ground. "The Champions in Jardin—" Zekiul said, "—are more than capable of taking care of their kids."

"Is that why you were hanging around Rogers' place the day after the envoy meeting?"

Zekiul glanced at me. "You saw me in the woods?"

"Um." I couldn't tell him about my natural powers. Not yet. "Yeah."

Zekiul lifted his face to the sun. "I wanted to make sure the substance had completely burned up. And it's a good thing I went back, because the poison stuck to the dirt clods in Rogers' pools." He sneered. "She didn't clean up properly. But I scooped out the clods and put them in her re-nutrification barrels."

"I saw that substance." I rolled onto my knees. "It smelled like gasoline."

"Gasoline?" Zekiul turned his handsome head to peer at me. "Of course. Gasoline must have leeched out of the valley Bots and trickled into the river system, which connects to Rogers' pools. Gasoline in Chaleur's water supply would have made everyone sick."

"Or everyone dead." I sat back on my heels. "I wonder who sent you the tip. And why?"

Zekiul shrugged. "Does it matter?"

"Maybe. A lot of stuff has happened over the last few weeks that doesn't make sense. I want to know what's going on."

Zekiul grinned, then nudged my shoulder. "One thing at a time. After we overthrow the government we can discover the mystery tipper."

My shoulder tingled from Zekiul's touch.

Uh oh.

"Why didn't you tell Oliver about the pool poison at the envoy meeting?" I asked as I moved away. Slightly.

"I was going to, but then he went on the offense so I figured —why bother? And Rogers should have noticed the gasoline and dealt with it, not us." Zekiul took off his jacket and stretched out on the ground, baking under the hot autumn sun. "It doesn't matter, though. I solved the problem. The Champions saved Chaleur and —hopefully—taught Rogers a valuable lesson about irresponsibility. If she'd managed her farm properly instead of harassing people on the News Alert network, the fire wouldn't have happened."

Slowly, I realized Zekiul wasn't a great person.

He was a hero.

So, the next day, when the Champions were outside the tiered chambers—foraging for berries for breakfast—I told Zekiul *my* truth: about Herra, and Mayor Billadeau's suspicions, and that I'd snatched his glints. I also told him I liked him, and said if he forgave me I would ask Mayor Billadeau to let the Champions join the Compassion Coplot.

Zekiul was angry, at first.

"I'm angry," Zekiul said. His frank directness was so refreshing. I never wondered where I stood with him, because he told me.

Frowning, Zekiul played with a wire that stuck out from behind one of his giant screens in the Intelligence Centre. Usually, on-the-ground vids rolled across the screens on repeat, but because of a quake that shook the tiered caves, the screens displayed nothing but grey lines and haze: like the fuzz in edited memories.

Zekiul fiddled with a cord, and the vid on the giant screen reappeared. Glancing at me, Zekiul moved around the chamber, fixing as he spoke. "You lied about why you came here—"

"Yes."

"—and you've been lying ever since—"

"Sort of."

"—and you snatched my glints—"

"Definitely."

"—but you think that's okay because you like me?" Zekiul straightened. The flickering lights from the multiple screens made his skin look red, then yellow, then pink, then green, then—"I don't know, Layla." He picked up a box of wires and set it on the nearest countertop. "Why should I trust you? You're strong enough to snatch glints without people knowing—"

"I've never snatched glints before," I interrupted. "And I only snatched yours because it was important, and I only did it while you were sleeping. I'm not that strong."

"So you say." Zekiul took off his sweat-soaked shirt, then tossed it to the side before moving to another screen. "But snatching glints—for any reason—is wrong."

"Yes." I kept my eyes on Zekiul's face instead of on his defined body. Me slobbering over his ridiculously-sexy self wasn't going to make Zekiul forgive me. "Very, very wrong."

"But the mayor of Chaleur is okay with it?"

I sat on a stool and pulled on the end of my hair. "When did you start caring about right and wrong? You don't follow the rules."

Zekiul snorted. "I follow rules that protect people. I break rules that hurt them."

I grinned. Oh, I *really* liked Zekiul Cox.

"And," Zekiul continued, "you think it's easy to snatch glints when people are asleep?"

"Well, yeah." I shrugged. "If it didn't break a law, I bet a lot of citizens would do it."

Zekiul laughed, then headed towards the last faulty screen. "You have no idea how strong you are, do you?"

Curiosity piqued, I followed him. "What do you mean?"

"Nobody can snatch glints," Zekiul said as he disappeared behind the screen. "Not even from people who are weak-minded, asleep, or completely unconscious. Since the war, I've worked with some of the most skilled criminals in the country. If snatching glints was easy, Canuckia would be a very different place."

Zekiul dropped an adaptor on the stone floor.

As he bent over to pick it up—and his pants tightened around his delicious tush—I swear I almost fainted. "That can't be right."

"You must have very strong mind if you can read glints without people noticing." Zekiul plugged the adaptor into the wall. As I shook away my glints that imagined Zekiul plugging *his* adaptor between *my* walls, he said, "It doesn't matter, though."

That cleared my head. "Why not?" I demanded. "Reading glints has been useful. If I hadn't snatched yours, I'd still be lying to you and we wouldn't be friends."

Zekiul grinned.

I turned red. Beet red. He was so handsome it was impossible to make eye contact. We had to formalize the alliance quickly, otherwise Zekiul and I would be*come* more than friends—and Oliver and I would be over.

The final screen snapped into focus, so *I* focused on the vid rolling across its face: a Champion backed away from a highland farmer as he shook his human-made hoe in the air. "I'm sorry I snatched your glints, but *how* I found out the truth doesn't matter. I know you like me, I know you want to be my friend, and I know you want to work with the Compassion Coplot."

Zekiul leaned against the screen, crossing his arms over his lickable abdomen. "You're reading my glints right now, aren't you?"

Yes. Yes, I was. "Listen, Cox. The Champions should work with Mayor Billadeau. She knows people in the Reclamation Party who can make your dream become a reality. If you stop posting twisted vids on the network—"

"Our vids are accurate."

"—and stop harvesting Bots, and stealing grain, and protesting outside the capitols, Mayor Billadeau will want to work with you. And she'll keep working with you after she's democratically voted into power in 2107."

Zekiul liked that I was finally being honest with him.

"I like that you're finally being honest with me," he said later that evening as we sat behind his gaming table, chess pieces scattered on the stone surface. "Even though you're the strangest person I've ever met," he said, "with your weird power and passive-aggressive attitude—"

"Passive-aggressive? Who? Me?"

"—I think we could work together, but only if I get to stay in charge of the Champions. Which means no interference from the mayor, or her sons. Or you."

I moved a pawn forward one square. "That's not how alliances work, Zekiul."

"My allies don't tell me what to do." Zekiul took my pawn with his rook. "So back off, or the deal's off."

"Or realize we aren't just allies. We're friends, and friends point out when one of them is about to do something stupid." I shifted my knight, setting up a move that would dethrone his king. "Like walk away from a partnership that could change the country."

"I'm happy we're friends." Zekiul slid his bishop up the board. "It would be nice to have you on my side if the Champions and the Coplot align—"

I gasped.

"If." Zekiul's lip lifted. "I said if. *If* we work together, I need to retain my autonomy. The Champions can't work for the Coplot. I won't work for you. You need to respect that."

"And you need to respect that I don't just *work* with my friends." I captured Zekiul's queen, then picked up the piece. Lightly tapping Zekiul's leg with the queen's crown, I said, "My friends and I have fun. Sometimes, we enjoy ourselves." I knocked over Zekiul's king with my knight. "See?"

Zekiul chuckled. His sharp face softened when he laughed. I wished he'd do it more often.

"You and I can have fun," Zekiul grabbed the queen from my hand and held it up to the lamplight, "but with one condition."

I raised my finger. "Friendship doesn't come with conditions."

"Okay. With a boundary."

I froze, my hand in front of Zekiul's face. A boundary? I didn't like the sound of that. Boundaries kept people apart.

"If we're going to be friends, you can't snatch my glints anymore." Zekiul twirled the queen in his fingers as he leaned back on the padded lounger that ran behind the gaming table. "I mean it. I'll tell you anything, but my glints are off-limits. I evaluate who enters my mind."

"Evaluate who enters, evaluate who enters." I smiled. "Do you always talk like that?"

"I mean it, Layla. It's wrong to read someone's glints without their permission. People have boundaries for a reason."

I dropped my hand on my lap. "To keep secrets."

"So what? There's nothing wrong with private citizens keeping a few secrets. Especially when they don't hurt anyone. But there *is* something wrong with you knowing secrets without the secret-keeper's permission. Some secrets are better off as secrets. Got it?"

I didn't get it: my head spun from Zekiul saying 'secrets' so many times.

"I want you to trust me, Layla, because friendship is built on trust." Zekiul dropped his toned arms on the lounger's back, still holding the queen in his hand. "I *will* tell you anything. You just have to ask. Go ahead, ask me about my secrets."

I scrunched up my nose. "But I can't tell anyone your answers, right?"

"Not *any*one." Zekiul shrugged. "But I have nothing to hide from the people I care about."

He cared about me? For the love of leaves, Zekiul was breaking *my* boundaries. And I wanted him to.

I had to change the subject.

Swallowing, I asked, "How old were you when you had your first kiss?" So much for changing the subject.

"Nineteen."

"Holy holly berries!" I giggled. "Like, last year?"

"Yup." Zekiul tapped his temple. "Check my glints."

I gathered my power to enter his mind, then stopped. "You said I couldn't read your glints."

"Not without my permission." Zekiul grinned, shaking his head. "I gave you my permission, you dork."

"Dork. That's different." I read Zekiul's glints and—sure enough—saw a memory of him smooching a rugged male inside a weathered farmhouse. "Who is he?"

"He was part of the rebellion before—" Zekiul fiddled with the chess piece. "An officer arrested him for picketing outside a factory that wouldn't allow a union to form."

I sank onto the lounger. "I'm sorry."

"There have been other kisses. Look."

Zekiul's glints showed me a memory of a female in a bathing suit swimming with him in an aquamarine lake.

I smiled. "She looks cute."

"She is cute," Zekiul said. "She's stationed in Jardin. I haven't seen her since the Champions moved here." He placed the queen on the chess board, then said, "What other secrets do you want to know?"

"What's your guilty food pleasure?"

"Fried grasshoppers."

"How many provinces have you rebelled in?"

"Three. Jardin, Fairfield, and Pluie."

"When was the first time you had sex?"

"Last year."

"Who did you have sex with?"

"The cute female from the lake."

"Where's the strangest place you've had sex?"

"In the lake, with the cute female."

"Your love life is thrilling."

"It would be more exciting if I wasn't busy saving the world."

I snorted. "Why did you start the Champions?"

Zekiul's mouth hardened. "I don't like the Reclamation Party. I think they're ineffectual. They could be doing more for Canuckians but, instead, the government spends its time reinforcing hierarchies of power so it prospers while the rest of us—"

"Hey." I placed my hand on Zekiul's knee; and accidentally knocked the queen off the table. "That last question wasn't serious. I know why you started the Champions, and I respect you for it."

Zekiul stared at my hand, then nodded. "Good." He swiped the queen off the floor.

I shook Zekiul's knee playfully, then backed away before I could rip off his trousers. "So, are we allies? Will the Champions and the Compassion Coplot work together?"

Zekiul agreed to form an alliance, so I sent a message to the mayor over the eyelinks. Mayor Billadeau *enthusiastically* agreed to form an alliance, after praising me for an embarrassing amount of time for setting it up. Zekiul broke the news to the Champions. His inner circle grumbled at first, but eventually accepted that working with the Coplot was the best way forward. We prepared for the trip back to Chaleur.

And I prepared to give my whole heart back to Oliver.

I'd been away for too long. Fantasizing about Zekiul had been sort-of fun, but I wanted to reunite with Oliver. Zekiul's charming smiles and shapely butt couldn't replace my stoic partner's soul. And I knew Zekiul didn't want to. His glints focused on serving the country, not sleeping with me.

It took us a day to make it to the town. Zekiul, Jolene, the inner circle of Champions, and I travelled down Peter's Peak in the Bot-gondola. It was a tight fit, but we managed. When the gondola stopped at the lowest plateau, I wrenched open the door and leapt outside. Then, after we hiked down the mountain pathways and the road straightened—and the dirt became packed from the trampling of many feet—my *heart* leapt. We were almost there.

When the Coplot cabin appeared at the end of Chaleur's main street and I saw Oliver through the window, I forgot about Zekiul's incredible body and inspiring soul. I squealed, then hurtled towards the cabin. Throwing open the door, I crossed the threshold. The afternoon sun streamed through the entryway and lit up my partner, who turned the moment I appeared.

Then I saw Oliver's face and my heart sunk into my boots.

CHAPTER FIFTEEN

Oliver frowned, then turned away.

Khleo and Dimitri—who were gathered around the leadership table—barely registered my arrival. I couldn't breathe. The auras humming inside the cabin mimicked Dimitri's usual anxiety-laden buzzing. It wasn't the greeting I'd expected.

"What's wrong?" Zekiul strode into the cabin and bumped into me, leaving Jolene hulking in the doorway. "Didn't Layla explain the alliance to your mayor? I watched her send the message. The Champions want to work with you, but if you can't get on board with us joining your precious Coplot, we might as well leave."

"No, Major." Dimitri's voice was harsh. "You're welcome here. You don't understand."

I walked over to Oliver, whispering, "What happened?"

Khleo answered in a tone that matched Dimitri's: "The Provincial Police know what you and Mom did: they saw the message you sent her. They know everything, Layla. They about the glint-snatching."

"Oli?" I reached for Oliver's fingers. "Is your mom alright?"

Oliver looked over his shoulder, but not at me. His eyes seemed to travel through me, like I was invisible. "They arrested her. She's in the Capitol, waiting to be tried for Glint Crimes."

I gripped the end of my hair. "What about—" I swallowed. "Are they looking for me?"

Oliver's gaze sharpened. "Right. That *is* what you'd be worried about, isn't it? Not my mother, or the people you hurt when you snatched their glints. You're worried about Layla. You're the only person you've ever worried about."

"Um—" Where was *this* coming from? "That's not true. Oli—"

"The Provincial Police don't know who sent Amelie the message," Dimitri interrupted. "A citizen noticed it—one of the highland farmers—and passed it along to the Capitol. The Police don't know you were involved, but they know someone snatched Zekiul's glints; and Amelie approved. Being complicit in a Glint Crime is a Glint Crime."

"But Zekiul forgave me for snatching his glints."

"She's right." Zekiul stood by my side. "I did."

"See?" I turned to Oliver, practically pleading. "Nobody was hurt. You can't be mad."

"What about Rogers?" Khleo moved behind his brother, feet planted wide. "You snatched her glints. Mom told us."

"I didn't!" My voice rang in the cabin. "I read Rogers' glints. It was different."

"Doesn't seem different to me," Khleo said. "Rogers didn't know you read her thoughts and feelings, did she?"

"That doesn't matter." I spun in a circle, trying to catch the gazes of the leaders. "We have to save the mayor."

"We are looking for Herra." Khleo met my glance with a condescending glare. "We have to run the town, now that my mom is gone. We can't go on a doomed rescue mission." He dropped his hand on Oliver's shoulder. "*We* have responsibilities."

"We have a responsibility to your mom," I said. "We have to go to the Capitol and explain what happened. If the Police knew that I was only—" I bit my lip. It wasn't the time to reveal my natural powers, or tell everyone I'd been testing them—growing them—over the past few weeks. But if I could explain to Mayor Billadeau's lawyer that we'd been trying to develop my abilities to help the community, the Police would have to let Mayor Billadeau go.

But nobody spoke. Nobody moved.

Nobody looked at me.

Except Zekiul. "I know I'm new here, but Layla's right."

The team turned to the Champions' leader.

"If your mayor—Amelie—hadn't sent Layla to speak with me, things would be a lot different right now." Zekiul's smile settled into his sneer, the one he used before we became friends. "Because of Layla, and your mayor, the Champions stopped protesting in Jardin. I have a team stripping our vids off the News Alert network, like she insisted. And we're here to help you find the missing girl. The Champions know how to survive in the wild. If Herra is lost, we can search places she might be sheltering."

Made braver by Zekiul's support, I lifted my chin. "See? My idea to infiltrate the Champions was a good one, and Mayor Billadeau didn't do anything wrong when she supported me. She was supposed to explain that to you. She would have, if she hadn't been arrested—but that wasn't her fault!"

Dimitri sighed. "Amelie did explain it to us, Layla."

Khleo shot my cousin a look of betrayal, but Dimitri just shrugged. "She did. Amelie told us everything. And—when she told us—everyone thought your plan was excellent." He pinched the bridge of his nose. "Be honest with Layla. You forgave her when Amelie told us the truth. Tell her you didn't care about the glint-snatching because it achieved a positive outcome." Dimitri dropped his hand. His buzzing aura quieted. "They didn't care: until Amelie was arrested."

"Well, that wasn't *my* fault." I took a shuddering breath. "The highland farmers are Anti-Techs. How was I supposed to know they could intercept eyelink messages? They aren't supposed to have eyelinks."

Oliver stared at the floor.

Holy holly berries, did *that* piss me off. "Fine. Be angry. I don't care. I didn't do anything wrong."

"It doesn't matter what's right or wrong, or who forgave whom and when or why." Dimitri glanced out the window as the wind beat against the cabin's walls. The community gathered on the street outside, waiting for the leadership team to unlatch the door so they could receive their daily search assignments. "We can't send someone to the Capitol to advocate for the mayor," Dimitri said, turning to stare at me sadly. "We need everyone here. We have to hope Amelie's lawyer can get her out of this, while the rest of us govern Chaleur."

Oliver looked up. He nodded. "Right."

"Three cheers for making a decision." Khleo crossed his arms. "I'm pleased as punch we're going to pretend Mom will be fine. But Herra—who's been missing for weeks now—is probably dead. But let's pretend she isn't and get the search teams looking for her—shall we?"

CHAPTER SIXTEEN

The next few days hurried by in a flurry of frantic activity.

Dimitri got Zekiul up to speed, and found a way to blend the Champions' advocacy ideas with the Compassion Coplot's. The two males often sat in the cabin discussing plans long into the night. It was the happiest I'd seen Dimitri since my dad left.

Khleo and Oliver were inseparable as they managed the child search; and the community. Not once did they mention how much their burden was eased when the Champions joined our ranks and I resumed my admin duties. Zekiul sent his rebels to scout places in the mountains civilians couldn't navigate, and he told Jolene to assist the Billadeau siblings personally. I spoke with the community about the benefits of a Champion-Coplot alliance, and soothed citizens' suspicion about the renegades' intentions. Soon, the community and the Champions searched the mountains together: because of me. I knew Oliver and Khleo appreciated the collaboration, but it would have been nice to hear them say it.

Or nice if Oliver talked to me at all.

Oliver avoided my company. When we were forced to work together, he spoke to me like we weren't a couple, or like I wasn't human. Like I was a Bot.

He was angry his mom hadn't told him why I went north, and angry I'd brought the Champions to Chaleur. He blamed me for his mom's arrest, even though nobody else held it against me. I wasn't able to read Oliver's aura or glints, but I knew how he felt. And it hurt.

But I gave Oliver his space. I followed Mayor Billadeau's advice and let him work through his feelings; and I trusted he'd come back to me after the mayor came home.

And she did come home. Mayor Billadeau had a powerful

friend in the provincial government: Councillor Whitley, our Reclamation Party representative. The rep got the mayor recused of her crime on a technicality and sent back to Chaleur. When the Reclamation Party's official coptercycle touched down in front of the mayoral offices and Mayor Billadeau leapt off the transport, I knew everything would be alright.

And it was alright. Even though Mayor Billadeau had been stripped of her title, her crime was expunged from the court's records and she was allowed to select her replacement. The mayor promoted Khleo, who—she felt—had handled the tumultuous time with surprising maturity. But when Khleo received his promotion and moved into the mayoral offices, Oliver locked himself in his attic for two days without speaking to anyone. The mayor—

Whoops. I had to start thinking of Mayor Billadeau as Amelie, since she wasn't the mayor anymore. But the informality of the address made my stomach flip.

When *Amelie* noticed that Oliver was missing, she rolled her eyes and said, "I knew Khleo's promotion would be a tough seed for Oli to swallow, but he'll get over it. That boy needs to be a tad more humble. Khleo has the perfect mayoral personality. Oli's strength is planning."

A new community routine was established. Amelie took over the partnership with Zekiul, and they became inseparable. Khleo stepped into his role as mayor with—as Amelie had stated—'surprising maturity.' His cursing stopped, his sarcasm disappeared, and he wore sensible canvas sneakers. The leadership transition was seamless. Citizens had no complaints about the change.

But Oliver stayed silent, obsessively intent on finding Herra.

I found that lack-of-change frustrating. Since Oliver didn't come to me after his mom returned home, the only thing I could do was take action. So, early one morning—as the cold autumn sun rose above the treetops—I kicked my way into the Billadeau's home (I didn't actually kick, I walked inside because the front door was unlocked). Then I ran up the steps that led to Oliver's attic.

Not tired at all—because running up several flights of stairs was easier than tree climbing—I pounded on Oliver's door. "Let me in," I yelled, not caring if I woke Khleo and Amelie. "You can't shut me out forever. You love me, Oli. Get over yourself and talk to me. Now!" I kicked the doorframe for good measure. "I mean it."

There wasn't a sound in the attic. No rustling bedsheets, or creaking from Oliver's stool, or the soft whistle that often spun from his nostrils when exhaustion caused him to pass out.

"Oliver Billadeau!" I hollered. "This is stupid! I love you, you mealworm." I banged on the door again. "Let me in—"

On my final *bang!* the door swung open and I tilted forward. Surprised, I stumbled into Oliver's room. Then I stopped, even more surprised.

Oliver's attic was empty.

His bed was made. His desk was cleared. His stool was tucked in the corner.

But Oliver was gone.

A cry clenched my throat. I'd been patient with Oliver—and supportive—but he couldn't treat me this way. I was lonely without my partner. I felt like Oliver had abandoned me, even though I knew independent adults couldn't abandon other independent adults. But my heart ached without Oliver, and my body missed his touch. I missed *him*.

I missed us.

As tears filled my eyes I searched the room for a cloth to clean my face. Rifling through Oliver's bedside table, I pushed aside his eyelink tube, a chalkboard, and a—

I paused, staring at the addition inside Oliver's bedside table drawer: a book, with its paper pages preserved in plastic.

A love story about feuding families and star-crossed lovers.

I scanned the story. It was written in an archaic language, and had a disturbing conclusion in which the lovers killed themselves, but it looked as though Oliver had read the script several times. His fingerprints were all over it.

I gasped, and dropped the plastic pages.

Did Oliver?—was Oliver?—had Oliver taken this story to heart? Was he somewhere—

My stomach lurched.

Was Oli planning to end his life?

Tears burst from my eyes. With cries wracking my entire body, I ran to the desk, looking for a tissue to blow my nose—and clear my mind—so I could think this new development through. As I shoved a stack of chalkboards to the side, a lightbulb rolled across the desk and onto the floor. Sniffling, I picked it up.

As my fingers touched the bulb's surface, the light ignited.

I stared, mesmerized, at the glowing glass. I turned the bulb upside down and squinted at the cap. Within the glass, beside the light's stem, a tiny nuclear cell hummed. I tilted my head, frowning. Dimitri must have designed tiny batteries to install inside the bulbs. But why?

I turned in a circle—searching Oliver's room for the answer (was he working on a tech project with my cousin?)—and another light ignited on the windowsill. Then a third lit up, just outside the frame. Clutching the bulb in my hand, I moved to the window and hoisted it open.

Autumn rain fell, but it was a cool rain. A gentle rain. And in the gentle rain, a line of nuclear lights trailed down the side of the Billadeau's mountain home and over the forest canopy. I stood on my toes and peered into the darkness. I could see the lighted path leading into the distance, deep within the woods.

Rubbing my nose with the back of my hand, I tucked the bulb into my trouser pocket. Then I hopped onto the window's ledge and swung outside. Clinging to the home's rocky siding, I climbed down the mountain and ran into the forest, following the lights.

I never wondered why I did it. I knew the lights led to Oliver.

I followed the line of lights to my grove. Stepping within the ring of trees I gasped, and my sadness popped like I'd stepped on a ponderosa pinecone. My birch tree was covered in strings of the nuclear lights. Its spindly branches twinkled in the darkness. Green afterimage coated the tree's heart-shaped leaves, making the birch look twice its normal size. Under the glowing branches—under the strings and twinkling—stood Oliver.

Smiling. "I hope you're okay with what I did to your tree." He glanced at the boughs. "Dimitri helped me out. We didn't hurt your birch—we didn't leave a mark—but I wanted to do something special." Oliver's smile broadened. "I wanted to apologize. I've been an ass about the whole Champions thing, and I didn't handle Khleo's promotion very well, but I feel a lot better and I—"

I ran across my grove and flung myself at my lover.

No, I didn't fling. I leapt into the air and wrapped my legs about Oliver's lean waist, clutching his shoulders to stay in place.

Oliver grabbed my thighs. "You like it?"

"I love it!" I squealed. "And I love you. I knew you weren't mad at me. You were upset because of Herra, and your mom, and your brother and the Coplot and Canuckia and—"

Oliver's mouth pressed against mine, stopping my speech with a kiss.

My legs slid off Oliver's body, and my feet found steady ground. With my lips on my lover's, my hands found Oliver's waistband.

"Wait." Oliver grabbed my fingers, then spun me around. "I want to try something."

Tingling with excitement, I stayed quiet, waiting for direction.

"It's been a long time since we—since we made love," Oliver said. I could feel his cheeks burning from embarrassment. "But I've missed you—every part of you—and I've hated that I haven't been able to touch you for weeks."

"Me too," I said, leaning into Oliver's warm chest. "I missed this so much."

Oliver ran his hands down my arms and wrapped them around my wrists. Slowly, he raised my hands over my head. "Do you trust me?"

"More than anyone."

Oliver reached towards the ground, under the birch tree. Fumbling in the grass, he yanked on one of the weeds that wound around the birch's roots: the weeds I hated. Oliver pulled the nasty fern out of the ground and wrapped it around my wrists. Then he tied me to my tree's trunk.

Oliver knelt on the moss. He pulled my trousers down to my ankles.

I looked down, then panicked because I couldn't see Oliver. The lights were too bright and my bound hands held me upright. Then I felt Oliver's fingers stroking my bared thighs; and my panic subsided. He ran his hands up the backs of my legs and pushed them as far apart as my gathered trousers would allow. I waited for excitement to spark—

—but fire didn't ignite.

The heat I typically felt didn't happen.

Maybe I was tired. I took a breath to clear my mind.

Oliver kissed my stomach. I squirmed against the tree. I let out a long, slow breath.

Nothing.

I felt nothing. "Oli—"

"Shh." Oliver's hands tightened about my backside. "Someone will hear you."

"Oli, I—" I shifted my stance and the weed snapped. I fell on Oliver.

Without hesitating, he rolled me onto my back and tightened the weed still wrapped around my wrists. Then he slipped out of his trousers. He pushed his bared knees into my calves.

I opened my mouth to ask him to wait—I wasn't ready—but Oliver winked and covered my mouth with his hand. "I said, be quiet."

Before I could move, the lights covering my tree burst in a shower of glass and sparks. With a loud, echoing *crack!* a branch snapped off the tree to fall—harmlessly—on top of us.

"What the—" Oliver rolled away. He shook glass out of his sandy hair, then pulled on his clothes. Eyes wide, Oliver stared at me, with my wrists bound together and the leafy branch spread across my half-naked body.

I looked at Oliver's shocked face, then at the branch that had broken us apart; and I laughed. "Are you—" I tried to catch my breath. "Are you okay?"

"Am I okay?" Oliver crawled across the ground—carefully—and tossed the snapped branch to the side. Unwinding the weed from my wrists, he helped me into my trousers. "You could have died."

I giggled. The stupidity of the situation was too much. "Because of a branch? And a few broken bulbs? No. My tree would never hurt me." I shook the weed off my arm, then pulled Oliver in for a kiss, hoping to alleviate his fears and ignite my familiar desire.

But I felt nothing.

Rain fell in sheets on the grove. Thunder rolled in the distance and wind whistled through the canopy, sending a shower of mint green leaves onto the shattered lightbulbs.

My birch tree's roots crackled.

I didn't listen to the tree's warning. I didn't pay attention to the crackle. So Oliver and I were still kissing when Khleo appeared, drenched from the rainfall.

We pulled apart.

"They found Herra." Khleo stood in the middle of the grove, staring at us with hollow eyes. He didn't seem to notice as mud seeped into his canvas sneakers. "Dimitri's search team found her."

Oliver stepped towards his brother. "Where was she?"

"She was at Rogers' place. The whole time. Rogers had no idea." Khleo's aura clacked like beetle pincers. The whole time.

"But that's good." Oliver said. "Herra's safe."

"Oli," I said softly. "Let Khleo finish."

Khleo laughed, but it wasn't a real laugh. It tore out of his lips, more air than sound. "They found her body, Oliver." *Found her body, found her body.* "It was buried in Rogers' mushroom field. Herra's been dead for weeks. The fire hid the evidence of her murder. When the cleanup crew put in the new field they covered up her corpse. Nobody looked there because—"

"They didn't think the two incidents were related," Oliver finished.

"Dimitri's team was searching Rogers' property and Justin Kendle tripped over a tree root. Except it wasn't a root. It was Herra's leg bone. The ground was saturated with water from the rains, so her skeleton rose to the top of Rogers' pools. Herra's body floated to the edge of the field and got lodged under a wooden board. That's where Kendle found her. Stuck under one of Rogers' planks."

"Holy holly berries," I whispered.

"And her murder was bad." Bad, bad, bad. "It was brutal." Brutal, brutal, brutal. "Dimitri's search team is struggling right now. Her head was—"

"Stop." Oliver backed away, hands over his ears. "You know I don't do blood. Keep the details to yourself. It's bad enough Herra was killed."

"This is awful," I said, reaching for Oliver. "Who would murder that little girl?"

Khleo turned his haunted eyes towards me. "There's one person who seems pretty obvious."

"No," I said, backing into my birch. The branches covered my head. "You don't mean—"

"The Champions!" Oliver spun around, pointing at me. "The Champions started the fire to cover up Herra's murder."

"The Champions didn't start the fire." Khleo's voice was steel. "Cox started the fire."

My legs shook. My glints reeled. "Wait," I said, placing my hand on the birch's trunk to hold myself upright. "You have to wait. I read Zekiul's glints. I *snatched* his glints! Zekiul started the fire to save us, not to cover up a murder. There was gasoline in Rogers' mushroom field." I ran over to Oliver, clutching his arm as he stared at his brother. "Don't do anything. We need more information. We need to—"

"Get rid of Cox." With that snarling statement, Oliver ran.

He ran out of the grove and away from my birch tree. Away from me. Khleo frowned, then followed his brother. His wet shoes squelched as he walked into the forest. I sat on the glass-shattered ground: emotionally and physically depleted.

My birch tree shrunk under the stormy sky.

PART THREE

"How did you know the victim?"
Councillor Georgie Whitley

CHAPTER SEVENTEEN

The Provincial Police arrived the next day.

Amelie said we had to tell the Provincial Police we'd found Herra's body. We *had* too, even though I begged the Compassion Coplot to keep it quiet. I knew Zekiul would be implicated in the affair, because Oliver promised he'd tell the Provincial Police his suspicions if Khleo didn't take action.

Amelie didn't agree with her sons about Zekiul's involvement in Herra's murder—especially after I told the Coplot about the gasoline in Rogers' pools—but she knew the law, inside and out. A missing child was one thing: a dead child was something entirely different. So, even though Amelie said she disliked the Provincial Police, she had to support Khleo when he reported Herra's death to Councillor Whitley.

In their matching tunics and trousers of navy blue, uniformed officers landed nuclear-powered coptercycles in Chaleur less than an hour later, ready to start an investigation.

But, to Oliver's dismay, Zekiul wasn't the first—or only—suspect. Everyone in Chaleur was questioned, including the grieving parents of the twins (who were under suspicion for not reporting their daughter missing when she actually went missing). The coroner's report revealed that Herra had been murdered—and her body hidden in Rogers' mushroom field—a full week before her absence had been shared.

"See?" I said from my place at the back of the Coplot cabin when the community met to receive the news. "The Champions weren't in Pluie when Herra was killed. Zekiul couldn't be the murderer. It has to be someone else."

But nobody listened to me. And the interrogations began.

Every citizen over the age of nineteen was pulled into the mayoral offices to be asked the same series of questions:

"How did you know the victim?"

Everyone knew Herra. It was a small town, and twins were rare in every community.

"Do you know how she died?"

Everyone knew how she died. News spread fast. Her jugular had been severed and she bled to death. Most likely by a shovel, or spade, or other tool: a tool every farmer had on their premises.

"Did you see Herra, or a member of her family, around the time she went missing?"

Nobody knew the last time they saw the girl. She was always with the other one—Havu—and the twins spent most of their time in the woods. Her parents stayed in their home. They were infamously anti-social, but not (necessarily) murderers.

"Did Herra say anything to you before she disappeared? Was she afraid? Or worried?"

Herra didn't say anything about her feelings. She didn't say anything to anyone about anything. Herra didn't talk. She was one of a silent pair: a strange, staring pair.

When it was my turn to be questioned, I parroted the same answers given by the rest of the town. Herra was in the constant company of her sister. I found out about Herra's death from the mayor, Khleo Billadeau. I couldn't remember the last time I saw Herra (and I didn't want to mention my last encounter with Havu, the day I read Rogers' glints).

I sat in Khleo' office, answering Councillor Whitley's questions and letting them read my glints. The councillor was an imposing official with pure-white hair and piercing black eyes. Whitley's blue uniform buttoned up under their chin, but the tight collar seemed to suit their personality. Their loose speech pattern mimicked the locals instead of taking on the heightened, overly-enunciated dialects most government officials adopted when they were sworn into office. But Whitley's movements were anything but sloppy. They sat perfectly still, eyes unmoving while I responded to their queries. But, every now and then, the muscles in Whitley's jaw would tighten and release.

Councillor Whitley was nervous, but I couldn't read why. Their aura droned with concern, like dragonflies hovering over summer grass, and Whitley's glints revolved around a single-minded goal: discover who murdered Herra. They seemed as though they were in control, but I got the sense Whitley was frightened.

I wasn't, though. I used my power to mask most of my thoughts and feelings. The government couldn't know about my involvement in Amelic's Glint Crime disgrace. I doubted Whitley's forgiveness would extend to a nobody female in a nothing town from nowhere. So I hid my glints, including Zekiul's reason for starting the fire. That was his story to tell.

But I let a few glints leak through to the councillor: glints of my birch tree, and reading in the library, and—for fun—a glint of Oliver with his hand between my legs. Despite the severity of situation, I had to admit I enjoyed watching Councillor Whitley wiggle as my sensual memory bombarded their mind. The government official squirmed the same way their squad had been making the community squirm all week.

When Whitley dismissed me I sighed with relief, then left to find Oliver. I wanted to tell him about my power—tell him everything—but when I found him in the Coplot cabin, it wasn't the right time. Again.

Oliver was furious.

"Why didn't you tell Whitley the truth?" Oliver stormed around the cabin, sort-of setting up for the Coplot's next gathering. "Cox is Herra's murderer. The Champions made an alliance with us so Cox could move here and protect his burial site: make sure Rogers didn't stir anything up. Why didn't you tell Whitley that?"

"Zekiul didn't kill Herra." I stood in the middle of the room as Oliver flung chairs around. "I'm not going to lie to our rep."

Oliver mumbled as he shoved a seat towards the front of the space. It crashed into the leadership table.

As the table flipped on its side and folded on the floor, I pulled on the end of my hair. "Louder, Oli."

"I said," Oliver yelled, spinning towards me, "why not? You lie to everyone else."

"I'm going to pretend you didn't say that." I flipped my hair over my shoulder indignantly. "Or, yell that."

Oliver mumbled again.

Fed up, I walked to his side and grabbed his chin. "Zekiul isn't the problem. The more time I spend proving that to you, the less time we can spend finding the actual killer."

Oliver jerked his face out of my fingers. "Why are you defending Cox?"

"Why won't you call him by his first name? He's been here for weeks, Oli. It's time you thought of him as a person, not just the Champions' leader."

"Because you think of him as a person?" Oliver's hands spasmed convulsively. "Or more than a person? Maybe more than a friend? Maybe you're together, and you're protecting Cox because you like having two males in your bed."

"You know you're the only male I let in my bed. Dimitri would never allow more than one at a time. He'd lose his mind over the piles of soiled sheets, and the used condoms tossed on his freshly-polished floor."

Oliver rolled his eyes, then bent over to unfold the leadership table. "How many condoms are you working your way through, Layla?"

"Oh, a few cases a day." I couldn't help but smile. "You'd know best. You're the only person who clocks my digicard."

"Clocks your digicard?"

"My work digicard. That tracks my hours. Because you said sex is work. You know? 'Working' my way through the condoms."

Oliver sighed.

I grabbed the end of the table and helped Oliver turn it over. "If you're so worried, put on your eyelinks and let me show you." I grinned. "You're the only male I love, and I can prove it."

Oliver thumped the table on the floor, then headed for the library.

I stamped my foot. It would be so easy to prove Zekiul's innocence—and my devotion—if Oliver let me into his mind: which I said out loud, since my partner refused to see the truth.

"I don't want to see your version of the truth. I know you can edit your memories. I can't trust you, Layla." Oliver slammed the library door shut.

"Why can't you trust me, Oli?" I leaned my forehead against the doorframe. "Why? I've never done anything untrustworthy." I paused. "Except for the glint-reading thing." I scrunched up my nose. "And the spying-on-the-Champions thing. And the not-telling-the-Coplot-about-the-gasolene-in-Rogers'-pools thing. But other than those teeny, tiny, inconsequential actions I'm solid." Pressing my cheek against the door, I sighed when Oliver didn't fling it open. "So solid."

When Oliver still didn't respond, I gave up. For the day. I slumped out of the Coplot cabin and went to my grove. My birch tree had been drooping lately, so I gave it some tender loving care.

That evening, when Dimitri lectured me about withholding important information from the leadership team—even though I'd reheated his favourite leftovers (pickled cabbage) so his dinner was hot when he arrived—I let him. I made one joke (I couldn't resist) asking Dimitri to pick up a case of condoms from Peevish Pear's the next time he went to the market. To my complete non-surprise, Dimitri didn't get my joke. So I went to bed, numb from the sequence of events that had kicked my mind-keister over the past few months.

I lay awake for hours, unable to fall asleep. I tossed under my river reed blanket. I turned on my side. I punched my pillow into a ball, then flung it across the room. But my glints continued to tumble. And I stayed awake.

CHAPTER EIGHTEEN

Annoyed, I flung my blanket onto the floor.

I couldn't lie awake in bed forever. I needed to tire myself out. I had to talk to someone.

I had to talk to Dimitri.

But where would my cousin be in the middle of the night? On the roof, behind his telescope, getting lost in the stars—like always. Which was perfect. I would go upstairs and interrupt him, then Dimitri could lecture me about planets and space monsters—or whatever—and I'd be bored and sleepy in no time.

I hopped off my bed and grabbed my night coat.

"What do you want?" Dimitri asked as I scuffled onto the roof in my slippers. He kept his eye on his giant telescope: a device my dad had assembled.

The metre-long tube pointed towards the sky, showing the stars overhead. Chaleur's high altitude made stargazing easy. Even though I didn't have an interest in things above the earth—I preferred things that grew within in—I had to admit the interstellar array looked beautiful.

I paused to get used to the cold night air, then shuffled to Dimitri's side. "I can't sleep."

"So you thought you would bother me during my alone-time because I have nothing better to do than talk to you?"

"Actually, I was hoping you'd bore my brain so it would shut down, but—" I shrugged, even though Dimitri couldn't see me: his face was pressed against the telescope's eyepiece as his hand fondled the focusing knob. "We can talk. Anything's better than over-thinking about Oliver."

Dimitri raised his head. "Are you having relationship trouble?"

"Don't say, 'I told you so.'" I shoved my hands in my night coat's pockets as I shivered. "Every relationship goes through

rough patches. We'll be fine."

Dimitri eyed me a moment longer, then turned back to his telescope. "What do you want to know?"

Grateful that Dimitri had spared me an 'Oliver lecture,' I leaned against the roof's railing and looked up at the stars, hoping he'd give me an astrology lecture. Or, astronomy lecture. "What's going on up there? What's happening tonight?"

"Nothing happens over one night, Layla. When you study space you have to think in months. And years." Dimitri straightened, then cracked his lower back. "Sometimes millions of years. It takes a long time for things to happen in infinity."

In infinity, in infinity, I thought. "What are you looking at right now?"

Dimitri's mouth quivered (into a smile?) then he lowered his face to the telescope's eyepiece. "There are a few interesting occurrences happening right now. Jupiter is unusually bright, and I'm watching a cluster of wandering meteors. One of them is nearby. Look." He pointed at the sky. "You can see it without the telescope. See that purple light?"

I could see the purple light: the streak of neon that had been illuminating Chaleur for a year. But the purple was the brightest it had ever been.

"I thought those were Northern Lights." I frowned. "Are we safe? Is that thing coming for us?"

"Don't be stupid, Layla. It's just a meteor: a tiny space rock. I'm more interested in a star that died." Dimitri frowned. "I *think* a star died . . ."

"You can see a star die?"

"No, but I can see an empty spot in the sky where a star used to be. There are only so many reasons light would go away. Death of a star is one of them."

"Huh," I said, craning my neck higher. "That's sad."

"Sad?" Dimitri sniffed. "It's not sad. It's not anything. It's just a fact. There's no need to attach emotion to it."

I grinned, then poked my cousin's shoulder. "I might not *have* to feel things, but that's not going to stop me. I'm a human, Dimitri. Not a Bot, like you."

"I must be a human," Dimitri said, adjusting his stance as he turned the focusing knob. "Unlike the Bots, I haven't killed anyone." He glanced at me over the eyepiece. And smiled. "Yet."

I gasped, shocked by the grin on my gloomy cousin's face. But I kept my surprise to myself. I didn't want to frighten away Dimitri's cheer. "You're right. You can't be a robot. Bots didn't have a sense of humour. At least, not a spontaneously-generated one. And there's nothing funny about upcycled humour."

"I thought I didn't have a sense of humour."

"That last joke was funny. It's hilarious you think you could kill me."

Dimitri sniffed, his focus back on the sky.

I gripped the roof's railing. "What else is going on up there?"

"You don't care about space, Layla. Go back to bed and think about your plants if you're having trouble sleeping."

"Plants aren't something I have to think about. I know them too well. Plants, and trees, and the earth are easy." I tilted my chin towards the stars. "Space is different. It's complex. *Too* complex. I can't remember enough about space to care about it. Like, why is Jupiter named Jupiter? What is a jupiter? And why does Khleo think a constellation in the shape of an animal decided his personality when he was born? And how is it possible you and my dad studied space for years and didn't meet a single extraterrestrial?" I looked over the railing, at the darkened ground below. "I know the earth. I understand plants. Trees aren't complicated at all."

"Space isn't complicated. Jupiter was the Roman god of the sky and—"

"See?" I scrunched up my nose. "I don't know what you're talking about. What is a roman? What is a god? I know about the sky, obviously, but—"

Dimitri shifted behind the telescope. "I'll skip the history lesson because there's no point in covering mythology nothing but a handful of humans remember, but I can answer your other questions. Khleo thinks the constellation Aries determined his personality when he was born because Khleo has a vivid imagination—"

"I know *that*."

"—and he isn't particularly intelligent."

"Is it possible for you to answer a question without insulting someone we care about?"

"Stating a fact about a person's intellect isn't an insult, Layla."

I crossed my arms. "Why didn't you and Dad do your jobs properly? Before the war?"

"We *did* do our jobs properly. Space is really big. Humans have been trying to contact extraterrestrials for hundreds of years. Would you rather we lie to the government about the existence of sentient species like scientists did in the twenty-first century? Or—" Dimitri peered over the telescope's tube, "—do our jobs properly and be honest? I'm not ashamed we couldn't make contact. Like I said, space is really big. And when the Bots started the war we lost the progress we'd made with assisted Artificial Intelligence. Which wasn't my—nor your father's—fault."

As Dimitri disappeared behind the eyepiece, I blushed. "Sorry if I'm being rude. I'm tired. And I'm worried about Oliver, but don't hold that against me."

Dimitri looked up. "You're welcome."

"For what?"

"You came up here because you couldn't sleep, but you just said you're tired. So, I fixed your problem." Dimitri smiled for a second time. "You're tired, so you can sleep. You're welcome."

Tilting my head, I said, "That's two jokes. Pretty soon you're going to be a regular—" I pointed at the purple streak overhead, "—comet-ian. Cometian. Get it? Like comedian, but with a 't'— because of the comet? You know, the meteor? Comet. Ian."

Dimitri stared at me.

"Don't worry," I said. "You'll recognize brilliant comedy once your sense of humour matures."

"I don't need a mature sense of humour to know that pun needs development."

I grinned at my cousin, then looked out into the night. Chaleur's lamplights twinkled in the misty darkness.

Taking a breath, I turned to Dimitri and said, "Why did my dad leave us?"

Dimitri straightened, hitting the top of his head on the telescope. The tube swung to side and Dimitri cursed.

"Sorry!" I winced. "Sorry, sorry, sorry."

"It's fine, don't worry about it." Dimitri rubbed his head as he carefully moved the telescope back in place. "Is that question another bad pun?"

"Nooo," I said slowly. "I've always wanted to know why he left. It isn't funny. Not to me."

"What brought this on?" Dimitri leaned against the railing and frowned, still rubbing his head. "Your dad left a long time ago. Why do you want to talk about it now?"

"We never talk." I pulled my night coat tighter. "I don't know, I guess—well—this is sort-of nice. Since we're actually in the same place at the same time, I thought I'd ask."

"You really want to know why your dad left?" Dimitri's green eyes dimmed under the purple meteor light. "I don't know the whole story, Layla, but what I do know might upset you."

"I think I can handle it," I said. "It can't be worse than living in a town that almost-certainly contains a child killer."

"Fair enough." Dimitri looked up at the stars, then said, "Your dad and I were best friends. We had a fight. He got mad and he left. End of story."

"End of story?" I leaned towards my cousin. "*End* of *story?* Dimitri. Fathers don't abandon their daughters because they had a fight with their friend. Tell me." I poked his shoulder. "Tell me the truth."

"We were good friends."

"*Good* friends?"

"Best friends."

"Dimitri!" I laughed. "You'd have to be best friends like Oli and I are best friends to have the kind of fight that would force one of you to walk out. You and my dad weren't in love. Tell me what happened."

Dimitri raised his eyebrow.

I gasped. "You and my dad were in love? Like, me-and-Oli in love? Oli-and-I-best-friends in love?"

Dimitri raised his other eyebrow.

I sunk into the railing. "Holy holly berries. Crumbly couscous. Mushrooms on fire, are you kidding me?" I leapt up and shook Dimitri's arm. "You and my dad are related. Ew! Ew, ew, ew!"

"I'm not actually your cousin, Layla. Adults say their close friends are family when they spend a lot of time with their kids. You know: auntie, uncle, cousin."

"This is a lot of new information I'm receiving at one o'clock in the morning."

"You *had* to know what was going on. You walked in on us a lot."

"Ew!" I swatted Dimitri's shoulder. "Ew, ew, ew!"

"You were young," Dimitri said, batting me away. "You didn't care."

"I can't believe this. You *love* loved my dad? My dad *love* loved you? How is that possible? I thought my dad was straight. Or—" I wrinkled my nose. "I've never thought about my dad's orientation. At all. Thanks for the uncomfortable glints, Dimitri."

Dimitri shrugged. "He was with your mom when you were born. After she died, I moved in. You were two years old when I started taking care of you." He narrowed his eyes. "You really don't remember?"

"I really don't remember." I shook my head, mumbling, "So much for having a strong mind."

"What was that?"

"Nothing. So, you and my dad were in love. And you had a fight. And it was so awful he left." I sighed. "I'm guessing you don't want to tell me what the fight was about?"

"Correct."

I could have snatched Dimitri's glints to find out what happened, but the ones I could read screamed, STAY OUT. So I let Dimitri protect his secret.

Maybe he'd reveal why my dad left after he started smiling more.

"Thanks for telling me the truth." I stared at my cousin—or, the male I'd believed was my cousin—then I slapped his forearm. "Anything else I need to know? For instance, *are* you a Bot? Or from another planet? Because only an alien would keep something like this quiet."

Dimitri rubbed his arm; and hid behind the telescope.

I gasped. "You *are* an extraterrestrial? From outer space?" Giggling, I said, "No wonder you like stars so much. You miss your home—"

"Enough." Dimitri glanced over the top of the tube. His dark cheeks burned. "There's one more thing I probably should have told you. Years ago."

Crumbly couscous. My fake-cousin was about to reveal something huge. Bracing myself against the railing, I asked, "And that is?"

"I have a sister."

I blinked. "A sister from outer space?"

"No." Dimitri looked everywhere and anywhere except at me. He looked seriously uncomfortable. "A sister from Bristol. I mean, she lives in Bristol. With her husband."

"Hold on." I lifted my hand. "You *do* have a sister? This isn't a joke?"

Dimitri shook his head.

I lunged across the roof and punched his arm. "You astronomical piece of shit!"

"Ow! Layla!"

"I've been so lonely," I said, pounding on Dimitri's shoulders as he shielded his head with his hands. "It sucked living with you—only you!—these past fifteen years! Why would you keep this from me? I would have *loved* to know about family on the other side of the country. I could have contacted your sister! We could have—" I dropped my fists and stepped back, away from Dimitri's cowering body. "But your sister isn't family. Not mine, anyway. Because you and I aren't family. So I shouldn't be upset—"

"You should be upset," Dimitri said, straightening. "Mira has been begging to meet you ever since your dad left." He ducked behind his telescope. "No, that's not true. Mira wanted to meet you when your dad and I started living together. But I, uh—" Dimitri's aura buzzed. "I'm sorry. I shouldn't have kept you apart. I can introduce you now, if you'd like. No, not now. In the morning. It's just—well—you see, my sister is a famous painter. But we aren't close. She pushes me off a cliff because her work is *all* she talks about."

"Wait. Shut up for a second. Let me think." I scanned my memories, then gasped. "Your sister is *MIRÆ* Mira? *The* MIRÆ?"

Dimitri's voice dropped into a guttural growl. "You should hear her gush about her successes. You'd think she was the only Artist in the family. Mitty," he simpered in an insulting female impersonation, "the Prime commissioned another portrait. Mitty, I'm using rotted reef oil to make paint and the locals love it. Mitty, Christoper—" Dimitri glanced at me conspiratorially. "That's Mira's husband: Christopher."

"Your sister calls you Mitty?" Even though I was furious, I had to remember Dimitri's nickname to use against him later.

"Christopher received permission from Bristol's Reclamation Party rep to harvest Bot metal from the sea and turn it into picture frames," Dimitri continued. "Mira goes on and on about it, nonstop. It makes me feel nauseated."

He did look sick, but not because of his sister's fame: because I was glowering as I cracked my knuckles.

"I *am* sorry," Dimitri said. "I know you've been lonely—but I really don't like my sister. When the war ended, Mira had the audacity to offer to move to Pluie so you'd have a companion."

"She did what?! That would have been great!"

"It would have been impossible. Mira is impossible."

I sputtered. "I can't believe you kept family from me. Or—" I buried my face in my hands. "Not family. Because you and I aren't related. But you kept a friend from me. A *female* friend." I looked up. "I needed a friend, Dimitri."

"I know." Dimitri had the grace to look ashamed. "She wouldn't have moved here, though. You don't know her, Layla. Mira makes bold promises but has no follow through. She's flighty. And, if she *had* moved out here, she would have left months later if an art opportunity came along or—" He pinched his nose. "Mira met Christopher days after the war ended. I knew what was going to happen next: they'd get married and you would become an irrelevant second thought. I couldn't let that happen. Not after your dad—" Dimitri breathed in sharply, then turned away.

I swallowed the sudden lump in my throat. "Well, that's—um—nice of you. I guess."

Dimitri shrugged. "Mira even asked us to move to Bristol, but I didn't want to take you from your home." He placed his hand on his telescope and looked at me. "*Our* home. We may not be related, Layla, but I've always done my best to take care of you."

Cursing the water that filled my eyes as I stared at Dimitri's beet-brown face, I said, "Alright. Um. Thank you."

Dimitri nodded. The colour receded from his cheeks and his buzzing aura quieted.

"Thanks." I shoved my hands in my night coat's pockets. "That means a lot." I coughed, clearing my throat, then tilted my chin towards the sky. "Tell me more about Jupiter. And your wandering meteors."

Dimitri smiled—again!—before disappearing behind the telescope. "Jupiter is the fifth planet in our solar system, and the largest. He's hot, and gassy—kind of like your dad—and he has many, many moons."

"Also kind of like Dad. He didn't like wearing trousers around the house."

"*That* you remember. You two are more alike than you think."

Dimitri chuckled, then said, "Meteors are balls of space rock that travel through our interstellar skies. I like to watch them move across our solar system because, sometimes, they collide with other meteors—or moons, or small planets—and the resulting spectral display is quite stunning. The mini meteor passing over Earth has high calcium content, which is why it looks purple—"

I let Dimitri talk, uninterrupted, as I stared at the heavens. In the cold night air, and under Dimitri's soothing word-blanket of scientific babble, my tumbling glints slowed and my fatigue disappeared. Dimitri and I—and the memory of my dad—stayed on the roof the whole night. With the knowledge of new, sort-of relatives out east (and a real caregiver in my home), I got up the next morning feeling strangely refreshed.

And ready for the next set of challenges Chaleur had to face.

CHAPTER NINETEEN

Days passed.

Autumn ended. And after speaking with everyone in the town, the Provincial Police moved onto the Champions. Or, at least, the Champions who remained in Chaleur with Zekiul. Most had gone back to Mount Champ when the winter rains started drenching the forest.

Zekiul was first on the Police's list of suspects.

Councillor Whitley led his interview, too. When they ordered Zekiul to join them in the mayoral offices, the Champions' leader messaged me over the eyelinks and asked me to meet him afterwards so he could show me his memory of the interrogation. Zekiul wanted to ensure he'd told his story properly, and adequately represented the Champion-Coplot alliance.

Touched, I accepted Zekiul's request when his energy rod knocked on my mind. I was honoured he felt comfortable showing me his glints after he'd insisted I respect his boundaries, so I suggested we meet in my private cave. Nobody would bother us there. Oliver was still avoiding me, despite my most recent attempt at reconciliation (I'd burst into his bedroom at six o'clock in the morning wearing nothing but a canvas coat and my rain-kissed skin, but Oliver had already left). So, I was pruning my birch tree—miserable—when Zekiul knocked.

We met after his interview.

"This is nice." Zekiul scanned the interior of my cave as he ducked through the entryway. "But I like mountain caverns, so it feels like home."

"If I'd known we were coming here I would have cleaned up," I said as I yanked a handful of weeds off a boulder.

Staring at the weeds clutched in my hands, my gut flipped over: like Oliver flipped me over the night he used a weed to tie me up. I hadn't been able to process my glints about our . . . sexual adventure. Other than my gut swooping whenever a reminder shoved itself in my face—or covered a rock in fronds—I didn't know how I felt about my lack of desire for my once-upon-a-time true love. And that wasn't alright.

But it was better than Herra's killer getting away with murder, so I figured I'd figure out my feelings after an arrest was made.

"Make yourself comfortable," I said to Zekiul. "The moss on those rocks in the corner is cozy, if you're okay with fungi."

"As a fun guy myself, I can handle the algae." Zekiul grinned as he settled onto the fuzzy stones. Then he blinked, took a deep breath, and widened his eyes. "Ready?"

I opened my mind and received Zekiul's recollection of his time spent with Whitley. Or, Zekiul's interpretation of his recollection. After a blur of confused glints, Zekiul's interview with Councillor Whitley appeared.

ZEKIUL 'ZEE' COX
NOVEMBER 17, 2106

This is stressful. Don't let Whitley see how stressed you are. Fuck fuckity-fuck, what the fuck did I get myself into? No. No, Zee! You can't spiral right now. Calm down. All I have to do is show Whitley what happened. Layla is counting on me. The Champions are counting on me.

That poor girl, Herra, is counting on me. Her soul needs peace, and her family needs justice.

I sit in the mayor's office—Khleo's office, the big guy who scares the shit out of me—and try to keep my hands still. I can't look nervous (guilty people always look nervous) but this councillor is as intimidating as the mayor. They both look at me as though they can see my glints, like Layla, though I know neither Whitley— nor Khleo—reads my mind without permission. Whitley acts with integrity, which in itself is intimidating, and Khleo doesn't have the strength. Mind strength, that is. I'm pretty sure the mayor could crack my skull without breaking a sweat.

Don't stress about that right now. Stress about the interview. Shit.

"Do you know why you're here today?" Whitley, who's sitting behind the mayor's desk like they own it, stares at me. Their bleached-white hair falls across their forehead, but they don't brush it off their face.

I've heard rumours about their hair. It went white during the war when Whitley fought in the final battle on Canuckian soil. The councillor was on the team of tech disablers who hacked the Bots' navigation systems so the machines couldn't manage their movements. Was that a risk? Sure, because the Bots indiscriminately destroyed towns when they lost control, whereas before all they did was target the capitols. But the confusion allowed the Global Government to speed through bureaucratic process so that bitch, RoboReiwa, could approve the Total Tech Takedown. Shit, I'm spiraling. I always spiral when I'm nervous. But I can't look nervous.

Focus, Zee. Focus.

I answer the councillor's question. "Yes, I do. You want to know about Herra."

"I need to know a little more than that, I'm afraid," Whitley says. "A witness saw you near Simone Rogers' property around the time Herra went missing. Where were you during the afternoon of September Twenty-Fourth?"

"Exactly where your witness saw me, I'm sure," I say. "I was here. I mean, I was around Rogers' property. Her farm. The mushroom farm. Like your witness said. Probably."

Whitley's jaw clenches. I can see the muscles in their face tighten. They weren't expecting me to answer that way: scattered, and insane-sounding. "Amelie Billadeau told me you started the fire on Rogers' property on September—" Whitley closes their black eyes, most likely scanning their eyelink memories, "—Twenty-First." Their eyes flash open. "You met with her envoy team on September Twenty-Third. Why did you stay in Chaleur? Weren't you needed at your base in the highlands?"

"Under the highlands." My lip quirks. I'm getting annoyed. I force my mouth into a straight line so I look like I'm taking this seriously. Because I am. "The Champions' base is inside Mount Champ."

"So, why were you here? Chaleur is a long way from your so-called home."

"I can show you." I press my temple. "If you'd prefer?"

Whitley agrees. I send them my glints from that fateful day: the day I lingered in Chaleur to see if the pools were still poisoned. Then I show Whitley the envoy meeting, the 'Rogers excuse' I gave to Oliver, and the real reason for Rogers' fire. Whitley watches my memories in silence, then sighs as their eyes refocus. "Well, I'll be a bowl of hot potato soup."

I nod. "I was equally surprised when I found out about the gasoline."

"I can see that." Whitley taps their temple. "Those were clear glints, Cox. Nice and clear. It's obvious you know nothing about Herra. But we should talk about the fire, and about the substance in Rogers' pools. I want to know who you tipped you off about the gasoline. I'd be nice to grab a sample of it at some point, too." Whitley frowns, then tugs on their collar. "Though, it might be best to investigate the poison problem after I find Herra's killer."

Good. Whitley believes me. Layla will be pleased when I show her this interview and—

I blinked, then shook my head to return to the cave. "Seeing your perspective is always an education. Your glints never stop, do they?"

I climbed to my feet and headed for the cave's exit. "Let's go tell Oliver that Whitley doesn't think you're Herra's murderer. Seeing him swallow his stubborn tongue should slow your mind."

Zekiul's raised voice stopped me. "There's more, Layla."

I paused, staring over my shoulder. "More? You showed Whitley what happened and they let you leave. You're cleared, Zekiul. Or should I say—" I grinned. "Zee?"

Zekiul patted the rocks. "It wasn't that simple. You need to see the whole memory."

Pulling on the end of my hair, I crunched over the dry leaves littering the cave's floor and sat by Zekiul's side. I received his memory and Zekiul was back in the mayoral offices, saying good-bye to Councillor Whitley.

ZEKIUL 'ZEE' COX
NOVEMBER 17, 2106

"Next time you get a tip about something that could harm citizens, report it to the Provincial Police," Whitley says. "Or to me. Don't wait for the worst to happen, or mess around with your vigilante friends. We have resources that can clean up these kinds of messes without ruining private property."

I wince. Whitley is right. But how could I have reported the gasoline to the Police when, at the time, the Champions were fighting the Police?

Relax, Zee. You can't debate how the real world works with the person whose job it is to deal with the worst of it. Just leave—walk away—and be grateful you aren't being dragged out in cuffs.

I wave as I exit, trying to look polite and not dismissive. Then I step onto the front porch. An officer is stationed outside. He glares at me as I zip up my coat. It's freezing out here. The sign hanging over the porch creaks as it sways in the wind. The street is empty.

Which is weird.

Cold weather doesn't force the community indoors. Pluie is the chilliest province in Canuckia and has more rain than anywhere else in the country. The locals embrace the wet weather like Jardinians embrace months of heavy snowfall. The community must be avoiding public places so they don't get roughed up by an officer. Once, years ago, Jolene and I passed through in a village in Bristol that was being terrorized by a squadron. Most of our peacemaking efforts were spent trying to convince the villagers to keep their heads down and not pick fights with officers, like they wanted to, but—

Shit. I'm distracted again. Get going, Zee. The last thing you need is to be accused of lollygagging outside the mayor's office when you should be reporting to him.

Double shit. I also have to show Layla what happened in my interview. But she'll be glad I stayed cool—

"Cox." The Provincial Police officer standing guard nudges me with his nuclear baton: a device which, when pressed against bare skin, causes instant cellular mutation. Nothing permanent, though: just a small discolouration. The damage is insignificant, but enough to frighten offenders. The batons don't paralyze criminals like the Bot-cops crowd management prongs used to.

I turn respectfully towards the officer. It's smart to show respect to people who have power, even though I'm trying to limit that power. "Yes?"

He tucks his thumbs behind his belt. "You going to hang around here all day?"

"No, sorry. I mean—" I'm stammering, which isn't good. Sketchy people stammer. Get it together, Zee! "I'm leaving. I had a meeting with the councillor, but they dismissed me."

"If Whitley dismissed you, what are you doing?"

"Good point," I say. "Off I go."

"Why did Whitley call you in?" The officer grabs my shoulder, holding me in place. "Are the Champions starting shit?"

"It was just a routine questioning," I say, pretending the officer isn't numbing my neck. "About Herra."

"Who?"

"The murdered girl." My lip quirks. "The one who was . . . murdered."

"You trying to be funny?" The officer's grip tightens. "I know you, Cox. I led the squad that tracked your crap on the network. I know what you're capable of. Don't be funny with me."

"Thankfully, that's all in the past." I spread my lips wide—smiling, I hope—then drop my head. With humility, I hope. "The Champions are allied with the Compassion Coplot now."

The officer leers. "That's a fucked up name for a government party: 'Compassion Coplot.'" He pulls me closer. "You can't fool me, Cox. Once a criminal, always a criminal."

My shoulder shakes, but I stay still. I've dealt with dillweed officers before, though rarely where they operate: in the open.

I prefer the shadows.

The officer narrows his eyes. "Nothing to say? No joke?"

I shrug, still in his grip. "What can I say? I already told you the Champions have changed. You'll have to let us prove it."

"You think I'm going to follow you on the network again? After everything you and your scum friends did?" The officer laughs. "You can't prove anything to me, or to anyone else in this province who matters. We know you. You're dirt. And there's nothing you can do—or pretend to do—to change that."

"There's no harm in trying."

The officer's grin slides off his face as though it were held in place with avocado oil. "There you go, being funny again. I don't like funny guys, especially ones who make jokes when they should be kissing my ass."

I'm about to say something stupid, but I stop myself. I shouldn't say what I want to say. Layla will *kick* my ass when she watches this later. I shouldn't say it. I shouldn't.

I say it. "I'd love to kiss your ass, but the Prime just passed a bylaw limiting same-gendered displays of public affection. If I did what you wanted we'd both be behind bars."

Before I can flinch, the officer pushes me down the porch steps. I stumble on the stairs' tread, then land in a heap on the road. The officer jogs down the wooden steps and places his booted foot on my outstretched hand, holding me down. "Make a joke now, funny guy." He leans over, putting more weight—and pressure—on my pinned palm. "Go on. You like making jokes so much, let's hear what you've got when you have a captive audience."

"I'm the captive here, *guy*."

The officer crushes my hand with his boot.

I yell, but nobody intervenes because the street is empty. No one can hear me howling, so nobody will pry this dillweed off of me. But I deserve it. If I was a quick learner I'd be Prime, instead of face down in the dirt with an officer putting me in my place—

"That's enough." I shook my head to free my mind from Zekiul's glints.

He was so frustrating.

"You can't think those things about yourself," I said. "You're right. I am going to kick your ass."

Zekiul's lip lifted. "I'll try to change."

"Don't change too much. I like your salty glints. You could get away with cursing more out loud. People in this town are too stuffy. Ever since Khleo became mayor—and his language became clean—we've needed some shit bombs and fuck grenades to liven up the place."

"Yes. Chaleur needs excitement. Kidnappings, and poisonous pools, and gruesome murders are boring."

"Boring my butt," I murmured. I held out my hand. "Show me."

"My butt?" Zekiul's smile grew. "It's already been kicked. I kind of hoped you wouldn't punish me since Officer Dillweed did such a good job."

"Not your ass, you ass. Your hand."

"Oh." Zekiul placed his palm on mine. "Ouch!" He yanked his hand away, wincing. "What is wrong with your fingers?"

"My fingers?" I glanced down. My fingers looked normal.

"Your fingers! They're rough and—I don't know." Zekiul cradled his arm against his stomach. "Your grip is more painful than

Officer Dillweed's tread."

"Do you mean my calluses?" I giggled, then waggled my fingers in Zekiul's face. "Ooo! Watch out for the thick, scary, hardened layers of skin that developed on my digits to protect against friction when I climb trees."

"That's an incredibly specific definition of calluses."

"Give me your hand." I opened my hardened palm. "And stop whining. You're too—" I swallowed the word 'sexy' and said, "—old to be upset over knobbly finger pads."

"Knobbly? You could rip open an acorn. Your fingers are steel-tipped, not knobbly."

"If it makes you feel better, Oliver hates my calluses, too." I flexed my hand. "Now, gimme. I'll be gentle."

"Oliver doesn't like your calluses?" Zekiul's face softened. He gingerly reached out and laid his hand on mine. "They aren't that bad."

I grimaced as I looked at the mess. Zekiul had tried to clean his wounds, but his mangled hand was swollen and a pattern of bruises in the shape of a shoe sole marked his skin.

Using the side of my finger—and not my acorn-ripping tip—I brushed a piece of gravel out of a shallow scrape. "I'm annoyed, Zee. And appalled. Annoyed *and* appalled. The last time I was both annoyed and appalled was when Oliver—well, when Oliver does most things lately."

Zekiul grinned while I worked on his ruined skin. "I'm still learning I'm not the leader of an all-powerful rebel organization anymore. I need to practice shutting my mouth when I'm around someone who can shut it for me."

"I'm not mad at you, Zee."

"Please stop using my nickname. My moms called me 'Zee,' but that's a private memory. You promised you wouldn't share my secrets."

"You're right." I let go of Zekiul's hand. "I'm sorry. I'm upset with that officer. And the town. Someone should have helped you when you yelled. I don't care how cold it was outside, the community needed to show up for you. Amelie never allowed that kind of negligence. You have to tell Khleo what that officer did. He'll talk to Whitley."

Zekiul frowned. "Uh. No."

"Yes." I leapt off the rocks. "Let's go."

"Layla, Khleo won't talk to Whitley. He doesn't support the Champions."

"Nonsense. Let's go."

"It's not nonsense." Zekiul mumbled to himself, "Not nonsense. That's an odd combination of consonants."

I stopped. I'd been thinking the same thing. "Let's *go*, Zekiul."

"The reason Khleo doesn't support me—why he won't help the Champions—is because your—" Zekiul swallowed.

"Out with it," I said. "Or I'll snatch your glints."

Zekiul's eyes twinkled. "That isn't an idle threat with you."

"I mean it, Cox." I stood over Zekiul, grinning in his face. "Tell me what you're glinting."

"It's Oliver."

I straightened. "Oliver what?"

"Oliver's been in Khleo's ear since the day Dimitri's search team found Herra. He and Khleo have been dropping—" Zekiul's smile broadened, "—shit-bombs about us for days."

"Which is why the officer hurt you and nobody did anything." I tugged on my hair, thinking. Then I shrugged. "I'll talk to Oliver. And Khleo. Don't worry, I know their weaknesses. If they won't accept your innocence, I'll—" I grinned. "I'll tell their mommy. She doesn't like the Provincial Police, and she hates divisive fuckuppery."

"I don't think I've heard that particular expression before."

"I told you, Chaleur needs more cursing. Especially when it's called for." I grabbed Zekiul's hand (his good hand) and dragged him out of the cave. "Amelie will stop her crybaby boys from being, well, crybabies. After she's done putting her youngest in his place, let's tell Oliver what Officer Dillweed said about the Compassion Coplot: it *is* a stupid name for a government party.

We have to come up with something better."

Zekiul skidded on a patch of loose stones as we made our way down the mountain. "You're going to insult Oliver's precious party? Today?"

"There's never a good time to criticize Oli, but that doesn't mean we shouldn't."

"Layla—"

"I can already think of several names that are better than Compassion Coplot." I stroked the white-and-black marbled trunk of a birch tree as we passed, then I leapt over a lichen-covered log. "The Awesome Party. The Tolerant Party. The More-Effective-Than-The-Reclamation Party."

Zekiul snickered as I pulled him along the path that led to the centre of the town. "The Awesome Party?"

"Yes," I said, picking up my pace. The evening meeting started in an hour, which gave us plenty of time to clear the air. But I didn't want to waste a minute. "It's true, isn't it? Combined, the Coplot and the Champions are awesome. Or, at least, we should be."

Zekiul didn't disagree. His aura fluttered with approval.

CHAPTER TWENTY

When Zekiul and I burst into the Coplot cabin and forced the leadership team to watch Zekiul's memory vid of what happened during, and after, his Whitley interrogation, Oliver and Khleo's jaws dropped.

And I wiggled with smug satisfaction.

And I almost burst with joy when Oliver and Khleo formally apologized to Zekiul. But it was Amelie pulling the Champions' leader into a hug—and Zekiul's face flushing—that sent me over my emotional edge. Finally my favourite people were united, even if we were up against the most powerful government-funded security sector in the province.

"Disgraceful," Amelie grumbled into Zekiul's shoulder. "I'm so sorry. I hate the Provincial Police. Imagine—abuse of power in my town. Mine!"

"My town, Mom," Khleo said as he watched Zekiul's memory vid replay. "But I agree with you about everything else. This is shitty."

"Le-Le!"

"This is unacceptable," Khleo corrected. He pulled on the hem of his starched mayoral uniform, squirming. "What are you going to do about it, Oli?"

"You're the mayor." Oliver stared blank-faced at the vid. "Khleo."

"Correct." Khleo bounced on his modest sneakers. Badges bearing the crossed branches of Pluie's provincial emblem were stitched on the shoe's sides. "I say we, uh, go to Whitley and, um, give them a piece of our—" he looked at his mom, "—minds?"

Wincing at the awkward interchange, Zekiul pulled out of Amelie's hug and said, "Before we confront the councillor, can I say something?"

Amelie waved him towards the front of the room. "Yes! Speak, speak. Speak!"

"Mom!"

"Sorry." Amelie waved at Khleo. "Tell him to speak. Speak!"

"Speak, Zeke." Khleo grinned as he settled on his chair behind the leadership table.

Zekiul slowly walked to the front of the cabin. He faced the assembly—made up of the Coplot's leaders and Jolene—then cleared his throat. "I'm glad you've acknowledged my innocence, but even though the Coplot and the Champions are working together—"

I raised my hand. "Before I forget, I want to add something to the Coplot's agenda. About a name change." As everyone in the room turned to stare at me I bit my lip, then scuttled to my seat. "Never mind. Don't worry about it. I'll remember. Keep going."

"Even though we're working together, the Provincial Police are powerful," Zekiul continued. "More powerful than us."

"I don't care how powerful they are," Oliver said. "They're abusing their power. The Police can't do that." He stalked to the back of the room; and dropped his hand on my shoulder.

My heart leapt. His gesture was a sign he'd forgiven me.

"Here's the problem." Zekiul glanced at me—and Oliver—then he sat on top of the table. Zekiul's aura quieted, but his voice stayed strong. "Actually, the best way I can explain the problem is if I tell you a story. But please understand I'm only sharing this with you because it represents several Canuckian experiences. I was told this story in confidence, and I never break trust with citizens."

"Never?" Oliver grunted. "Maybe you should skip the story and make your point."

Amelie rolled her eyes. "Your story will stay here, Major. Please, tell us the tale."

"Remember who's in charge, Amelie." Dimitri sniffed by his window. "Your son, not you."

"Her eldest son." Khleo smirked in Oliver's direction.

"If you're in charge, Le-Le," Amelie snapped, "act like it."

"That was a mean micro-aggression, Mumsy." Khleo pointed his toe at Amelie. "Don't be patronizing. Unless mayors are supposed to be patronizing? Then you're doing a terrific job modelling the virtues of a rural government: hypocrisy, and irony, and—"

"Let Major Cox speak." Dimitri glared around the room, then he winked at me. He winked!

"Mayor Cox." I giggled loud enough for Dimitri to know I got his joke. Life was so much easier when everyone sort-of got along.

"Go ahead, Zekiul," Khleo said with an obscene amount of magnanimous foot waving. "We're listening."

Zekiul nodded. "Here's the problem. If anyone reports Officer Dillweed—"

"Dillweed." Khleo snorted. "Love it."

"—to Whitley, he'll get in trouble. Then he'll be embarrassed and tell his officer friends. Then the rest of Herra's investigation is going to be Hell on Chaleur until the Provincial Police leave. *If* they leave. Which takes us to my story: about an incident in a town in Fairfield where a teenaged girl complained to her Reclamation Party representative about local law enforcement. The Provincial Police were throwing their weight around to get extra rations from the townspeople, and they 'subcontracted' their security services to vigilantes so they could get some 'R & R.'" Zekiul paused. "You can tell when I'm quoting the Provincial Police, right? They weren't subcontracting, or resting and relaxing. They didn't want to do their jobs, but they wanted to keep their authority and paycheck. You know, all fun with no responsibility?"

"Sounds like the perfect career for you, Khleo."

"Sounds like—bite me, Oli."

"Oh, very mature."

"Takes one to know one."

"Know one what? One mature?" Oliver grinned. "What's a mature?"

"So—" Zekiul continued, "—this girl told her rep, and the rep pulled the police force from the town and replaced it with a new squadron, fresh from the Capitol. All of a sudden, the town gets hit by marauders, pilfering food and supplies. And the new squadron does nothing. Then the girl figures out that the old force told on her, and the new squadron backed up their friends. So she came to me. The Champions gave the new squadron way more trouble than a small-town gang."

"Please don't tell us about the illegal things you used to do," Amelie said, rubbing her fringe of hair. "We're still supposed to be giving you a second chance."

Zekiul drew a finger across his lips. "Zipped. Let's just say we distracted the Fairfieldian police so the townspeople could have peace."

Amelie nodded. "Much better."

"HEH," Jolene barked.

Oliver looked at the broad-shouldered Champion standing in the corner of the cabin, then he whispered to me, "Did you know she was here?"

"She's Khleo's personal assistant." I patted Oliver's hand. "She's always here."

Oliver frowned at Jolene. "Right."

"So, to summarize," Zekiul concluded, "the Provincial Police are horrible. And dealing with them directly—you know, like adults—will get us nowhere."

"What should we do, then?" Khleo planted his feet on the floor. "We can't let them get away with this."

"That's exactly what we should do," Zekiul said. "Nothing."

Oliver removed his hand from my shoulder and shoved it in his sweater pocket. "Not an option."

"They'll crush us," Zekiul said as he faced Oliver. "And we have to find Herra's murderer. Nobody has resources like the government. The Provincial Police are the Boucher family's best shot at justice."

"I—" Khleo paused and lifted his finger, commanding the attention of the room, "—agree."

"I agree with Zekiul, too," I said over the collective exhalation of breath gathered during Khleo's pregnant pause. "We can't waste time arguing with the Police. We need to know who killed Herra."

"Or—" Khleo raised his finger again, "—we could retaliate another way."

The auras in the room peaked. Everyone inched forward on their chairs, closer to Khleo—who sat with a small, sneaky smile on his ruddy, round face.

"Well?" Amelie said. "What do we do?"

"Micro-aggressions." Khleo twirled out of his seat, ousting Zekiul off the table. "Micro-aggressions are hard to identify because they're easy to dismiss. You can make someone feel powerless without any kind of consequence. If your victim calls you out, you can simply claim your attack was misinterpreted." He spun around, then said, "Layla? The next time you come into this space wearing muddy boots you won't be allowed back in. Cleanliness is how we show respect for the room: the room in which we conduct our Coplot meetings." Khleo tapped his toe. "You want to show the Coplot respect, right?"

I choked on my tongue. "Yes—I do—yes! I respect the Coplot. But it's winter. I can't control how muddy my boots get. And nobody has complained about this before. It's unfair to threaten me with expulsion when this hasn't been a problem and—"

"New leader, new rules," Khleo said. "You want to show your *mayor* respect. Right?"

My jaw dropped: like Oliver's had ten minutes earlier. I sputtered, "But—but—but—" before snapping my mouth shut. For once, Khleo's glints didn't match his behaviour: but they were as obvious as a glistening glacier.

I grinned. "Good one."

"*That* is how we retaliate." Khleo clicked his heels with glee. "Micro-aggressions."

Silence followed his statement.

Zekiul raised his hand. Slowly. "You want us to ask the officers to clean off their boots before they stomp all over us?"

Khleo grinned. "That was an example. If I'd actually been up set about mud in the cabin I would have pulled Layla aside after the meeting, in private, to ask her to clean her shoes. Or I would have added an item to the Coplot's agenda so I could inform the entire collective about my expectations. But I didn't care about Layla's boots, or the mud. I wanted to establish dominance, so I used her sloppiness as an excuse to publicly humiliate her. She couldn't defend herself without looking unreasonable. Nobody likes muddy boots." He glanced at his high-tops, then beamed around the room. "See? Micro-aggression."

"Why did you want to dominate me?" I smirked. "Are you jealous of my filthy footwear?"

Khleo rolled his eyes. "Always."

"That was wonderfully explained, Le-Le," Amelie said, pink with pride. "I couldn't have done it better myself."

"I'm more than just a sexy set of sneakers, Mumsy. Here." Khleo turned to the wall and pressed his temple. A vid projected onto the space. "While Layla was drowning like an ant in a puddle, I found examples of micro-aggressions on the network. Look."

A series of scenes played on the wall. A line of marching officers tripped over a log placed on a darkened path seconds before they turned onto the street for their nightly patrol. An officer bent over her shoes, trying to undo a knot tied in her laces by a local who'd snuck into the barracks while she dressed in the cleansing closet. A squadron of officers sat in their mess hall, making faces as they ate their military rations: the town cook had 'accidentally' added too much salt.

The vids continued. Oliver chuckled every time an officer was bested and citizens got away with it.

I shook my head in awe. "Khleo. These are so petty."

Khleo grinned. "Petty, but effective."

"Well, now," Amelie said. "I don't know about this. The Coplot takes the high road. We don't string weeds across it to trip our enemies. That isn't how good governments operate."

"We aren't a government," Khleo said. "Not yet, anyway. Right now, the Coplot is a small town collective that manages the small town tasks associated with small town life."

"But the Coplot is applying for Party status in the new year," Oliver said, his laughter cut short. "Our submission won't get approved if we play pranks on the Police."

"Micro-aggressions, Oli. Not pranks. There's no way the Provincial Police could prove any of this stuff. They can't punish us for innocent accidents." Khleo turned to his mom. "Can they?"

"I don't know," Amelie said. "I've never seen anything like this before."

Zekiul grinned. "I like it."

"And the town would love it," I said. "This is exactly what we need to improve morale. Nobody wants the Provincial Police here. Peevish Pear was complaining about them yesterday. She'd be the first to pull a prank. You know, sell the Police wormy grain, or torn socks, or something."

"Torn socks." Khleo cackled. "I like that. Jolene?" He raised his voice and called to the corner, "Write that down. Peevish Pear has to poke holes in the police officers' underwear."

Jolene nodded sluggishly, then lumbered out of the cabin. Her glints told me she was on the hunt for a chalkboard, even though there were plenty stacked in the storage room.

"I don't like these mini-whatevers." Amelie crossed her arms. "I dislike the Provincial Police more than anyone, but we should talk to Whitley and tell them what their crew is up to. They'll get rid of that officer. I vote no."

"We're voting? One moment, please." I widened my eyes and mumbled, "I need to get in the headspace to record an official vote."

"I promise you, Mumsy, this isn't one officer," Khleo said. "Policy always starts at the top. You taught me that. Whitley could be encouraging their squad to take their frustrations out on people who can't fight back, like Zekiul. You need to vote yes."

"I'm a yes," I said. "Yes, yes, yes."

"I'm a yes, too," Zekiul said. "But Oliver's right. These are pranks, not micro-aggressions. And Layla's right. Pranks could help with town morale."

Oliver shot Zekiul a side glance.

"What do you think?" Khleo tapped Dimitri's calf with his toe. "Not that it matters. The yeses have the majority."

"Please stop forgetting I exist," Oliver said as he pushed away from the back wall. "I'm right here, for the love of leaves."

"You agree though. Right, Oli?" I blinked, stopping my vid recording. "Won't this be fun?"

"Not fun, but I can see it's necessary. Just—" Oliver raised his hands, "—no blood, please. Or violence. I don't do blood."

"Well, Dimitri?" Khleo pressed his temple and the projected vids disappeared. "Your opinion may not matter, but we still want to hear it."

"Democracy at its finest." Dimitri sighed, then said, "I agree with Amelie."

Khleo kicked Dimitri's shin. "Boring."

"These games are a waste of time," Dimitri said, massaging his leg. "You shouldn't play these pranks—"

"Micro-aggressions," Khleo said.

"—so you don't have my vote." Dimitri's green eyes faded as he straightened. "And when this ends terribly I'm going to say I told you so."

But it didn't end terribly. The pranks played on the Provincial Police were exactly what I hoped they'd be: a way to alleviate the suffocating stillness in the town as Herra's murder investigation continued; and a way to solidify the bond between the Champions and the currently-named Coplot.

The entire community participated. Every day a Provincial Police officer was pranked. Boots were left out in the rain, nuclear batons lost their power cells, and bad luck seemed to follow the officers everywhere they went. And the town stayed quiet.

The town—supposedly—stayed in their homes, complying with every police request. The community even went out of their way to help the officers when they needed it, but the help 'accidentally' led to more 'accidents.' The only person who escaped torment in the days that followed was Whitley, because I sort-of liked the white-haired rep, so I kindly (demanded) everyone leave them alone. But despite the councillor's shoes staying dry—and their food staying perfectly seasoned—Whitley couldn't identify Herra's killer.

That should have dampened the morale in the town, but the pranks were too fun; and the community was determined to bring the Boucher family justice.

The Coplot continued our private investigation with the Champions by our side. We conducted searches in the parts of the mountains the Provincial Police wouldn't go: the bogs, gullies, and places too steep and too high to scale. But we found nothing. Not a clue, not a trace, not a hint leading to the person who'd killed a young girl.

Until one day, weeks later, the case cracked wide open: along with my mind.

I was hiding in my grove—high up in my birch tree—as I waited to prank the Police. I'd found a wasp nest in a Douglas fir, and I planned to drop it on the midday patrol when they marched through my part of the woods. Then Jolene wandered by.

Or, stumbled by. Just Jolene wasn't much of a wanderer.

I was bored because I'd arrived too early—earlier than the officers marched—and the wasps weren't around to keep me busy. They flying insects disappeared after I climbed my tree, almost as if they'd smelled something offensive. So when Jolene stumbled into the grove, I decided to practice my glint-snatching skills. It had been weeks since I'd tested my powers, and I wanted to stay sharp in case I had to use them again. I needed to remain strong.

I knew Jolene wouldn't notice if I practiced on her—Jolene didn't notice anything—so I only felt a little bit of guilt when I snatched her glints and absorbed her aura.

I felt pain, though. Searing pain. Because when I entered Jolene's mind, a grey haze infused my head and I fell out of my tree. Landing in a patch of felt-ringed agaricus with a *thump!* I shook the toxic fungi off my body, then rolled onto my hands and knees, heaving.

Jolene stumbled away. Oblivious.

I clutched my head as the grove spun. Jolene's glints pounded against my temples.

Within Jolene's grey haze—the fuzz—her glints stood out with perfect clarity. Glints of a memory: a memory of the Champions sneaking through the forest to set Rogers' field on fire. Zekiul reached the base of Rogers' hill and moved towards the field, leaving Jolene stumbling behind. Then Jolene heard a sound. She stopped and turned towards the aspen tree. There was nothing there: except another sound.

Snap!

Surprised, Jolene stepped forwards, towards the forest. Her glints gurgled with fear as a male appeared behind a bush. He was shaking a girl. A small girl, with staring eyes. Then the male picked up a shovel—Rogers' mushroom shovel—and thrust it into the girl, up under her chin.

The girl crumpled to the ground. The male straightened. From Jolene's solitary hiding place she gasped—

—and the male turned, drenched in blood.

The clouds let up and moonlight shone through the trees, illuminating the sandy-haired, blood-soaked figure holding the spade in his shaking hand: a fiery-eyed male with hunched shoulders and an expression that glittered with malice.

He had murderer's eyes.

Angry eyes.

I turned over and vomited under my tree.

CHAPTER TWENTY-ONE

After I cleaned myself up—and kicked leaves over my puke (vomit made good compost, but it also made a mess if a citizen stepped in it)—I paused.

Even though my whole body itched to hide in my grove and avoid the messes *I* kept stepping in, I forced myself to stay still. I took a deep breath. I hugged the trunk of my birch.

The birch's marble bark vibrated beneath my hands. A single leaf floated onto my face, leaving a drop of rain on my forehead. I fingered the velvety soft leaf, then let it fall softy to the forest floor. Calm restored, I straightened my shoulders and sat, cross-legged, under my tree.

I replayed Jolene's memory—twice. Then I played it twenty more times. Then I flipped my hair over my shoulder and headed for the Coplot cabin, where I knew Oliver would be working since he refused to participate in the Provincial Police pranking.

With certainty guiding my steps, I strode into the cabin and over to my partner, who sat behind the leadership table—alone—with his eyes on his chalkboard. Feeling a little wild, I swept Oliver's board onto the floor and cleared my throat. Loudly.

Oliver sighed. "What now?"

"Come with me." I walked into the library, confident Oliver would follow.

He did. As soon as Oliver stepped into the back room with its shelves stocked with plastic pages, I shut the door. "We're fucked."

Oliver twerked his eyebrow. "I know it's been a while since that magical night I tied you to your birch tree, but the Coplot's agenda has been under-managed for months and my list is ten times its normal length. I don't have the energy to fool around."

Ignoring the shame battering my belly (because I *still* hadn't spoken with Oliver about how awkward that 'magical night' had been for me) I said, "Not that, you dillweed."

"Dillweed?" Oliver grunted. "*Dillweed?*"

I leaned against a stack. "I don't want to sleep with you. I'm telling you we're screwed. Hooped. You and I are in trouble."

"Cut the dramatics, Layla." Oliver headed for the exit. "I don't have time for games. Once you have something real to tell me, I'll be ready to listen."

"Why did you kill Herra?"

Oliver froze, his hand on the library door's handle. "What?"

I smirked. "Ready to listen now, huh?"

Oliver turned around. "Why do you think I killed Herra?"

"I don't think you killed Herra."

Oliver squeezed his eyes shut. "I'm going to kill *you*."

"I was in my tree—"

"Yes."

"—getting ready to prank the Police—"

Oliver grumbled.

"And Jolene walked by."

Oliver opened his eyes. "And?"

"I snatched her glints."

"Layla!"

"Cut the dramatics, Oli. Once you calm down, I'll be ready to talk."

Oliver clenched his hands. "I'm sure you had a good reason for breaking the law. A law that landed my mother in jail. A law you've been told to stop breaking. Frequently."

"I didn't have a good reason," I said, annoyed and wanting to bite back. "I was bored."

Oliver sighed. "What does your boredom have to do with me killing Herra?"

"Jolene has a memory of you murdering the twin on the night of the mushroom fire." Annoyance gone, I swallowed the bile pressing against the bottom of my throat. "She thinks you're the killer."

Oliver stayed still, his eyes glued on my face. "But you don't think I'm the killer?"

I laughed, which—apparently—was what I did when I felt uncomfortable. "Of course you didn't kill Herra. You were with me the night of the fire. And you don't do blood." I pointed at the scar on Oliver's chin. "There was a lot of blood in Jolene's memory."

"Stop." Oliver shuddered. "Why does Jolene think she saw me that night?"

"That—" I said, "—is why we're in trouble. When I snatched Jolene's glints, her memory felt wrong."

"Wrong how?"

I stamped my foot. "I'm trying to tell you how! For the love of leaves, Oli, can't you bend a bit? Let me be a little showy. Not everything is a graph, or table, or cake chart."

"Pie chart."

"You know what I mean. Let *me* tell the story of how you didn't murder a little girl," I twirled my hands in the air, "with pizazz."

"You're twisted."

"And you love it." I knew I was being over-the-top—my glints felt as out-of-control as a teenager's—but I didn't care. "Jolene's memory was blurry. Or hazy. Or, something." I breathed in slowly, then said, "Jolene's memory was altered."

"Altered?"

"Altered. Either someone told Jolene they saw you there and Jolene is so simple she thinks she saw it herself—"

"Which is possible," Oliver said. "Jolene is very simple."

"—or someone forced a false glint into Jolene's mind, though I can't see how that's possible."

Oliver groaned. "See, Layla? This is why I hate the eyelinks. They open people up to manipulation. Connection makes people vulnerable, and weak-minded people like Jolene can be tricked into believing things that haven't happened."

"It doesn't matter, though."

Oliver frowned. "What? Why?"

I walked across the library to stand in front of Oliver. "Jolene didn't tell anyone what she saw. The Provincial Police have questioned the Champions—every single one of them—and Whitley hasn't arrested you. So, Jolene must be strong enough to hide her memory."

"Why wouldn't she tell Whitley I killed Herra?"

"Because, Oli-my-love—believe it or not—the Champions are on our side. This is proof. Zekiul told the Champions we're allies, and his people trust him."

Oliver pursed his lips. Then he said, "Let's pretend that's true. Why was Jolene remembering this *today*?"

I thought for a second, then snapped my fingers. "Because Jolene's going to tell Zekiul—or one of us—today. She wasn't sure about the memory, so she had to think about it, but now she's—"

"Jolene's going to tell someone?" Oliver threw his hands in the air. "What if Jolene tells Whitley?"

"Oli." I hugged his hunched shoulders. "We're just talking. We don't know if any of this is true. All we know is that Jolene has a false memory that makes you look really bad. We need more information."

Held in my arms, Oliver sighed. "You want to snatch her glints again, don't you?"

"No." I lifted my chin, beaming. "I want to snatch everyone's glints."

"What? Why?"

"I want to find out why Jolene has the false memory. I need to know who put it in her mind. The only person who'd claim you committed the crime is the murderer, and the murderer has to be in Chaleur." I released Oliver, who'd tightened in my arms with every word I spoke.

I understood. I was tense, too. But now that I'd told Oliver my plan, I had to *do* my plan. So, I turned to leave—

—and my eyes stuck on the bookshelf closest to the door. The shelf was stacked with detective fiction. I skimmed the titles: 'A Sneaky Secret,' and 'The Manipulative Miscreant,' and 'That Troublemaker Who Terrorized A Tiny Mountain Town.'

For some unknown reason a memory popped into my mind. "I wonder if the troublemaker and the murderer are the same person."

Oliver peered at me. "Which troublemaker? Cox? Rogers? Peevish Pear? There are a lot of problematic people in Chaleur."

"The troublemaker your mom worried about, months ago. The person who glinted anger and excitement at the same time. You remember: the Min RoboReiwa doppelgänger."

"You think the troublemaker is the murderer?" Oliver fingered the spine of 'Pay Attention To the Evidence, You Moron' (a Canuckian classic) then said, "You could be onto something."

As another memory surfaced, I said, "So, you don't mind if I go on a glint-snatching spree?"

"A spree?" Oliver spun around. "A *spree?*"

"Your mom gave me the idea. Take it up with her if you don't like it."

"Right." Oliver rolled his eyes. "I'll take it up with the female who has a history of making decisions that don't *put her in prison.*"

I kissed the tip of Oliver's nose. "You need to let that go."

Oliver sagged against the shelf. "Go on your spree."

"Oli?" I pretended to be shocked, fluttering my hand over my chest. "Are you bending a bit?"

"Maybe," Oliver said. "Alright, yes. I am. You—and my mother—have shown me that, sometimes, it's okay to break the rules. Not everything is a cake chart."

I grinned. "I adore you."

"I couldn't stop you, anyway," Oliver said. "You don't need my permission. You're going to do what you want, no matter what I say."

"That is so sexy." I stroked Oliver's sandy hair. "Take me now."

"Layla." Oliver grabbed my fingers. "You need to be careful."

"I'm always careful."

"Layla." Oliver's eyes bored into mine. "Pause for a second. There is someone in this town who is powerful enough to either influence a person's memory, change it entirely, or embed new glints in their mind. And that someone could be Herra's killer. *And that someone wants to hurt me.* Murder is a life sentence, Layla, and a source memory is the only proof a jury needs to convict."

"Well, then," I said, patting Oliver's head. "I should find out the truth as soon as possible, shouldn't I?"

I whisked out of the library and through the Coplot cabin, confident I'd prove my partner's innocence.

And hopefully catch Herra's killer in the process.

CHAPTER TWENTY-TWO

That afternoon should have been one of the best in my life.

Finally, I was able to use my glint-reading power to help; and I was desperate to exercise my ability. Finding the glint-alterer, or murderer, or troublemaker, provided the perfect opportunity to flex my strength. So I made my way through Chaleur and snatched the glints of every citizen I passed without any inconvenient guilt holding me back. I invaded citizens' privacy, but it was alright because I had a good reason. A great reason. And I learned a lot.

As their glints quickly proved, citizens worried—a lot—that their authentic self was strange and, if anyone knew what they glinted, they'd be ostracized from society. But the community glinted about the same things. Pretty much all the time.

I wandered along Chaleur's streets and down the pathways that wound around homes, quietly snatching glints. Nobody knew what I was up to. Citizens assumed I was just being me: the female who traipsed through the town taking care of my plants or passing along Coplot directives. So nobody questioned why I wandered. But, as I traipsed, I consumed the community.

EMILY AINS FERGUS
DECEMBER 5, 2106

—oh, great. Another wrinkle under my eye. Every day I wake up, look in this Bot-forsaken mirror, and see more wrinkles—

CRAIG STUART KOVALCHUK
DECEMBER 5, 2106

—where in the green earth is my other sock? Jeffrey did the laundry last night, and when I put the socks away they were all in the drawer. So—where did the left one go? And why is it always the left sock that goes missing? Who is taking my socks? And why only the left ones—

MICK TEMPLETON
DECEMBER 5, 2106
—if I ran against myself in a race would I finish first or last? If I raced myself I'm pretty sure I'd win, because I'd be racing myself. Or would I lose? Or would I tie—

ELOISE WREN FLORENCE
DECEMBER 5, 2106
—I'm sooo tired. I don't want to pick up Dara from school. I want to take a nap. Maybe Fredrick can pick her up. I should message him. But he might say no, and I don't want to fight right now because I'm sooo tired. But someone has to pick up Dara—

LIZBETH FLANAGAN
DECEMBER 5, 2106
—the next time Agnes leads the cauldron circle she has to use rosemary in the brew. Fierce Female Fairies won't be able to commune with the Divine Mother if Agnes uses bay leaves, like last time. Every truly-connected female knows rosemary is much better than bay—

SORCHA KATHRYN SCOTT WALLACE
DECEMBER 5, 2106
—holy holly berries, Ashleigh is so hot. I wonder if she thinks about me. No. Ashleigh is *too* hot. She'd never think about me the way I think about her. Layla Douglas, however, is the kind of female who'd screw every person in the town if she wasn't with Oliver—

I glared at the teenager who had that glint: a pimpled girl who hung around Peevish Pear's market.

Then I shook my head. I didn't want to police people's minds.

So I kept snatching.

JUSTIN AARON KENDLE
DECEMBER 5, 2106
—and after I catch that Provincial Police officer (the short one, with the spot on his earlobe) I'm going to tie him up, and steal his pants, and make him walk back to the barracks with his rear end flashing for everyone to see, and then his friends will point and laugh, and he'll rue the day he criticized me for hanging my laundry on the line outside my house the one day this week it didn't rain—

ALICE LEE LANDRY
DECEMBER 5, 2106
—did I order enough sandbags to barricade my field when the floods come this spring? I did. I *did* order enough sandbags. Did I, though? If I didn't, I need to place a second order—today—because it takes months for shipments to arrive from the capital, so if I didn't order enough sandbags I can't barricade my field when the floods come this spring. But . . . I *did* order enough. I'm *sure* I did. Except . . . what if the floods are unusually heavy? Did I order enough sandbags to barricade my field if the floods are unusually heavy this spring—

LILLIAN CLAIRE PASKUS
DECEMBER 5, 2106
—I'm going to kill Kamal. That son of a spider didn't pick up oat milk—again!—and now I have to drink my tea black—

SIMONE AVERY ROGERS
DECEMBER 5, 2106
—where in tarnation did I leave my eyelinks—

SERGIO ALEJANDRO LUIS XANDER
DECEMBER 5, 2106
—what should I have for lunch? What should I have for dinner? What should I have for breakfast tomorrow? And for lunch? Ow,

my head hurts—

~~~

I dismissed those glints. Even the threatening one, which I didn't take seriously. Citizens were so consumed with their everyday lives they wouldn't have the time—or the ability—to plan and execute the murder of a little girl.

The Coplot leaders—and Councillor Whitley—were no better.

Whitley was focused on finding Herra's murderer, but they didn't know who it could be. Khleo worried about his new position; and his mom. Dimitri couldn't stop glinting about Zekiul: Zekiul with his shirt off, Zekiul standing under a water-fall, Zekiul running through the woods—naked—with sweat streaming down his rock-hard abdomen . . .

I didn't snatch Zekiul's glints. I didn't want to break my promise.

Amelie's glints were about infrastructure. *Infrastructure.* Not a dead child, or her time spent in jail. She did have one glint that considered speaking with Whitley about the officer who'd stomped on Zekiul (Amelie wanted him gone and was ready to do anything within her limited scope of power to make it happen), but—mostly—she glinted about infrastructure.

Infrastructure.

Amelie obsessed over how much gravel was needed to pave the paths that summer, and the cost of glass to upgrade the window in the Coplot cabin. She wondered if Khleo would remember to find someone to spearhead the spring cleanup, and how long it would take before the shipment of government-grade eyelinks arrived from Oakland so the community could communicate with citizens in other countries.

Community could communicate, community could communicate, community could—

My head spun. Based on Amelie's headspace alone, I wasn't sure if leadership was for me. Would it be better to stay a subordinate instead of letting my life be controlled by numbers and dates?

I shook my head. That was another problem for another time. I hadn't been promoted, and it didn't look like I would be soon. The most important administrative duty I had at that moment was my spree.

Apart from the commonplace glints every citizen in Chaleur seemed to have, I was touched—and surprised—when I picked up on an interesting emotion woven within the words. Beneath the rumination and worries, citizens' glints pulsed with—

—hope.

They wished for a better future. They knew tomorrow would be different. They believed in their hearts, and souls, and bodies and minds that they could live the life they wanted if they tried a little harder, or waited a bit longer, or put their faith in someone who would show them the way to achieve happiness.

As the hopeful glints swirled, I had to stop in the copse of hemlocks to catch my breath. The amount of optimism coursing through the people in my town was overwhelming. I reeled from the force of their mindset.

But I couldn't rest for long. I had to find the person who'd altered Jolene's glints before she shared her memory. So I swallowed my pride for my people, and kept snatching.

I only had a few adults left to snatch when I realized I should read the glints of Chaleur's children, in case they'd stumbled upon information our elders missed. I changed direction and found a cluster of kids playing in a park. But they revealed nothing. The local children glinted about their curfews, how unfairly they were treated by their parents, and spicy stories their friends told when the adults weren't around.

Then I spotted Havu and the blonde sitting outside Peevish Pear's market, so I paused to prod their minds: the girls were watchers—and listeners—so they'd probably seen—or heard—something.

Nope.

Havu's glints were still simple: almost Jolene-like in their sluggishness. She wasn't thinking about her sister, or her family.

Or anything, really. As Herra's twin sat on the market's front step and poked a pile of dirt with a stick, Havu glinted about the dirt (it was brown and had pink worms in it) and about the stick (it was rough in her palm, but it felt good to stab the mud).

The blonde wasn't helpful, either. Her glints were calm and steady—she seemed to have gotten them under control—but they pulsed with concern for her younger friend and sadness she'd lost Herra.

Shrugging, I strode towards Peevish Pear's market. I'd saved the grocer's glints for the end of my spree because I was certain Madame Perrault was the memory-alterer. Or, at least—as the town gossip—she'd have an idea who the culprit could be.

As I walked by the girls, the blonde spoke: "No, you idiot. If you want to spear an insect you have to poke it with the sharp part of the stick."

"I don't want to spear it," Havu said. "I want to crush it."

"Crush it?" The blonde pushed her wavy hair out of her eyes. "Yes. Crush it. That's better. Okay, if you want to crush insects you have to aim for their bodies, not their heads. The long part, Havu. The part with the goo."

Havu smushed a millipede as it scuttled across the step. Yellow fluid burst from the insect, staining the stone. Havu looked at the blonde—and grinned. "How did you know that would work?"

The blonde winked. "I'm good with weapons."

Shaking my head (the girls were so strange), I entered the market. The bell Peevish Pear hung over the lintel tinkled as I shut the door, cutting out the sound of citizens making their way through the town; and the blonde's bug-killing encouragement.

Perrault shuffled plastic sheets around her checkout counter. She glared down the long bridge of her nose as I hovered by the entryway. "Dimitri already picked up your household's order for the week. Don't complain to me if you ate your allotted rations. I've told you time and time again, Layla: fair's fair. The town has to do its post-war share."

Peevish Pear thought she was so clever, but I could have invented a catchier rhyme dangling upside down in my birch. I fingered a coat hanging on a rack by the door, then shot a sweet smile at the sour grocer. "My rations are fine, thank you. I need a new winter jacket. If that's allowed?"

Perrault scoffed, then went back to her plastic pages. "Don't get your muddy fingerprints on my merchandise. I see you in the woods. I see what you do." She mumbled under her breath, "I see you rolling around under that hideous tree with Amelie's son."

I bet you do, I thought. I bet you spy on Oli and me all the time. You like watching us roll around, since you've nagged away every human who might have wanted to roll around with you. Pleased, I pretended to search the rack, running my 'muddy' fingers over the canvas coats with their silkworm-spun lining. But my mind was elsewhere: reading the glints of the grocer.

If she ruins my jackets I won't be able to replace them until next summer, thought Perrault, intent on her pages. With the anticipated influx of imports from the Separated States, I can't absorb the cost. I'll be lucky if I make my minimum targets this quarter, and—

Wincing, I pulled out of Peevish Pear's mind. Targets? The town's most-informed gossip was glinting about her business goals? Not juicy secrets about citizens? Or awful rumours she'd heard? Not a single evil scheme?

I resisted stamping my foot. I had to dive deeper. If anyone in Chaleur could help me find a murderous glint-alterer, it was Peevish Pear.

With a jolt, my mind split in two. A sharp pain hit the back of my head and cut straight across my spine. Gasping, I grabbed my face. Then, as suddenly as it arrived, the pain disappeared.

I dropped my hands and looked up, into Peevish Pear's pinched face.

"Are you alright?" The grocer frowned down at me. "I can send Havu and Erika to fetch Dr. Munroe. You don't look well."

I straightened. "I'm sorry, I—" I massaged my neck. "It's a cold-weather headache. I get them sometimes."

Perrault frowned. "I don't believe you."

I rolled my eyes, then winced as my head pounded.

"You look horrible," Perrault said. "Come with me. I have an armchair in my office. You can rest until you feel better."

Without protesting (because I wasn't alright), I let myself be led into the back room. Perrault motioned to an overstuffed chair sitting in a corner, then she handed me a blanket. "I'll make tea. Sit tight."

Perrault closed the door. I sighed with relief. Alone, I could relax and let the pain in my head recede. After three slow breaths—and after listening to the repetitive *clink!* and bubble of Perrault boiling water—I thought back to the moment the pain in my head hit. Had I been close to something? Did Peevish Pear know I was reading her glints? Was the pain the grocer's defense system?

Gritting my teeth and wrapping the blanket around my knees, I gathered my power and channeled it into the glowing orb. With stealth—and subtlety—I sent the orb into the grocer's mind. Perrault's memories appeared and I was caught by a clear one.

A memory of a night that summer.

CHAPTER TWENTY-THREE

AGNES JOYCE PERRAULT
SEPTEMBER 14, 2106

Gosh, it's late. When I was young I could finish long before the sun set. Now I'm here past midnight. I'd better close up, and try to get some sleep. Tomorrow's another day.

I walk out of my office and into the market. The single light I left on shines on a—*fuzz fuzz*—light I left on catches the silver lock on the front door. I forgot to turn the bolt at closing.

My memory isn't what it used to be. I hope nobody wandered in when I was in the back. No, they couldn't have. I would have heard the bell.

I walk to the door to turn the lock: I'll leave by the back exit tonight.

fuzzy FUZZ]

Oh!

When I place my hand on the silver bolt, a figure jogs up the street. I see them through my front window.

How odd.

I can't see who the figure is—it's too dark, and they're staying away from the streetlights—but they shouldn't be outside.

This is wrong. Citizens are supposed to be in their homes. It's not an official rule, but it is best practise, and it's my responsibility to make sure the town follows best practise for their own safety.

People shouldn't wander around in the dark.

I leave by the back door, then head for the path I saw the figure run along. Soon, I've caught up. I'm quiet, so this hooligan doesn't know I'm following them. I can't see who they are, though. They're wearing a dark sweater that's pulled over their head to hide their hairstyle and colouring. Not that I'd be able to pick out those details. The moon is behind the clouds.

I hurry after the hooligan. I need to see which path they're taking to the forest, but I can't get too close. If the hooligan looks around, they'll know I'm behind them.

Oh! They take the path that leads to the big aspen.

I know where the hooligan is going. There's only one property by the aspen trees: Simone's mushroom farm.

How very odd.

We reach the edge of Simone's acreage, and I stop at the tree line. The figure keeps moving over the planks that lead to Simone's cottage.

Should I say something? Call out? Simone's cottage is dark, so she can't be expecting anyone.

I stay quiet. If this hooligan is out to cause mischief I could get hurt, and I can't protect myself the way I used to.

The figure stops in the middle of the farm, pausing on a plank. There is a sound.

The sound of a child crying.

What is a child doing on Simone's property after midnight? This is wrong. Very, very wrong.

The figure moves. In a few strides they've crossed the remaining planks. They disappear into the shrubbery that surrounds the base of Simone's hill. A moment later, they drag a little girl—who is sniffling and sobbing—out of the shrubs and into the forest. Before I know it, I'm following them.

I don't know why.

I should be running to tell someone: Simone, or Amelie. Or I should message the Police. But, instead, I'm running into the woods. I head towards the spot the figure dragged the little girl.

There they are!—I see them. The hooligan is shaking her.

How horrible!

She's a small girl, with dark hair. She's—gosh! The girl is one of the twins! Havu, I think, or the other one. I take a step forward to stop the hooligan. They're going to hurt her. They're shaking her too hard. They—oh!

OH!

[SMASH into grey]

The hooligan—who is a male, I can see him now—picks up a shovel. Or a trowel. It's hard to know which, because the male is waving it in the air. At any rate, he's holding one of the nuclear tools Simone leaves around her acreage. I'm always reminding her to put them away so someone doesn't stumble over them and get hurt, but—OH!

The hooligan is—

He lifts—

The male slices the twin's throat.

Gosh.

The twin falls to the ground. The male straightens, then turns.

I can see him. He's holding the spade in his hand, holding it to the sky. Is he?—he is! The hooligan is happy.

I need to get out of here. I need to run. But I can't. I'm too scared. If I move, the male might see me. What if he throws the shovel at me next? There is blood everywhere, all over the ground. It's horrible.

Horrible!

I have to get away.

[*rapid fuzz that blurs the grayscale*

GREYSCALE SMASH]

Oh. No.

The clouds move. Light fills the forest. The male's face—*fuzz fuzz*—face and form are visible.

I've made a terrible mistake.

I need to leave this place, now. I need to leave, and never tell anyone what I've seen—No! I need to wait until the time is right, then report what I've witnessed to Mayor Billadeau. I need to make sure the hooligan is locked away forever, once and for all.

I run.

I run away from the scene of the crime and away from the

hooligan who isn't a male after all. The horrible hooligan is a female. A familiar female.

Layla Douglas.

I knew orphans were untrustworthy. Now I know they're capable of murder.

CHAPTER TWENTY-FOUR

"You ran?"

"Yes."

"You ran out of Peevish Pear's market? Ran here?"

"That's what I said."

"You ran out of Madame Perrault's market—after watching a memory she has of you committing the worst criminal offence in Canuckia—and you came to the home of a female who just got out of jail for committing the second worst criminal offence in Canuckia, and you didn't think that might make you, and my mother, look incredibly suspicious?"

"What was I supposed to do?" I flipped on my side, then hopped off Oliver's bed. Rain pounded the attic's window as I frowned at my partner, who sat rigidly on his stool. "This is the second false memory I've seen today. Someone is altering glints all over the place. They're trying to blame other people for a crime they committed, and they're coming after us. What would *you* have done? Run for the border? Gone to Whitley to tell them I snatched everyone's glints? Our options are limited, and they aren't good." I sat on the bench under Oliver's window and braided my hair (a habit that showed up when I was nervous—really nervous). "I need to think."

Oliver chewed on his tongue: a habit that showed up when *he* was nervous. Then, after what felt like an eternity, he said, "Let's go through the facts. What do we know and what don't we know?" He grabbed a blank board off his desk and held a piece of chalk over its surface. "Go."

I sat up, strangely invigorated. "Um, what we do know?"

Oliver nodded. "Yes. Tell me what we know."

"Alright." I closed my eyes and recalled my memories of the past few months. "We know that your mom—and Dimitri—sensed a disturbing glint in a Coplot meeting."

Oliver scribbled on his board. "Got it."

"And we know that your mom said the disturbing glinter was disturbed."

"Mmm."

"Wait." My eyes opened as a memory revealed a forgotten point. "Did anyone investigate the three original suspects? Ashleigh Smythe, Peevish Pear, and—"

"Justin Kendle?" Oliver smiled ruefully. "Khleo followed up with them when we were at the envoy meeting. They had alibis."

"Crumbly couscous."

"What else do we know?"

"We know that Herra was murdered a few days before the disturbing glint was noticed. And her body was buried in Rogers' mushroom field. And Zekiul set fire to that field. Holy holly berries!" I leaned forward, brimming with excitement. "Do you think the murderer put the gasoline in the pools so they could tip off Zekiul, knowing he'd set the fire and destroy Herra's body? That would explain the mystery messager."

Oliver's chalk flew across his board. "Keep going."

"Alright, um—" I closed my eyes. "We know that Whitley was tricked by the glint-alterer—"

Oliver's scribbling stopped. "Tricked? Why?"

As my mind scrambled through my memories I said, "The glint-alterer probably killed Herra, otherwise Whitley would have learned the truth during the investigation. We know the glint-alterer-aka-murderer can change other people's memories, so the murderer-aka-glint-alterer must be able to change their own memories. Whitley read everyone's glints—and no arrests have been made—so they had to have been tricked by the memory-altering murderer."

Oliver hmmm'd. "You're making assumptions. The glint-alterer-aka-murderer could be two people working together. And I know for a fact that Whitley didn't read everyone's glints because they didn't read mine. During my interrogation, I answered

Whitley's questions out loud."

My eyes flashed open. "You didn't wear your eyelinks for your interview?"

"The government can't force people to use assisted technology," Oliver said without looking up from his board. "Eyelinks are a convenience, not a communication requirement."

"Oh." I closed my eyes, annoyed by Oliver's admission. He was right—the government couldn't make people wear the eyelinks—but his choice made discovering the truth more difficult. What if other people refused to let Whitley read their glints, too?

Then I shook my head. It didn't matter what Whitley read, because *I* knew what everyone glinted. Then I shook my head again: if someone was able to alter glints then—technically—everyone in the Chaleur could have memories that weren't real.

When I said as much to Oliver, he replied, "Don't pull on that filament. We have to assume most people glint authentic thoughts and feelings. The murder—or glint-alterer—has a job and a life. They wouldn't have time to change everyone's memories. Right?"

"Right." I kept going: "You didn't kill Herra—"

"No, I did not."

"—so Jolene's memory isn't real. *I* didn't kill Herra—"

"No, you did not."

"—so Peevish Pear's memory isn't real. Zekiul didn't kill Herra—"

Oliver hand clenched.

"—and neither did anyone else in the Coplot-Champions combo collective. So, who killed Herra? And who is the glint-alterer?"

The wind howled outside, shaking the window frame.

Oliver grabbed a fresh chalkboard off his pile. "What don't we know?"

"We don't know who killed Herra."

Oliver rolled his eyes.

"We don't know who the troublemaker is, or the glint-alterer, or if they're the same person. We don't know why Herra was killed—"

"Yes, that *is* odd," Oliver said, pausing his scribbles. "What did that kid do to make someone kill her?"

"—and we don't know who had the opportunity to kill her. Herra was murdered days before the Champions came to Pluie. I've gone through my memories of that week to see if I heard anyone's aura around Rogers' field, but there wasn't any residue. The town did what it always does: socialize, sleep, and screw."

Oliver choked.

I banged on his back as he coughed, then said, "There wasn't any aural activity around Rogers' that week. Which doesn't make sense."

"What do you mean 'aural' activity?'" Oliver gasped in air, then swallowed as he wiped his eyes. "Is that a glint thing?"

"Um, yes? I thought you knew about auras."

"I don't know anything about the eyelinks." Oliver swallowed again, then went back to his board. "What else don't *we* know—about Herra's murder?"

"That's it. That's everything."

Oliver held up the two chalkboards:

What We Know

- Mother and Dimitri sensed a disturbing glint in a Coplot meeting (September)
- disturbing glinter is a troublemaker, but they aren't Kandle, Smythe, and Pear
- Herra was murdered early in September
- murderer put gasoline in pools
- when Cox set Rogers' field on fire it should have burned Herra's body, but it didn't
- most people glint authentically
- Jolene and Pear's memories were altered, because Layla and I aren't murderers

> ## *What We Don't Know*
>
> WHO KILLED HERRA?
> WHO IS THE GLINT-PLANTER?
> WHO IS THE TROUBLEMAKER?
>
> ARE THEY THE SAME PERSON?
>
> ### WHY WAS HERRA KILLED?

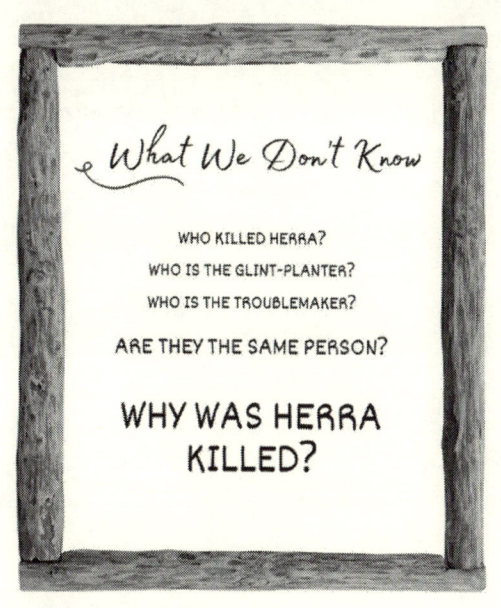

I read the lists, then nodded. "Looks good."

Oliver frowned at the boards. "We define 'good' differently."

"You know what I mean. We can figure out what to do now that we know what we know and what we don't." I leaned closer to the chalkboards. "You have really nice handwriting."

"Mmm."

"Like, *really* nice handwriting."

"Thank you."

"Did you know you can tell someone's mental stability based on their handwriting?"

"That can't be real."

"It is. Dimitri was glinting about it the other day. He's a scientist. He knows things."

"Scientists aren't psychologists, Layla."

"Your printing is pretty, too. I like your swoopy underlines."

"I added a little flair. Not everything is a cake chart."

"Aw, Oli! I love that you're a good listener. Most people are talkers, but people who listen have all the power—" I stared over Oliver's shoulder. Not at his desk, but at a space he couldn't see. My glints took over my mind as a pattern emerged, inspired by my last statement. Blinking, I refocused on Oliver's face. "I have an idea."

Oliver dropped the boards on his lap. "You?"

"I want to check something. On—" I breathed. "On someone. I *knew* we missed something important, but I didn't think—"

I pulled on my hair, hesitant to reveal my theory. Oliver wasn't going to like it.

"I don't think anyone will support this idea," I said. "Not even your mom. Definitely not Dimitri."

"Is it illegal?"

"No, but—" I withdrew into my mind, reviewing the pattern. "It's immoral. Or, morally messy. What I mean is, I don't think people will *want* to believe my idea because it's unpleasant. It isn't romantic."

"Not everything is about romance."

"If I learned anything from snatching glints today—"

"Just today?"

"Alright, not just today. If I've learned anything about people it's that underneath their worries, and distractions, and lists—"

Oliver grinned.

"—underneath everything, people are romantic. They're soft."

Oliver frowned. "That's not good."

"You don't understand." I leaned against the window, trying to find the right words to explain the hopeful emotion I'd sensed that afternoon. "Not 'soft' as in 'weak.' Soft as in sweet. *That* kind of romantic. People, deep down, are gentle. Everyone." I smiled at Oliver. "Whether they admit it or not."

"So, your idea isn't romantic, but because citizens *are* romantic, you think they won't accept it?"

"Some of them might," I said. "Some people are more willing to accept the scarier side of human nature. You know, cynical people. Or people who are self-aware. And smart. If I tell this to the correct people, my idea might be understandable."

"Who are the correct people?"

I stared at my hands. "Khleo would believe me. And Zekiul."

Oliver grunted. "Right."

"And Whitley. Though, they're pretty ooey-gooey under their official persona, so they might not hear me out."

"What is your idea?"

I looked at Oliver's face: his expression was guarded. My idea wasn't going to make him feel better, but I had to tell him. So, I breathed again—seeking a deeper reserve of strength—and said, "I think the glint-alterer is Havu. And I think she's the murdering troublemaker."

Oliver smirked. "Oh, people will believe that. If anyone in this town is a sociopathic mind-fucker it's that little kid."

"Oli!" I giggled, shocked by his use of profanity. Normally, Oliver avoided curse-words as though they crawled with mountain pine beetles.

His eyes twinkled, then he moved across the room to sit beside me on the bench. "I'm sorry."

"It's fine," I said, patting his leg. "I won't tell your mom you cursed."

"Not about that. I'm sorry about—about—" Oliver mumbled as he stared at his bedspread, then he pulled me onto his bed; and rolled me onto my stomach.

For a brief moment, I thought Oliver was about to try a position that had been unsuccessful for both of us in the past, but instead of running his hands down my back to slide off my trousers, Oliver placed his hands on my shoulders. And he *massaged* my shoulders.

Face down on the bed, I grinned. "You *are* sorry."

"It may not have been apparent lately, but I do love you." Oliver's hands melted. His thumbs worked on a knot under my shoulder blade. "I know I push you—and I expect a lot from you—but you have showed me, on more than one occasion, that you can handle it."

"Several occasions," I said, face smushed in Oliver's pillow.

"What?"

I turned my head to the side. "Several occasions. I've handled a lot, extraordinarily well, on several occasions."

Oliver's fingers tensed, but I liked it. Not *like* liked—tingling desire still eluded me—but Oli's strong hands felt good on my tight neck.

"What I'm trying to say—" Oliver said, "—or, what I'm trying to *show*, is that I want to trust you."

"Aw—"

"Let me finish. If you want to find the glint-planter—"

"Ooo! That's clever. It's the opposite of glint-snatcher, and you know how much I like plants—"

"Let me finish." Oliver's massage moved to my lower back. "If you want to take charge of the situation, I support you. I trust you."

I sat up. "What if the glint-planter-murderer-troublemaker isn't Havu?"

"You'll find out the truth," Oliver said. "I trust you."

"What if Whitley gets mad at us? What if Khleo blames *you* for my idea?"

Oliver sighed, then he said through gritted teeth, "I trust you."

"What if I'm wrong and your Coplot agenda gets disrupted again?" I tugged on my hair. "And your lists? And your legacy?"

Oliver grabbed my hands and leaned forward. "Do whatever you want."

That was all I needed to hear. "I'm *not* going to tell anyone my suspicions about Havu. I'm going to discover the truth myself."

CHAPTER TWENTY-FIVE

I started stalking Havu.

Yes, stalking. I knew what I was doing—and I knew it was creepy—but Havu was creepy (and possibly evil) and, sometimes, you had to go low to get a job done.

Because Havu tended to stick to quiet places, or places children didn't play, it was easy for me to find her. I stayed in my trees—moving without rustling even so much as a leaf—and before long I spotted the dark-haired child doing what she always did: strange stuff.

That day, Havu and her blonde friend—

I frowned. Why couldn't I remember the blonde's name? I snapped my fingers as mind found the teen's title: Erika! Havu and Erika, the unlikely duo. There they were, in another bush.

Why did they like bushes so much?

I scaled a pine tree and perched over the girls' heads so I could read their glints: except I didn't have to read their glints. The girls were speaking loud enough to be heard on the other side of town.

Erika picked up a pinecone, then tore it into tiny shreds. "What did your parents want?"

"They're upset." Havu spun her stick in her hands. "Because of Herra. They didn't want me to leave the house. But—" she stabbed the stick into the ground, "—they don't actually care. They didn't stop me when I said we were going to play in the woods."

"Good," Erika said. "They don't have any right to stop you. You're your own person. You can do what you want."

I giggled. Quietly, that time.

Stupid kids, I thought. They think they can do whatever they want? Havu is a baby, for leaf's sake. And Erika isn't much older. Judging by the shape of the blonde's curves and the self-conscious way she adjusted her shirt, she had to be fifteen. Maybe younger.

Fourteen, or even twelve.

I shook my head. I was a disaster at guessing ages. Not that age mattered: thoughts mattered, and actions mattered. Anyone—at any age—was capable of awful thoughts and actions, like glint-planting. I leaned lower on my branch, closer to the girls.

Havu was mid-speech: "—and I'm bored. This place is boring. I'm tired of crushing bugs, and I don't like the network anymore. Can we play another game? Please?"

"Not right now," Erika said. "Maybe during New Year."

Havu pouted. "You said we could play a game *before* New Year. I did what you asked. Why can't we—"

"Havu." Erika raised her hand. "Shut up for a second."

Havu closed her mouth. Sullenly, she poked a wandering slug with her stick until slime oozed out its side.

With her eyes searching the canopy above her head, Erika rose to her feet. She lifted her chin.

The forest rustled, and the pine tree's roots creaked.

Erika smiled.

I grabbed my face.

Sharp pain—constricting pain—pierced my skull. If my legs hadn't been wrapped around the branch in a steel-tight grip I would have fallen. But I'd learned my lesson after snatching Jolene's altered memory, so—as my head shrieked and blood filled my vision—I stayed in the tree.

It saved my life.

When the pain receded, I opened my eyes and checked to make sure I was alright. I didn't taste any blood, and I didn't have a lasting headache, but the girls were leaving: moving farther into the forest. Havu kept chattering about games, and playing, and playing games, and game playing—

—but Erika stayed silent.

Then, as though my head had exploded again, I realized who'd caused the pain. Who had been present at every one of my mind-splitting headaches. Who had the opportunity, strength, and snark to spare.

Who had the ability to manipulate citizens in order to keep her secrets safe.

Erika.

I scrolled through my memories, high in the pine tree: memories that confirmed—with total certainty—Erika's guilt in my gut.

ME
SEPTEMBER 22, 2106

"If it's a test," Erika continues, "We should take out Zekiul Cox."

"That's extreme," Dimitri says, turning to glare at the girl. "Banishment should be our last resort."

Erika crosses her arms. "I didn't say we should banish him."

"What was that?" Dimitri rubs his temple. "Did you glint something?"

"Me?" Erika bats her lashes at Dimitri.

"I could have sworn I sensed an odd—"

ME (VIA DIMITRI ORION SIMARD)
SEPTEMBER 22, 2106

Dimitri sits back. "What's wrong?"

Amelie glances at Oli. "Did you sense that strange glint over the eyelinks?"

"When?" Oli looks upset. "In the Coplot meeting?"

"I sensed something," Dimitri says. "What did you sense, Amelie?"

"Anger combined with—" Amelie pauses. "I'm a little embarrassed to say this, because it's such a strange combination of glints, but I swear I felt excitement. Excitement mixed up in the anger."

ME
SEPTEMBER 24, 2106

"I'm helping Madame Rogers. I didn't know you were playing back here." I smile at Havu. "I wasn't aiming for you, little bug."

"That tool was sharp," Erika says. "You could have killed her. Why did you throw it at us?"

"That is none of your business," I say, being much too kind.

"Go play somewhere else."

Erika gives me a nasty look, then pulls Havu towards Rogers' hill.

I sigh. Then I grab my head. A searing bolt of pain hits my mind out of nowhere. The pain disappears. My head throbs and my glints spin.

ME
SEPTEMBER 24, 2106

"Layla and I need to be going." Amelie lifts her feet out of the mud.

I step on the nearest plank, the one Amelie is already halfway across, and a sharp pain—the same pain from the forest—hits me between the eyes. Gasping, I bend over, clutching my face. Then the pain goes away like before: unexpectedly.

A shrill laugh peals through the forest.

ME
SEPTEMBER 27, 2106

"But Herra was my friend." Erika drags Havu into the Coplot cabin. "You have to let us look for her. It's only fair."

"Don't fuss," Amelie says. "Go home. You'll only get in the search team's way."

"Sure." Erika sneers at me and Oli. "You have enough to worry about."

ME
DECEMBER 5, 2106

I don't stamp my foot. But I want to.

If there's anyone in Chaleur who can help me find the glint-planter, it's Perrault.

With a jolt, my mind splits in two.

The pain disappears.

"Are you alright?" Perrault is in my face, frowning. "Erika can fetch Dr. Munroe."

ME
DECEMBER 5, 2106

Erika looks up, into the trees.

Sharp pain—constricting pain—pierces my skull. If my legs weren't wrapped around my branch I would fall. But I stay in the tree.

It saves my life.

~~~

I opened my eyes.

For the love of leaves. Crumbly couscous! Staying out of Erika's way *had* saved my life. Erika caused my headaches. And—holy holly berries, I was on a roll!—I knew the teen was more than a sneaking, lying, head-splitting sicko. Erika was the glint-planting murderer. She'd been manipulating minds since Rogers' fire. She caused my pain when I got close to learning the truth: close to reading her glints. Why else would she hurt me? Erika had to be guilty!

But I had no evidence. No real evidence, anyway. Without Erika's glint confirmation, my recollections meant nothing. They suggested a possibility instead of proving it.

I leapt out of the pine tree. As I wiped sap off my hands a new idea popped into my mind. Just like I'd breeched Zekiul's mind-world in Mount Champ, I would break Erika's boundaries: by snatching her glints while she slept. Then I'd show Whitley Erika's truth, and Erika would be arrested; and Oliver and I would be safe. It was the perfect plan.

But for some reason, I couldn't move.

CHAPTER TWENTY-SIX

I stood under the pine tree, rubbing the tips of my callused fingers together.

I couldn't think. I had no thoughts. Or feelings. And for a female whose head overflowed with the glints and auras of other people as well as her own, that was a strange sensation. I knew I had to take action—I had to snatch Erika's glints!—but something held me back.

And I had no idea what it was.

So I went for a walk.

The wind rustled the canopy overhead and shifted withered leaves across the mountain pathways as I moved deeper into the forest. I didn't know where I was going. To my cave, maybe? All I knew was that I couldn't stay still.

I climbed higher—past moonlit waterfalls and limestone cliffs—until I reached a flattened pasture midway up Caloscypha Mountain. Without slowing, I walked into the pasture, following a dirt path lined with goldenrods. The clouds shifted, then cleared, and bathed the pasture in light. A series of sulphur ponds appeared, nestled within the grass.

I pulled my hair over my shoulder, then sat on a stone seat placed beside the nearest pool. Normally the sulphur ponds smelled like rotten eggs or burning matches, but the wind blew across the pasture—away from me—so the only scent that rose to my nose was the flowers' honey perfume. The moonlight should have made the sulphuric water glow with an opal sheen, but Dimitri's meteor still hung in the sky, so the ponds looked blue-black, like the exoskeleton of a jewel beetle.

"What are you doing here?"

I swear I jumped six meters into the air before spinning around on the stone seat. With my heart pounding, I bent over—laughing

—when I saw the questioner: Zekiul, who was (apparently) also out for a nighttime stroll.

"I should ask you the same thing," I said after sitting up. "These are my mountains, Cox. I belong here."

Zekiul grinned, then sat beside me. He kicked his long legs out in front of the seat until his boots almost touched the edge of the pond. "I've been restless lately, so I thought I'd clear my head. I haven't explored this side of Chaleur before, but Jolene told me about the sulphur ponds and said I should visit. She discovered them when we first arrived." His eyes warmed as he turned to me and said, "This place is peaceful. I understand why she likes it."

"It is peaceful." The wind picked up, rippling the surface of the water. I shivered.

Zekiul's lip lifted as he unzipped his jacket and placed it over my shoulders. For once, he wore a shirt under his coat, but the tight cotton fabric didn't mask his defined chest.

I looked back at the ponds. The inner fire that was quenched when Oliver tied me to my tree suddenly sparked: which was mortifying. There was a teenaged killer in Chaleur and, instead of proving her guilt, I was sitting in the dark with the most attractive male in Chaleur—in the most romantic spot in the province—tingling with desire and the uncontrollable urge to abandon my principles for one great night with my too-beautiful friend. What was wrong with me?

"Are you okay?" Zekiul's aura fluttered. "You look like you're going to be sick."

"I feel like I'm going to be sick." Yeah, I was going to puke because I was a sex-addicted female who needed to be spanked. No! Not spanked. Removed from society. Maybe I should let Peevish Pear tell everyone I'm the murderer. If I'm put in prison, I can't 'accidentally' tear Zekiul's tight shirt off his hot body.

"What's going on? Did something else happen?"

I glanced at Zekiul. Rather than indulging in my fantasy, I decided to tell him what was on my mind. Or, what wasn't. "Something did happen, but I really shouldn't be talking about it with anyone except—" I stopped.

I was going to say 'Whitley' but, instead, Oliver's name lingered on my lips. Then I realized why I was stuck: the second I found out Erika was the troublemaker I should have gone straight to Oliver. I should have talked with him about snatching Erika's sleep-glints, then asked if he'd come with me to report her crimes to Whitley.

But I hadn't.

"You don't have to tell me anything," Zekiul said. "We can just sit here. Silently."

That wouldn't work either. Talking broke tension, and Zekiul's presence stretched me tighter than molasses taffy between two twigs. "I found out who killed Herra."

Zekiul blinked. "I didn't expect you to tell me *that*."

"I snatched Jolene's glints today. Someone planted an altered memory in her mind that made it look like Oliver killed Herra. So I snatched everyone's glints. That same someone planted an altered memory in Peevish Pear's mind that made it look like *I* killed Herra. So Oli and I talked about it and decided that Havu was the killer—because she's strange, and strange people do strange things—but when I tried to snatch her glints, Erika sent lightning into my head, so I realized *she* had to be the murderer who altered Jolene and Pear's memories, and she's—probably—a diabolical egomaniac because she—probably—likes causing people pain in order to hide her real glints."

Zekiul stared at me, then winced. "Fuck."

"I know!" I spun around to face him. "And I know what I have to do: snatch Erika's glints so I can claim her memories and show Whitley the truth. But I need to talk to Oli about Erika before I tell Whitley, except I can't—" I tugged on my hair. "For some reason, I don't want to tell Oliver what I learned. I want to go to Whitley as soon as I snatch Erika's glints, and I want to snatch Erika's glints right now. But if I don't tell Oliver first he's going to be really angry."

"Angry? Why? It sounds like you—probably—figured out

who killed Herra."

"Oli and I figured out who killed her. We went through the facts together."

"But you did the work." Zekiul tilted his head. "You snatched everyone's glints—"

"Not yours, though. I promise."

"—and you put all the incredibly messed-up pieces together in this incredibly messed-up puzzle. And you still have more puzzle piecing to do. Nobody else can snatch Erika's glints to prove she's the problem. So, nobody else can decide what you should do next." Zekiul glanced at the sulphur ponds, then frowned. "You don't need to talk to Oliver to make this decision, Layla. You're the one who has super glint-reading strength, not him."

"He doesn't know about my strength," I said, compelled to defend Oliver. "He doesn't know anything about glints, or auras. He thinks I'm good at using the eyelinks. I haven't told him about my power."

"Why not?"

I paused. That was a hard question to answer. "Oli doesn't trust the eyelinks. I guess I'm worried he won't trust me if he knows how strong I am. He might think I'm evil, like Min RoboReiwa."

Zekiul grinned, then shook my knee with his hand. "Anyone who knows you would never think you're evil."

My cheeks burned: but they weren't as hot as my leg under the weight of Zekiul's heavy palm. "Oli is complicated. I get the sense he'd be upset if he knew about my strength. I don't know why. I can't read him."

"You've never snatched Oliver's glints?"

"Nope. I love him. If I read his glints without his permission, it would hurt him a lot."

"You're definitely not evil." Zekiul shook my leg again, then winked. "And it's nice to see that you can respect *some* people's boundaries. I must be rubbing off on you."

I smiled. Then I stared at Zekiul's hand. He kept holding onto my knee, and the heat from his grip spread up my thigh and all I could think about was rubbing *him* off and—

For the love of leaves. I was evil.

Zekiul let go of my leg. "It's remarkable how strong you are. I've never met anyone with power like yours. Are your family members gifted readers?"

"I'm not sure." I'd never wondered where my powers came from. "My dad left when I was nine years old, so I don't know much about him. And my mom died when I was a baby. In 2083."

"Oh, shit." The colour drained from Zekiul's face. "During the pandemic?"

"Yup. The Big One."

Zekiul slid across the seat until our sides touched. "I had no idea. I'm so sorry."

"It was a long time ago. And it doesn't matter, right? I don't care why I'm powerful. I just wish I could use my power better."

"You're already exceptional at glint reading. Look at everything you've accomplished these past few months! If it wasn't for you, Erika might have gotten away with Herra's murder."

"She still could. I haven't snatched her glints yet, or told Whitley what I suspect."

"Then go!" Zekiul clutched my shoulders, pretending to shove me off the bench. "Get the evidence. Erika can't get away with murder."

I smiled again, but didn't move. Zekiul's embrace felt nice. "Erika also split heads. And planted glints."

"Then what are you waiting for?" Zekiul stood and held out his hand. "Come on, Layla. You forced me to prove my innocence to the town, so I need you to prove—to me—you're an all-powerful advocate. Fight for justice! I'm on your side."

I stared at his outstretched palm, then lifted my fingers. "Even with my scary calluses?"

"Your whole body could be covered in calluses and I'd still think you were the most incredible person I'd ever met." Zekiul dropped his hand, then flushed. "I mean, incredible friend."

I grinned; and got to my feet. "Admit it, Cox. You love me."

Zekiul's smile split his face, brighter than the moonshine and the glowing meteor. "Very funny."

"You're obsessed with me." I flipped my hair over my shoulder, then walked down the dirt path. "You followed me to the sulphur ponds because you can't get enough Layla."

"Ha ha." Zekiul grabbed his jacket. He joined me as I walked into the woods. "If I was in love with you, Oliver would drown me in sulphur ponds."

"Then I'm glad we're just friends." I didn't look at Zekiul's face. I couldn't. If I did, I knew what I would read: we both wanted more than a friendship, and we both knew it could never happen. I loved Oliver. That wasn't going to change.

"Since we're such good friends, I have to tell you that you're about to do something stupid." Zekiul stopped, forcing me to pause. "You need to snatch Erika's glints tonight and tell Whitley—right away—what you find. Don't worry about Oliver. He's a grown male, Layla, and you're the love of his life." He grabbed my hand, then squeezed—before letting go. "He'll forgive you for doing the right thing."

Without saying another word, we walked down Caloscypha Mountain. I didn't read Zekiul's glints or listen for his aura. The comfortable silence told me everything I needed to know: I'd found a true friend I could trust who made me feel more powerful than my natural abilities ever could. And even though we weren't holding hands, I wasn't going to let him go.

CHAPTER TWENTY-SEVEN

After we reached the town—and Zekiul nodded goodbye—I made my way towards the residential area at the far end of Chaleur's main street.

I knew where Erika lived (I could hear Madame Graham's whining-mosquito aura) so I stood under Erika's bedroom window until the lights were put out and the household fell asleep. It was easy.

And, surprisingly, snatching Erika's glints was even easier. Asleep, the teenager wasn't as strong as I'd thought. Or, I was stronger.

I dove into Erika's mind, then claimed her memories from the entire year.

And I recoiled.

—stupid stupid stupid town, they think they are so superior, they do not know, they do not know know know. How dare they look at me like I am less, how dare Dimitri Simard talk to me like that. AHHH!!! Say words they will accept, feed them lies lies lies. Ha! They believe it. Dimitri Simard is confused. He thinks I am a child, just a silly, silly child—

—Herra Boucher and Havu Boucher are too close, it is not fair not fair. I was pleased when they both listened, but now Herra Boucher wants them to stay home, with their mummy mummy mummy CAPTOR instead of doing what *I* want, what *I* say, what *I* need, NO. Herra Boucher is the problem. Herra Boucher has to go. Havu Boucher belongs to me, belongs to me me me—

—tell Havu Boucher that Herra Boucher wants to hurt her.

Tell Havu Boucher she hates her. Tell Havu Boucher that I am her best friend, her only friend, the only person who will take care of her, forever ever ever. Make Havu Boucher ask me to get rid of her sister. Make Havu Boucher distract my mama so I can do what needs to be done. Tell Havu we are playing a game, play play—

—perfect timing, slowly now, into the wet field where Simone Rogers lets us stay. Ha! Simone Rogers does not let us, I *let* her let us. Stupid farmers, they do not know. Simone Rogers cannot know, she cannot wake up, cannot light her lamp and see me in the dark with her spade and Herra Boucher as I shovel mud over her not fair NOT FAIR face—

—get Havu to siphon gasoline from the Bots in the valley, put the gasoline in a canister, hide the canister under her bed, sneak out after her mummy falls asleep, run to the wet field, pour the gasoline in the pools, oh! Ha HA! Let the games games games keep going—

—flick the lighter, unleash the flame, and run run run back to town, back into bed before the fire reaches the forest—

—make Zekiul Cox think he received a tip about the gasoline. Make Simone Rogers think she spilled secrets on the network. Make Zekiul Cox think he took advantage of Simone Rogers' spill by making him think he set the fire to burn the gasoline. Put the memory of their choices in their deepest, darkest places where they will not look too closely. NO. Ha HA!!! They do not want to look closely at the lies I put in their hearts in case they realize they are true true true true—

—there is a message coming from Mount Champ and the Champions. It is a message from the tree female, the one in the birch. I hate it HATE it. She is strong, her message is from far far away. I do not like her, do not LIKE her. She could see the truth, the true truth TRUE TRUTH. Grab her glints, catch the message. OH! The tree female and Amelie Billadeau have been lying, are being bad, are stealing glints ha HA! I will tell on Amelie Billadeau. Pretend to be a highlander. Tell the Capitol she is a LIAR, but do not report the tree female SHE IS BAD too SMART too too. Hurt Amelie Billadeau, send her to prison, get her gone—

—look at them looking. They do not know! Look at them searching. They cannot see! They blame each other, blame the Champions, which is good gooooood for me. It is easy to get away with—

—I do not like Layla Doug // do not think her name NO NAME NO NAME NO. I do not like the tree female, she sees too deeply and too much. Have to get rid of her, dig her grave, but not too deeply or too much. She has to hurt herself, with her thoughts and feelings and certain certain certainty. Fix the memories again, fix them more, fix them deeper. Make Oliver Billadeau the guilty one to Jolene Jones, such a shame, such potential, and make the tree female the guilty one to Agnes Perrault, not a shame SHE IS BAD. Make them all guilty guilty wrong—

—she knows she knows, I know the tree female knows. Does not matter, it is too late, in the morning Agnes Perrault will go to Georgie Whitley and tell them what she saw. The tree female with the spade. The tree female burying Herra Boucher. The tree female locked in a prison of her own certain certain mind—

—does not matter what they think. Does not matter what they say. I am ERIKA GRAHAM GRAHAM ERIKA, so it only matters what I think and say, what I think and say, what I want and feeeeeeeeeeeel—

I pulled out of Erika's glints, gasping. Her final memory was from that evening. Erika knew I knew she killed Herra. She knew!
But I didn't care.
I gathered my power, then lifted my chin. Braiding my hair into a plait and tucking it into my shirt, I jogged up the main street, heading for the police barracks. I arrived at the single-story wooden structure a few moments later, then I moved into the forest surrounding the back of the building. In the darkness, I channeled my power into the glowing orb and sent it into the barracks. The orb entered a large, rectangular space filled wall-to-wall with bunkbeds that were filled end-to-end with snoring officers.
Whitley wasn't there, so I sent the orb into the barrack's central hallway. Whitley's aura appeared, droning in a private room at the front of the building. Clutching my braid, I gathered my energy and sent the orb directly into Whitley's snoozing subconscious.
COUNCILLOR WHITLEY! WAKE UP!
Their aura peaked as Whitley jolted in their bed, disoriented. I used their half-aware state of mind to my advantage and took over Whitley's mind. I forced them to roll off their bed, into their boots, and out the barrack's back door. They stumbled into the forest, their mind screaming in panic.
"It's me! It's Layla," I whispered, steadying Whitley as they jerked to my side.
As soon as their glints calmed, I released my grip on Whitley's body. They leapt away, backing into a Western Red cedar after they realized what I'd done. "How could you—how on Earth is it *possible* you—"
I raised my finger to my lips, shushing the confused councillor. "I can explain. But not here. Can we go to Khleo's office? I know who murdered Herra."
Whitley's aura peaked. After they regained control (impressively fast) they said, "Lead the way."

We walked along the main street, sticking to the lamplight's shadows, then we snuck up the mayoral cabin's front steps, across the wraparound porch, and into Khleo's office.

After I showed them my memories, Whitley's jaw looked as though it was about to unhinge. "You're a strong natural glint reader? And you can control people's bodies?"

I nodded. "And I can snatch glints, if I have to."

Whitley's eyes scanned my face as they sat on Khleo's chair. Their spine was so straight it could have been made of Bot-metal. "How do I know *you* haven't altered your glints?"

"You don't." I shrugged. "I could be lying. But I'm not."

Whitley's jaw spasmed, but their droning aura confirmed what I already knew: Whitley believed me, even though my story—and memories—were unbelievable. "Here's what has to happen next: I'm going to summon Erika and her mother, Madame Graham, here tomorrow morning."

"Why are you questioning Erika's mom?"

"I'm not. Erika is fourteen. She's a minor. Her parent has to be present. I could bring in an officer who's certified in sociology, but our child-psych expert stayed behind in the Capitol." Whitley opened the top button of their pinstriped pajama collar and cracked their neck, which was the most movement I'd ever seen Whitley, well, move (other than when I controlled their limbs). "I'll show the Grahams the memories you claimed, then ask Erika contradictory questions while I insult her abilities. It's a tactic that works with arrogant criminals. It confuses them and hurts their pride. If Erika is like the other riff-raff I've dealt with, she'll admit to her crimes."

"Why are you telling me this?" It was out of character for the councillor to be candid with a civilian.

Whitley didn't need to answer. Their glints practically shouted, You already know why. You can read glints, so you'll find out what I plan to do eventually. You're reading my glints right now. Right, Layla? "I never—in a thousand years—would've guessed Herra's killer was a kid," Whitley said after I shot them my *I'm-*

sorry smile. "And that two abnormally-strong natural glint readers lived in Chaleur: Erika and you. Makes you wonder if people like Min RoboReiwa are actually unique."

Tucking that point away for later rumination (*more* people like me?) I said, "Erika isn't just a killer."

"No," Whitley said. "She's not. I'll charge her with lying, theft, coercion, spreading false News on the network, glint-snatching, *and* murder. Everything you saw her doing. By the way . . ." They stood, pushing their unbrushed white hair off their face. "What you've done is illegal, too. I should charge *you* with glint-snatching. You broke into Erika's mind, and Zekiul Cox's."

Cox's, Cox's, Cox's—

"Speaking of Cox, his fire-starting incident will formally be removed from his record, since he didn't actually start the fire. And I know Cox doesn't care you snatched his glints," Whitley tapped their temple, "but the government does."

"But snatching glints helped catch Erika. I figured out who committed a premeditated murder, pretty much by myself."

"Pretty much?"

"Um, yes." I'd hidden my glints that showed me and Oliver scheming. "Completely by myself."

"We haven't caught Erika yet," Whitley said. "Your snatched evidence was obtained illegally, so she has to confess."

And she did. Twenty minutes after Whitley hauled the Grahams into the mayoral offices the following morning, a squad of officers was called in. Ten minutes after that, Madame Graham left the office—weeping—and Erika was dragged, literally kicking and screaming, into the Provincial Police barracks.

"I don't care if she's fourteen," Whitley said to Khleo that afternoon (who later told Amelie, who later told Oliver, who immediately told me). "That girl is troubled. Her mother didn't want to believe it, but Erika admitted everything. She seemed proud of her crimes. But when my officers arrived, she changed her tune. It would be best for the country if that girl was placed in a permanent holding facility—you know, a life sentence—but her mother begged me to put her in rehab. But, between us—" Whitley said to Khleo (who said to Amelie, who said to Oliver [aka me]), "—no amount of rehab will change the way that girl glints. There's something not right with her. Not right, at all." They placed a finger on their nose. "But this stays between us, Monsieur Mayor. It doesn't look good for the Reclamation Party if the public finds out we're stuffing teenagers into prisons. Sorry—*not* a prison. It's rehab. Though, like I said, no amount of rehab will fix Erika Graham. When she gets out in six to eight months, some other community will have to deal with her problems. And she will cause problems. I guarantee it. Not that I can do anything about it. She's a minor, so her record is sealed. But Erika Graham will hurt someone else, and it won't be a little kid she has a petty grievance against. I guarantee it."

Whitley dealt with me next. After explaining everything to Khleo (who later told Amelie, who—for some reason—did *not* tell Oliver) the councillor and the mayor insisted I never intrude upon a citizen's privacy again. For any reason. No matter what.

"You aren't going to be charged with a Glint Crime—this time," Whitley said as the three of us stood nose-to-nose-to-nose inside Khleo's tiny office, "but the Reclamation Party is giving you a warning. Your snatching is going on your record for five years, but if you stay out of people's heads, we'll clear it."

"I had no idea you were insane, Layla." Khleo sprawled across his desk, wiggling his feet with impatience. "Not going to lie, I'm totally judging Oli for dating you. Only a crazy person would fall in love with a wacko."

"The Justice Department in every province has been notified, and your National ID has been Red Flagged. If you move to a different city within the next few years, any glint-snatching activity will be noted and your warning will immediately turn into a criminal charge: a retroactive criminal charge."

"What were you thinking? Are you that fucked up?"

"The Reclamation Party appreciates that you were trying to help—and your unconventional choices did lead to the arrest of a murderer—but your behaviour is unacceptable."

"What the fuck, Layla? What the fuck?"

"Mayor Billadeau has agreed to keep this matter between us, so nobody else in the town knows about your abilities—"

"What the fuck?"

"—which means you can return to your normal life, but I cannot stress enough how important it is you learn to control your powers and *not* use them." Whitley stared at me, unmoving. "Do you understand?"

I nodded at the floor. "I understand."

What the fuck, Layla? Khleo leapt off the desk. "What the fuck?"

And that was the end of the investigation. Erika admitted to murdering Herra, starting the fire, and planting glints in Zekiul, Rogers, Jolene, and Peevish Pear's minds. She *was* a troublemaker. But Havu wasn't implicated in any of it: Whitley said they couldn't stomach punishing an innocent child since it was clear the twin wasn't twisted like her blonde counterpart. So the Coplot resumed our meetings, Zekiul and the Champions stayed to maintain the alliance, and Oliver went back to tackling his agenda (undisturbed).

I went back to my birch. I'd neglected its care during the town drama. My tree's branches drooped, its mint green leaves were pale, and thick weeds wound around the roots. It needed a little love, which I willingly provided.

As Pluie plunged into the deepest part of winter—and the rain and wind fell harder and blew faster—I tended the grove. I sliced away the weeds, cleared the trees' densely packed twigs that sported stunted leaves, and tilled the soil until every birch in the grove hummed with health.

Surrounded by life—and purpose—I should have been happy. Really happy.

But I wasn't.

In the middle of a healthy forest, my birch tree should have thrived.

But it didn't.

I had no idea why. And, for once, I didn't know what to do.

But I did know I wasn't going to stop using my powers, no matter what Whitley—or the government—threatened.

PART FOUR

"We can't let anything stop us this time."
Oliver Billadeau

CHAPTER TWENTY-EIGHT

"Well, now."

Amelie sat beside Khleo in the Coplot cabin, tugging the waistband of her trousers over her love handles. "Well, well. Well."

"Now that the unnecessary violence is over," Oliver said, "can we start the meeting?"

The rest of the Compassion Coplot's leadership team sat—and stood—in their typical places, debriefing. I sat in my typical place, recording the atypical meeting: which was the only task Khleo allowed me to take on after Whitley let me go uncharged. There wasn't going to be a Coplot promotion. Ever.

I didn't care, though.

That afternoon, Erika had been escorted to Fairfield by a squadron of Provincial Police officers. Her mother—along with Havu's parents—were in the process of relocating to a different community. They didn't want to stay in a town where their private problems had been made public.

That *morning*, Oliver and I sat in my grove, under my wilted birch.

"The Bouchers shouldn't leave." I stroked Oliver hair as he lay in my lap, hoping the easy energy that once flowed between us would return, but my fingers were stiff and Oliver didn't melt. "Havu deserves a second chance. I know she was part of the problem, but she was manipulated by Erika. Now she has to start over somewhere else. And Havu sucks at socializing. So do her parents. We could help them if they stayed here."

"Havu isn't innocent," Oliver said, tight-lipped. "She helped Erika. Regardless of Havu's potential, she's too much of a risk. We can't let anything distract us again. I can't—can't do it." He shut his eyes. "It's been too much, Layla. I need it to stop."

I nodded, then wound my fingers through Oliver's. But I didn't understand. I knew how Oliver *felt*: I didn't have to read his glints to know he was stressed. But I didn't get why he thought Havu would become a problem on her own. Without Erika, Havu had the chance to start fresh. I knew she'd be alright. I knew it.

But Oliver didn't. And he wouldn't listen to me.

"Don't forget, Jolene thought I was a murderer." Oliver picked up a handful of loose stones and tossed them, one at a time, on the ground. "That can't happen again. Erika might be gone, but I'm still a leader in this town and I have a reputation to maintain. Nobody will trust me if they believe I'm a bad guy."

I should have paid attention when Oliver said that, but all I could sense was his pain.

Like his brother, Khleo wanted the Bouchers and Madame Graham to leave. He wanted Chaleur to process what happened and move on, which was why the Coplot leadership team had gathered that afternoon. Khleo wanted to discuss our upcoming Party status submission and get back on track. But things couldn't go back to normal. Not the way they'd been before.

The officers hanging around the town while Whitley wrapped things up proved it.

After we left my grove, Oliver and I made our way to the Coplot cabin; and Dimitri joined us on route. "I thought I saw you two up ahead. Are you ready for the meeting?"

"As ready as we can be." I smiled at Dimitri shyly. He'd been nice to me since our night on the roof. He didn't know about my glint-snatching—and that I'd told Whitley about Erika—and I worried he suspected something, but Dimitri didn't push, or press, or lecture me in any way. We stayed cordial. Almost friendly.

I liked it. "Are *you* ready for the meeting?"

"I suppose." Dimitri smiled and his green eyes folded into the crinkles made by his cheeks. "If I'm being honest, I've spent more time studying space these past few weeks than I have thinking about town matters. In fact, I wanted to talk to you, Layla."

"Me?" I stopped, holding Oliver in place. "What about? Am I in trouble?"

"Of course not." Dimitri pointed at the sky: at the indigo spectre rising over the top of Niccola Peak. "I wanted to talk to you about our meteor. The purple one we spoke about."

Warmth flooded my cheeks. Tears almost flooded my eyes. "*Our* meteor?" I whispered, using my power to control my sudden surge of emotion. I couldn't believe Dimitri remembered the details of our conversation, let alone thought they were meaningful.

But before I could say 'Yes! Yes! Let's talk about our meteor right now!' a loud *blast!* exploded in the centre of the town.

Wide-eyed, I spun around. A dense, dark aura hummed over Chaleur like a cumulus cloud, but nobody else could hear it.

"Something's happening by Khleo's office." I tugged Oliver's sleeve as I said to Dimitri, "We have to run. Hurry!"

We hurtled towards the main street, skidding to a stop when we saw what was happening: the Provincial Police officer who'd stepped on Zekiul was standing in front of the mayoral offices, screaming at Amelie.

Who shrieked back. "I don't care what you say! I don't care what anyone says!" Amelie waved her arms as she backed the officer into the porch. "If you touch a single hair on another citizen's head while you remain in Chaleur, I will squash you flatter than a freckle on a fruit fly!"

The officer sputtered, and his face turned pink. "Get away from me!" He shouted over his shoulder, "Whitley! The locals have lost it!"

Whitley stuck their head out the office door. "What is going on?"

"This shit-kicking officer beat up one of my leaders." Amelie placed her hands on her hips. "He kicked Cox while he was down. I wanted to deal with it discretely, but he—" she glared at the officer, "—had to make a scene."

"I'll give you a scene, lady," the officer snarled.

"I'd like to see you try." Amelie drew back her fist. Whitley yelped and tore across the porch. Khleo stuck his head out the cabin door, then shouted, "Mom!"

As Whitley and Khleo tried to pull Amelie off the officer, Zekiul appeared behind me. "For fuck's sake," he whispered in my ear. "Is this about me?"

I nodded, smirking.

Oliver grumbled, "Look what you started, Cox."

"I didn't start this. I thought *this* was over because we played the pranks. I didn't ask Amelie to go after the guy." Zekiul grinned as Amelie's shrieks hit a higher pitch. "Your mom's approach is effective, though. Look at Officer Dillweed. He doesn't know what to do with himself."

Sure enough, Amelie had broken out of Whitley and Khleo's grip and was smacking Officer Dillweed with her flattened palm. "We—do—not—use—feet—to—share—feelings!" Amelie cried, hitting the officer on every word.

"Mom!" Khleo looked mortified. He stood—frozen—behind Whitley, who was rolling up their sleeves as though they had to prepare for battle.

The officer ducked away, then ran up the street. Baring his teeth, he snapped at Amelie, "Back down, you bitch!"

It took Whitley, Dimitri, Zekiul—and Jolene, who showed up out of nowhere—three minutes to pull Amelie and Khleo off the officer. Oliver stayed on the sidewalk, muttering about 'blood,' but I helped by taking over Officer Dillweed's mind to freeze his body. I couldn't let him get away before Whitley put him in handcuffs.

I also sent a wave of soothing sound into everyone's minds: the string-like hum of a chorus of grasshoppers. In the numbing haze, the Coplot leadership team stumbled into the cabin, followed by a snickering Zekiul and the sluggish Jolene.

"I don't know what got into me," Amelie said as Dimitri handed her a cup of water. "One second I was heading here, and the next thing I know I'm giving that officer a firm talking-too. Suddenly, bam!" She clapped her hands together. "He's backed into the building and crying like a kid."

"Mom." Khleo sat on his chair, shocked. "Mom!"

"I'm sorry, Le-Le, but there have to be consequences when

people make mistakes. Citizens can't keep hurting each other."

Dimitri squinted as he leaned against his window. "But you can hurt people?"

"Well, now," Amelie sputtered. "Well."

"Now that the unnecessary violence is over," Oliver said, striding towards the storage room, "can we start the meeting?"

We settled in our places.

Khleo crossed his legs, then said, "How long is your list now, Oli?"

"It isn't helpful to focus on the entirety of his list," Dimitri said. "I recommend we break it down. Tackle each item one at a time."

"I was joking," Khleo snarled. "I know how the Compassion Coplot works."

"Item One: Change the name of the party, " I said, half-joking. "Compassion Coplot is too long. We need a name that's catchy, and easy to remember."

"Changing the name we've used for years isn't Item One. It's Item One Thousand and One." Oliver sat behind the leadership table, then looked at the chalkboard he'd grabbed from the storage room. "No. Item One Million and One."

"If we aren't the Compassion Coplot, who are we?" Khleo thrust his camo-canvas sneaker in my direction. "Enlighten us."

"Weeeeeeell," I drawled. "We could call ourselves the Awesome Party."

Khleo's mouth quirked. "Love it."

"Or the Tolerant Party," I said. "Or the Better-Than-Every-Government-Ever Party."

"Because Better-Than-Every-Government-Ever Party *isn't* too long," Oliver said.

"Are we really going to apply for Party status? Still?" Dimitri asked. "We're months behind. Wouldn't it be better to wait and submit before the next election?"

"The next election is next fall," Oliver said. "We have to send in our submission next month."

"Not that election," Dimitri said. "The *next* next election."

"In four years?" Oliver swung around to glare at Dimitri. "No! That's not going to happen. Tell him, Mother."

"Coplot business is town business, and town business is Khleo's purview. I've learned my lesson after the whole . . ." Amelie waved her hand over her head. "The officer business. I've clearly lost my touch. I shouldn't have approached that shit-kicker." She blushed. "Sorry."

"Language, Mumsy."

"I *said* I was sorry."

"Well?" Oliver glared at Khleo. "Tell Dimitri we won't wait!"

"Uh, we need to consider all the options," Khleo said with a sharp nod. "Every voice is important."

"No!" Oliver clenched his hands. "I don't accept this. We've been working too hard, and for too long, to abandon our plan. I will not wait four years to apply. Who knows where we'll be in four years!"

"Oli," I called from the back of the cabin. "Nobody's going anywhere."

"My mother was put in jail this year, Layla." Oliver spun around. "Jail. And a girl was murdered by a teenager nobody noticed. And the Champions are our allies. Look how much has changed. You can't guarantee this group is going to stay together for four more years. You can't!"

"Those are excellent points," Khleo said. "Layla, are you recording this?"

"Of course," I lied. I didn't have to consciously record anything anymore. My natural ability was so strong I could recall everything that happened without any effort.

"Does anyone have anything to add?" Khleo snapped his fingers at Jolene, who lumbered in her corner. "Can you grab us some drinks? We're going to be here a while."

Zekiul shifted on his seat as Jolene left the cabin, mumbling to herself. Her glints reeled as she attempted to figure out how many trips she needed to take from Peevish Pear's market and back to the cabin in order to bring everyone a bottle.

"We'll have to work overtime to get the application ready," Dimitri said. "The government won't accept our submission unless it's perfect."

"Oli has been working overtime for weeks," I said. "His list is shorter than it should be because he's stayed up late, every night, keeping us on schedule. Right, Oli?" I smiled at Oliver, but he refused to look at me.

Instead, Oliver stared at Zekiul, whose aura zoomed after Khleo's abrupt dismissal of Jolene.

"Don't worry," Zekiul said after swallowing his irate glints, "the Champions can pick up the slack."

"That's right." I leaned towards Dimitri, pointedly. "Things aren't as disastrous as you design."

"That sounds alright, but be honest," Dimitri said. "Can we complete every item on Oliver's list in order to get the submission prepared so it meets the government's standards? In three weeks?"

"It's possible." Amelie smiled around the room. "This group is the most capable—and resilient—assembly of people in Canuckia. Oliver's dream for a brighter future is attainable. If we stick to his plan, I believe the Compassion Coplot will be accepted as an official government party and we'll be voted into power next fall."

The leaders' tense auras eased.

"Yeah," Khleo said, after a reassuring pat from his mom. "And if we're not voted into power, the Billadeaus will definitely land seats in parliament."

"Or the Coplot might become the official opposition," Zekiul added. "Wouldn't that be great? We could take on the Reclamation Party where *our* ideas make a difference."

Oliver's cheeks burned. "That's the plan."

"Well, now!" Amelie perked up. "Le-Le?" She ginned at her son. "Shall we—I mean, you—begin assigning duties?"

"Good catch, Mumsy."

"I'm getting there," Amelie said. "Slowly but surely. Le-Le?"

"I shall." Khleo clicked his heels together. "Oliver? Did you send your agenda to Layla?"

"I did."

He had—the night before—when I visited him in his attic to explain why I hadn't told him about my plan to snatch Erika's glints and report her to Whitley: an explanation he sort-of accepted. I didn't tell Oliver about my pep talk with Zekiul, though. I didn't have to apologize for everything I did without Oliver's knowledge.

"Peachy keen, Lima Bean," Khleo said. "Layla, project the plan so everyone can see it."

I blinked. Oliver's agenda appeared on the wall.

Dimitri sniffed. "That is a tight timeline."

Khleo rolled his eyes. "Loosen up, Dimitri."

"My point, Monsieur Mayor—" Dimitri said, "—is that there isn't any room for error on Oliver's schedule."

"Then we won't make an error," Khleo said. "*You* might, but the rest of us will be perfect."

"What if something happens in the next three weeks?" Dimitri asked. "Something bad? Again? If anything goes wrong in the town, or the country—or the world—we won't get our application finished. Shouldn't we come up with a contingency, just in case?"

"The world, Dimitri?" I snorted into my fingers. "The *world*?"

"Yes," Dimitri said, narrowing his eyes. "The world could end, and we'd never get to submit."

"You think the 'something bad' that will stop our submission is the end of the world?" I had to laugh. "The *end* of the *world*?"

Dimitri shrugged. "Anything is possible. The purple meteor is getting close to Earth. Closer than I expected. For all we know, it could be a comet and smack into the planet. It might destroy a village, or a city, or—"

"We get you," Amelie said, "but Khleo's right. You could loosen up a little. We don't need a contingency."

Oliver frowned at the wall projection. "Maybe we do."

"You agree with Dimitri?" I leaned forward, giggling. "You think a *comet* is going to kill us?"

"I agree with an idea that makes sense," Oliver said. "And a contingency makes sense. We can't let anything get in our way."

"Oli." Amelie reached for her son's hands, but before she could make contact, Oliver shoved them in his sweater pockets. Amelie sighed. "I know these last few months have been rough, but we need to relax. If we don't, we'll bust. And if we bust, we'll make poor decisions. Canuckians need us to be smart. For the country."

"Yeah, Oli." Khleo sneered. "You want what's best for the country, right?"

"I'll change the schedule," Oliver said. "It's not difficult to add a contingency."

"Son." Amelie shifted on her seat. "We've got this. We'll be able to apply for Party status next month. Nothing's going to go wrong."

I thought about Amelie's statement—later that night—after Whitley entered the Coplot cabin with their news. And I thought about Oliver's stubborn certainty when Dimitri and I returned home. And I thought about pushing Dimitri off his roof instead of maintaining our fragile friendship, because he wouldn't stop smiling.

Dimitri didn't like a lot of things, but—apparently—he loved being right.

CHAPTER TWENTY-NINE

"Son of a bitch!" Oliver hollered the next morning after I took him to my grove to vent his pent-up frustration.

Frustration wasn't the right word. Oliver was out of control. He stormed around the rain-drenched grove kicking tree trunks, overturning logs, and swearing like a Curse-Bot: my favourite Bots.

"Don't call your mom that," I said, covering my head with my hand. I tried to ignore the downpour as I watched Oliver try to turn over a boulder. "Amelie is a badass, and she doesn't deserve your anger—"

"Layla!" Oliver leapt in the air, pulling on a branch to break it.

"Don't hurt my trees, Oli. They don't deserve your anger, either."

"Layla, for the love of leaves, if you don't—" Oliver stalked across the grove, then collapsed. He sank into the moss at my feet, burying his face in his hands. "I can't believe this. Four years," he groaned. "We have to wait another four years. The Reclamation Party will be in power for four more years." Oliver looked up. "Do you know what that means?"

I grabbed Oliver's hand and kissed the tips of his fingers. "Corrupt politicians, government officials who lie to the public because they don't think we can handle the truth, rations forever, rust forever, confusion forever, apathy forever—"

Oliver groaned again. "For four more years."

I sat with Oliver in silence, holding his hands as the rain fell.

The news Whitley told us the night before had been bad. So bad, I couldn't believe I hadn't seen it coming.

When the Boucher's were packing up their house, Havu escaped and followed Erika—and her escort—to Fairfield. Havu stole an officer's nuclear baton, revved up the power, then tasered the entire squad. Erika and Havu ran away.

Whitley was inconsolable. *I should have prevented this*, their glints cried as they knocked on the cabin's door, readying themself to tell us what happened. *I knew Erika was rotten. I could have kept Havu here until she was safely locked away. Why didn't I stop her?*

Nobody blamed Whitley, but the Provincial Police had to stay in Chaleur until the girls were found, which would definitely take longer than three weeks. And Whitley needed our help. They sent Zekiul—and the Champions—back to their base so the officers could live in Mount Champ while they searched for the girls. Which meant the Compassion Coplot—or, name-to-be-determined Party—had lost a leader and a team of support staff.

Oliver was a wreck; and I wasn't sure if my life would include happiness in my grove again.

That following morning, Oliver stared at me as water ran down his face. He looked like he was crying. "What am I supposed to do, Layla?"

His pleading broke my heart. But I couldn't fix it. "We have to be patient, and help the Provincial Police." I was going to work with Whitley and scan the mountainside for Erika and Havu's auras, though Oliver didn't know that. I still hadn't told him about my natural power. The last thing he needed was another complication in his already chaotic life.

"I hate this," Oliver said. "I wish I could find those girls and make them—" He looked over his shoulder towards the break in the trees. "You know whose fault this is, don't you?"

"Yes," I said, wiping rain off Oliver's furrowed brow. "Erika and Havu's."

"No." Oliver turned around. "It's my mother's fault."

I blinked. "How do you figure that?"

"If she hadn't gotten arrested she'd still be in power, instead of Khleo—who's incompetent. Why did my mother make him mayor?" Oliver staggered to his feet and laughed until his voice broke. "Oh, right," he gasped. "My mother is incompetent, too!"

"Oli—" I scrunched up my nose. "You don't mean that."

Oliver's words came out in wheezes. "I'm right about this. If my mother had remained in her role, she wouldn't have let the Provincial Police come to Chaleur. And they wouldn't have been able to, because my mother wouldn't have a criminal record. Whitley respects citizens who don't have criminal records."

"Khleo doesn't have a criminal record."

"Khleo is an idiot and everyone knows it."

"Oli! If your mom was the mayor, Whitley—and the Police—still would have come here. A child was murdered."

"No." Oliver shook his head. Water flew out of his sandy hair. "I know my mother. She would have let us handle Herra's death."

I reached for Oliver's fingers. "This isn't your mom's fault. If it was, it would be mine, too. She got arrested because Erika intercepted my message, remember?"

"I'm very aware you haven't been adequately punished for your glint-snatching, Layla."

"Hey!" I leaned away, raising my hands. "If I hadn't glint-snatched everyone in the town, we never would have found out that Erika was a killer and Havu was her horrible henchperson."

"But we *would* be able to apply for Party status in three weeks."

"Are you saying Erika should have gotten away with murder so the Coplot could make your time target?"

"It's my legacy, Layla!" Oliver clenched his hands as he hollered at the sky, "Why don't you understand what I'm trying to do here?"

"I understand," I said, leaning against my birch. "Your legacy is more important than the people who love you."

The roots under my tree crackled.

Oliver stared at me. "Erika and Havu don't love me."

"Your mom loves you. *I* love you. And you're talking about me—and your family—like we don't matter."

"Stop, Layla."

"Do you know what love looks like?" I stepped forward. "Do

you know how to love someone?"

"I said, stop!" Oliver roared, then lurched towards the forest.

"Oliver!" I yelled as he ran out of the grove. "Where are you going?"

"I'm going to find those girls," he called, "and protect my legacy!"

I sagged under my birch tree's sheltering canopy, watching him run away. The pines circling the grove rustled, even though the wind died down as Oliver disappeared.

A single heart-shaped leaf fell to the ground.

I didn't notice.

Because as soon as Oliver vanished, I gathered my power and dove into Khleo's mind. *I need you. Oli's in trouble.*

Oliver's brother appeared by my side two minutes later, sucking air in through his nose. "Where did he go?"

I closed my eyes. I could sense Oliver's aura zooming around Dimitri's property. "That way," I said, pointing. "If we cut him off, we can talk to him before he does something stupid."

Khleo peppered me with questions as we headed into the woods. "He blames our mom?"

"Yes."

"And you?"

"Yes. And you."

"What a dick. But not the girls?"

"He blames the girls, too," I said as we jogged up a path. "He wants to punish them."

Khleo rolled his eyes and laughed. "My brother is insane. Always has been. What does he think he'll accomplish if he hurts two little kids?"

"Erika isn't little."

"You know what I mean," Khleo said as we slowed to hike up a steep incline. "If he finds Erika and Havu—and hurts them—the girls will still go to rehab, and he'll be thrown in prison." He stepped over a puddle. "Bye-bye, legacy."

"And the Coplot," I said. "It'll be finished without Oli."

"Yeah. The Compassion Coplot needs a united Billadeau front to be successful."

I looked at Khleo out of the corner of my eye. Oliver's brother rarely showed real enthusiasm for the Coplot's future—despite his role in the local government—so his sudden commitment seemed strange. Carefully, I read Khloe's glints: but they didn't tell me anything new.

Hey. There he is. "Look. There he is." Khleo turned towards a line of shrubbery that shook as though someone had recently pushed through it. "Good thing we're fast."

"And subtlety isn't Oli's strength." I grinned at Khleo, grateful to have him there. "How do we want to tackle this? Good Officer, Bad Officer? You scream in Oli's face while I kiss it?"

"I have a better idea," Khleo said. "I'll tackle Oli."

We reached the field in front of my house as Oliver stalked through the grass. Picking up our pace for the final strides, we intercepted him (or, I hung back while Khleo flung himself on his brother and pinned Oliver to the ground).

"AHHH!" Oliver yowled, spitting dirt out of his mouth.

"Listen to me, baby bro." Khleo positioned his broad body on top of Oliver's leaner one. "You are not going to hurt those girls. Do you get me?" he asked, doing his best imitation of Amelie.

"What is wrong with you?" Oliver scowled, then wiggled to get free. "I'm not going to hurt anyone."

"Botshit," Khleo said. "Layla told me everything."

In that moment, I realized Oliver hadn't told me he was looking for the girls so he could punish them. It was something I'd read. Without realizing it.

I was getting stronger.

I shrugged innocently, then said, "I know you, Oli."

"You think I'd hurt those girls?" Oliver turned his harrowed eyes in my direction. "Layla."

I winced. I wanted to spend the rest of my life with Oliver, but I could never tell him what I was reading in that moment. Not only was he capable of hurting the girls, but he also wanted to hurt me, and his brother, and the whole town, and—

I shook my head to get rid of his glints. Oliver was upset. He didn't mean any of it.

"Get off me," Oliver said, wiggling harder. "Damn it, Khleo. When did you get so heavy?"

"I've been working out." Khleo pushed his palms into Oliver's shoulders. "You never know when a politician might need to get rough."

"You?" Oliver snorted. "Mayor Sparkly Sneakers?" He jerked again, then stilled.

The rain fell harder.

Under the rhythmic patter of water droplets, Oliver's aura settled. "I'm not going to hurt Erika and Havu," he said. "Please let me go. It's wet. And I'm wet. And I'm tired. And—"

Khleo climbed off his brother. He pulled Oliver to his feet, then smiled over at me. "See?"

I did see. Sometimes family made all the difference.

"Come on." Khleo slipped his arm through Oliver's. "Let's get you home and dry."

Oliver shot me a mournful look as his bother pulled him away. My heart melted. "It's alright, Oli. We all have bad days."

"Bad years, Layla," Oliver said as Khleo steered him towards the path that led to the Billadeau's property. "It's been the worst year of my life."

"Come on, Grumpy Garlic." Khleo patted Oliver's arm. "You'll feel better soon. Mom's with Whitley in my office, but she'll be home in an hour. We can make a new agenda, with new lists. You'll be alright."

I wanted to follow them, but I sensed what Oliver needed: support from his mom and brother. So I lifted my fingers in goodbye.

Oliver stopped, staring back at me. "I love you, you know. I'm not good—I'm not good at showing it. You were right. I need— I need—" He clenched his hands. "I'll do better."

"You'll do better *after* you dry off and eat some food." Khleo pulled Oliver towards the forest. "And after you get some sleep.

I'm locking your chalkboards in Mom's den for a month."

I stood in the field, in the rain, as the Billadeaus headed home. I stayed until the downpour let up, and a beam of sunlight pushed through the clouds.

Oliver *was* going to be alright. But he—no, we!—had work to do: real work, if we wanted to have a real relationship. And I had to keep my power a secret until Oliver was back to his stoic self.

But I needed him to feel better soon. If Oliver found out I was a natural glint-reader from Khleo, or his mom, he'd never forgive me. A betrayal like that would end our relationship. I knew it would.

Again, I was wrong.

A ray of sunshine fell across my face and I looked up, distracted.

I forgot about Zekiul, and my abilities; and Oliver.

In the sky, passing in front of the sun—within the space created by the tops of the trees—a huge, swollen spectre of fire crossed the clouds. A purple spectre, with heat and black smoke trailing in its wake. There was a comet in the sky. And it was heading for Earth.

I couldn't believe what I was seeing.

It was the end of the world.

CHAPTER THIRTY

I saw the end.

Fire came from the sky. It *fell* from the sky. I was helpless. My powers couldn't do a thing to stop it. The comet made that clear.

When the News Alert network flashed its warning over the eyelinks and the world witnessed the indigo orb descending from the clouds, fear descended on the global population. They saw. They knew. And they accepted what was to come. There was nothing *anyone* could do to stop it. The world shouldered its fear and stood, side-by-side, in silent solidarity.

But when I stood in the field outside my home and looked up, I was affected differently than the rest of the planet. I didn't see the comet. I didn't feel its heat on my face, or the dry, brittle wind trailing in its wake. I felt the collective soul of the world scream. And it broke me.

My mind snapped, clean in two. If anyone nearby had looked away from the sky, away from the comet, they would have seen a girl with walnut-coloured hair trembling from head to toe as I grappled with the magnitude of what I faced. Because it *was* the end. Of everything. I felt that certainty inside billions of hearts. Even if we survived the comet's collision, my world—the world, *our* world—was over.

After I snapped, a hole remained. A large hole, larger than a meteor. Larger than death. I didn't know a human could hold a hole inside their body. I didn't know it was possible to be empty and, at the same time, filled with suffering. I didn't know what it meant, or how I could keep going when I was hollow. When *I* was death.

When I was dead.

How? I wondered as the comet drew closer. How do you live when you aren't alive? How do you look people in the eye without them seeing your secret? What kind of person can survive when they carry death everywhere they go?

These were the glints—reflections—within my broken mind that I had the luxury of experiencing. Because I was frozen, *not* dead, and I knew my body would make it through the comet's collision. I knew with the same certainty that sustained me during my dad's disappearance, during a lonely upbringing with a distant male, during the Bot War, and during the years order had been restored.

Order was over, too. I knew that. I was certain chaos would come, and I was certain there wasn't a single person on the planet who was equipped to deal with the aftermath.

I was right. But, again, I wouldn't know that for sure—I wouldn't have proof—for a long time. The comet had to hit, and the ending had to arrive, for my predictions to come true.

So I stood, staring at the sky with the others—with the living and the damned—and glinted my glints. Broken in pieces with a hole in place of a soul, I waited.

I didn't have to wait long.

The comet came. Because of my powers, I saw the universe—and time—unfurl. My incredible strength connected my consciousness to every person on the planet. I saw through their eyes. I felt with their hearts. I died, a little bit more, every time someone had their life stolen.

When the comet hit the southeast quadrant of the planet, everyone on Earth knew. If they hadn't been outside in the hours prior to impact—if they hadn't stood under the sky, mouths open, bodies shaking in anticipation of what was to come—they knew when it landed.

The comet crashed just below The Island. Millions were gone, instantly. Swallowed by boiling oceans, buried in a tidal wave, and crushed under the weight of water. In the resulting earthquakes—and tsunamis, and fire—oh, the fire! the end! the end!—the lower half of the planet was covered by salt water. The northern hemisphere mourned with salt tears. It was worse than war, during which only hundreds of thousands were killed. It was worse than government control; and murder.

I didn't know any of this when the comet hit. I learned what happened later. What I experienced—what my community felt, and Canuckians felt—was the aftermath: the ripple from the comet's collision. When it hit, the planet shuddered. I was pitched off my feet.

Not right away. It took time for the ripple to reach the North. But when it came, it came with a fury. It tossed the town to the side, discarding Chaleur like it was an uprooted dandelion. I fell to the ground and my palms ripped open. My blood stained the earth. I crawled to my house and pushed my back against the closed front door, then watched several things happen at once.

Later, I replayed the resulting scenes in my mind too many times to count. I saw and heard multiple glints and auras in several places at once: I was that powerful. My eyes saw Dimitri. My heart heard Amelie. And my broken soul screamed for Oliver and Khleo, who was sheltered under my birch tree.

When the brothers passed through the grove on their way home, the birch ripped out of the ground and toppled to the earth, knocking the brothers unconscious while it—simultaneously—protected them from an avalanche that hurtled down a mountain after the comet hit: an avalanche that would have killed the Billadeaus if they'd made it out of the grove. Oliver and Khleo didn't see the purple streak strengthen in the sky. They didn't know about the end of the world.

But they were alive.

And my birch tree was dead.

It didn't matter, though, because love died, too. It died when Chaleur's main street split down the centre, pulling Dimitri into its crack. I saw his head hit the side of the concrete. I saw his skull smash, saw his lifeless body fall into the crevice. I saw his blood stain the deepest grave anyone would ever know.

I never forgot the blood.

I watched love die with Amelie. I watched her wave her hands as she tried to maintain order in the chaos that consumed the community. I watched her shouting directions, heralding the weaker citizens—the children, and vulnerable adults—into places where the ground didn't heave. Where trees didn't fall. Where the earth stayed flat and still. And safe.

I watched the shit-kicking Officer Dillweed grab Amelie's arm as he tried to take control of the scene. I watched Amelie jerk out of the officer's grip.

I watched the officer's face turn red.

I watched—and felt—the officer's soul harden. I felt his glints tilt with maddening anger towards Amelie: BITCH, STUPID BITCH, CRAZY BITCH, FUCKING BITCH. Then, in the resulting rage, the officer grabbed Amelie's head with his hands and twisted.

I didn't hear Amelie's neck snap, or her spine—or her light—but I felt her aura extinguish. I watched Amelie slump, boneless, to the ground: in the centre of the town she served her whole life within the country she fought to restore.

I felt Whitley's horror as they stood behind the Coplot cabin and watched Amelie die. I felt Oliver and Khleo regain consciousness and scream, then run from the grove. I watched Mount Champ fold in on itself, killing every Champion and Provincial Police officer who used it as a shelter. I didn't know exactly what the rest of my community was doing—hiding, fleeing, howling—but I felt them *try*. They were trying to live, which made me laugh.

I couldn't hear my laughter, but my mouth was open and my throat throbbed, so a tiny part of my soul must have remembered mirth.

What a joke! The world thought the Bot War was the end. Chaleur thought renegades, poisoned pools, murderous teenagers, and lying citizens were the worst the universe could throw at us. I thought a nerve-wracking relationship was my biggest worry but—all along—the cosmos had a trick up its starry sleeve: an astronomical catastrophe that made every Earth-bound effort, wish, and woe irrelevant. I had to laugh, or else I would die.

Oh, wait. Too late.

Ha ha ha.

Later (when?—I didn't know) someone found me. Laughing. Pressed against the closed front door of my home not Dimitri's home, Dimitri is gone with laughter rocking my body like the comet rocked the world. I didn't stop laughing until that someone placed their hand on my leg.

I fainted. I stopped thinking, feeling, grieving. It was the end.

It was *an* end.

CHAPTER THIRTY-ONE

When I woke up in the Billadeau's house, in Amelie's den—Amelie was dead dead dead—Zekiul sat next to me on the couch, holding a cup of water.

Blinking at the sight of my friend (who I'd assumed was dead—dead dead dead) I glanced around the room. If I hadn't known about the comet, I would have thought it was a typical afternoon. Amelie's den was in perfect condition: her comfortable furniture was intact, the books were lined up neatly on the shelf, and the thick mountains walls blocked out the sounds of the world falling apart.

Outside of my mind. Inside, the screams were becoming intolerable.

I shook my head. I sat up.

The green room spun.

"You were in Mount Champ," I said to Zekiul, using his face to focus my vision. "Mount Champ collapsed. I saw it. You shouldn't be here, Zee." I laughed hoarsely. "Remember Zee? Zee's gone."

"I'm right here." Zekiul put his hand on my leg.

I couldn't feel it.

"You know that trapdoor you asked me about? The one under my bed? It was attached to an escape tunnel," Zekiul said. "When the network released the News about the comet it showed up on our screens in the Intelligence Centre. Everyone else was out, looking for Erika and Havu. I wanted to warn them, but there wasn't enough time." He lifted his hand to his temple. "I'd taken out my eyelinks. So I ran through the tunnel. And I made it here."

I stared at his face. He'd made it when so many others hadn't.

"Go slow." Zekiul pressed the cup into my hand as he helped me settle into the couch's cushions. His skin looked green, like the paint on Amelie's walls.

Dead. Amelie was dead.

I took a sip of water. It poured through my hole. "How long have we been here?" I took another sip. "Is it over?"

Zekiul nodded. "It's over."

"Why are we here? How did we get here?" My hand shook, so I placed the cup on Amelie's desk. Dead Amelie's desk.

Dead Amelie's desk, dead Amelie's desk, dead Amelie's—

"I saw you," Zekiul said. "Outside your house. But Mount Ryndle was shaking, so I brought you here. Niccola Peak is solid. The Billadeaus were smart to build here. But I don't know what happened, or what's happening." He looked up at the lowered ceiling. "Communication technology is down. Our eyelinks, the network. Everything." His lip lifted. "It might not come back."

I closed my eyes and let the truth take root. Information flooded my mind from auras across the planet. Tech might be down, but my glint reading ability was stronger than ever. I pursed my lips. What a convenient trauma response.

Then I nodded. That was how I could keep going when I had a hole instead of a heart: I'd sense the stories of others to share.

And serve.

I claimed the stories. I opened my eyes. "I know what's going on. I can tell you." I tapped my temple. "I know."

Zekiul inched closer. "What do we do?"

"We wait for the Reclamation Party to reach out. The federal government—in Oakland—was unaffected by the comet. It was one of the only places on the planet that escaped the ripple."

"Shit. I guess we should be grateful, but—fuck."

A sudden surge of terror emanated from the East. "Oh—no," I said, shutting my eyes. "That was them. The federal government. The Reclamation Party is falling apart, right now. They don't think they can handle this." I squeezed my eyes tighter. "We might be on our own."

Zekiul's hand found mine. "What else do you see?"

I breathed in his strength: his steady confidence in my ability.

"The Southern Continents—south of the equator—are gone. Billions of people drowned. *Are* drowning. I can feel the water in their throats. It's filling their lungs and they're trying to cough, but they can't and I—" A sob caught in my mouth. I swallowed it: forced it into the hole. "The land above the equator is shifting. Our land. Not a lot right now, but the continents will move. Boundaries will be reformed. There are survivors above the equator, but not many."

"Are there enough survivors? Enough to rebuild?"

I opened my eyes. I grabbed the cup of water. "Rebuild what?"

Zekiul's mouth hardened. "Tell me about Chaleur."

I stared at Zekiul's lips. My hand holding the cup trembled. I sipped the water, then said, "Oliver is alive. When the comet hit he was protected by my—" I stopped. My birch tree.

My beautiful birch was gone.

I swallowed my sorrow. "Oliver was protected by a tree, and he was with Khleo. Whitley is alive, too. They were in the Coplot cabin when—when the comet came. The Provincial Police are—" My knuckles whitened around the cup. A crack split in its side, sending water trickling onto my wrist. "The Police scattered. They're running away. We won't see them again."

"Good." Zekiul took the cracked cup from my bleeding hand—when did I start bleeding? I'd better be careful Oli doesn't do blood—and placed it on Amelie's desk.

Amelie was dead. Amelie was DEAD.

Zekiul sat down. "Is Whitley still here?"

I breathed. "They are. They're helping the other survivors."

"And Oliver?"

I closed my eyes. My hole shrunk a hair. "He's on his way. He's hurt, but he's with Khleo. He's coming home with his—with his mom."

"Amelie?"

"Amelie's body." I had to keep talking. "Amelie was killed."

Zekiul said nothing.

I stared at his green-tinged face. He didn't understand. Maybe he hadn't heard me? I leaned forward and raised my voice.

AMELIE IS DEAD

Zekiul didn't move. Didn't flinch. Didn't blink as a single tear crested his lower lashes and rolled down his cheek.

I watched the tear. Watched it fall.

Watched it roll onto Dimitri's outstretched hand.

No. No no no. Dimitri was—

Dimitri was dead. He was empty, he was over.

Mitty, Mitty, Mitty, Mitty—

It was the end.

Zekiul stared at me. His fluttering aura vibrated, almost lifting away from his body. Then he leaned forward to kiss me—

—and Oliver burst through the front door with a sobbing Khleo not far behind.

Zekiul wrenched back. His green face paled. I didn't care.

His attempted kiss meant nothing.

Oliver stumbled into the den and stopped. Khleo bumped into him, then gasped when he saw me. He fell onto my lap, crying and clutching my hair. Zekiul moved to the door and offered Oliver his hand.

But Oliver waved Zekiul away. He pulled his brother off me, then held me tightly, burying his face in my neck.

My heart gave a thud. It was faint, but movement was there. Oliver's embrace coaxed a spark. He eased the edges of the hole.

"You know what happened, don't you?" Oliver looked up. His hair was plastered against his forehead. "You can read people. Read the eyelinks and tell us." He grabbed my shoulders and shook. Hard. "Tell me, Layla! Tell me what I'm supposed to do."

"Stop, Oli." Khleo pulled on Oliver's arm. "She can't tell us anything if you hurt her."

Oliver's hands fell away. The Billadeaus stared at me hungrily. Zekiul moved behind the couch, backing me up with his presence.

I opened my mouth. "Where did you put her?"

Khleo stumbled away from my words.

"We buried her," Oliver said. "The dirt behind the house was turned up from the comet. My mother's grave is under

Niccola Peak. Beside my father's."

I breathed in. "Do you know anything that happened?"

Oliver's eyes grew larger—and darker. "Tell us."

I took another breath, then shared the world's story. All of it. When I finished, Oliver walked over to Amelie's wall and punched a hole where I'd once played a vid of meeting that was supposed to bring peace. It wasn't a large hole, but now Oliver and I had matching hands, covered with blood.

I'd *never* forget the blood.

"What about the Provincial Police?" Khleo spoke quietly. His mind was in complete control, which—somehow—frightened me more than Oliver's display of aggression. "Where is the officer who killed my mom?"

"Dead," I said, after scanning the memories still siphoning into my mind. "An avalanche crushed him. The officer is dead."

"And Dimitri?" Khleo knew the answer—I'd already explained—but he asked anyway. "Is Dimitri really gone? And Rogers? And Perrault? And—"

"Everyone, Khleo." Oliver spoke to the hole in the wall. "What about the girls? Erika and Havu?"

I closed my eyes, scanning.

Scanning.

My mouth twisted into an ironic smile. "They're alive. They're running south, towards the border. I can hear their auras: Erika and Havu are moving towards the Separated States. They won't come back."

"Sure," Khleo said. "My mom is dead and our lives are ruined, but those bitches get a fresh start. Fuck."

"I wouldn't go that far," Zekiul said. "There's no fresh start for any of us. Just survival."

"And the Champions?" Oliver's voice hardened as he turned towards the couch. "Did the Champions make it?"

I looked at the grief-stricken face of Zekiul and answered for him. "Mount Champ is gone. There's nothing left."

Zekiul nodded. "There's only us."

"And Whitley." I closed my eyes. "They're in the Coplot cabin. It's still standing, so that's where everyone is gathering. Everyone who survived."

With a cry, Oliver picked up Amelie's chair and threw it against the wall. As it shattered I winced, but I didn't move. I watched Oliver work out his pain on Amelie's carefully designed furniture: designed by Dimitri, whose hopes for artistic longevity had been destroyed by a force stronger than human will and imagination.

When Oliver moved towards the bookshelf, I intervened. "Oli."

My partner froze, halted by the authority in my command.

I crossed the room until I stood by Oliver's side, by the entryway where Amelie told me I was special. "We have to go to Whitley. I can sense—" I shook my head. "People are struggling. Their glints are terrified. If someone doesn't take over—if we don't go to them—they'll fall apart. The comet has brought out citizens' cruelty. They're worse than weeds, Oli. The community is about to destroy everything good left in Chaleur. We have to help them. We need to find a way to bring everyone together." I held out my hand.

Oliver didn't take it.

Flames ignited inside my hole: fire sparked by Oliver's disregard. I channeled the fire, using it to feed my power. I headed for the foyer. "I'll do it myself."

I stormed out of the house. I was ready to step into the position I'd dreamed about so many memories ago. I was going to lead the community. A better way for dimmer day.

But before I could make it under the archway that ran in front of the Billadeau home, Oliver grabbed my arm and whirled me around. "Where do you think you're going?"

I didn't have time to argue. I had to act. So, I strode around the broken searchlights sending sparks across Oliver's walkway and headed for the path that led to the town. Whitley needed me, I could sense it. I was coming. I was going to help. I was—

Stopped by Oliver again. "I need you here, Layla. With me."

"Listen to me." I shook Oliver away. "Chaleur is in trouble. People need someone strong to get them out of this crisis."

"And that someone is you?" Oliver laughed.

He *laughed.*

"Don't be stupid," Oliver said. "You aren't a leader. My mother is dead, and Khleo almost—" He shuddered. "We have to stay together. You, me, and Khleo. Everyone else has to fend for themselves."

"That is a shit idea."

"Layla!"

"That is the shittiest idea you've ever had."

"This isn't the time to play Prime. You may be good at understanding people—and citizens used to like you—but smiling and being empathetic aren't leadership qualities. You have to know things, Layla." Oliver tapped my head. "You have to *know.*"

"I do know, Oli." I grabbed Oliver's face. "I KNOW!"

Holding Oliver's head in my hands, I broke into his mind. I destroyed his boundaries with my power, even though I'd promised myself I'd never intrude upon his privacy. But the comet had changed everything, so I bombarded Oliver's mind with the truth: with *my* truth. I showed him my natural glint-reading strength. I showed him my visions of the world, during and after the comet. And I showed Oliver the wild glints racing through the survivors in Chaleur.

I lowered my hands and headed for the town.

Oliver followed. "I can't believe you did that to me."

"You didn't trust me," I said. "Sorry, Oli, but *you* needed to know."

"Not that." Oliver ran in front of me, halting my strides. "You lied to me. You lied about your natural ability. You've been lying for months. Why would you keep that from me? Why?"

"Stop it, Oli."

"NO!" Oliver grabbed my wrist. "You stop it. Stop lying."

"Let go of me, Oli."

"You don't love me, Layla. That's the biggest lie of all. You can't love someone you lie to."

"I'm not lying," I said, my eyes filling with tears. Oliver was hurting my arm. "I do love you. But the town needs a leader, and I can—"

"Shut up, Layla!" Oliver's grip tightened. "Don't you understand? My mother is dead. Dead! Chaleur doesn't matter."

I choked back a gasp. "What about—what about your legacy?"

Oliver bared his teeth. "I don't care."

"But—but what about us?"

Oliver stepped away, his face blank and staring. "I don't care."

My head split. The pain was worse than Erika's mind-vice and almost as bad as the comet. My glints reeled from Oliver's words. I stumbled backwards, under the archway. "You don't mean that."

Oliver headed into his house.

"You're upset," I said, running after him. "You're sad about your mom." I reached out and grabbed Oliver's sleeve. "Don't leave me, Oli. Don't leave—"

"Shut *up*, Layla!"

"You love me, Oli!" I yelled—no, screamed!—until my throat ached. "For always!"

Oliver whirled around, lifting his arm. His upraised hand hit my cheek, directly beneath my eye. I saw sparks, then fell to the ground.

"Know *this*." Oliver stood over me, glaring. "I'm done. You chose the town over me and Khleo. We're your family, and we should *always* come first."

"Oliver!" I climbed to my feet, holding my throbbing face. "Forget Khleo. Are you going to say anything about this?" I moved my hand, revealing my rapidly-swelling cheek.

Oliver laughed like he was shocked, or surprised. Or delighted. "That's nothing."

Straightening my shoulders, I ignored the pain in my face— and I spit. Spit blood.

Oliver's eyes widened as he stared at the red staining my

mouth. But he said nothing.

I walked away. Councillor Whitley, I sent to the councillor's mind—without using technology. I'm coming.

I didn't see Oliver step back into his home. I didn't notice Khleo, who stood in the entryway: watching. And I wasn't aware of Khleo's glints as Oliver spoke to him. So, even though I was the strongest natural glint-reader on the planet, I didn't know what was about to happen next.

And I couldn't have prevented it if I had.

CHAPTER THIRTY-TWO

I had a busy day.

Zekiul and I—with the help of Whitley—dealt with the immediate danger from the aftermath of the comet: the fallen buildings, destroyed farms, and rock piles from resulting avalanches. Relieved, the surviving citizens gathered in the Coplot cabin. Their glints soothed and temporary order was restored. Plans were made to put the dead to rest in the coming days. Then the night came, the stars appeared, and darkness descended upon Chaleur: darkness worse than the comet's smothering ash, which blew into the town on a hot, harsh wind.

As Whitley handed out flashlights powered by Dimitri's nuclear batteries, Zekiul offered to raid Perrault's market for food and supplies. He stroked the back of my head, then left the cabin, leaving me and Whitley alone with the survivors.

Unable to handle the silent cabin, I left too. I walked through the town, heading for Rogers' mushroom field to harvest fresh nutrients. Even though my heart was broken—and my face was a mess—my body needed nourishment. Everyone needed food.

I'd lied to Whitley and Zekiul about my bruised eye. I said a rock dislodged from Niccola Peak and clipped me as I headed into the forest. I didn't care if they believed me. I cared about Oliver: if he apologized, I was ready to give him a second chance. Despite everything, we were supposed to be together. I loved him.

But Oliver had to take the first step toward reconciliation. I wasn't going to beg him to apologize for hitting me. But I knew, once he cooled down, Oliver would find me.

I was right.

And very, very wrong.

I squatted in Rogers' mushroom field after midnight, harvesting the fungi. Oliver appeared. I dropped my handful of mushrooms as he walked over the cherry-wood planks to the base of Rogers' hill. The house on top had collapsed, but the farm beneath it remained intact.

Oliver stopped in the shadows. I couldn't see his face.

I wasn't sure if I wanted to.

"Can we talk?" I couldn't see his mouth move, but Oliver's voice gave me hope. It was soft and steady. He was calm.

I stood, then wiped my shaking hands on my trousers. "I'd like that."

"You can't tell anyone what happened today," Oliver said. "At my house."

"I wasn't going to," I said. "We all do stupid things when we're upset. I wouldn't want anyone to hold it against you—"

"No." Oliver huffed: an uneasy laugh combined with an inhalation of air. "You can't tell anyone about—" he gestured at my face, "—about your accident."

I touched my cheek. "My accident? Oli—"

"Your accident," Oliver said. "Nobody will believe it."

I smiled, then winced. My face hurt. "I know how strange it will seem to everyone that you could do this to me—" I pointed at my bruised cheek, "—but they'll believe me. They know you, Oli. You get upset all the time."

"I might get upset, but I would never hit anyone." Oliver grew taller in the shadows. "And even though I don't love you anymore, I don't want you to be embarrassed."

"I—what? What do you—" I couldn't move. "What do you mean, embarrassed?"

A shadow detached from a tree.

I shrieked, then covered my mouth with my hand when I realized who the shadow belonged to. "For the love of leaves, Khleo. You scared me."

Khleo gave me a tight-lipped smile as he crossed the wooden planks. Clasping his hands behind his back, he stopped at the base of the hill and rocked forward on his sneakers. "Here's the thing, Layla. We've got a problem."

I frowned at Oliver, who'd slipped behind his brother. Sighing, I said to Khleo, "I've been solving problems all afternoon. Tell me the trouble and we'll work it out."

"No, uh, you don't get me." Khleo rocked backwards on his heels. "I've called an emergency meeting of the Compassion Coplot. I have to tell everyone what happened: you lost your mind when the comet hit and are on some kind of power-mad trip to become Prime."

The shadows around Oliver shifted as he straightened his hunched shoulders. "We want to help you, Layla."

"What are you talking about?" I stepped back, into the hill. "I don't need help. And I don't want to be the Prime. I want *to* help."

"You're seeing things," Oliver said. "Things that didn't happen. You think I hit you, right? You think you can read glints without using the eyelinks?" He stepped into the moonlight. Oliver's eyes shone with pity. "Khleo helped me see the truth. You aren't well."

"No." The field spun, even though I could feel Rogers' hill behind my back. "I'm a natural glint-reader. I am."

"You aren't, Layla."

"Tell him, Khleo." I turned to Oliver's brother. "You and Whitley know I snatched Erika's glints to prove she killed Herra."

"Look, I know what Whitley said, but until *I* see proof I can't believe it." Khleo's smirk glowed in the moonlight. "What kind of politician would I be if I took people at their word?"

"Your mom knew about my powers and she believed me," I said. "Don't you believe her?"

"My mom is dead." Khleo bristled. "And you're crazy. You can't lead the country. Nobody will be a better Prime than Oli."

"Oli?" I frowned. "Not you?"

"Me, Oli—what's the difference? A Billadeau needs to be in charge and Oliver understands real power." Khleo sneered. "Not delusional power." He chuckled. "Come on, Layla. You think you have power like Min RoboReiwa? You?"

"I'm more powerful than RoboReiwa." I planted my feet, then

breathed in deeply. "You have no idea."

I dove into Oliver's mind. I needed to see why he thought he had to undermine my abilities. But—after I entered his head—I froze. Because Oliver was empty.

He didn't have glints. The zooming aura I'd sensed when we'd first met was gone. Instead, there was a tiny kernel of sound buried deep within his core. It throbbed with an intensity that pushed me away. Radiating from the kernel was effort: Oliver had locked himself up so tight he couldn't access the human thoughts and feelings that made him, well, human! He was as empty as a Bot, with nothing but a void where his heart should have beat. He was dead inside.

Like me.

I *thought* I understood. I thought I knew what he was going through. I thought I could empathize with his pain, and his struggle, and the despair that forced him to protect his heart.

I was wrong.

I withdrew from Oliver's mind. "It's going to be alright, Oli. We can help each other."

Oliver offered me his hand. "We're here to help *you*."

"You know I'm a natural glint-reader. I showed you my power. And you know the survivors need to be led by someone strong. We can work together."

"I'm sorry, Layla." In a single movement, Oliver jolted forward and grabbed my wrist. "Khleo and I have to fix you."

A force more powerful than a comet exploded in my belly. I shook Oliver away. "You bastard."

Oliver flexed his fingers, frowning. "That's not very nice."

"I don't need fixing."

"Layla—"

"And you can't tell the community I'm crazy," I said. "I can show everyone the truth, remember? I can send everyone the memory of what you did to me."

Oliver clenched his hands. "You're just like Erika."

I stepped back. "Excuse me?"

Oliver's face drifted in and out of the moonlight as clouds passed overhead. "You know how to plant glints. You planted a false memory in my mind."

"No." My palms began to sweat. "No, that's not—that's not true. I would never do that."

"You're a glint-planter, Layla," Oliver said. "You've been breaking into people's minds for months. You're a criminal. Everyone knows it."

"It—it doesn't matter," I said as I inched to the side, glancing over my shoulder to see if there was a path out of there that led in a direction I could run run fast run now. "Zekiul will believe me. So will Whitley."

"They won't." Oliver drew closer. "They'll believe me; and Khleo. He's the mayor, and he's never done anything wrong."

Khleo smiled. "At least, nothing anyone knows about."

My throat constricted. "I don't need to show people what you did." I moved around the base of the hill, closer to the forest. I had to run run run run. "I'll yell. Right now. And people—people will hear me. Someone will hear me. They'll come and help."

"No, Layla. They won't," Oliver said. "Everyone is in the Coplot cabin."

"And everyone else is dead," Khleo said. "Dead people can't hear."

The clouds parted, bathing Oliver and Khleo in light—too bright, moonlight, I'm not going to get away—and I froze as the male I loved—my partner and soul mate—reached out and took my hand. He raised my knuckles and pressed them, softly, to his lips. Then Oliver looked into my eyes; and terror exploded in my head.

Oliver was gone. He'd been replaced by

nothing

"I hate this," Oliver said, still holding my hand. "But we have to make sure you can't lie anymore." He sighed. His breath grazed my knuckles and I trembled, unable to move. Oliver squeezed my hand—too hard too HARD—then said, "I don't do blood, but sometimes you have to make exceptions. You taught me that, Layla. You said I need to bend the rules. So, I'll bend. For you."

I bit his hand.

Oliver yelled in pain, then backed away—and I ran.

I ran around the hill, then stopped behind the aspen tree, breathing heavily. There had to be an easy way out, easier than running. Why didn't I think of this before? I had to gather my power so I could take over Khleo and Oliver's bodies. I'd force them to stay on Rogers' property while I ran to the town. Then, after I told Zekiul and Whitley what happened, we could restrain the Billadeau brothers until—until—until—I don't know! Until something else happens!

I breathed. I'd think of the second part of the plan after I completed the first.

Channeling my energy into a rod, I split my power into two prongs. I aimed the prongs at Oliver and Khleo's auras, which flanked the hill as they tried to flank me, and—

From behind, Khleo's fist hit my face with a sharp *crack!*

I didn't see him coming. Why didn't I WHY DIDN'T I see it coming? I crumbled to the ground.

I didn't feel much after that. I knew Khleo was hurting me. I could sense him dragging me back to Rogers' field, but a small *hummm!* of consciousness seemed to have detached from my limp body to float, invisible, over the farm.

I watched Khleo kick my ribs, then kick the side of my head. I watched my breathing slow. I watched Khleo rinse his bloody hands in Rogers' pools and walk across the planks. I watched Oliver watch everything.

He *really* didn't do blood.

After Oliver followed his brother into the forest, my consciousness—my weakened aura—hovered in the air. My body still clung to life, though you'd never know it. In the dark I could see my clothes, torn and soaked, and I could see my face: a kaleidoscope of cuts and bruises. Khleo hadn't broken my ribcage, though, or any of my bones. My body remained whole.

I lay beneath Rogers' hill, completely still. Battered. My body reached for my humming aura as I spun in a tortuous circle for hours and hours and hours and hours and—
HOW?
WHY? HOW?
WHY?
But it wasn't the end of my world.
My aura floated into my shattered body—
—and I took a breath.

CHAPTER THIRTY-THREE

The moonlight shifted.

I winced. What now?

I kept my eyes closed as feeling returned to my body. I didn't have the strength to endure more, but I was alive. And awake.

Strong arms lifted me in the air. A voice spoke in my mind. I'm sorry I didn't get here sooner. The major sent me, but I was too late. Don't worry. You're safe now.

I stared at the stars overhead as the citizen carried me through the forest.

Dimitri's stars.

I'm taking you to the major. He's in your cave, waiting for us. I know where it is. The major and me got out of Mount Champ before the comet hit—we escaped through his tunnel—then the major told me to hide in your cave and wait for him. He was worried . . . The voice trailed off. You need to hide for a while, too. But the councillor will help you, don't worry. They'll fix you, and then you can get out of here. The major has a plan.

The arms tightened around my limp body as they carried me up an incline, higher into the mountains.

The major told me what happened. He said you can read glints—the voice gave a quick 'HEH,' then continued—and he said you could save us. But then the old mayor and his brother told everyone in Chaleur you went crazy and tried to kill them before you ran away, so . . . you probably can't save anyone anymore.

The major didn't believe the brothers. The councillor and him snuck out of the cabin and came and got me, and the major told me to find you. There's a new mayor, now—the old mayor's bad brother—and the major doesn't like that. The bad brother wants power. He wants to control the country. The bad brother doesn't want anyone to stop him, which is why he lied about you. The voice paused. The major told me the bad brother lied. The major said you wouldn't hurt anyone.

I felt tears mingle with the cuts on my cheeks.

You have to escape, the voice said in my mind. The major and me looked for you at your house, but we didn't find you—because you were at the mushroom farm with the brothers. But the major found something that can help you: the designer's Will. The designer left his money to you. The brothers can't change the Will, so you'll be able to use the money to survive. You're lucky the designer left you everything. He must have cared about you a lot. The voice shook, but the arms stayed steady. The major cares, too. So do I—so don't worry. You'll be safe after the councillor comes here. The major told me they're on their way. We all have to leave.

Dimitri's stars disappeared. The arms carried me into a warm, dark place. I turned my head to the side and winced. The pain was too much. But I could see. We were in my cave. My saviour had brought me to my cave.

She laid me on the ground, on the moss, on the earth. A lighter ignited and the wavering flame let off a fierce glow. Zekiul's face appeared at the back of the cavern, and Jolene—the voice—patted my hair. Then she moved away, to stand by her leader.

I kept my gaze above the fire. "I didn't know."

Zekiul nodded, his eyes kind. "You couldn't know."

I sat up, ignoring the pain in my ribs and the haze in my head. "This is wrong. *We're* wrong. Oli is upset, he isn't evil." I crawled towards the cave's entryway, hoping I'd find Oliver quickly so I could make amends before anything else happened. "I'm the best natural glint reader in the world and I know Oli better than anyone. He made a mistake."

"Where are you going?" Zekiul grabbed my shoulder. "Layla, stop!"

I folded, gasping.

"Sorry!" Zekiul raised his hands. "I'm sorry. But—what are you talking about?"

"He made a mistake," I said again, gingerly testing my arm. "I have to find Oli and apologize."

Zekiul knelt in front of me. "You didn't do anything wrong."

"If I'd told Oli about my natural ability this wouldn't have happened." I turned towards the mouth of the cave, but Jolene lumbered forward, guarding the exit. "Please, let me go. I have to explain that I love him, and love is stronger than everything. Please!" I tried to crawl around Jolene, but it was a pathetic attempt at escape and I collapsed again. I lay on the ground, squeezing back the tears that filled my eyes. "I don't want Oli to hate me. I love him."

"But he doesn't love you."

Zekiul's words should have crushed me, but they didn't. They fluttered in my chest.

"He deceived you, Layla," Zekiul said. "He deceived all of us."

"No," I said. "I know!"

"None of us knew," Zekiul said. "Why do you think Oliver never wore his eyelinks?"

In that moment I actually knew.

And I felt like a fool. Then I looked into Zekiul's warm eyes; and felt sadness siphon from my soul. "So people couldn't know he was empty."

"He wasn't empty. He was hurting." Zekiul knelt beside me as Jolene moved away to sit on the mossy rocks. "You were too close to Oliver—and the Billadeaus—to see what was really going on," Zekiul said. "Everyone was hurting. Amelie indulged her sons because she lost her husband. When they fought each other, or acted immaturely, she didn't intervene. She encouraged it, to a certain extent, by laughing it off. Amelie was a great leader, and her intentions were good, but her weakness was her sons. She refused to see the harm they caused—to themselves and others—because she needed them to love her back." He frowned. "Or she chose not to see it because her sons worked for her. Ambitious idealists ignore the truth all the time."

"HEH."

Zekiul and I looked at Jolene, who frowned and sent her glints into my mind. The major is wrong. The nice lady was the brothers' mother. She was supposed to love them, no matter what.

"Jolene is right," I said, after telling Zekiul what Jolene sent. "Amelie was a great person. There's nothing wrong with loving someone unconditionally."

"But she expected her sons to reciprocate unconditionally, instead of teaching them how to reciprocate in ways that came to them naturally." Zekiul smiled sadly. "And great people do stupid shit—and ignore the stupid shit other people do—all the time. Look at the Billadeaus: Khleo bullied Oliver. It wasn't funny. It hurt him, I could tell. And Amelie didn't defend Oliver, which—as his mother—she should have done. And *Dimitri* didn't help the leadership team's culture, with his doomsday predictions and worst-case scenarios."

Jolene grunted.

"Dimitri was right about the comet," I said. "How can you say that about him?"

"Dimitri got lucky." Zekiul winced. "Wrong expression. There was a one-in-a-billion chance his meteor would turn into a world-ending comet, but he acted as though odds like that were possible to predict. And his constant negativity effected the Coplot. And the Champions." His face darkened as his aura quieted. "Sometimes I wish the Champions had stayed in Mount Champ. We were happier before—" Zekiul looked away. "Never mind."

"Before I came along," I said. "Be honest."

"Regardless of what my glints are saying—because I know you're reading them right now—I don't believe that, Layla." Zekiul lifted my hand and kissed my palm. "I don't regret meeting you for a second."

He *was* being honest. His aura fluttered with affection.

I pulled my hand away. "You agree with me though, right? About Oli?"

Zekiul sighed. "I don't think his pain was his fault. He's an emotional guy, anyone can see that. I understand why he had to protect his sensitivity: the world is awful! I respect that Oliver wanted to change things, and I understand why he was angry—look at me, I'm frustrated all the time—but I chose to lead the Champions, and we chose to rebel. Oliver and Khleo didn't work for the Coplot because they wanted to help Canuckians. They wanted to please Amelie. Now that their plans are broken, I don't blame the brothers for breaking, too. The resentment Oliver must feel seeing his life's work squashed has to be suffocating. But I do blame him—and Khleo—for what they did to you." He growled. "I don't care how hurt they are. Nobody has to beat the living shit out of another person to 'protect' himself."

My gut clenched. "I did."

Zekiul stared at me. "What are you talking about?"

"I hurt people." I closed my eyes. "I broke their boundaries and snatched their glints. I controlled their bodies. I didn't have to do that."

"That was different." Zekiul placed his hand on my cheek, very gently. "You can't compare snatching glints to Khleo trying to kill you while Oliver stood by and watched. Especially someone like you, who just wanted to help."

"Oliver wants to help," I insisted. "He's doing his best."

"Oliver wants to help himself. And his best isn't good enough."

A low *roar!* sounded in the distance. Trees broke and cascaded down the mountainside. We stared out the cave's mouth, at the mountain littered with broken pines.

"Layla?"

Zekiul's low voice brought my attention back into the cave. I stared at him—waiting.

He leaned closer, then said, "You understand that none of this is your fault, right? Your power is incredible—and it has allowed us to access some really important information—but being a strong natural glint-reader doesn't make you responsible for other people's glints, nor their thoughts, words, or behaviour. Even if you'd known what Oliver was glinting, you couldn't have changed him;

and you can't change him now. So, you can't blame yourself for whatever he does next. Okay?"

"Maybe if I—"

"Layla. Listen to me. Oliver isn't your responsibility. The community isn't your responsibility." More trees slid down the mountain in a torrent of snapped bark and broken stones—and Zekiul sighed. "Everyone is responsible for the choices our society makes. Nobody is innocent when the world falls apart."

"I get it." I rolled onto my knees, then looked away. I couldn't let Zekiul's words affect me. He was wrong; and I didn't deserve his misplaced kindness. "Where are they? Where are Oliver and Khleo?"

Zekiul growled. "Probably still in the Coplot cabin, lying to the survivors. You should have seen how happy they were when they told us you abandoned the town because you were crazy."

"How did you know I wasn't?" I sniffed, then bit back a cry. Everything hurt, including my nose.

"Layla." Zekiul placed his hand on my leg. "I know."

Zekiul's face filled my eyes and—suddenly—*I* knew. I understood what I'd missed, and what I couldn't sense.

Even though I could read glints better than anyone, I couldn't accurately interpret glints, or predict how they'd affect the choices and actions of the glinter. But Zekiul understood human nature.

He knew.

But Zekiul was wrong about my responsibility. I was the most powerful person on the planet, and I was supposed to use that power to help people. I should have realized Oliver wanted to cause more harm that a killer, comet, and controlling government combined, so it was my responsibility to make things better.

But I couldn't

"So, they're going ahead with it? Oli is—" I stopped. My heart hurt. "Oliver's going to form a government?"

As the words left my mouth a vision appeared in my mind.

Oliver stood in the cabin with Khleo by his side. The survivors surrounded the brothers while Oliver gave the speech of his life:

an inspiring speech, full of promise and hope. And deception. Khleo gazed at his brother with rapt, adoring attention, and—following Khleo's lead—the rest of the town listened to Oliver, too.

He was going to make them fall in love with him. Everyone was going to love Oliver. The country was vulnerable, and he had a plan. Oliver Billadeau was going to become Prime. It was that simple.

His path to power was that easy.

I dismissed my vision of the present and the future. Shaking my head, I said to Zekiul, "We have to leave, right?"

Zekiul nodded.

"And I can't go with you?"

Zekiul glanced at Jolene, then sighed. "Layla . . ."

Zekiul's glints were clear: he and Jolene did have to leave Chaleur, and I couldn't go with them. The second they left Pluie, Oliver would send people to track them to make sure Zekiul didn't come back; and he would find me. That couldn't happen.

I gathered my hair over my shoulder and clung to my tresses. "Where will you go?"

"To the Separated States," Zekiul said. "Or what's left of it. You can join us, eventually, but right now your best hope at survival is to disappear. If we could be together I'd want that, but—"

I lifted my fingers, stopping him. "We can't."

Zekiul wanted love. All I could offer him was suffering, and a life in hiding. Oliver would stop looking for Zekiul someday, but he'd never forget me.

Zekiul nodded curtly. "Jolene and I are leaving tonight, before the Billadeaus realize I snuck out of the cabin." He pulled a cloth out of his pocket and pressed it against my bleeding forehead. "Whitley will be here soon with supplies. Once you're on your feet, they'll help you get out of here. While the Reclamation Party's still in power, Whitley has resources to protect you."

"Where should I go?"

"Bristol, or Jardin," Zekiul said. "But don't go to Union. Once Oliver takes over, he'll move to the capital city: Oakland. You can't let him find you."

I grabbed Zekiul's cloth, forcing him to look at me. "So, it's over? We're giving up?"

"For now." Zekiul stood, then helped me to my feet. "There's nothing we can do. Oliver and Khleo's story is compelling: two young brothers who devoted their lives to public service under the guidance of their mother, only to have their dream for a better world destroyed by a comet and their mom murdered by an officer working for the province. If I didn't know the truth, I'd support them, too. And Oliver has made sure the Billadeaus are in a position to wield legitimate power. He—and Khleo—know how to spin facts and manipulate citizens' emotional vulnerability so Canuckians will vote the Coplot in as the majority government."

"We could fight," I said, climbing to my feet; and biting my broken lip so I wouldn't scream. "We could speak against him."

"Nobody will listen to us, Layla." Zekiul pointed out the cave's mouth, towards the town. "A comet destroyed the planet. Citizens won't tolerate leaders fighting against each other right now. People want someone to fight *for* them, not for control over them. You know that."

"So—" I trembled. I could barely stay on my feet. "Everything is finished?"

"I'm sorry," Zekiul whispered, "but this is just the beginning."

CHAPTER THIRTY-FIVE

It took several months to make it across the country to the second easternmost province in Canuckia: Jardin.

The landscape was destroyed, so I had to navigate craters formed from earthquakes, and pits of gas that sent noxious steam into the sky. And burning forests. Everywhere the trees burned.

I avoided the other survivors. I didn't know who was an enemy anymore, and I'd promised myself I'd never read anyone again—ever!—so the journey was long, and lonely.

But it was worse when I arrived in Jardin. Before Whitley snuck me out of Chaleur, I used Dimitri's Will to withdraw his fortune from his federal finance account, but I couldn't spend a cent or my whereabouts would be Flagged. So when I got to Jardin I had to live on the streets.

I had to stay invisible so Oliver couldn't hurt me again.

Once the Reclamation Party restored some semblance of order, I got a job as a dishwasher in a rations restaurant, and rented a room within the row of apartments built into the back of the building. As spring turned into summer, then into the voting autumn, I watched the News Alert network in horror as Oliver—and the Tolerant Party (the name Khleo stole to distance the Billadeaus from their past)—came into power.

I hid in my apartment when the celebrations began in the winter of 2107: citizens cheering on their new leader. Some said the Tolerant Party started a revolution, Prime Billadeau was their saviour, and his brother—Khleo Billadeau, the new Chief Justice—was a maverick.

When I heard the shouts, and felt the building shake from the celebrations thrown by my neighbours, I felt sick. I thought about sharing the truth—that Oliver was a lying scumbag, and his brother was a treacherous abuser—but I knew nobody would believe me.

Oliver's promises were too wonderful, and his energy was just what Canuckians craved. They wanted a post-catastrophe leader: someone who could be ruthless and make the country right.

So I stayed silent, and hid in my apartment.

Over the following months, I was promoted from dishwasher to restaurant server. Then from server to host. While I worked, Oliver implemented his agenda for Canuckian culture—which looked nothing like the vision Amelie encouraged.

Prime Billadeau updated the Acts established by the Reclamation Party. He made them "clearer," he said, "and easier for citizens to understand." But when I read the revisions posted on the News network, the Acts didn't seem clearer. They were controlling.

Oliver stripped away the bylaws: the specific rights that catered to the minority. He removed gender and orientation protections from the Inclusivity Act. He made it mandatory for every citizen over the age of nineteen to attend post-secondary schooling at institutions that taught *his* curriculum. He simplified the Intimacy Act, and outlined the boundaries of how, where, and when physical touching was allowed (citizens called it the Slut Act). The Health Act banned non-essential food stuffs—like sugar, alcohol, and caffeine—and required citizens to participate in mandatory exercise hours. Prime Billadeau passed the Creation Act: Artists were required to pay a 30% tax on everything they created and get a government certificate of approval to guarantee quality. No more romance stories were protected by plastic pages. The Creation Department—which published practical narratives instead of frivolous ones—refused to approve them.

Prime Billadeau built walls around every city. "To protect us," he said, "and keep those who won't comply with our peaceful ways out." Everyone complied with the 'peaceful' ways. They didn't have a choice. The Acts had so much grey in them—so little specificity—that the Justice Department had no problem manipulating the Acts to serve the Tolerant Party's unlawful agenda. Khleo was put in charge of Action Specific Consequences: a system that gave his department the power to determine punishment when citizens broke the rules.

The Acts weren't the only grey addition to the country. Citizens had to wear uniforms: grey jumpsuits with hoods. The Tolerant Party claimed uniformity made it impossible to impose authority over others and, in Oliver's utopia, hierarchy was a tool of oppression.

The irony wasn't lost on me when, in 2115—and Prime Billadeau was voted into power for the third time—the Tolerant Party declared they were going to modernize and combine a democracy with an autocracy. The Tolerant Party shed its old name and chose another.

The Complot.

*Com*passion Co*plot.*

The name was catchy, and easy to remember.

I knew what Oliver was doing. I *knew*. He was giving himself unquestionable influence by removing the check-and-balance systems citizens used to advocate for their individual needs. But Oliver—and the Complot—rejected individuality, so how could anyone complain?

I couldn't complain. If I spoke up, Oliver would know I was alive. Only my continued anonymity kept me safe. So I said nothing.

Not even when Oliver went for my heart.

Prime Billadeau razed the forests in Canuckia. He started in Pluie, clearing trees from city spaces and telling citizens they had to "make sacrifices to Nature, Canuckia's enemy, so the comet won't come again." But I knew—I *knew!*—that destroying nature was Oliver's symbolic way of separating from me. Completely.

He knew I was alive. He knew I watched everything on the large screens the Complot installed on the facades of public buildings. When he hosted a live event in Chaleur—his "corrupt hometown"—and set fire to a fallen birch tree as the kick-off for the country-wide razing, I knew my face filled Oliver's empty soul. He wanted me to remain empty, too.

The fallen birch burned blue as its branches caught fire and its leaves shriveled: leaves in the shape of hearts with lateral roots running outwards from the tree.

My tree.

I watched it turn to ash—

—and I said nothing.

I heard things, though. From my friends. Zekiul and Jolene *had* gone to the Separated States, and were hiding in an advanced city-state called the Rivet. After they found a safehouse, Zekiul asked me to join them—and he tried to form another rebel group to overthrow the Complot—but I'd found safety in Jardin; and nobody had the energy to fight when they couldn't survive.

Whitley didn't survive. They thrived.

After they helped me escape Chaleur, they gathered up the weakest survivors and snuck them out of Pluie. Whitley set up a base in Fairfield, and worked underground to continue technological developments inspired by Dimitri's nuclear batteries. The ex-councillor coached young scientists, and discovered a female with a mind more brilliant than mine: a girl named Frances who'd been born mute.

Under Whitley's tutelage, Frances rediscovered a device that hosted private lines of communication so we could talk without Oliver—or Khleo—knowing. Whitley couriered Frances' prototype to me, and to others who knew the truth (like Zekiul, Jolene, and their old friends in Jardin). When I opened Whitley's parcel—wrapped in cloth and tied with string—I blinked as a wrist band fell into my hands: a wrist band attached to a tiny screen. Frances said the nuclear-powered device was called an ArmCom. Before the war, ArmComs had been popular, but they'd fallen out of fashion. ArmComs allowed users to speak, read the News Alert network, and send messages while remaining anonymous. They were a safer version of the eyelinks.

Zekiul direct-contacted me over our ArmComs, trying to change my mind about moving south—but after years of telling him 'no,' he finally stopped asking. He kept sharing his concerns about a revolutionary kind of power Whitley and the scientists were developing, though—fusion power, he called it—but I didn't pay attention. Zekiul always worried about the next catastrophe, and I didn't care. I could barely get out of bed each day long enough to care for myself.

But years passed. And I got out of bed. I went to my job, every day. And I worked hard: every day. I was promoted to assistant manager, then manager and, soon, I helped the restaurant's owner manage the finer details of the business.

Then a new person direct-contacted me over the ArmComs: Mira Simard, Dimitri's sister. Whitley had found Mira so they could tell her how her brother died; and that Dimitri left his fortune to me. But Mira didn't want Dimitri's money. She wanted to tell me she was sorry: sorry she hadn't reached out sooner, and sorry her brother was such an astronomical egoist he hadn't let us connect.

Mira's husband, Christopher, was an Angler, so she'd shut down her art business and joined the fishing guild after the Complot took over. She kept painting, though, and sold her pieces in secret. We became friends and stayed in touch, and Mira told me everything that happened in Bristol. She told me about her most recent creations—dedicated to Dimitri—and about her pregnancies. Two of them.

The day my sort-of nephew was born, Mira held the infant in front of her ArmCom so I could bond with the boy. I liked the child (his name was Doyle, which was sweet) but I didn't feel any real affection for him.

Broken people couldn't love.

But when Mira's second child was born—curly-haired wretch named Cordelia—my empty heart filled.

The baby was so vicious—squirming and screaming in her mom's arms—that I couldn't help but be impressed. The tiny child had more vigour and *oomph!* than I'd been able to muster in years. So, the morning after I met Cordelia, I shook off the last of my grief and went to work with hope.

Which was a considerable improvement over the hole I'd

learned to live with.

The timing couldn't have been better. That day—Cordelia's birth day—the owner of the restaurant retired and, to my surprise, left the business to me. As I grew older, and more settled, the tenuous ties I had to my job, friends, and family grew stronger.

Oliver's power grew as well, and the reigns he'd roped around Canuckian throats tightened.

His influence within the Global Government increased and, soon, nobody could question his authority. Nobody wanted to. Not Khleo, or the premiers, or the councillors in their chambers. Canuckians were grateful Oliver led the country out of the worst catastrophe in history with only several thousand deaths (recorded). They didn't question the increased taxation, or the immediate punishments the Complot Members inflicted upon constituents if they stepped a toe over Oliver's line.

His power was the price citizens paid for peace.

I kept my head down. I ran my restaurant well, and used Dimitri's fortune to establish a legacy I knew would continue beyond my aging years. I made a Trust that would go to Mira's children so, when I died, Doyle and Cordelia would have financial security. I secretly hoped Cordelia would use the money—and her strength—to challenge Oliver's world order.

I made more than a Trust. I cleared out the apartments behind my restaurant and turned them into food storage units, which were completely legal and definitely important as the agriculture sector continued to suffer. Then, in one of the units—hidden from the spying eyes of the Complot—I built a room.

A beautiful room. A room with a single picture, painted by Mira, of a tree covered in heart-shaped leaves. When it was dark outside and cold, and the restaurant patrons cowered in their bungalows, I invited my friends—the people I'd met since 2106— to sit with me in the room. Under the painting.

And there, beneath the birch tree, facing a suffering generation of Canuckians, I finally spoke. I shared my story—the real story— and people listened.

They didn't use the eyelinks. They didn't share information on public forums or in the streets, and they met under Mira's artwork to discuss a united vision for a true utopian world.

And I let them.

I never once wondered if it was the right thing to do. I never doubted the importance of telling the truth, even if my truth wasn't accepted by everyone. I knew my love for Oliver had been real that day in spring—when he looked up into the birch tree's branches hanging over his head—and I knew it was my fault I'd closed my eyes to the anger in his.

Oliver had always been himself. He never deceived me. But I wanted so badly to believe I could turn his scowl into permanent smile *I* lied—to myself—over and over, while he pushed me away.

Over and over.

I believed I needed Oliver's love, but really—in the end—the love I needed was my own.

Which was difficult to provide when I believed I was partly responsible for the collapse of civilization.

Then, in 2127, a perky blonde cabinet member and her sullen, staring friend ousted the Billadeaus. Erika Graham and Havu Boucher had spent years establishing influence within the Complot, unnoticed. They achieved their positions as Cabinet Members legitimately. Then they killed Prime Oliver Billadeau, and replaced the entire Complot Cabinet; and they dissolved the Canuckian senate. And *not* because of a petty grievance. They craved power.

So I told my friends another story: a story about a murdered child and the girls who destroyed her. When Erika Graham became Prime and Havu Boucher was made her torturous Chief Justice, Canuckians fought back.

And I finally forgave myself.

I was human. I believed in love, and I'd chosen love instead of doubt all those years ago in Chaleur. And that was alright. It was better to make a mistake and love the wrong person than be like Oliver, and Erika, and the countless other Complot Members who couldn't love at all. Because despite the lies, and the loneliness—

and pain—I was romantic. Just like everyone else. But I was born in an era when the people in power couldn't see in the strength of softness, or respect the voices of those who were sensitive enough to believe in it. But my hope, and need for love, helped me find others who could love me back; and who knew that community-nurtured love was stronger than natural empathy.

I didn't regret falling in love with Oliver, but I regretted caring for that love after it began to wither and die; and that's what I told my friends when they sat beneath my tree

You had to *know* love before you could help it grow.

Love was certainty.

Love was connection.

Love was understanding.

My friends understood. And they loved me. I never once wondered about their love. I never doubted if I should love them back. I knew.

I knew.

NOTES

Beneath the Birch Trees

Hello!

Writing this book was . . . interesting. The process I used to get it from brain to page was the longest—and messiest—creative journey I've taken as a writer to date. The story I initially wrote is nothing like what you've just read, which proves the value of revisions, reader feedback, and thoughtful introspection over a long period of time.

This story was supposed to be about a bold young woman who innocently—and optimistically—attached herself to a withdrawn young man with the intent to "save him from himself." The world (and plot) was supposed to serve Layla's journey of self-discovery—and self-love—with a tidy ending in which she learned it was best to leave people as they were. The book was also supposed to showcase Frances, a secondary character in *We Call Her Rose*; and it was supposed to allude to *We Call Her Rose's* chaotic world. There was little mentioned about the eyelinks, Layla's power, and the systemic dysfunction in Cancukia that shaped a deeply individualistic community.

So much for creative intentions.

After receiving feedback from many *many* voices (including the ones in my head which are super noisy), I shifted the tone of the story so I could highlight different ideas: that people are unpredictable and (mostly) well-intended, and that humans make assumptions about *everything*. I also explored questions about the implied responsibility of caregivers (to serve others regardless of personal sacrifice?) and the importance of having an interconnected awareness of the needs, and desires, of unfamiliar personalities within our global society.

So! That's how this book came to be. I'm proud of what evolved; and I hope you enjoyed the end result.

acknowledgments

Thank you to everyone who helped this story become a book.

    Thanks to my husband, who pretends to enjoy my dramatic performances when I have to check complicated sequences of dialogue. Many thanks to the team of beta readers—Paulette Burgess, Rachel Burwell, K.L. Neidecker, Emily Newell, Stacey McGregor, Stephanie Martin, @yara_loves_languages, and Brittney Sasseville—for sharing their thoughts about the book. The feedback they provided greatly improved the novel. A special thanks to Stephanie for her intuitive understanding of the work, and her commitment to hashing out the finer points of the narrative (without her enthusiastic attention to detail aspects of the final story wouldn't have been developed); and special thanks to Brittney for her invaluable cover art creative comments. Thank you thank you *thank you* to the ARC readers who took a chance on a relatively new writer. And thank YOU—reader—for reading this story.

And an especially special thank you to Stacey, who introduced me to cro-muffins.

biography

STEFANIE BARNFATHER is a Canadian author. Previously, she taught high school arts and inclusive education. Stefanie graduated with honours from Sheridan College's Music Theatre—Performance program, and has a BFA and BED in secondary fine arts from the University of Calgary. When Stefanie isn't writing she enjoys painting, hiking, and spending time with her husband and pug.

If you want to read more stories by Stefanie Barnfather, feel free to show your support by following **@stefbarnfather** on Instagram and TikTok. Star ratings and reviews on Goodreads are always appreciated.

Other Books by Stefanie Barnfather
available on Amazon, Audible, and iTunes
– and bookshops and libraries –
and on Barnfather Books' online store
www.barnfatherbooks.com
in paperback, eBook, and audiobook

Novels
WE CALL HER ROSE

Short Story Collections
YOU KNOW WHAT I THINK?
YOU DIDN'T HAVE TO

Rapid Release Flash Fiction
JOSHUA
HAPPY NEW YEAR! LOVE, THE COMPLOT:
and other stories
CHARMS IN THE AIR
FRESH NUTRIENTS: and other stories

Manufactured by Amazon.ca
Bolton, ON

39650325R00173